THE
STUDY
CIRCLE

Haroun Khan

THE
STUDY
CIRCLE

Haroun Khan

dead ink

dead ink

First published in Great Britain in 2018 by Dead Ink, an
imprint of Cinder House Publishing Limited.

Paperback ISBN 9781911585336
Hardback ISBN 9781911585329

Printed and bound in Great Britain by Clays Ltd, Elcograf
S.p.A.

www.deadinkbooks.com

Let me write of the students
Those seekers of the truth.
Who came seeking the truth at the doorstep
Of the great and mighty.
These innocents who, with their dim flickering lamps
Came seeking light
Where they sell naught but the darkness of long endless nights

Dedication by Faiz

1.

Circles never end, but they close.

Ishaq stole a look at the darkness descending outside. Week after week you could find him here, kneeling on the floor in respectful attentiveness. The coarse rug, unable to hide the numbing resolve of hard ground, forcing him cross-legged and back again as the lack of feeling in his limbs became unbearable. Unlike the others, he was not used to sitting in these positions. He envied and felt reproached by their ease. It exposed the lack of time he had spent in these gatherings.

The orator continued:

'As Allah, glorified and exalted be he, says in Surah Ikhlas: "Say: He is God, the One and Only, Allah, the Eternal, Absolute, He begetteth not, nor is He begotten, and there is none like unto Him"'

Ishaq adjusted his long cotton tunic so as to avoid it getting stuck under his loose salwar trousers. He felt a bead of sweat gather on his forehead, threaten to break free and drip.

Uncomfortable as it was, he waited until he was sure no one was looking before taking a swipe at it with a embroidered cuff. He continued on to massage his forehead as he struggled with the pungent aroma of agarwood oil that wafted through the room and enveloped all.

He had attended this gathering for so many years now, listening to discourses on subjects ranging from those of the theologically highest import like Tawhid – the indivisible and absolute oneness of God – to areas of basic Islamic jurisprudence such as performing your prayers exactly in accordance with the prophetic tradition.

'*As the prophet, peace be upon him, told us: "Just this sura or chapter is like a third of the Quran, in that it contains a third of the message and beauty of Al-Islam that we have been honoured with. In the days of ignorance, and even in our times, people have worshipped Fire or Stone. They have taken statues and shrines as objects of worship, their ancestors or even the sun and stars. They have put intercessors, priests or saints and holy men, between themselves and the Creator.*"'

He admired the speaker's delivery. Sometimes sombre, sometimes solemn, occasionally austere, the style was slow, measured, and pensive. It bestowed added authority on the knowledge that was imparted even though the content had become all too familiar. In unison with the speaker's steady drum-like intonation it produced a soporific effect in Ishaq. His eyelids felt heavy. He wanted to close them and rest. But was all too aware that other eyes watched. Still, Ishaq took great comfort from the feeling of communality washing over the group, their familiarity eliciting an undercurrent of ease, comfort, and even frivolity, that contrasted with the hefty burden of the subject matter.

'*However, Islam came continuing the true message of Abraham, Moses, Noah, and Jesus. Strengthening our natural inclination, our fitra, and affirming that the Creator is above and separate from creation and there is no likeness unto him. That we worship him alone, the most Beneficent, the All-merciful.'*

For nearly five years now Ishaq had attended this pure assembly. Persevering. What Ishaq found in the undiluted form of Islam was wondrous and timeless. The Quran and Hadith held answers to the most fundamental of our questions about life. Why am I here? What is my purpose? How do we live a good life? What happens when I die? Alongside came a body of knowledge and ideals on how to organise society, and economics, and politics, contemplated and ruminated on by scholars in works over hundreds of years, and across numerous civilisations. Indians, Arabs, Turks, Persians, Africans and so many others; an endless torrent of thought instigated by an unlettered man promulgating a divine revelation in another millennium.

Looking around, he saw all of that diversity and unity around him. Black, brown, and white. Brothers in Islam, in flowing garments, all listening with intent, deliberating on an eternal and unalterable message. This brotherhood of man across all races and strata nourished Ishaq. All were equal before God, only differentiated by their goodness, piety, and knowledge. A life of dignity was within reach of all. One could be rich or poor, surrounded by loved ones or alone, have a life of ease or of hardship, yet Allah would judge them all equally within their means. No secret knowledge. No priests standing between you and God. No church with a hierarchy claiming a sole path of access to the divine.

Ishaq had internalised all of this and felt blessed in being party, but day-by-day he had grown uneasier within the circle. Yet, on this occasion, just as on all others, he stayed, listening on as the speaker made a finishing supplication in Arabic.

'How perfect you are ya Allah and I praise you. I bear witness that none has the right to be worshipped except you. I seek your forgiveness and turn to you in repentance'

The circle's attendants relaxed as the sermon ended. With their large beards and smiling faces, they faced their neighbours and started to indulge in smaller talk, catching up with their beloved friends. They poured each other generously laden vessels of steaming tea, as was the traditional custom in this, Ishaq's native land.

Not wishing to engage them in case they noticed his unrest, Ishaq pushed himself up from the floor with his hands and grabbed his shoes, stumbling while putting them on in haste. He gathered his overcoat, opened the door, and spilled out into the South London night.

A delicate chill spread over his body. His skin tingled, his face smarting and glowing as the heat generated by the Islamic gathering collided with the solitary cold of the English night. Closing the residential flat's door behind him and moving onto the balcony, here on the 17th floor of a twenty-storey block, the vast council estate was revealed to Ishaq. A sterile panorama of ashen granite that, from most vantage points, dominated the totality of your vision. Blotting out the rest of the world. A demand to be your sole reality. Spawned from the popular post-war Brutalist style, the estate consisted of half a dozen twenty-storey towers. Monolithic structures that thrust upwards and stood like forbidding sentinels, forever gazing. Joining them were ten, small, four-storey blocks that interlocked with the larger buildings through bridges and tunnels. A cold grey stone covered the larger blocks, peppered by the grubby windows of their constituent flats. In the daytime, sunrays ricocheted downwards between the buildings, adding a grimness to the light that trickled down to those below. At night these huddled edifices looked giant and conspiratorial, their intentions opaque and inscrutable; they created not so much a blackness but a quiet abscess in the loud and beating heart of the city that was London.

The Study Circle

Ishaq's estate covered half a square mile between Tooting and Streatham, in South London. The word 'estate' evoked the idea of a large manor in a green and pleasant land, but this place could never be mistaken for that. In other parts of the world they used words like 'project', which seemed even worse, as if the inhabitants were lab subjects to be experimented on. However, in line with the inceptive vision, this may have indeed been more appropriate. In the sixties, the white working-class that originally inhabited the estate were swept up from other parts of London and placed here, in order to uplift their conditions through this architects' utopian idyll. Those imperious and idealistic town-planners had talked about '*streets in the sky*', a benefaction they could bestow on the common folk so they could live in harmony and solidarity cheek by jowl. The thought went that high density housing, while solving the issue of space and poor post-war housing in London, could also promote community and sharing. That was the theory, an idealised and proletarian Laputa, except the cold reality was an underclass, forced to live in confined spaces, pent up in frustration, immobile and stagnating, with no say in who they lived beside.

Former subjects of the British Empire, such as Ishaq's parents, joined these initial settlers and came to claim what had been promised. Many of his elders laughed when Muslims were accused of ghettoising themselves, as if there was some planned idea to congregate and concentrate themselves in the most rundown parts of the UK. Their faces had seen the white scrunched-up stares that welcomed them. Quickly urging the council to move their accommodation, and pulling their kids out of schools, these initial white families started a cascading effect that actually resulted in their own complete displacement. Over the last couple of decades they had moved out to areas around Croydon, and to hidden and less salubrious parts of Surrey and Kent. There was no need to be in London, as they didn't seem to want to do the jobs of serfdom that the Pakistanis and Ghanaians and West Indians and Bangladeshis did. The jobs that made London run; stewarding buses and trains, steering the underground, driving mini-cabs, and cleaning offices. The jobs that kept this city, this great money-making engine, well-oiled and firing, churning out wealth for an international elite.

Deep in thought, Ishaq's body jolted as he felt a strong hand clamp onto his shoulder.

'Ishaq, assalmu alaikum, what's the rush? Been a while since I last saw you. What's up?'

He looked round and saw Ayub giving him a mischievous smile that radiated from a bearded face. Ishaq turned to face him, gave a limp shake of the hands and a half-hearted embrace.

Ayub, like Ishaq, was of Pakistani parentage, though a decade-and–a-half older, with salt-and-pepper hair that seemed well matched to the estate. The main speaker for the circle, it was Ayub's manner that so impressed Ishaq. Ayub was respected by all of the brothers for his Islamic knowledge, as well as being someone of patience and warmth. A man of good judgement and gentility.

Ishaq replied with polite formality. 'Alhamdulillah, I'm good, may Allah reward you for the tadhkirah. It was really beneficial as usual. How are things with you? Your family?'

Ishaq had been employing a more refined mode of speech as of late. Regularly using Islamic etiquette and salutations. Nice manners, but others noticed how he used it as a stick to ward off intimacy. Ayub said, 'Alhamdulillah, thank you. Same as normal. Work, and family. My younger brother and sister are growing up quickly. I'm having to keep an eagle eye on them…I haven't seen you around for a while. Hope you and your family are doing well. Do you still go with them to the car-boot on Sundays?'

'Of course. It's boring, I don't like it but they're getting old. I want to spend as much time with them as possible…other than that I'm just busy with Uni.' Ishaq's face forced a smile then retreated to its previous aspect, he hunched his shoulders and made himself small in an attempt to ward off any further inquisition.

'Of course. It's your final year, right? Subhanallah, makes me feel ancient. I remember you running around the estate with your gang of really heavy ten-year-olds, creating havoc. You were like the Bash Street Kids, with you as Dennis the Menace' said Ayub, with his face struggling between cheer and concern.

Ishaq always found Ayub's stilted attempts at small talk both painful and endearing. Not recognising Ayub's reference at all, Ishaq forced a laugh, 'Aha, yea…probably looked something like that…'

Ayub nodded slightly, his face drew more serious. 'Brother, you looked a bit preoccupied in there and then you bolted. Like you had seen a jinn. Anything you want to share? It's not like you.'

'Uhh…nothing. Just busy with studies…deciding what to do once I've finished…' He didn't want to get into anything with Ayub but, seeing his care and out of respect, he felt obliged to offer some form of answer. 'I know…I'm sorry…but we do seem to cover the same stuff every week.'

'I'm sorry Ishaq, but I'm not an alim. I cover what basics I know and pass it on. It's like a tadhkirah, as you say, a reminder to everyone and myself.'

'Akh, I really appreciate that…but it's more …' Ishaq paused, and scanned Ayub's face.

'Go on, I won't be offended. Saying that, it's hard not to be after you've just been told your talks are really boring,' Ayub said, once again breaking out a smile. 'As I said, I'm not a scholar, and nor is anyone else here. We do what we can and do our best to remind each other of the basics. Striving to improve our piety and character, right?'

Ishaq studied Ayub, this man who did so much for everyone but who somehow seemed from another era. It was best to not stray, move to safer subjects. 'Did you hear about the march? Those English Defence lot wanting to march right past the mosque sticking two fingers up at us; I've been thinking about that a lot.'

Ayub laughed. It looked genuine. He placed an assuring hand on Ishaq's shoulder. 'Subhanallah, well that's another set of matters. I admit they are a concern. The worst people. They only want to cause trouble. They don't know us, or want to know. All they are certain of is that they want to start something. To kick-off big time. Like the mosque says, best to stay out and let the authorities deal with it. Ok?'

Ishaq nodded. 'Well let's see what happens, inshallah, and hope for the best. Anyway, may Allah bless you for the advice. I'll definitely bear it in mind. I'm just tired…Listen, I'd best get back to the books.'

'Ok Ishaq, you know that my door is open anytime. Just remember, be soft of heart, go easy. Give my salams to your family.' Ayub gave Ishaq a quick embrace and walked back into the flat.

Ishaq gave his hood a controlled pull up and fastened the zip so that his black coat was tighter. He always took the stairs when in the big blocks, no matter how high up. There was no way he would risk being stuck in a lift with some of the characters around here. Ishaq, like Ayub, was lucky to reside in one of the smaller buildings. Although the situation had drastically improved in recent years, the large blocks, especially the upper floors, were a law unto themselves. You could find yourself trapped, like a battery-caged chicken. He thought of Mrs Siddiq, up on the 20th, varicosed hands clutching at her shawl waiting for his mum's weekly visit, while the council placed a procession of ashen-faced users either side of her.

The Study Circle

Ishaq scrunched his nose as he passed a set of lifts, the smell of warm urine stinging his nostrils. Like the piss-stained lifts, the floors stank of squalor and menace. Ishaq bounded down the steps three at a time, jumping and using a hand on the bannister to swing round to face every new tier. Graffiti adorned many of the levels; slurs about who slept with whom, who reputedly gave free and easy blow jobs, which flat numbers sold drugs, defiant messages to the police, and badly drawn tags on behalf of a gang or, more likely, a bored teenager. Gliding by the tenth floor, Ishaq saw the all-too-familiar mural that had been sponsored by some bygone well-meaning youth trust. It featured multi-ethnic faces from the youth of the estate, with beaming smiles enveloped in the patronage and radiated-light and white wings of an angel behind them. Ishaq liked it, something of beauty that looked even more luminescent given its location. He always slowed down to take a look before careering back off. On this occasion he saw that someone had scrawled 'ROZ WOZ ERE' in thick black spray paint across the whole facade, leaving those once beaming faces looking bereft and disfigured. *Nothing ever lasts*, he thought.

Arriving on the 4th floor, Ishaq used one of the grey stone bridges to get to the adjacent shorter building. From there he could access street level and hop, skip, jump to his place via memorised routes, minimising the time he spent exposed on the ground in the hope of bypassing trouble. As he reached a blind spot of the Estate, Ishaq raised his pace. It was possible to get on with your life, shuttling between work and home, without spending too much time on the streets or getting involved with the neighbours' issues, good or bad. Still, during long, black, winter evenings when walking through shadows, Ishaq felt like he was rolling dice at a casino. Eyes forward. Body tensed. Breath held. Hoping that you weren't the next victim of being in the wrong place at the wrong time.

Before the corner, he heard footfalls, their padding magnified by the glassy silence into loud pounding. Anytime he encountered someone unfamiliar, even from a distance, he made a quick, automatic assessment. Size. Weight. Gender. Race. Split-second decisions made about whether to walk past or try another route. Groups of young men were especially intimidating, both to older residents and to each other. Ishaq rounded the bend and saw that this time the way was clear. He inhaled rapidly, his fluttered breath grabbing new life, feeling a dangerous joy at a small survival, and a victory, however pyrrhic.

Nearing home, he saw the crawling lights of a police car creep around the outskirts of the estate. Xenon beams blinding him, exposing him. And then passing over – writing his silhouette against a wall. Police rarely came into the estate proper and then only in large groups, for show or an armed raid. This car moved like a coiled cat, ready to pounce on any unsuspecting mouse that was brave enough to try and escape. Any criminal activity below the threshold of a large drugs arrest or a terrorism charge was normally allowed to fester. A tacit acknowledgement that the police were fine with the estate functioning like a loose anarchy. Haphazardly self-regulating through hidden allegiances and networks.

Their empty presence meant that in the case of crime there was little hope of restitution. You could resort to paying other, rather more robust, members of the estate to distribute natural justice, but that could always have blowback. It was best to try hard to avoid unnecessary interactions and just keep your head down. As the car slinked off, Ishaq, the only rodent around, spotted a decent sized rock. He put the toe of his right trainer over it, rolling it around to fathom its heft. He looked at the car, at the rock, at the car, savouring the possibility of defiance. But this gave way to a feeling of pettiness. It wasn't becoming, it was the act of a reactionary, and he could be better than the police. Ishaq gently rolled the rock under a bush at the side of a road.

2.

Shams loved that dank, metallic smell of the underground. The caressing whoosh of air across your face as chained carriages shot by the platform – bullets exiting a gun barrel. Brap, brap, brap. His first experience of the tube had been on a shopping trip with his mum. The clandestine nature of stations far underground was thrilling. A dark parallel world, under London streets. He loved the danger, the violent rush of trains that could take your life in an instant, and the loud tannoy warning to 'Mind the Gap'. He remembered that he had always been terrified of that pitch-black gap, that one small step between train and platform. Scared of falling into an abyss, scared of the unknown.

Shams rose with the escalators and exited Tooting Broadway station. He stood outside, squinted pupils sipping in the once familiar area, his small but stocky stature lost in the shadow of Edward VII. The regent's plinth lay adorned with bronze plaques of the female personifications of *Peace* and *Charity*. From 1911, this King of the United Kingdom, British Dominions and Emperor of India had stood here, day after day, on his granite stage. As the seasons revolved, through sun and sleet, he looked outwards, surveying his lands and family's acquisitions, his depilated head decorous with bird poo. Shams wondered why this bloke was looking to the horizon, away from the station, rather than to what was behind, when he just needed to gaze downwards. Under his metal cast feet all of those dominions were now waltzing around him, hurrying to and fro, paying the loveable bearded anachronism no heed.

The station felt comforting. He had spent his early years as a local. As he grew into his early teens and gained the autonomy to explore without his parents' searching eye, Shams often played truant from school. He ventured with friends, to random tube stops just to see what was out there, the underground map and its rainbow lines a vast landscape of possibility and adventure, new worlds other than the constricted horizons of the council estate: a city of millions; hundreds of square miles of mysterious territory; abandoned docks and stretches of rust-dappled water in the east; Heathrow, dispatching winged emissaries around the Earth, in the west; and, on a map's blurred edge, pastoral tableaux and verdant fields, in his mind's internal reckoning.

They used to kick around by asking people for their unused Travelcards and gathering knowledge of which stations were unmanned and un-gated. As more stations started to introduce electronic gates, they crossed rail lines and cut across private property to avoid capture. Modern day mudlarks scavenging for excitement, adept at jumping over barriers or tailgating other passengers before the gates slammed shut. Shams had enjoyed that time with Ishaq and Marwane. Spending hours talking about random subjects: the experiences of their parents and what they would do in the future. He had a big interest in animals and entertained the possibility of working in a zoo or helping to save the giant panda. On occasion, he dragged them out to the more bucolic edges of London to see what the countryside was like. Marwane used to point things out. 'Ok lads, this thing is a 'Cow', say "Mooooo." These people are 'good folk'. This air that smells like shit is 'fresh'.' When they were about twelve, Shams took them to the Chalk Farm underground stop, because there must be a farm there right? They got there and found it was smack bang in the middle of North London, about as poshly urban and residential as you can get, and in fact also held its own dingy council estates. Ishaq and Marwane took the piss so much that day. They chastised him for being simple. He ran off in tears, promising never to speak to them again. But of course, as always, he returned.

Now, shuffling on Tooting Broadway, his soles scraping as they barely escaped the ground, Shams glimpsed the college that he used to attend. It was wedged above a large Sainsbury's supermarket in what was called a mixed-use development. Ishaq used to rib Shams about how the grocer's and school shared the same building, that there was probably a revolving door that churned, thrusting hapless students out into good shelf-stackers. In other places, they would probably have a major bank or an accountants sharing the building; Marwane said that in South London they were just lucky it wasn't a Maccy D's or Carphone Warehouse.

Shams hadn't stayed the course. His attendance hadn't been great and he was fed up of being upbraided by teachers. He quit. Trying to get work, he sought apprenticeships at mechanic's and at builder's but these got filled before he'd even deposited his application form. It really was who you know; his teeth clamped shut every time he found out someone like the son of a contractor's mate had taken his position. Not even a gofer job, even if he was willing to get paid at a really low rate like some Eastern European Piotr. One day he replied to a nearly hidden ad for sales staff, in the Metro. Getting an interview straight away, he dressed in an aquamarine suit with silver flecks that his mum found in a charity shop. It was nice, a bit oversize, but looked spanking after a brush-down. Mum's proud face gave him confidence as he went to their office on the edge of an industrial estate. It went well, they complimented him on his wonderful suit even as they saw him struggle with the sleeves flowing over his hands. That same day they told him that he had passed, and as nervous as he had been he was just as excited for Monday.

On his first day, face flushed with nerves, but psyched, he was given a bunch of papers to sign. Halfway through he realised he hadn't quizzed his new employers on what they sold. Better not to make waves though, this was a fresh chance, an opportunity to impress. Someone had seen his potential.

That done, he was introduced to Clive. Tall, skinny Aussie who looked slick in his three-piece suit, a senior member of the team who he would be shadowing. Fast talker. Too fast for Shams to butt in, Clive gave some patter about the freedom of the job and how it built independence. 'The sky's the limit,' he said. At the end, Shams managed to ask where the shop was and watched as Clive reached under a desk and handed him a polyester duffle full of t-shirts and electronics, an assortment of Chinese phones, GPS, and language translation devices. The tees looked cheap, the tech archaic. It all moved quickly, Shams stayed quiet as the senior proceeded to take him out of the office and into high-street shops. He saw, an impassive external observer, as animated Clive, all flailing tapeworm limbs, pitched their wares to sales staff. About half-way through the day, he just went with it. It was an opportunity. Just go for it. Suck it up. So off he went with this stranger onto the streets of London, suited and booted, selling electronic diaries made in Taiwan and t-shirts made in Bangladesh.

After a few days of this, it was obvious to Shams that the whole thing was an elaborate setup with a blurred legality. The business worked as a pyramid, so if you hired any of your friends or others then you gained a percentage of their sales. The ghost ship of an office was laid out with empty desks and chairs, and business dress codes were enforced in maintaining the pretence. Fiery, motivational speeches were given every morning. Then again at the evening count up. The lead salesperson, an American, would give a pep-talk citing how much they had earned. Shams never used the word but it popped into his head that this was a real live 'Yankee'. A cowboy. A proper bullshitter.

Lead man tried to instil his sales technique into everyone, reinforcing the same points again and again.

1) Maintain firm and friendly 'Eye Contact' with the customer. It builds trust and gives you their attention. Build that confidence. Build that rapport.

2) 'People are Sheep' – Try and drop into your spiel how their neighbour has bought a load and see if they follow.

3) 'Fear of Loss' – Invoke the fear of missing out. FOMO, my friends, FOMO. Talk about how scarce the products are, how you'll only be in the neighbourhood today. Let the buyer handle the item. Then once you see they are interested, tear it, no, rip it out of their hands. Mention that the discount is a one time deal or gone forever. It all helps to nudge the customer along.

4) And finally 'Hit Rate'. You need to hustle. To see as many people as possible to maximise your chances. There's a sucker born every day. You only need one.

With revelatory astonishment, Shams found this actually worked and he enjoyed it. He would practice facial gestures in the mirror before work. He took pleasure in polishing his sales patter, and relished the feeling of holding someone under your sway, the feeling that you could nudge them one way then the other like a hypnotist's pendulum. And he was travelling all over London on the tube, finding greenfield areas to sell his wares. It was like being paid to indulge his childhood.

He wasn't scrubbing around, had some decent cash in his pocket, bills he could feel in his hand, but sometimes the doubts gnawed. The inclination that they were skirting the law and teetering on society's edge. For so-called independent traders they were told what to do a lot. You could only go to shops. You could never knock on residences. You couldn't tell friends.

He managed to get a copy of the form he had signed and it was all complicated verbiage. He thought about the unctuous nature and credulity of the senior salesmen; individuals who had bought their own snake oil, taken a resolute gulp and blissfully slathered the rest all over their greasy bodies. The whole thing was iffy. Why didn't they just say what they were, just upmarket vagrant hawkers. The company had a couple of hundred pounding the streets every day, so the barons at the top earned well. The chief constantly harped on about the Corvette that he had bought; no one had the heart to tell him that here we thought American cars were shit.

The leader regularly took Shams and a few other high earners out to lunch. He would tell them they were the chosen few, waxing on about how he had skipped uni for this business and that it was the best decision he had ever made; that there was no need for a degree when there was so much money to be made. Behind women's backs, he would also regale them with stories about how much sex he was getting because he earned so much. Tongue licking the constant enunciation of 'shagging', his American twang enjoying the novelty of the word and thinking it showed how down he was with the locals. Shams didn't believe the chatter but enjoyed the attention and couldn't help admire the American's manic energy, his complete lack of shame. It was novel. One co-worker, a concerned Nigerian girl, who was most definitely going to university to become a lawyer, always told Shams not to believe the man's hype. Just nod, earn some cash and get out.

The mornings before everyone went out with their lumpen duffle bags were fun. Energised voices reigned loud as people practiced their pitches. The smiling American, or 'septic tank', as some would have it, would get people to shout out his sales mantras, geeing them up for the day ahead. Shams caught him ditching that greasepaint smile behind the backs of some beggars whose recital wasn't up to his theatrical standards. Shams met a lot of new people. He enjoyed looking around his group. Aussies on their travels, immigrants from around Europe, loads of Irish and Saffers, students, even some single mothers who he did feel sorry for. This was a beginning for him, a means to an end, not a final destination.

Then, one day, it all came to a crashing halt. The day started bright. In fact by 11am he had achieved his best sales tally ever. He had sold his whole bag of goods to one guy. While pitching at a mechanic's an onlooker was having his car serviced. He had taken one look at Shams and his bag and called a mate, who he said would be interested. That mate gleefully bought everything, even the bag. Shams went back, proudly boasting of how good his spiel had become. He had even sold the bloody duffle bag, over 300 quids worth. He finally had the honour of ringing the golden bronze hand bell. As he had actually sold three times the qualifying amount, he revelled in ringing the bell multiple times, tenor and peals imparting his glad tidings. He was all smiles, cheeks rosy like an angelic choirboy, as his colleagues gave him high fives, just like they had been drilled to. He relished their envious faces as they offered begrudging handshakes and covetous ovation. His team leader was colder, more sceptical as

Shams handed her the guy's payment. She eyed the paper cheque and gave Shams a strange look. In her Afrikaner accent and with slitted eyes she said, 'You sold the bag…and they gave you this?'

'Well they needed something to carry everything, and I got a good extra price for the bag. They gave me the cheque for everything. What a bonus, right?'

As a child of the digital age, Shams had never seen a cheque before. He didn't realise that you needed a card to guarantee it and a few days later it promptly bounced. He had been had and defrauded. A street kid himself, he had not even been duped by a sophisticated trick. He was just a credulous fool. But that's life, shit happens. He went for the next day's pick-up and sensed people stealing quick looks, conversations dampening as he walked by. He was greeted with grim-faced aggression by his team leader, and managers further up. They brought out his forms, forced him to recognize the shaky scrawl of his signature. They told that him that it was a disclaimer and he had agreed that he was a separate entity. In effect he was acting as his own company and was liable for the cash. After an argument Shams got out, limbs shaking. They threatened legal action, started calling him constantly on his mobile and at his mum's place. His mum was already weak at the time and he made up excuses to keep her happy. The job wasn't right. He was moving onto other things. It was all a misunderstanding. Shams was too ashamed to tell Marwane or Ishaq about the hawking and what had happened. Would the hawkers now call the police, or take him to court? Everything about them was dodgy. Would they dare? A couple of weeks later, the haranguing calls stopped for good but left him with an elemental fear.

So once again he was on the look out for a job, and after finishing his brisk walk from the station he was standing outside the bright red door of this 10th floor flat. He stared at the chipped entryway and took in a sedating breath. He could see his reflection in a circular portal at the top that was turning to a silver silk with his breath, and shepherded back a few wayward strands of matt black hair. He took a look back at the landscape that he had sped through, hoping no eyes had stalked him and only saw tower blocks of caried teeth in a consuming black maw. He did a flight check of his jeans to make sure his fly was done up. This was a regular problem, forgetting, sometimes only to be informed by the abashed look of a shop assistant. He moved through life with an uncertain feeling that his privates were undone for all to see. Ready, Shams pressed the doorbell. He heard a muted chime go off within the flat to the tune of Greensleeves. He had a vague recognition of the melody from his childhood but struggled to place it. After waiting a while, he pressed the bell again. Still no response. Shams' feet started to scrape and shuffle. He swore that Mujahid had said midnight sharp.

Shams tried the ringer once more. On this third time he used a clenched fist to pound the door. No messing around, even if it was Mujahid. Impatient, he looked around in case of any other doors peeking, then he looked at the letterbox, lifted the cover and bent over, peeping through the opening. He heard some heavy steps on the stairs, lethargic thuds, and dropped the cover, quickly straightening himself.

'Who is it?' Shams heard Mujahid say in muffled bass from behind the door.

'It's Shams. You said to meet you tonight.'

Wiping his bleary eyes with a shirtsleeve, Mujahid poked the door ajar and took a peek at Shams in his puffer jacket and a strange cap. Satisfied, he opened a gap just about large enough for Shams' wide frame.

While nodding, Mujahid said, 'Ok, ok, Assalamu alaikum, bro, you want to calm down with the knockin'. I was getting out of bed. No rush.'

'Wa alaikum salaam. I'm sorry, I wasn't sure if you were about.'

'I heard the letter box. You weren't about to try and snoop, were ya? In Islam, a man's privacy is serious business.'

Mujahid yawned, his mouth creating a cavernous opening before he remembered to cover it with a hand, and then continued with baffled speech after it passed.

'You know in the Sharia I would be allowed to poke your eye with a stick through that letterbox. Blind you if I need. A house is a man's castle.' Mujahid took a look past Shams left and right on the landing and beckoned him in with a firm grasp on the shoulder which made Shams shift under the nettling touch.

Shams walked in and heard the door shut and the lock click into place. 'No, I was knocking. I wouldn't peek. You know me. Anyway bro, what's with the ice cream van music?'

'That thing? The doorbell's from ages back. Just never got round to changing it. So you stayin' cool? What you been up to?' said Mujahid

'Just, you know, mixin' it up. Trying to keep my head above water. You see that police sign down the road. Some stabbing?'

On the way to the flat, Shams had seen one of the police's yellow signs appealing for witnesses. If anything had gone down Mujahid would have a sniff of what happened. He was known for patrolling the estate dishing out his version of justice. A righteous enforcer, both judge and jury. Someone you could go to if you had problems from less salubrious residents. Mujahid had recently been given a warning about harassing a Lebanese Muslim shopkeeper, sinful parasite who sold cheap alcohol to the local community without care. No one was sure what Mujahid actually did for a living. There were rumours. He gave out odd jobs. Ishaq and Marwane warned against him, but Shams reminded them how they always said you should think the best about your brother, and how they shouldn't indulge in unsubstantiated whispers as this was a form of back-biting – *ghibah*, a major sin.

Dismissive, Mujahid kissed his teeth. 'Yea, same ol' shit. Rats taking bites out of each other. Some outsider. Whenever I see strangers round the block I make sure that they know not to mess around here. I don't accept no messin'. Anyway, I wanted to see you, you're looking for work right?'

Shams paused, standing feet fixed in the hallway '…yea, I just need some seed money for this business I'm doing. But I don't want to get into anything dodgy.'

'Bro, c'mon man, I wouldn't ask you to do anything funny. That's proper offensive. Dodgy?' Mujahid laughed off the suggestion as he wiped a bit of grit from his eye and then started rubbing both. 'What's this business about?'

'I have this cousin in Bangladesh who knows a lot of clothing factory owners. He says he can hit me up with the contacts and start doing some imports if I get the cash. Start off small you know, then try and build up.'

'Mashallah, that's good. Brothers should be earning their own way. Not relying on the kuffar for their jobs and income. The centre of our struggle, our Jihad, is money, bro. You can't do anything without money. If that means taking from and exploiting the enemies of Islam, then so be it.'

Shams looked unsure, 'I…don't know…what do you mean about taking? Stealing is haram. I'm talking about trade.'

Mujahid returned a hand to Shams shoulder. ' Of course it is bro, but stealing ain't stealing when you are taking from an unjust, oppressive system and giving it to people living under that oppression. Just sayin'. Nothing meant by it. Chill.'

Entering the living room, Mujahid brushed some soft toys and a heap of children's clothing off a sofa that had seen better days. Holes in the couch's green fabric allowed the upholstery to make a break for freedom in sprouting tufts. Shams took a seat, being careful to avoid a wet patch. As he sunk deep, the cushioning made a despairing sough. A few wrinkled books were cast around the floor. *The Crusades Through Arab Eyes*, *Foucault's Pendulum*, and what seemed to be a compendium of medical diseases. Mujahid sat down on a plastic folding chair opposite, picked up another book and showed Shams the cover in triumph. It showed a picture of Christian and Muslim knights on horseback, flailing their sword and scimitar at each other.

Mujahid rubbed the cover of the book in a caress, while still warding off his slumber. 'I've been reading see. Taking from the warmongers who once stole from us is not stealing. You feel that don't you? Our countries have been invaded for 1,000 years, since the Crusades, bro. And they've kept invading, killing, and taking ever since. That's how they made their money. We owe no loyalty to that. In this book, I was reading once about this one Crusade. There was a town the Christian invaders lay siege to called Ma'arra. After they took over the town, they killed the survivors and ate them out of hunger. Butchered them, and roasted children on spits. All these animals blessed by the pope. Cannibals. They've been hungry and biting bits of our flesh ever since.'

Shams eyes widened. 'Seriously bro, I never heard of that.'

'Yes, I read, see. All the time. All those friends of yours think I just hustle, but I spend a lot of my time learning. Learning our history. Learning is power. I think and make plans.' Muajhid looked at Shams, checking to see that he was suitably impressed, 'Anyways, I do have some errands that you can do for me. Pays good cash.'

Shams looked down at his seat, making as if he was examining the sofa. 'I'm not sure that I'm interested. If the brothers from the halaqah found out, I'd get in trouble'.

Mujahid stopped shifting and went quiet, the atmosphere altered as if Shams had uttered a taboo that petrified the air. Mujahid had attended the same circle as Shams and the boys, but his attendance became erratic and he faded from the scene. Some didn't think anything of it. It was weird for Shams, being back on this estate but not going to that group. They were his crew. He respected Ishaq, who he also thought was strong but in a different way. Ishaq didn't get drawn into crowds and always tried to do the right thing. Shams remembered when a local pusher offered him a different odd-job, a courier gig, by bringing out a wad of bills. To Shams, the man was like Willy Wonka. He held little tickets of freedom bound in a shining gold money-clip. As he had reached to take it, Ishaq had stopped him. It was not our way. Shams had pulled back. The grubby, pockmarked dealer then lent over Ishaq, held him by the throat and asked everyone who the little cunt was. He told Ishaq that there were no other ways here and, with a gravelled hoarseness, said, 'Everyone does it, do you think you're better then them, better than me?' Shams remembered the chill down his spine, how everyone had frozen. He remembered how Ishaq's eyes widened and body went rigid, but then how clearly and without his voice breaking he had said, 'You're a drug dealer.' Ishaq closed his eyes, already flinching in anticipation of the blow. The dealer stared at Ishaq, licking a shrivelled lip, hesitating, and then told everyone to fuck off. Shams asked Ishaq afterwards whether he was being brave or stupid. Ishaq had replied, 'I don't know, Shams…it's just right and wrong.' Since then he had always turned to Ishaq for advice. But those days were gone. Ishaq and the others had left him.

Mujahid wiped his lower lip with a finger, his face all angles and flatness like hewn stone. 'What those poodles? Praying in the mosque and having their religious conversations but doing nothing. Do you think they respect you Shams? You're like me, like the guys I met in prison. In there, there was true brotherhood. That's where I found Islam. We fasted and prayed, and we were there for each other. Coming out, it's every man for themselves. No nothing, no one has time for anyone else. You see this?' Mujahid pointed to a sinuous trail on his right cheek, 'In prison, one of those racist white pigs had a go at someone like you. A brother. A brother in Islam. I weren't having it, so I stopped it. The guy had a razor and slashed me. I hit that guy so hard, his cheek caved in. No mandem dared try cut me after that. Or touch my friends.'

People converted in prison, came and went through the circle and local mosques, sometimes never to be seen again. Their temporal needs sated or a return to being misplaced in the world. Mujahid was different. With others that he had met or connected, it was rumoured that he had indeed started down the path of his old ways, but this time with a tincture of Islamic-based defiance against the establishment. He forged his own way and Shams liked that.

Shams tried not to stare at the scar. Seasoned, curling almost into a coil. Paid for with trauma, a currency that could never be taken away. Mujahid didn't take any crap and had respect. Respect meant no one would try to mess. He enjoyed being a fly in the ointment. Early on, his ragtag group was called the 'Muslim Boyz'. Their very basic graffiti tag was seen around a lot of the estate. Shams remembered Ishaq laughing at it, he thought the changing of the 's' to a 'z' in the spelling was predictable and comedic, yet the group so unpredictable and tragic. He said their use of Islam was 'a stain on us all.' Shams had stayed quiet. Ishaq never seemed to understand the need to have a group that had your back. He mentioned the tag's spelling to Mujahid once. Mujahid had given it the dismissive grunt it deserved.

Mujahid continued, 'Now, out here, no one was helping me out so you have to do your own thing. I know you feel that way too, Shams. You want to do something properly for our Ummah, our nation. I'm trading away and I've got big plans.'

'Like what?'

Mujahid grinned. In the evaporating light cast, by a sole naked lightbulb, his tarred yellowed teeth blended into one long strip.

The Study Circle

'Well, you can't expect me to tell you everything straight away. You have to earn and deal yourself in. There's loads of people that I could have called in to start helping us out, but I see something different in you. Something special.'

'What do you mean?' Shams asked, growing unsteadier.

Mujahid's paternal smile pushed down and held Shams, their eyes fixed in an unyielding vice, 'You struggle like me and my boys. You know what hardship is like. Those circle boys and the old men in the mosques are soft. On these streets we are living in times of war, and we are the warriors of Islam. We must live our lives like mujahideen in this land, not like those others spending their life pretending.'

Mujahid stood, his smile dissolving into a look of fizzing anger as he banged his right fist into the other open palm, as he continued a righteous oratory.

'Pretending that we are going to be here forever. They don't like complaining or raising a fuss. Just want to get on. Just pretend that everything is all right. That this is a just society. And if you don't, pretend everything is ok. If you say that you're a victim of the police or racism, people say you've got a chip on your shoulder. They start blaming you, the victim, instead of the oppressor. And if you continue going on about it then they become uncomfortable. Uncomfortable that a man can feel. That a man can feel injustice deeply. They don't like being reminded of the truth. So it's easier to wear masks. Happy ones. Busy ones. Positive ones. Never showing our real faces. The painful and angry ones. We all wear these masks you see. Oils our way through life. Lets us be comfortable with each other. And if someone's mask drops we crap ourselves, because we might see ourselves as well as them. People like Ayub. I refuse to be like him. I refuse to wear a mask. I refuse to pretend. I think you feel that way too.'

Shams felt a tingling down his body, a new sensitivity to his surroundings, a craving swelling inside. Mujahid's reddened face loomed, like a preacher delivering a fiery sermon. But, as impressed as he was, Shams knew other preachers. 'But Ayub says we have to stick within the laws. Try and be good. Try and be better?'

Mujahid mouth contorted. 'Laws? The only law is Allah's law and Ayub has no control over that. His word isn't divine.'

'But he is learned,' Shams said, almost in a whisper, sinking further into his seat as Mujahid's form bore over him.

Both of Mujahid's arms were out in front. Fists clenched, one finger out, stabbing at Shams. 'A few phrases in Arabic don't make you learned. See, what people like him don't understand is that outside in the real world laws are there for other people. People who have their family to support them. People who live in areas where the police come. People who have backup. People who live in nice warm houses looking at crazy events on tele from ways away. They live in delusion. They think that there are laws, rules that govern our society. But there are no rules, not for us. And those types of people are hypocrites anyway. They'll look down on a gangster hustling to feed his kid. But a banker earning millions from doing haram, from doing what harms all of us, well as long as he has the big car, nice suit and big house then they give that guy big time respect. They gather like flies to honey. They can't help themselves. They make laws to keep people like us down. Especially Muslims. They always create new laws for us and pretend it's justice. We owe nothing to that unjust system, made by men with bad souls. Tell me Shams, all these laws, how do they help you?'

Shams had never seen Mujahid so animated. The air itself shook as if in fear. In a world of lies these words were a howling wind of truth. He felt as if this knowledge was implicit, that it had always been lying there unspoken. Mujahid had chosen him to share this deep well of experience and obvious hurt that lent gravity to his speech, his passion sanctifying inviolate truths.

'I dunno…they…don't.'

'You do know. I see it. People like you and me who have none of that, know the truth. All I want to do is give you an opportunity to start being a man. Making your own way. Nothing dodgy, just legit work.'

Shams' eyes flashed, labouring to take in the feeble light. '… What do you want me to do?'

'Nothing dodgy, and this isn't stealing, this is a business transaction, pure and simple. All you need to do is take some cash and hand it over to this guy who works at the airport. He'll give you a package and that's it bro. All legit.' Mujahid pulled out a thick wad of banknotes.

Shams rubbed the side of his head up and down, motioned to say something, stopped, then said '…What's in the package?'

Mujahid took his seat again and his voice settled on a more soothing tone. 'Trust me brother, nothing dodgy. You can take a look yourself if you want, once you get it. And if you do well, I'll cut you in on the profits.'

'Why can't you go yourself?'

'Hey, hey, questions. As you can see, I'm a busy man. Let's not kid ourselves that you wouldn't be here if you weren't interested in doing the job. Come on Shams, you know I have people doing jobs for me all around the place, all the time. This place is miles from here. I can't spend all day going back and forth. This is just one more on my list. I'm really relying on you. You can earn your cash for whatever business you need, then be off on your way, but I think that you'll stick around. You're the boss of yourself. Your own master.'

After the street hawking Shams had searched for other jobs. He managed to get work at a local supermarket. He remembered his row with a supervisor that no doubt was racist. The guy always made a beeline for him, only him. Shams refused to handle bottles of booze. Other Muslims and a Jewish guy who complained about pork had been given other duties, but Shams was forced to work the alcohol aisle. He quit after they asked him for ID to buy his mum a simple paring knife. They knew him, what was the need? He wouldn't accept being treated like some potential thug. Always the same.

Shams looked at the thick pack of money '…Ok, but I will take a look at what it is?'

'No problem, here's the address. Take this phone too. He'll be expecting you. Drop the cash off, and he'll give you another day to come and pick it up.'

Shams looked on as Mujahid placed the notes carefully in an envelope, sealed it and placed it on a child's pink play table in front of him. He had never seen so much cash. He wanted to reach out and touch it. Here, now, at night he felt the room whirl with endless possibilities, but he carried a fear that if he reached out and clutched a strand it would all wither to a earthly reality.

Mujahid said, 'So we safe?'

Shams replied, 'I still need to think about it, I think.'

Shams watched as Mujahid nodded, slid the envelope back and tucked it into the band of his trackie bottoms. 'Ok, but decide soon. Take the phone, it's got one of my numbers and the guy's digits.'

Mujahid offered the phone. An old Nokia candybar, it had a low-res picture on its scratched and dilapidated screen that Shams barely looked at before stashing it in a pocket. Mujahid stared at Shams, who was forced to return the gaze. 'I'm doing you the favour here, working for me, remember that. It won't come again. Opportunities like this don't come often. As you know, other people round these ways are doing stuff for me and doing well. You could be like them. If you say no, I've got a line of them looking for a chance. You know that's truth, but you were alright with me way back so I want you to be the one.'

Shams nodded. 'Bruv, I appreciate it. I'll definitely give a think and give you a shout.'

The men stood up, Shams needing a second attempt to bounce upwards from the couch. Shams gave Mujahid a hug. He left the flat and could feel Mujahid's gaze follow. He looked out high over London, cars going to and fro, scurrying like ants. He heard the door shut once again, felt his body relax, felt its thirst, and quenched himself on the cooler air like a man coming out of a fever. As he walked and saw London walking with him, he remembered that Ishaq liked to climb to the top of these towers to stare at stars and memorise constellations. It had always been a pain, getting Ishaq to come along with him and Marwane on those tube adventures. Ishaq was reticent about steaming behind a passenger, and preferred to ask commuters for their unneeded passes. Shams thought it a strange code of behaviour when they were completely dodging fares either way. Ishaq said that his dad worked in transport and could get into trouble if they were caught. Shams remembered laughing as he called Ishaq a pussy, and how irritated he became when he was coolly ignored. Ishaq would say jumping the barriers only worked a few times, until you finally got caught. It was better to work through the system as much as possible, even if it was a total sham.

Ishaq and Marwane were not that far from where he now stood but they were as distant as those ants. At some point the adventures stopped. The thrill had gone. They had been frontiersmen bucking boundaries, making their own stories and histories. Now they were just ordinary travellers.

Shams took the lift down and exited the block, once again walking past the police sign that was partially obscured by a mound of consolatory flowers. The notices were so common now. Yellow harbingers of peril. There was probably no alternative, no real substitute for the police anyway. You had to bring focus to the crime and they didn't have the manpower to go door to door for potential witnesses. Still, they added to an underlying feeling of gloom. Shams felt it whenever he came back. So permeated and soaked through that locals didn't even notice it. That took an outsider's eye.

In the shadow of one of the large towers, Shams passed a rare grassy patch and remembered one such interloper: a well-dressed woman, well put together, in a royal blue suit jacket and pleated skirt with pearl earrings and necklace. From an affluent part of Surrey, she woke up one day, and took the train all the way into London for a trip. Once there she boarded a bus and somehow arrived at the estate. Probably the first set of high rises that could be seen when entering the city from the south, away from her own home and community, ready to make her statement to the world. She proceeded to climb one of the tall towers, ascending as far as possible, one floor below the roof. She took in the view. And then jumped. As her body fell, revolving, descending from the heavens, crashing into the indifferent earth, a febrile whisper dashed around the estate like lightning. Upon hearing, Shams, with Marwane and Ishaq and some other friends, ran to take a look at the body. Getting there just before the medics, the ten year-old boys egged each other on as to who would dare touch the body. Shams didn't take part. He just stared at the cadaver. He had expected a pool of blood, but the body had hit that rare grassy bank and somehow remained intact. Her skin had turned a translucent pale and her face was fixed, not in fear or despair, but in peace. The medics arrived and took the body away. The first dead body Shams had seen. Some gatherers strained their neck to take a gander, and said it was such a shame, and voiced some quiet sorrows. A white youth with a more prosaic mind called her a dumb bitch and jogged on. Shams ignored them and went home. No words, his face showing no reaction or emotion. But he felt anger. The first real anger he had experienced. Anger that someone rich had come from outside to inflict their misery on the estate, as if they should simply accept it as a humdrum part of their lives. It wasn't enough that they had all the chances that people here never had: they had given up, and in that capitulation wanted to make their suffering more important than anyone else's. Shams thought that he would never end up that way. He would get out. Whatever it took.

3.

Ishaq reached the block's entrance. There was no lighting again, the lamp had been smashed. He swiped his electronic fob over the lock, its buzzing sound taking a chainsaw to the dead stillness. The door, made of thickly cast steel, took a violent tug to heave open. Ishaq found it harder than usual, hearing a high pitched metal scraping as he struggled. He looked down and saw a collapsed can of lager braced at the bottom. Since the door locks had become electronic, the cost of a replacement key was enough to keep a family in take-aways for a couple of days, so the solution of some tenants was to wedge the door open with anything expedient. As a result, errant groups of kids sometimes converged in safety on the stairways. They would huddle, sleeves over their hands, passing around joints. This led to tests of wills, as Ishaq was very guarded about his small block. If you were soft on small incursions, your block could get altogether too hospitable a reputation around the estate and be infested by druggies, and other undesirables squatting. He didn't want his mother and sister to navigate that. It was supposed to be their refuge, not some safe haven for exiles. Ishaq reached down, picked up the intruder and flung it, not caring to see where the projectile arced and fell.

Compared to others, his block was in a tolerable state. The rubber flooring on the stairs was tired and eaten, but largely intact. The walls were painted with an off-blue anti-graffiti paint that contained incongruous glittered flecks as if it had been vomited by a lost and hung-over fairy. On the stairs, lamps fizzed and flickered as if inhabited by forlorn spirits striving to communicate through Morse.

At the foot of the stairs, Ishaq saw a couple of familiar silhouettes trying to climb. Getting nearer, he could see Frankie, an old school friend, giving his partner Rice a hand up. The other hand bidding to cope with both a spliff and a can of lager that washed and slapped the sides of the tin as it was haphazardly cast about. Frankie was tall. He was scrawny where once he was muscular. All the fat had been sucked out of his face, his skin now taut and stretched over his skull like a living, breathing tsantsa from some South American tribe. A walking, talking, shrunken head that served as an admonishment to all.

Ishaq spotted him every so often with a new woman in tow. Every time, Frankie always looked just that little bit worse. A decline just at the edge of the envelope of perception. Too young yet for his sunset years, more a sunrise in reverse, a thwarted blooming. Frankie's obsidian eyes were dilated. His skeletal face held a permanent look of desperation, made even worse as the stairwell light alternated, exposing his face to harsh fluorescence and then burying it back into darkness.

Frankie had shacked up with the older woman, Rice, after her last man had done a runner. As of late, both of them had started to make regular trips to a flat on the other end of Ishaq's block. Ishaq didn't care to inquire into what they were doing there as long as they didn't cause a fuss and left quickly. Hoppy alcohol and weed conveyed their musty essence over all three of them. Having never touched the stuff, they smelt to Ishaq of boundaries violated. Piss, beer and dope. Eau de toilette, eau d'estate. He had faint hopes that they were sticking to the lower end of intoxicants. A better analgesic for coping with reality than many of the other options available. Although, even now, experimenting around had siphoned away their youth and cauterised any chance of perception.

'Hey Issy, long time. Hey, I went to school with this guy,' Frankie said with pride, letting go of Rice and pointing at Ishaq. Frankie's speech was slurred but it was more the dimness and lethargy of it that confirmed to Ishaq that something of Frankie had departed permanently. Rice, however, was too busy to look. One hand on the stairs' metal handrail, both feet looked bound together, pivoting on the edge of the first step. She was struggling to gain traction or put one foot in front of the other, see-sawing away. Seeing her straining, Frankie raised his voice, 'I TOLD YOU TO STAY DOWNSTAIRS. I said I'll only be a second. Why do you always need to come up?'

A plaintive Rice started to wail, 'I want to come too, help me.'

Body straight like a plank, Rice looked like she was about to topple. Ishaq motioned to put a hand out to help her, then pulled back, his arm left in stasis as his calculating, guarded brain rebelled against a palpitating heart. One of the first rules of survival was to never get involved. Your business is your business and theirs is theirs. He had learned long ago that the process of enduring meant shutting down. Refuting yourself. Inuring yourself to bad news. Not getting involved. Not getting dragged into the consuming vortex of others, at any cost. Especially those who had a hand in their own downfall. There was no hope there. You couldn't make things better, but you could make things a lot worse for you. See no evil. Hear no evil. That was more important than surviving by dark wiles. Ishaq hated this. Your God fearing, your moral code, your basic human decency. Suppressing it. You had to. Loathe yourself if need be, for impotence, or your fear, but survive. Meddling was a vanity, a luxury.

Frankie caught Rice just in time. 'I SAID STAY!…So Issy, how are you? Things going good? You safe, yea? Sorry about the spliff, yea?'

Glad to see that Rice didn't crack her head open, Ishaq replied, 'Alright. Nothing to report really. Just surviving as usual.'

Frankie looked vaguely like the pasty ginger guy whom he had known when younger. Ishaq remembered that he had been a mouthy gobshite, but a massive laugh. Feisty, full of beans, he had been a great baller in the local youth league whenever his manager hadn't banned him for turning up late or skipping training. Now, his rapid ageing made him look like a badly maintained thirty something, when he was around twenty just like Ishaq. None of the old sparkle. Ishaq tried not to pity him, he could try and give him that at least that, but he did. The funny thing was that back in the day when Frankie was whole, he would never have apologised for the spliff. He wouldn't have given a crap what Ishaq thought, or deferred in any way. There was always some beef back then. Ishaq felt it wasn't even politeness, now, but Frankie's knowledge of his own fall. He detested Frankie for that. It made him uncomfortable. Yet another old friend. But still. He felt. Something. That these two were of his tribe. More than the money-changers of his local mosque, or the ya-yas he went to university with. Here, in this occulted space, even through the haze, they saw each other. They were his and he was theirs.

It was hard to tell Rice's age, her pock marked face had gone the other way of Frankie's and bloated, giving her the look of a confused puffer fish. Her varicose legs were exposed by her half-leggings. She wore a red beanie, with the embellishment of a soiled Hello Kitty that gave a mocking look. It was pressed down so tight that it partially covered her eyes. Rice gave up hope of climbing and initiated full sobs, inhaling and exhaling loudly. 'I want to go! I never get to go!'

Ishaq had seen enough, he looked at Frankie. 'Alright bruv, good seeing you. I'll see you about, yea.' Frankie looked disappointed, his lips wavered as if he wanted to talk on, but he took a glancing look at Rice, 'Alright safe yea, yea, you too, I'll see you around. Keep safe, yea.'

Ishaq thought about what they would do if…not if, when, one of them moved on and made a new friend. How do they survive? When they go in to collect their money from the job centre or wherever, do they get stopped and asked if they needed help? Where was their family? As brief as this empathy was, the thought was crushed, his mind pushed it out.

He left the duo behind, walked up to the second floor and to the fourth door. He passed the smell of fish that the quiet Sri Lankan family was making. A welcome change. He thought he could detect cinnamon and saffron. Tentative, he put his key into the lock and twisted it slowly. Once in, he made himself small and crept up the stairs, clinging to the walls. He took care to avoid the third step from the top. It held the threat of a loud creak that could alert the house. And as usual, this didn't work. 'Issy,' his mother called, 'why are you back so late? Have you eaten, baita?'

Ishaq followed the trail of sound to the largest bedroom and saw his mother sitting on the floor with a copy of the Quran, giving dhikr using green tasbih. Only a side-table lamp was lit, enveloping his mother with light, glancing off the golden calligraphy on the holy book.

The Tabrizis lived in a maisonette. Three bedrooms upstairs, with a kitchen and small lounge downstairs. His parents had thought that they would only be in the UK a few years. This transitory feeling, along with constant remittances home, meant that they had never felt secure enough to buy a place outside the estate. Ishaq resented that drag of relatives on his mum and dad. Some amorphous face, a second-cousin twice removed that they were obliged to give a hand. They were lucky to have gotten on the council list, and here they had been ever since. Not sitting on a paper fortune like some of peers who had purchased their Edwardian terraced houses, and ridden the ridiculous London housing bubble ever since. But still able to purchase the property at tuppence when Thatcher allowed right-to-buy. It was a good home. A constant. Something to be thankful for.

'Assalmu alaikum, I was with the brothers at the study circle, I got a shwarma from the Lebanese place before,' he said.

Leaning over to kiss her on the cheek, Ishaq recognised the familiar smell of sandalwood that came from her favourite Pakistani soap. While returning the kiss, his mother brushed a hand over his face. A feather touch that held the assurance of someone's unbroken concern.

'Always with the 'brothers'; I hope they are good boys.'

'Of course, you know Marwane. Ayub still gives the talks.'

'Yes, nice boys. Good families, but I don't know the others. You need to eat healthily Ishaq, you are too skinny.'

'Well, I eat enough, I don't know where it goes. Do you want me to be a doughboy like some of the other Asian kids? You need a forklift truck to get those guys out of bed.'

Ishaq's mother shook her head in admonishment but mixed in a smile that always made him happy. They smoothed her wrinkles and gave her a serenity that he yearned for. Ishaq had the slim profile of his father, who he saw snoring away in bed. They shared thin but aquiline noses that could lend them a haughty look when not careful. His father worked as a bus driver, taking overtime whenever possible, and was generally found here sleeping the previous shift away. Rude boys creating disturbances, swearing passengers, aggressive car drivers cutting him up and honking away, overtly risky or overly timid cyclists close to his blind spot while he was turning, none of this fazed him as long as he could come home and have a nice cup of chai.

It could…no, it should, have been better. When Ishaq's parents came from Pakistan in the sixties, his father came proudly armed with a mechanical engineering degree from a college in Rawalpindi. Highly expectant that he would soon be of service to the once famous manufacturing industries of the UK, hope was quashed when he found that his qualifications were of no use. Whatever his knowledge and experience, they were treated with contempt. With a wife in tow, extended family back home expecting financial support, and the desire to raise a family, Ishaq's father got work wherever he could. This meant taking anything, whether it was unregulated building work, driving taxis or delivering food. It meant constant aggro with tempermental customers and being ripped-off by unscrupulous employers. What stung the most was that he was even exploited by members of his own Asian community, who wanted to rinse out every penny of possible use from needy and desperate newcomers. Living in such a fragile and insecure way, without recourse from the law, meant that getting a job with London Transport on the buses had been a boon. Constant work in a secure structure, and supported by a marvellous entity known as a trade union. It felt like a working man's nirvana.

Ishaq sat on the bed, careful not to dislodge his father's slumbering mass, and took a habitual sniff. He held early recollections of his father smuggling him a slight sip of whisky when he had flu or a sniffle. On occasion, his slightly inebriated father would arrive home supported upright by a colleague. Ishaq would help him up the stairs, take his shoes and belt off, and usher him into bed, overseen by his grim-faced mother. If his father ever caught her gaze, he would say, 'God will judge me, no point you being angry with me too, woman.'

The funny thing was that it wasn't his wife he should have been wary of, it was his kids. Ishaq and his sister had started taking up Islamic practices seriously in their early teens. His father was initially concerned when he saw his offspring become unnecessarily pious. Coming to the UK, he had worries that they would be too Anglicised in culture. Brown sahibs who were lost and alien, foreign to him. He could never have guessed at this other outcome. To Ishaq, it looked like the done thing. Like the rest of his cohort, there was a knock on the door, or a recommendation from a friend, sometimes it started with a dars or reading at a mosque. The religion Ishaq was introduced to seemed strange, so alien from the Islam of his parents. Theirs was a religion of Indic customs, saints and homage to ancestral ways. A servile deference to the past that could not hold in the full glare of western interrogation. The new way brought a broom to that superstition and insouciance. Their parent's unquestioned Islam was entwined with cultural practices. A Gordian knot, so dense and tight that unravelling it was impossible. The only option was a desperate cut, right through. Other children had come home enflamed with religious zeal. Fearing idolatry or corruption, they prohibited anything not supported by a scholarly text. An Islamic state at home. Year Zero. Forcing a head covering on their mother and inveighing against their fathers if they didn't pray. The strictest Muslims banned music in their homes. Ishaq remembered a pair of brothers so enraptured that they went home and tried to destroy every old CD, tape and vinyl record of their parents by burning them. A bad idea in the confines of a badly ventilated flat. The whole estate came out to see them carted off to hospital with toxic smoke inhalation.

His father once said to his children, 'Religious knowledge is like a deep ocean; if you go down too far, you will drown.' Ishaq had replied, 'But with time, dedication, and the right training, you can find pearls at the bottom.' This earnest, meditated answer had made his father arch back in laughter, showing paan-stained molar teeth, while lightly patting his boy on the head. Ishaq was not like the others, he had not tried to change his parents after he became more observant. Along with his sister, he did try to wean them away from what he felt were the more outlandish practices that conflicted with Islam. Those superstitions about protective amulets or special wristbands. His mother used to send money to a so-called holy man in India so that he would pray for them. Ishaq put an end to it. As well as being in conflict with the rules regarding intercessors and God, he saw a shabby scam. A scam that he saw repeated across the estate. Here was fecund soil for all sorts of chancers to capitalise on the downcast. A marketplace of sorts, the hawking of blind hopes disguised as truths. He had seen people use African faith healers, to cure sickness or try and get a disabled child to walk. Spiritual mediums offered succour to the elderly for the right price. Rich outsiders used indigent locals as proxies to sell even more impoverished people their pyramid schemes. Payday loans at extortionate interest rates, once offered by spivs and loan sharks, were now being pushed by large corporations. Ishaq remembered he had to chase one out when he was fourteen. Stumbling in, as his mum was about to sign something more out of politeness than understanding, Ishaq hurled Anglo-Saxon at the salesman. Effing and blinding at the man while his shocked mother admonished him for being so rude to a guest.

There were many other religious groups as well. Ishaq's home was always being pamphleted by some zealous new convert to Seventh Day Adventism or a new Christian sect. And of course there were the Mormons. Slickly combed young American missionaries, doing a tour of duty for their army of God. Wandering around the estate, with oiled and well-combed hair, dressed in suits and ties in a way that only a 1950s American could possibly think was refined, they actually came across as sinister within the ragged environs of the estate. Always unerring in their politeness and smiles, they never got mugged or harassed. Their total ignorance of the area seemed to give them such mental freedom of their surroundings that they came across to residents as totally alien, and stark raving mad, rather than replicable models of civility. His mother always invited them in for tea and cake until, one day, Ishaq was finally at home for a visit. His house must have been blacklisted as a lost cause and they as perished irredeemable souls. In an inversion of the Lamb's Blood of Moses' tenth plague, whenever a new tour of Mormons started wandering the estate they now always passed over his place. His mother of course chastised him for once again being so rude. Offering any sort of counter-opinion to any guest was deemed disrespectful by his mother's standards 'Just let them talk Ishaq; they seem like good boys.'

Ishaq felt Islam was above this. Yes, Muslims believed in a great omnipotent being, but not in a man or men. It felt so systematic. It concentrated on deeds as well as faith. It offered the certainties of ritual that inculcated healthy habits of discipline while also focusing on the brotherhood of mankind, and conditioning of the heart. From its inception, it offered a universality that was lacking in other faiths. His view, and that of his generation's, looked to his parents like a new and exotic way of practising the religion. Theirs was still a localised Islam from the sub-continent, that seemed isolated and superstitious. A return to a more textual way enabled Muslims to reach out to each other across language, race and nation. Ishaq wasn't pushy though. He had seen how hard his parents had struggled and did not see how he could justify being harsh towards them like some of his peers were with their own. He reassured his parents with his behaviour, and his dad even started to pray. He remembered the saying of the prophet, peace be upon him, 'Islam began as strange and it will return as strange, so give glad tidings to the stranger.' The house had settled into a heartening rhythm of prayers interspersed with normal life. When asked questions by his parents, he just provided books in Urdu about Tawhid, the oneness and indivisibility of a God that created and transcended the universe. Maybe this meant that his faith wasn't as strong as his friends. But his mum was always praying in the night. He didn't do that and he doubted his friends did, so how could he judge her? He did not stop his mother playing her radio. In fact, he secretly found a lot of the old Urdu and Hindi songs soothing in their reflective melancholy. No one could invoke loss, pain and nostalgia as well as those songwriters and poets. Ishaq would find himself laden with the yearning that his parents must feel for home and loved ones. As well as praying, cooking and fretting, Ishaq's mother also loved poetry. He would marvel at how she could recall classic verses and couplets written by Ghalib, Faiz, Iqbal and others. Enchanting verse about longing and belonging, that could easily be talking about lost homes as well as loves. His parents were generous people and he wasn't sure he knew any other genuinely nice people, including himself.

Bringing him out of his thoughts, his mum said, 'Ishaq, son, I have a question, about something I saw in the newspaper this morning.'

Ishaq asked, 'Which newspaper?'

'Daily Mail.'

He felt his blood heat, quicken and rise. Ishaq was exasperated by his mum's continued purchase. But when he had time to kill and the paper was just lying there, ready to hand, he was always tempted by it too. It was like being seduced by a schoolmate's dodgy late night doner kebab. The shame and disgust existing before, during and after the event.

'Mum, why do you buy that rubbish?'

'I told you it has special offers and good shopping deals.'

Ishaq found his mother's simple nature infuriating at times. Maybe simple was unfair, more hospitable was about right, open, able to take everything at face value. Raised among her own people as the majority, she hadn't needed to assess risks, or develop street smarts. Not been born into those feelings of insecurity and quiet paranoia that are borne of being from a conspicuous minority. She would strike a conversation up with pretty much anyone on a bus or the underground, with Ishaq smouldering, feeling agitated and protective when his mother was engaged by a potential threat. His parents lived on the estate but they lived a remarkably different life. From childhood onwards he saw how smiles evaporate as puppy fat disappeared, cheekbones became defined and muscles grew hard. Society's pattern of fear and reaction, fight and flight, was set off by seeing boys of brown and black skin growing into men. Not by some tiny elderly woman in a salwar kameez pushing along a polka-dotted shopping trolley from the budget supermarket. A shopping trolley that did in fact get stolen when Ishaq's mum left it at the bottom of the block's stairs for five minutes while she fetched him to carry it up. That had been one of the rare times he had seen his mother angry. She had made a meal for an elderly neighbour and couldn't believe that someone had dared to steal a beautiful fresh chicken biryani. Ishaq had enjoyed telling his mother how much this validated his view of estate life.

Ishaq shook his head. 'What did you read?'

'Something about Muslims…'

Ishaq started laughing, catching his mouth in case he woke his father. 'Well, it's always something about Muslims. Did a burka wallah steal toffees from a baby and do a runner?'

'No, it was about something called FGM. I wanted to ask you, what is that?'

'Uhhh…' Ishaq's face took on a rose hue. He puffed his cheeks as he tried to think of an appropriate answer, 'uuh…

well…you know how…men…get circumcised…well…in some countries in Africa they do something like that for women. It's pretty gross. Nothing really.'

Ishaq avoided eye contact as his mother stared, even more intrigued. 'Ok…what does that actually mean?'

'Mum, seriously, I'm not going into detail with you. It's too gross, ask Maryam instead. Anyway, don't worry. It's some local culture thing, even if they are trying to pin it totally on us.'

His mother grabbed a copy from behind a chintz-patterned pillow and started flicking through the pages, pointing at a picture. 'I've asked your sister, she goes too shy as well. Why have they got a big picture of a niqabi next to the article? Nothing like this happens in Pakistan.'

Ishaq took the newspaper, held it as if he were wearing asbestos gloves, folded it and handed it back. 'Well because, as if they don't have enough to slap us around with, they like finding any little thing that happens anywhere among a billion-and-a-half and then blaming everyone. It's an called an agenda, Mum. Don't. Buy. That. Newspaper.'

Ishaq's mother nodded, calmy taking the newspaper and putting it away. 'You haven't explained. So what exactly happens, and in which countries?'

Ishaq scanned through the list of news reports in his mind. It wasn't just that paper but so much of the outside world. Always hysterical. Anything from the serious, like benefit cheats and grooming gangs, to the surreal, like articles stating that Muslims are trying to implement Sharia law and ban Christmas. Ishaq was surprised they didn't accuse Father Christmas of being a clandestine Muslim; that guy had a massive beard, avoided airports, and enjoyed breaking and entering into their homes on their sacred holidays.

Still, the stories continued. Every minor infraction by anyone remotely 'Muslimic' diffused into multiple headlines, conflating the many fears of a crepuscular nation in decline. Rather than reflecting on our times, the media acted as the Pied Piper of public opinion. Merrily leading their aroused charges over the meridian to a blurry destination that was not even within their own purview, but probably somewhere where Winston Churchill was in charge, blowing hard on a cigar while listening to Vera Lynn.

'I'm tired. Please ask Maryam again. I can't do it. Can I go please?' Ishaq said, hoping his abruptness would end the conversation.

Ishaq's mother paused, looking at him. 'Ok, Ishaq get some sleep. You have school in the morning.'

'University,' he said firmly.

'Ok, big man, university.' His mother scrunched both eyes as she smiled.

Ishaq kissed his mother and left, relieved that he had averted an excruciatingly awkward conversation.

4.

Iron bars of rain enveloped Ishaq. Running for cover, he felt their weight batting at him. Looking to the horizon he took in heady cumulus clouds laden, ready to dump their load onto an already dank university campus. The sky spread a grey-blanketed pall over already leaden buildings. Ishaq found this most London of hues a comfort; far preferable to those rare, hot, and somehow inappropriate summer days. No, London was better in a nice restrained grey, like a regal elderly statesman. Less of a stygian gloom than the palette of the estate but nevertheless muted and understated. Ishaq liked grey. He lived in grey. There was contentment in grey.

He reached the entrance of his university's administration building. Standing in the portico, within the shadow of one of the giant Doric columns, Ishaq fumbled around in his backpack for a hastily-scribbled post-it note. Once retrieved, he checked the room number of his final year tutor.

The Study Circle

Ishaq had gained admission as they raised tuition fees. With the money saved from living at home, and summers working at a call centre, he could just about make ends meet. Get through the years, keep the plates spinning without a crash or smash. His parents had always talked about university. It was a given. An article of faith that education solved all problems. It was the match that lit the generator of material wellbeing and security. When they had come to the UK higher education was free and it made their struggle worthwhile, knowing their children could work their way up. Now he felt like the drawbridge was being raised.

He made his way to the east wing, climbed the winding terrazzo stairs and located his tutor's door. On first inspection it looked like an impressive hardwood, in accordance with the grandeur of the building. On closer scrutiny, Ishaq noticed that the door was blistering and cracking in places, and in fact peeling away in others like chapped skin. He pulled on one strand of the hardwood veneer, felt it ease away and reveal cheap chipboard. Ishaq caught at another section. The door opened. Professor Harrell saw Ishaq looking slightly abashed, with a sliver of hardwood veneer in his hand.

'I do wish you students would just come in, rather than insist on stripping my door of all its dignity. No time for gawping, come on.'

A harassed-looking man, constantly pushing his unkempt hair one way then the other, Professor Harell always acted like he was late for his own funeral. He had been Ishaq's tutor for a while, although they met intermittently. This suited them both fine. Don't bother them and they won't bother you.

The door opened onto a room a little bit larger than Ishaq's bedroom. Just enough to hold a wooden desk, a couple of haggard chairs, and a wall-to-wall bookcase haphazardly packed with papers. A likely indication of this tutor's disheveled mind; though, in this digital age, Ishaq found that musty smell of old papers reassuring. They held the ready nostalgia of recorded history and the reclamation of minds long gone. But then it was not his history and nor were they related minds. This whole institution, its architecture, its discussions, its concerns, always reminded him how the West culturally and romantically traced the total lineage of human knowledge and wisdom back to the Romans and Greeks.

The decision to study History had been a difficult one. Friends of his parents would raise eyebrows or ask abrupt questions of what their son was up to. It was axiomatic to his parent's generation that getting a university education involved studying something of substance, something that had a direct link with job prospects. There was so much risk in migrating, and the future so uncertain, that you needed skills that were easily transferable. Abilities rooted in the real world, to do with things you could feel and manipulate. Doing, not thinking. Action, not prevarication. Competencies that were physical, not incorporeal. Ideas were too abstract and the subject of whimsy. They were beholden to extraneous judgement, and only as good as contacts, and any assurance bred-by-birth, allowed. The ability to make money from ideas fed on distant audiences and inaccesible networks was a charmed confidence trick that they did not possess the guile for.

'Excuse the mess. Come in Ishaq. Quickly. Take a seat.' The professor took one of the chairs and indicated another, moving a bundle of yellowing papers.

The professor settled on the other side of the desk and Ishaq went to take his seat, having to evict one final book.

'*The Catcher in the Rye*,' the professor noted. 'Have you read it?'

'Yea, good book. A classic,' Ishaq said, as he mirrored the other man's nodding. 'Is everything ok? I don't believe that we had anything in the normal schedule.'

Sitting with one leg over the other, the professor wrung his white liver-spotted hands. Like a spry gymnast preparing for action, thought Ishaq. Often this could look like nerves but Ishaq thought the man was the victim of an energetic and overactive mind, what with his constant fidgeting and irregular nodding while talking.

'Yes, everything is fine, don't worry…unless there's something you want to tell me?' The professor stared.

Ishaq shook his head slowly and frowned, embarrassed by the ensuing silence, feeling that he was at a confession, prompted by a preceptor rather than a pedagogue. 'Uhh…no…nothing that comes to mind. You called me in…'

The professor continued with an attempt at an appraising stare. Something about the way the man was trying to look grave whilst lost in an oversize orange jumper, pilling from age, made him want to laugh.

Professor Harrell said 'Ok…well…Look, I've been meaning to have a chat to you about your future plans. Do you know what you want to do after you graduate?'

Now this sounded like Mum or Dad talking. What about the future? Yea, what about it? He had romantic ideas of university as the opportunity to think and analyse and explore; they saw it as more of a passport to a secure livelihood, but this was all guesswork. This journey was just an idea that had never been tested. One part conjecture, another part founding mythology. He did accept the need to be more calculating. Be responsible, earn money. Cold decisions were required, not quixotic ideas. When applying for degrees he had flirted with the sciences and engineering, but had no interest in becoming a doctor or staring down at people's manky teeth. The prohibition on usury ruled out banking. He even looked at pharmacy, but the idea of that was soul-destroying. Yea, the final choice was a bit carefree but the only opportunity to study something fascinating. One fleeting window in a lifetime, one narrow chance, that had flown so quickly that here he was now, in his final year. Resigned to applying for jobs and entering that so-called real world.

'Well...I'm not too sure. I'll probably go through the milk round, see what's out there.'

'Anything else?' The professor's eyes widened.

Ishaq shook his head and pursed his lips, 'No...not really... should there be?'

'We, the department and I, have kept an eye on you... and think you have promise. I wanted to talk to you about the possibility of staying on.'

Ishaq, slumping in his chair, straightened up. 'To do what?'

'Masters, Research, a Phd track maybe?'

He had mastered the art of low expectations yet this felt different, it piqued his interest, but then surprises were not always a gift . 'Why me?'

'Well, we are getting a lot of funding for more research on the Muslim community in Britain, and as a promising student, presumably with germane experience, I thought I would see what you think.'

If this is what patronage is, there's always a premium to be paid, thought Ishaq. 'So I would be the token Muslim guy? Great, what would the work exactly entail?'

'No, no, no! You've been mentioned because of the quality of your work and dissertation this year. As for the work, well, that would be what we would decide together. There's not enough that has been done on the history of Islam in Britain, reform movements, leadership, the media, mosque development, development links to activities overseas. The list is endless. I think you would find it interesting as it seems to be in line with your elective choices.'

The venerable Prof was right; it was interesting. Social and economic shifts, groups uniting and dividing, ideologies prospering and declining. It was so engrossing. He couldn't help comparing what he had learned here to his own community. It was as if he was experiencing history at an accelerated pace, the peculiar awareness that he was both an observer and participant. Some lefty students maybe dreamt to be a part of it. He saw their romanticisation of the downtrodden, the allure of a cause. As if he had been given a mysterious gift. If only they knew the truth of it. A cocktail of race and class struggle was begetting an inchoate future, abutted by periodic violence. So many questions but no time to sit down and think. He wanted some sense of understanding. His own perceptions. Some control, even if it were illusory. Some notion of agency, even if ultimately a mirage. He felt his community, if indeed it was a community, lurched from one crisis to the next. Society clubbing with one question after another, a wall of sound so sonorous, so resounding, that many started to tune out its constant pitch, to clamp weary hands to their ears and retreat inwards. He was the same as a boy – as a man – with a slushed foundation and no guide. Every movement forward a new frontier, a naked step, knee deep into virgin snow. Pioneering yet exhausting.

He put a hand forward to make a point, but paused and retracted, took a brief look at this elderly white man, and pressed his thumb into the table, testing its solidity. Was it worth attacking that deep dive, the risk of drowning to find treasure?

'That sounds interesting but I have to ask, what would be the point? Lots of papers passed between university and government departments. What does it ever achieve?' said Ishaq.

'Again that depends on you. You could use the research to help Muslim groups, it can be used to formulate government policy. It's not an ivory tower project, Ishaq. It's a niche area, you could make a good career. Who knows…if you are possibly interested in academia, this is a good opportunity. It's a fascinating time and we could do with people like you researching it.'

Government and its policy? There were many well-connected right-wing institutes that resolutely held them as their targets. You had shadowily-funded think tanks with Orwellian names such as the Centre for Social Cohesion, which aimed at spreading in-cohesion. One called 'Student Rights' that existed solely to attack the rights of Muslim students. Dog-whistle talk on how large the Muslim population will be or why the name 'Muhammad' is popular for babies. Questioned on why they were producing such papers, they would cower and say, 'Just leaving it out there' and 'Let's have a debate'.

'People like me? You make it sound like paid-spying or government-lackey work,' said Ishaq, insistent.

Professor Harrell went silent. Taking a deep breath he said, 'Again it's not that…but it does tie-in with something else I wanted to speak to you about. This is difficult, but…don't know how to put this…but we have had requests for information about you.'

Ishaq felt his cheeks go warm, and struggled to push out his words 'Re… requests for information? What does that mean? By whom?'

'Well, to be frank, there are not many openly observant muslims on the social sciences courses here. There was a Home Office liaison unit that wanted to gather intelligence from lecturers here on Muslim students…'

Ishaq cut the professor off. His voice raised slightly, 'So in plain English, that means you were asked to spy on me. Is this what this is all really about?'

Harrel's voice declined to nearly a whisper as he took an obvious gulp. 'In plain English, yes. We were asked to…report on people fitting your profile. Although we didn't comply. They are interested in quiet or isolated students. People who may be vulnerable.'

Ishaq stared at the man in front of him, somehow looking smaller, diminished. 'I'm starting to feel this conversation is really inappropriate. I don't want to be rude. But this is bollocks.

What does that mean, "quiet or isolated"? I don't drink, so avoid those circles. I also have like-minded friends like anywhere... just like anyone. "Quiet or isolated" from the perspective of who? People like you judging people like me?' Ishaq's tone had raised and he rose from his seat.

'I understand, but you must admit that you're not very active in extra-curricular matters around the department. You just turn up and go.'

Ishaq berated himself at being surprised. He should have expected it. He knew idle gossip could destroy. It was everywhere. Fear or maliciousness, it didn' matter. Fake letters produced Trojan hoaxes. Inadequate men looked for fifth columnists under their Sunday papers and cereal. On campus, they were supposedly the best and brightest in English society, yet upon hearing of his background he had actually been asked for drugs once. During terrorist scares, he caught students' double-takes of him and his backpack, saw their dread as they jumped out a lift. Ishaq's response was a quiet compliance. Just endure. All these incidents; it was draining to start a long, detailed conversation every time you were at odds. There were some arguments, once even a brawl that Ishaq had felt rueful about afterwards. The other boy would not meet people like him on many occasions, so he had probably solidified a lifetime view. That kid could plead temporary dickheadedness, he did not share the burden of being emblematic of a people. No, it was best to avoid, rather than spend all your time being in discomfort or in confrontation.

'You or most of the researchers in the department don't take part much, either. You're too busy with your own work. I don't see you or them under investigation. Look, what's the Phd got to do with all of this? The offer sounds shady now.'

Professor Harrell looked downwards and his fidgeting increased. Ishaq was placated by the man's show of nervousness and timidity. 'Genuinely...please...it's got nothing to do with the other matter. Naturally, I expected you to be slightly perturbed by this all but it is an honest offer, however strange it may seem. In fact we're telling you the whole story, because if you decide to stay, we don't want you to find out through campus gossip. As you well know, this type of activity on the part of government has been raised higher up within the university, and by the Student Union. Please. Take some time. Think about it.'

Ishaq settled back in his seat, closed his eyes, and tried to generate some anger. That seemed to be most appropriate. That which was expected of him, right? That would be normal? In truth he didn't feel anything. Taste, touch, feel, was numb. He was not distressed or frightened. He did not feel upset or nervous. It was this resignation that saddened him. The professor was right: he had heard the stories on campus, read the national newspapers, so in the back of his mind he had known. He had a limp acceptance of it and it had been that way for a long time.

'They did also ask that if you knew of any vulnerable people, or people of concern, then would you come forward…' said the professor, who looked at Ishaq expectantly.

Ishaq, his tone deadpan, said, 'Well if I find someone making a suicide belt to blow themselves up during rag-week then I'll be sure to dial 999. If they want to gather people who are concerned about Muslims issues, in other words concerned about their lives, then they can round-up hundreds of random students themselves. In fact why not just report anyone who wears a keffiyeh, except of course the rich white students, because they look cool right?'

'No, no, it's exactly what we don't want. That's why we're pushing back. But we're a university, we don't exist in a vacuum. We can only do our best.' The professor slumped into his chair.

'I appreciate your candour, but being frank and honest like you have, academia is for the rich, and theory is for bystanders. I'm neither. I hope that you'll understand that for people like me, I need to get that piece of paper, hopefully with a First, and start earning some cash. That's my reality. Look, I am really tempted but I don't think it's realistic.'

'As I said, there is some funding available. You won't be amazingly comfortable but you will not be in penury. You can still go for a job with a more lucrative salary, and armed with another qualification. Entering the world of economic meltdown and armageddon can wait another three years for you, Mr Tabrizi.' He was wringing his hands again, looking to Ishaq like a moth-eaten Pontius Pilate seeking absolution.

'Ok. Thank you, I'll have a think about it…thank you for telling me about this.'

'Please take your time. Please think long and hard about it.'

The professor extended his hand. Ishaq looked at it and gave it it a cautious shake. As he left the office, a conciliatory Professor Harrell said, 'Interesting times, aren't they?'

Ishaq gave a reply devoid of feeling. 'Yes, just like the Chinese say.' He opened the door, paused before stepping through and then twisted back, contorting himself to interact with his lecturer. 'By the way. I lied.'

In the middle of gathering some papers, the professor's body stiffened, and after some time he asked the question, 'About what?'

'*Catcher in the Rye*. I hated it. I hate that book.'

Ishaq left the building, hunched, gears of his mind in steady rotation. He had taken care when interacting with students. Obviously not enough. There had been stories of the security services hiring other students to befriend suspects. He had met one post-grad who insisted on coming to talks and fasting with them during Ramadan, yet was insistent that he was not interested in converting. The boy said he was simply practising empathy. Something that horrified Ishaq. Empathy? In London? Maybe this was a middle-class thing, that he didn't understand. The guy had also said that, in private, he sometimes cried at the pain and suffering of the world, which wound-up Ishaq even more. He later turned out to be part of some radical Christian sect proseltysing in Egypt.

One well-to-do white girl on his course had been approached by MI5 to apply for their graduate training program. Told to tell no one, she immediately brought in the prospectus, and a group of them had a great laugh at the pictures of actual MI5 graduates. Stills of them in awkward poses where they were facing a wall, or their head was lost in a file, or so close together in discussion that their faces were never revealed. Their security upheld in a kind of photographic niqab.

He had tried the political and international organisations but found too many people who thought they were the next Gordon Gekko or Mother Teresa. Ishaq could only share details on how his summer was spent stacking shelves in the local supermarket, trying to pay his tuition fees. Others bonded over building homes in South America, or teaching English in some ramshackle Nepalese town. About villages like his parents'. How hard it was to shit in a hole while squatting, haha. Or wide eyed as they talked about how spoilt they were with their western comforts. Oh, the colour, oh the vibrancy. How poignant it was to see locals be hospitable in the most impoverished of circumstances. It was like an amazing revelation, some truth had been endowed on them.

Ishaq would sit there, astonished when they had the audacity and impudence to lecture him on the realties of those other worlds. Even if they were nice, he could not shake-off the feeling that the world was just an exotic backdrop to their own self-realisation. Their story. Hobbyists who could dip in and out. They could safely play, import the struggle of the other without real peril.

His one outlet was sports. He actually made the first/second team squads for the football team. A darting and crafty winger with a wicked right foot, he played a couple of games pretty successfully, but soon enough both sides came to realise his face just didn't fit. A coach ride, back from a game, where a lot of the players proceeded to get drunk and strip naked, was the first sign. Then a WhatsApp trail where everyone took a picture of their penis and provided full and hilarious commentary. On excursions to nightclubs, those boys played 'Pull a minger' and 'Ride a beast'. His refusal to join in the 'banter' and compulsory nights-out drinking meant being frozen out, until he inevitably quit. Ishaq didn't find this behaviour shocking. He had seen and been inured by far worse on the estate. He didn't openly show any disdain or contempt. He just found them incomprehensible. Their interaction was so foreign it was like looking at hieroglyphs without the Rosetta stone.

But there were others. Starting at university had also been, in many ways, a massive shock . The first time that he had met relatively intelligent English teenagers who could hold a conversation. During his first year he couldn't help stare at them. Exotic creatures from houses in the countryside somewhere outside of London, whose parents somehow earned enough money to send them to schools where you had to pay. From places where they trusted the police, who you weren't afraid of if you called. He knew that for most them this was a period of unalloyed freedom, that could be looked back on as the best years of their lives. A time to explore, a finishing school for the scions of the well-to-do.

Even now he didn't really understand them. He could understand working class types like him who wanted to get on, and strangely he had no problem understanding the really posh ones who generally acted like they didn't give a crap and were killing time. It was the ones in the middle that perplexed. Like black boxes, and he could only guess at what drove or motivated them to do anything. So different from what he knew, where everyone flailed with little control and direction. Ishaq recalled that he used to wonder about this, when a child. Like children that had headaches spending hours thinking about a universe without-end, or the concept of nothingness before the big bang, or even the possibility and existence of an all-powerful deity, the twelve-year old Ishaq struggled during countless hours with how the English could have possibly procured such a gargantuan empire once upon a time. How was it possible that these people, from this small, unruly island had claimed the world as their own? He thought that his own ancestors must have been truly pathetic, if they had been conquered or subjugated by the English as represented by the crowd from his estate. At school he did study Shakespeare, poetry from the First World War, the Elizabethans, and the Victorians, so he knew there must have been capable people here at some point.

But that history was not so much of a foreign country, but of a people so alien, to the point that sometimes the young Ishaq thought it had to have been made up. Maybe it was 'Once Upon a Time'. He would ask his white mates anything of this history and they would shrug their shoulders, or say they weren't a swot. All the intelligent kids at school were brown. Now, those same white mates were starting to be deadened by alcohol, or drugs , or petty crime, some blaming their plight on people like Ishaq usurping them. Ishaq thought it iniquitous that he was surrounded by students who also indulged, yet somehow they made it through unscathed. These students took for granted the support networks and role models of friends and family, the fuel-of-ambition and career-hopes of which his estate mates had none. They could make assumptions of the future, were not left to be condemned by the age of sixteen for not taking chances they never had.

But he had been given a chance now. He had never considered staying on, past graduation, but now that the opportunity had been dangled in front of him, he was nearly sold. He knew that he would really miss the clarity he felt here. He had always thought of university as just a means to an end, living at home and never far away from the early responsibilities he saw closing in.

Ishaq stood in front of the neo-classical building, under its colonnade, taking sanctuary. As he edged towards the threshold, he gazed upwards at the heavens being drained. When still a child, he thought he could push rainy skies away with his mind, and now he raised a hand as if trying to nudge those heavens away. He felt a vitalising tickle of water travel down his arm and took a ponderous step outwards onto the quadrangle that was thronging with students. People without a care in the world, or at least only caring about themselves. People who, in a deluge, would have him tiptoe between raindrops and blame him if he got wet.

Many, with their self-ordained sophistication and enlightenment, merely saw the universe in ceaseless entropy; that humanity was just a chain of chemical reactions that were indifferent to right and wrong, good or bad. Ishaq could see their listless ennui as how pointless it all was and how they busied themselves trying to forget its crushing banality. And he didn't believe this came from godlessness or a lack or faith. It came from comfort – ease. Everything had been done in their society. All the big battles had been fought, all their needs for shelter and safety sated. There was nothing left. The only challenge they could conjure was their success as an individual, their success as a lonely entity.

Maybe he was being harsh but, even though they traced the same footprints and shared the same spaces, they lived separate human realities, a vibration of different frequencies existing in the gaps of each other's oscillations. Standing here alone as estranged crowds buffeted him, swirling and dancing, he thought of those who told him that he needed to try and fit in more. He thought of the professor's words. He thought that he expended enough energy just to hold ground and stand still. They can't ask anything more. He had done enough.

5.

The rain dwindled to wadding spits, Ishaq trudged his way to the bike racks in the front quad, head down, grazing shoulders when passing others. By the bicycles he saw a rake-like figure, lounging in box fresh hi-tops, shaking off droplets from a fuzzy ball of hair. Marwane. Languid and laconic, the boy who never seemed to take anything too seriously. One of his closest childhood friends and also an estate lad, Marwane was studying Computer Science at another uni nearby. Ishaq always admired how it all rolled effortlessly off his back.

Marwane saw Ishaq, straightened and mock saluted him, 'Assalamu alaikum, bruv, why didn't you call me back? I gave you a missed call.'

'Why didn't you leave a message?'

Marwane looked at Ishaq as if he were simple. 'I never leave messages, you don't know who is listening in, right?'

Ishaq looked over his friend's face, uncertain, searching for the source of such a sinister query. It could be a knowing taunt, or some test, but all he saw was a smile and that glib innocence. His own dependable Shaggy.

'What was so important?'

'I was going to ask what you wanted for lunch? Chicken or a shwarma?'

Ishaq shook his head. 'Don't care. We can eat at the prayer room or the Student Union. Don't mind.'

'You look happy as usual. Droopy dog ain't got nothing on you,' Marwane said, clocking Ishaq's sullen look. 'Ok, let's do the Union, we can pray afterwards.'

They started walking, the rain now a drizzle but the gloom not lifting. Marwane rushed to fill the silence. 'I really hate this crappy weather, it's not one thing or another. Sometimes I wish we had been colonised by the Spanish or Italians and ended up there.'

'But you're Algerian. Your parents should have ended up in France, not here.'

Marwane let out a sly whistle as his body, all large jutting bone and sinew, danced side-on to Ishaq's shorter athletic marching.

'Man, that was a missed bullet. At least the English were just honest and just after cash. The French want to colonise your mind, bruv. Proper messed up. Look at how angry Algerian bros are.' Marwane tapped the side of his head to emphasis the point.

Within sight of the Union building, Ishaq noticed a crowd around the entrance to the canteen. This was pretty usual. Placards brandished like an army's herald, beseeching all to heed their proclamations. The Union building was a lightning rod for the pet concerns of protest groups, or for people with too much time on their hands. One woman held a sign saying 'NO TO ANIMAL CRUELTY. SAY NO TO ALL RELIGIOUS SLAUGHTER'. Dour faced, she was jostling for position with an older man, trying to grab his sign that said 'HALAL MEAT TODAY, SHARIA LAW TOMORROW'.

Ishaq caught Marwane rolling his eyes, as they came closer and saw that one group consisted of animal rights activists. To their obvious discomfort they were backed by conservative groups, and those even further to the right, whose cluster of signs indicated that they saw the issue as a threat to British identity. Divided by ascending Union steps, the other side saw some of his co-religionists, aided and abetted by picketers from the Socialist Workers lot. Whether this was bridge-building or just unholy alliances, it looked to Ishaq that here was his own cognitive dissonance manifest, anthropomorphised, made into human form.

'Man, more protests, Pakistanis love it, don't they? Even the ones here. I wonder if they have an effigy? I've always wondered at how quick they manage to bring one out. Someone's got an effigy factory as a good sideline, bruv,' said Marwane.

'Yea whatever, just like Arabs somehow always have a spare American or Israeli flag to burn. Your lot's banners are even more psycho by the way. Like I saw one with a knife stuck into Masjid al-Aqsa and blood gushing out. How mental is that?' replied Ishaq.

'Ah, so Droopy lives. Well he can shut it. Anyway, you want to get out of here, this is busted,' Marwane said, as he took in the rest of the jumbled scene.

'I'm cool like Scooby or even Scrappy; you're a proper muggy bone-head Shaggy.'

'Get stuffed, at least Shaggy is a geezer. You're that bare dry wannabe preppy one no one remembers the name of.'

Ishaq laughed. As they neared the stoop a white boy with grubby dreads, and in a military coat, shouted out to Ishaq, 'This is barbaric slaughter. Look at these pictures? Are you seriously going to eat out of this canteen?' The kid thrust a leaflet into Ishaq's face. Ishaq took a look and saw pictures of distressed sheep being slaughtered, their eyes pleading and betraying fear. Ishaq looked at the boy. After nearly three years he still struggled to maintain eye contact with people. Here and in the outside world it was a form of assurance and confidence building, while at home firm eye contact was a hostile challenge, a prelude to confrontation. Grinning outside your close social circle was seen as naivety and weakness, while here he noticed everyone gave rapid smiles that caused distrust if not reciprocated. Ishaq still had not mastered the continual fluctuation between the two codes and walked around worried that he was too stern faced. His vex-up 'screwface' as Marwane put it.

Ishaq pocketed the leaflet. 'Sorry fella, I can't afford to eat in the canteen, I live at home and my mum makes me a pack lunch, but thanks for the info.'

Marwane was given a leaflet too, he took one look, squashed it into a ball and threw it on the floor. 'Yo Duuude, why do you rich kids love to dress down so much. Need a cause to fill that empty hole, do ya? I would listen to you if you were a little less smelly.'

Ishaq put his hand over his eyes and whispered to Marwane, 'C'mon Marwane, give it a break, let's just go.'

'Fucking animal-killer arsehole. You people should know better. Karma, you know? You need another Gandhi,' the boy shouted, as Marwane laughed.

'Mate. Totally wrong people.'

Ishaq looked around at other students, making a subtle disassociation from his friend and his new mate. He spied another student. Looking like an experiment gone wrong, dressed like the lovechild of *Where's Wally* with one of those Mormon missionaries, he could only be from the Conservative Party. The man held aloft a blown-up version of a tabloid front page, which read 'BRITAIN SECRETLY GOES HALAL. WHAT NEXT?'

'Ok, you're right. Let's shift.'

Seeing the duo turning on their heels, one of the Muslims, a girl in a bright red headscarf with a flowered pattern, came up and said to Ishaq, 'Brother, it's your duty to get involved. We must defend our rights.' Ishaq noted her accent – in his world of glottal stops, Received Pronunciation nearly always meant Received Wisdom.

Before Marwane could make an inappropriate reply, Ishaq said, 'Uh…sorry sis, but we're late for a class.'

Marwane ignored Ishaq and the obvious lie. 'Look sis, I respect your activism, but I'm really not bothered about this. Like your hijab by the way, mashallah, is it from Laura Ashley?'

The girl gave Marwane a terse look, 'But it's about halal meat first, then everything else. Prayer hall. Women wearing hijab at uni. It's the thin end of the wedge. People like you want to avoid issues but the reality of our life is that we can't avoid them. It's on all of us to pitch in.'

'Well a lot of Muslims in this country are too lazy and fat.' Marwane puffed out his cheeks and started waddling around, arms outstretched, mimicking an over-fed belly. 'So eating a load more veggie stuff might be good for them.'

'This isn't a joke, brother, this is about our rights as Britons.'

Ishaq put a mollifying hand on his sidekick, and smiled at the sister. 'Well, how much so-called halal meat is really halal in the UK? There are strict rules on animal care in the Sharia. I doubt battery-farmed chickens qualify for that.' He saw that the girl was unhappy with this reply. 'Ok, well, just settle on Kosher meat. It's halal for us, and most non-Muslims will be too scared to complain about Jews.'

'That's really helpful,' she said, deadpan and with a look of disapproval. 'Maybe you would be interested in this instead?' She gave Ishaq a leaflet with the headline 'THE ISLAMIC REFORMATION' and a list of talks that were taking place over the next week. 'It's a conference on integration of Muslims. They are covering all the issues, with major European political leaders talking as well. You may not want to take part in demos but you should stay informed.'

'Ok, jazakallahukhair, I'll have a think.' Ishaq showed the leaflet to Marwane. 'What do you think?'

Marwane slipped on a pile of soggy pamphlets, the ground a paper flood. 'What is it with all these leaflets and conferences? Seriously, I couldn't care less. Whoopee doo, we've got politicians talking about us…again. You're the cafe latte socialist type. That's more your thing, isn't it? Thinking too much and being moody.'

'Go on Marwane, it looks interesting. You can keep me company.'

'What? Are you like five years old and need me to hold your hand? I'm playing footy tonight in the cages on the estate. You should sack this conference off and come with.'

Ishaq pulled the leaflet back and stashed it in a pocket. 'I think I'll go to it…If it's dry I'll see if I can make the game.'

Marwane kissed his teeth as he peeled a mashy sheet off the bottom of his new hi-tops. 'I really don't now why you bother. It's a load of hot air. The Muslims there will be the oh-so-into Persian poetry, airy-fairy, magic-carpet types. Really annoying.'

'Well, maybe I'll buy a copy of some Rumi or Ferdowsi, wear a kaftan and start whirling.'

'I swear bruv, if you do that I'll definitely come.'

Listening to their conversation, the girl politely tried to offer Marwane another option in her Oxford English. 'Brother, if you are interested, we are also creating a flash mob to feed the poor. It is for the homeless in the East End.'

Both boys took one glance at each other and started cracking up. Ishaq couldn't hold himself and doubled-over in hysterics. Tears streamed down Marwane's face as he held onto Ishaq to keep him up. Slowly, as the laughter subsided and Ishaq composed himself, he saw the sister's face had contorted in offence.

In between dampened chuckles he said, 'Sister, I'm really sorry, I don't mean to offend but seriously, a bunch of guys, in big beards, and veiled women, appearing out of the middle of nowhere. And then descending on a bunch of unsuspecting homeless people, trying to shove samosas in their mouth? It'll have them scared out of their wits, no? Even I'm scared thinking about it. They'll think Bethnal Green is being invaded by the Taliban and a bunch of ninjas. The Prime Minister will call in COBRA.'

Holding her disdain for the two, she scolded them like wayward children. 'It's important we try to help the local community, Muslims and non-Muslims alike. Immature attitudes do not help. You guys are real idiots, you know that?'

'I know, sorry sis, sorry. I'll definitely make the conference. May Allah reward you for your time and patience with us.' With this Ishaq pulled the still sniggering Marwane away.

'Let me ask her about the scarf again.'

'You're not asking jack. Let's go.'

Just a few steps past, Ishaq and Marwane saw a third group, slightly removed. Garbed mostly in black, they held aloft placards: 'CAPITALISM = SLAVERY', 'THE CALIPHATE IS THE ANSWER', 'ISLAM WILL DOMINATE ALL'. The ringleader of the third group, a rotund individual, was looking their way. Ishaq dipped his eyes and lengthened his stride. Marwane whispered, 'I told you we should get out of here. As night follows day, these flippin' jokers would be here.'

'You told me? Idiot. We wouldn't be hanging around if you hadn't created a flippin' tamasha,' hissed Ishaq in reply.

Abdul-Majid's mass filled their path, his chubby cheeks framed by a dense but scraggly carpet of a beard. With his wide but short frame this gave him the look of a sweet but alarmed hedgehog. Ishaq resisted the impulse to grab one of those cherubic prickled cheeks and give them a good wiggle.

Early on in their university days, Ishaq had spent some time with him through the Islamic society. Abdul-Majid was once a gauche kid from some vague coastal town in Dorset. It was obvious that this was the first time he had been to a big city and been surrounded by Muslim company. They had bonded slightly. He would listen as Abdul-Majid articulated the painful racism he had experienced. About having no backup. No one to talk to.

As time wore on, when around them, he started to talk as if he was from the 'ghetto'. He would lower the register of his voice, and descend into what must have seemed a semblance of street talk that he probably coined from bad grime records, and YouTube clips of people he thought were like Ishaq and Marwane. Lots of 'yea, blud' and 'wagwan'. The boys tried to sympathise but couldn't help smirking, at which point he would ask why they were 'gassed', which only served to crack them up. But that was back then, now Abdul-Majid had realised an ambition and wasn't funny anymore. An ersatz youth from the streets, he grew into a self-constructed Golem.

'Assalmu alaikum, my wasteman brothers. Doing a runner from the issues as usual?'

'Wa alaikum salaam. Not really. Brother. Just busy getting some munch. Hope you are doing well,' said Ishaq, tasting that empty word of kinship as he brushed past.

Abdul-Majid took a skip backwards and held a hand out, pressing it slightly against Ishaq's chest. 'Woah, what's the rush. Just trying to be civil, bruv. You lot always 'praying' and 'studying',' he said, while making quotation signs. 'Let's catch up. You should look around a bit...at the protests, no? When it comes to the reality of the lives of the Muslims you lot do nothing, see nothing, as usual?'

This group always did a great line in righteous indignation. These people saw themselves as the intellectual renewers of

Islam. Abdul-Majid himself became skilled at bombast and histrionic speeches about the debased state of Muslims, and how his group's way would be a panacea to all their ills. Ishaq did his utmost to avoid them, and now he grinned, took a lethargic look from left to right, finishing with a once-over of this crew. 'Done. Well it was nice to see you too. I'm sure you are busy making safe that supply of halal hotdogs. We'll move along. Ta.'

Abdul-Majid skipped back again, this time with a firmer touch that was almost a push. 'Hot dogs! You like mocking. Number one at taking the mick, aren't ya? People like you are the root cause of all our ills? You focus on one small part of the religion and forgo the other bigger responsibilities. Like that hidden pillar of Islam, creating an Islamic state and upholding the law so we don't have to deal with petty issues like this halal meat nonsense.'

Abdul-Majid once had little idea of Islamic practices. At uni he fell in with, and then became a leading light for, the Party for the Restoration of the Caliphate. The group that would reanimate the concept of the Islamic State that was lost with the fall of the Ottoman Caliphate. Everything else was subordinate. They saw it as incumbent on all to fight for such a state, via word and maybe deed. The change had felt sudden, but maybe there was always something there, some resentment, waiting for a vessel to hold it. Some grievance, waiting for a channel. Ishaq wasn't sure what he should have looked for, it hadn't occurred to him that he should be looking for anything. Abdul-Majid's jovial demeanour fell away to reveal a boy puffed up in anger.

'Yea, Abdul-Majid. Brah. You know why it's so well hidden? It's because it doesn't actually exist. You've just made it up. You help yourself and those around you, and that spreads through the community. Any decent state can come through grassroots change. We've been through this loads of times, just be cool and let us through.'

'Ah ha, so you do believe in an Islamic state?' Abdul-Majid pushed a finger on Ishaq's sternum.

Marwane pried the finger off and grabbed Ishaq's shoulder, while checking his friend's tensing face. He had seen this circus before. 'C'mon let's go, proper rubber dinghy rapids, bro.'

Ishaq shook his head, pawing off Marwane's hand, and poked his antagonist back. 'What do you mean "*believe*"…I can't "*believe*" I get drawn into this again and again with you lot. Yes, an Islamic state in theory is all nice. Self-determination without Western invasion. Without all that constant interference. But you have to be balanced. Be reasonable. Look back in history, look at Hajaj Bin Yusuf. He was a tyrant, and by your ideas we would be forced to live under his fist. Just shouting 'Islamic State' won't solve anything until the people change first.'

'I know my history. I have read far more widely than you. You can't tell me jack. We had safety and dignity under the state.' Abdul-Majid's stance relaxed, as he put his hands on his hips and looked to his colleagues.

There were some fond memories of this guy. A proud Abdul-Majid had showed him his collection of pretty much every Star Trek novel available. He was passionate in talking about which books were 'canon', and had forced Ishaq to sit and watch his favourite film *The Wrath of Khan*, and went on and on about how *The Empire Strikes Back* was the best Star Wars episode. Now Wesley Crusher had become Che Intifada.

'Look in history, that wasn't under people like you. Going on about revolutions and illegitimate rulers. You're more like brown chocolate Bolsheviks.' Ishaq's hand rose with his voice. 'If you want to go and do that, then go abroad and try your luck. Don't bother me. You lot couldn't pull this stuff, these demonstrations, in most Muslim countries, because you'd be arrested'

'Arrested, because we fight for the haq, the truth? Any

72

oppression we get just proclaims our legtimacy and strengthens us. What we need is a political struggle against the imperialists and their agents, those government scholars who give fatwa against the righteous for money and power, and their lapdog acolytes.' Abdul-Majid's popping eyes looked at Marwane and then Ishaq. 'And you talk about character and being religious, but look at how haughty and disdainful you talk.'

The boys were used to this strangely formal speech. The upright tone. It was a disguise. An unwavering certainty used in offence and defence. An act of self-reinforcement. Assert something strongly enough, without pause, and any doubts were purged in fiery righteousness. 'I'm sorry, we do this dance every time and it's tiresome, bruv. All you do is get angry and talk about politics. I've been taught that if there is no sincere belief under all of your bluster, no mention of Allah, of being humble in worshipping him, then there is no point. Listen, sincere advice. You go on like this then in ten to fifteen years' time you're going to be an empty husk, dried out by all that fiery talk. All your beliefs are built on vapour.'

'And what? We should sit in the mosque and pray all day? We uphold the good and forbid the evil. We want...'

Ishaq watched this old friend rant. Meekness buried by the armour of God. Residual softness hidden under impenetrable verbal screeds. Ninety percent political and ideological, with a dash of religion on the end. It was so disheartening; no good could come of it.

'Where's the religion, the *deen*. The balance of the heart, mind, and action. You guys are so angry. You put people off Islam. How about talking about pleasing Allah? Abdul-Majid, people can't build whole lives around defiance and hate. You must work for something, not against all the time. These placards...it just seems like you enjoy spitting in people's faces and trying to wind them up. Where does that get anyone?'

Abdul-Majid felt this was pleading and looked pleased that he had entrapped Ishaq. Surrounded by his party colleagues who were urging him on. 'No, we are just proud and brave Muslims, who uphold the truth anytime and anyplace. The same truth everywhere. The prophet peace be upon him said, "Whoever of you sees an injustice, let him change it with his hand. And if he is unable to do so, then let him change it with his tongue. And if he is not able to do so, then let him hate the injustice with his heart – and that is the weakest level of faith." Not cowardly like you, skulking away when it gets difficult.'

'Don't twist things like that Shams...I mean, Abdul-Majid,' shouted Ishaq, his voice swelling, 'you lack integrity, you encourage extremists on the sly with words that you think are fancy, but don't want to get your hands dirty. You take proper liberties as well, you use and abuse the rights in this country. A proper lack of honour.'

'We support the mujahedeen everywhere in spirit. We take the prophetic message that forbids harming non-combatants, and children, and the old. That is far more than the western jackals. We are open that we have a pact of security in that we live in Western lands and the party will not cause harm here as long as we have our right to speak.'

'You can't even think for yourself, just regurgitate speech because you think it sounds deep or smart. You guys couldn't and wouldn't do anything anyway. As for the lot you support "in spirit", look at what they did in Algeria, and then Afghanistan, then Syria. They get impatient and kill, and this results in a cycle of killing more. And you guys just sit on the side-lines, passively encouraging this behaviour of the jahiliyah by not condemning it, and so you yourselves are part of that jahiliyah.'

Dumb mistake. A word that shouldn't be idly thrown. A jahil! One of those pre-Islamic, uncivilised creatures. Those tribal days of idol worship, female infanticide, and spilling of blood. Times before the call of conscience and submission to a higher purpose. Abdul-Majid's cheeks puffed even further and flushed, his arms outstretched to bring in his mates for support, and he started stabbing in Ishaq's direction, 'How dare you call us jahil? You, who live in mental and religious poverty. You, who collaborate with the authorities against the Ummah. I bet you're working for them now.'

Ishaq lip wavered. He bit to dampen it. He could feel other students look around as voices became raised. The discussion with the prof was fresh. Even though he had just been threatened an hour previously, his silence made him feel complicit. He was hauling around a secret that was a burden. Abdul-Majid's colleagues crowded around further, cutting off his view. He could feel the erratic rhythm of the other boy's breathing. He did always desire a civil conversation with them. Tell them that he felt their anger, at the treatments of their parents, their ancestral countries, how hard it was for all of us today, how they should work together and try to open their hearts as Islamic brothers. He wanted to say all of these things…

'Man, you lot are so full of crap. A complete bunch of muppets,' Ishaq spewed, the words out in a venomous torrent. 'I spoke to one guy who hangs around your circles…he says you don't need to pray or give to charity until the Khilafat is established. You know you really piss me off. I wouldn't trust you monkeys to run a kebab van, let alone an Islamic state. You think the authorities are really worried about a bunch of puffed up Ali G boneheads like you?'

Marwane started laughing but turned his face away to avoid Ishaq's gaze. He had seen the same cycle before, of Ishaq trying to be reasonable and restrained, and then getting so hacked off and hyped that he effectively blew up. And he had seen how he handed this group a victory and greater vindication. But he had never seen Ishaq this unrestrained. Real anger deformed his face.

Ishaq's nose was nearly resting on Abdul-Majid's forehead. 'Also plain foolishness. The thing about the nutters you encourage is that they go on and on about Sharia and rule of law, but somehow they then think it's ok to be the whole law themselves. Like they see someone with a Teddy bear called Mohammed and they think it's legit to go and do that guy over for blasphemy. Sharia is law, a set of jurisprudence, not some petty excuse for mob rule or to use it against the poor. Waxing on about Sharia and Khilafa without character or community building. I'm not dealing you with Maj. You're proper retarded. Which, by the way, is why you don't know that no one here past the age of ten uses the word 'wasteman'.'

Abdul-Majid was red-faced and shouting. An inflated space hopper about to burst. 'Astagfirullah, that is a slur. Ishaq, you're an ignorant jackal. I will testify against you on the Day of Judgement for defaming all the righteous Muslims.'

'You'd love that, wouldn't you. Yea, I'm ignorant, alright, but at least I know it. I know my limitations. Hundreds of years of Islamic scholarship and you're so certain about everything. Abdul-Majid, you're like me. You hardly know any Arabic. We're basically kids. Just children. If you think you know it all then you're a proper fool. Seriously, get out of my face, I've had enough.'

Ishaq's voice was cracking. Marwane pulled him back. 'What's wrong with you? Let it go, bruv. You always let these guys get to you.' Marwane looked to his friend's opponent. 'Abdul-Majid. Just leave it out, right? This kind of stuff doesn't solve anything. You got your kicks.'

With a disdainful wave, Abdul-Majid said, 'Go, take him. This is the reason why we are in such discord – people like him.' Abdul-Majid smiled at his entourage in triumph, acknowledging their nods and a couple of congratulatory back-slaps. As he moved back to the picket he muttered to the others, 'His boy Shams knows better, and he knows it'.

Pulling him away by his collar, Marwane saw that Ishaq was shaking. 'I'm always telling you, there's no point. It's just a show for them. It makes them feel better. Seriously, they get off on it. It's their go-go juice.'

'I know,' Ishaq said, wiping at his face, brushing fingers through his hair.

'Yea, but it's not up to you to solve everyone's issues. You're intense today. What's up with you?'

Ishaq looked up at Marwane then down to the ground, as they started walking. He thought about telling him about the conversation with his tutor but felt queasy in his stomach. It was a bad idea. He needed to keep dragging this around, hug it tight, so that it didn't fall and break into pieces.

'…nothing. Just, it's annoying. The world is going to pot and all people seem to care about is whether they're going to be attacked in their canteen by bacon sarnies or a jihadist pizza.'

6.

It was just after sunset, and blushed rays transformed the white steel and glass of the Excel Centre. Bubbled laughter greeted Ishaq as he arrived in East London. Looking in the direction of the sound he saw a puce-faced white man standing outside, on a small set of builder's steps. Mounting a solitary, puffing vigil against the conference, his fist pounding the air while he bellowed to the skies.

'We are the new aborgines. We're forced to keep shtum... Islam is an ideological cult that is all about death and hatred. It's a threat to our country, our great land that is Britain, our sacred Albion. But ohhhh noooo, we're not allowed to say that are we?' He said. Through a megaphone.

His voice bounced off the bobbing heads of the horde that teemed around him. A niqabi woman draped in black, only her sparkling jade eyes to communicate with, floated by. Her words ringing like Bow Bells, drifted in her wake, 'We get it. You hate us. Wanker.'

He had heard it all before. The man was King Canute raging. For his people, history was out of sight. Never to remember their society's own sins. No recall or retention. The privilege of yesterdays, falling light as a feather into a void. The prerogative to forget. No ancestral memory of indiginity or humiliation. No struggle to to pay homage to your past, to your forefathers, whether they were antecedent through blood or belief. And why should they? They were triumphant in modernity. Every war, every structure and conveyance, all-enveloping construction and creation, exulted all that had preceded, and sanctified all determinations. It reinforced any sense of what was right and just. Anything that curdled ill for others was not an inherent flaw, just the slag of history, unfortunate by-products of creating in iron and steel, enforcing man's will on the world and realising their fitter destiny.

Ishaq fled the ranting. Inside, a blue-grey carpeted concourse ran down the centre. To the left and right was a stream of fast food chains and coffee shops. Ishaq noted how many had put up signs, some in hastily written scrawls, proclaiming how their meat was halal so as to attract delegates' cash. He allowed himself a smile as he thought that maybe those university students should bring their protest here.

Taking in the full vista, he could see all the varieties of Muslim. To an acute observer, a believer's choice of clothing and grooming habits helped indicate their religious and political leanings. For men: length and type of beard, whether they were clean shaven, the presence of turban or type of hat, a full face of hair, a shaven moustache line, wearing leather socks, wearing trousers that stopped above the ankle, western clothing, type of foreign clothing, were they openly wearing something silk or gold. For women: presence of a head or face covering, if so how they wore it, was it patterned or plain, an abaya or a burka or skirt, use of jewellery and make up. And so it went on and on. All formats in all types of configurations were present, but nowadays it was just a free-for-all. Cultures within cultures, a din of apparel and clashing accoutrements like some mystifying border town.

Adding a layer to this reverie, half the building seemed to be taken up by a Dr Who exhibition and fan-meet. Abdul-Majid would have loved it, or at least loved it in his heart. Ishaq looked over the poster of some bloke with what he recognised as a sonic screwdriver. At least he knew that much about this stuff. He wasn't a fan of superheroes. As a kid he had read the comics and watched them on tele, he still torrented the odd movie but, as he grew, they disappointed. Too jarring against the backdrop of the real world. Characters who could save lives and planets at the last minute with a rubber band or a bit of sticky-back plastic. Super-powered beings, or implausible geniuses in robotic suits, making last-minute reprieves, and thwarting reassuringly obvious evil. *No*, Ishaq thought, *they should make more realistic movies. They should make the same film, but where life, family, or planet is in peril and you can only watch on and do nothing. Impotent, unless you're prepared to do something monstrous yourself.*

Ishaq rushed to find a room so that he could make salat al-magrib. Having found a space and made his prayer Ishaq marched back down the walkway. He saw a man in his eye-line wearing a blue steel suit. He raised his pace, altering his route, zigzagging through the other attendees as if he was trying to thwart a sniper. Too late. Zulfi had seen him. A son of one of his father's friends, Zulfi did something in the city. Not a full-blown banker but something involving project management, and trading metals on the side. Zulfi always wore a suit with pride, his speech always rushed as though he were a man of great import. It pressed upon the recipient that he was busy and they should be appreciative of the attention.

'Assalmu alaikum, dude, surprised to see you here.' Zulfi took Ishaq's hand in a way that was more of a gregarious slap than a shake. He felt that Zulfi always tried to overwhelm with a display of energy that conveyed his dynamism.

'Wa alaikum salaam, well I'm trying to open my horizons.'

'Good, good, we need smart people like you. You studying or done yet?'

'Still there. Not long to go, how about you?'

'Well you know, business is going from strength to strength. I got hitched. You might see my wife around here, she's doing an Islamic fashion stall. Not a hijabi herself but she used to be a model so it's a good starting business for her. Just got a new car and house…yea so all good.'

Ishaq forced the best smile he could and nodded. He paused, not knowing what to say, '…Mazeltov.'

Zulfi, his hair oiled a little too well to a gleaming wetness, pushed back curved strands as he regarded Ishaq.

'Haha…you've still got that sense of humour. Like I said, I didn't expect to see your face here. Had enough of the fundies have you?'

Zulfi's overfamiliarity made Ishaq resentful. It was an encroachment, an intrusion; but maybe that was the point. Zulfi didn't pretend to be a sympathetic character. In every part of his life he had a mission.

'Uhh…no, not really. Still friends with those *fundies* . Just wanted to take a look around.'

'Well good, good, that's exactly what we're about. We want Muslims to indulge in blue-sky thinking, think outside the box and challenge any traditional or retrogade paradigms.'

Ishaq looked at Zulfi for any signs that he was having him on, wishing Marwane was here to hear that sentence. Ignoring the exotic use of language, Ishaq decided to take Zulfi's bait. 'Backwards? What do you mean?'

'You know, cultural vestiges, ghettoised mindsets.'

He tried to let the comment pass. Zulfi seemed to think that he had ascended past the primitive social mores of the working class into a new dynamic form of Islam that was in harmony with modernity. Ishaq would have been more interested in this mystical journey of advancement if Zulfi did not come from an uncomfortably frank family. When Zulfi's father ever encountered Ishaq alone, he would talk about how much Zulfi was earning, what property he had purchased and the latest BMW that he had acquired. Zulfi's father would also tell him how much of that wealth had been illegally earned, how much cash had to be kept in a safe to avoid the taxman. All told in such a resigned manner that he could never tell if Zulfi's father was proud or ashamed. But then again, maybe Zulfi had it figured out like his English peers. As Ishaq used to tell mates, there's no point doing lengthy jail time for nicking a pair of trainers or a mobile phone when you can play a longer game and get a slap on the wrist for white collar crime. That was real gangsta.

'But all the organisations here seem to have partnered with banks. You can be as sophisticated or *paradigm*-challenging as you want, but making money from money is usury. It's haram, right?' said Ishaq.

'See this is the backward thinking that we are trying to challenge. With that train of thought, we wouldn't have engineers, doctors, teachers, or be able to participate in any western industry.'

Ishaq caught his reflection in Zulfi's buffed, shiny shoes. His face distorting on the leather.

'No...hmm...not really, everything else you mentioned would be fine. Just the banks would stop making excess amounts on the backs of the poor.'

'Well, we are involved with Islamic mortgages and loans. Loaner and loanee sharing the risk in a sharia-compliant way. I don't expect someone like you to know about sophisticated financial instruments.'

He knew well enough about these 'sophisticated financial instruments'. It was funny how those at the top of the pyramid, pilfering and *earning* shed loads, were so confident that they knew better. As if the simple plebs could only understand it as magic, and need only trust them. Once, ships from all over the Empire traded their timber, sugar, grain and textiles here. Trade in actual things. Things that you could hold and feel, taste and eat. History had left behind a lifeless husk that showed little of its former glory. This light and airy building itself had been built in the regeneration of formerly moribund London docklands. A building that had now been bought by the Gulf Emirate of Abu Dhabi. White men created white elephants, printed money and debt, bailed out by the illiterate and bare-footed who siphoned wealth from the earth. He knew how it worked.

'Well, that's a joke though. They are just repackaged interest bearing loans and are even more expensive than the high street stuff. Everyone knows it. Those bankers definitely know it and just laugh at it. And laugh at us.'

Zulfi's Gillette-shaved face edged downwards. 'See, you lot are always negative. We want to support visionary thinking, but anything we say, people like you put a downer on. It's not all about sitting in a mosque, praying while the world burns.'

Ishaq could imagine Zulfi shaving in the mornings, pleased at his mirror image, thinking, *The best a man can get.* 'Maybe, but you guys go on about being visionary and in reality that means jettisoning the fundamentals. I'm not interested in being a cultural Muslim.'

'How very noble of you, Ishaq,' Zulfi said with dripping condescension, 'but that's not how the world works. We need people who are active and integrated, who are politically networked through the power structures of this country. Rational and modern, who are accepted as equals in this society...'

Ishaq cut Zulfi off, 'You can do both!'

As they conversed, a woman and two men passed. Ishaq figured they were his age but the sailing manner of their walk made them come across younger. One was wearing an autumnal frock coat, a ridiculously long stripy scarf, and a puffed up brown wig. Next to him, a pimply boy, with shocking pasty skin, wore a cream jacket and trousers, teamed with what was most definitely a cricket jumper. The woman wore a tweed jacket and bow tie, her hair shaped into a short, masculine, floppy style with a subtle comb over. Ishaq and Zulfi cut to silence as they passed.

The girl said to one of her companions, 'I'll kill myself if they change canon, willy-nilly.' The pimply boy replied in the affirmative. 'Yes, me too. They'll have to be really smart to do a retcon like that, otherwise it's all an epic disaster. I won't get over it. I don't know what I'll do.'

As he had learned, Ishaq gave them a quick reassuring smile, and they responded accordingly. Once out of earshot, he said, 'Look, that's not true.' He could see Zulfi stiffen, clench his fists slightly. 'I don't disagree with your politics, Zulfi. Maybe you're right, I should do more. Which is why I am here – listening. Doesn't mean that you need to harangue everyone who doesn't do what you want. Just remember, the Prophet peace be upon him, said, "Actions are only by intentions, and every man has only what he intended." So both the intention and action has to be correct.'

'Ah, typical preacher boy. So what do you do?'

Ishaq stalled. What do you do? More like what *should* you do. These were always the questions that followed him about. 'Look, I'm sure you work hard on your causes but I'm not going to give details of my life just to win an argument.'

'Ah ha, so that means you probably do nothing. Just another person stuck in analysis paralysis.'

'Yea, well, I never see you in the mosque on Friday, in the community you want to save. And I'm being careful here, I'm not chastising,' said Ishaq, his own fingers crimping, almost claw-like.

Zulfi looked vulnerable, his face reddened and strained. 'I'm busy. I can't make it most weeks.'

Ishaq had hit a sore spot and he felt regret. Threatened by Zulfi's accusations of inaction, he had hit with a petty counter-attack rather than genuine brotherly concern. He looked at Zulfi's eyes, a bit more uncertain but still holding that lupine glare. If you couldn't count it, size it, value it, own it, then this guy couldn't comprehend. Ishaq was a bit like his dad. He tried to make do without causing waves, he believed in caution. That you should watch, examine and study before charging ahead. Yet he had this feeling, like a lancing needle at the base of his spine, that his community was trapped. Captive in a burning building and all he was doing was standing back, looking on as the heat encroached; that maybe, by the time he was ready, it would be all too late; that the stabbing needle was making a relentless piercing of his skin, penetrating layer upon layer and inducing the panicked desire to do something – to do anything.

He felt his body judder and took a deep breath through his nose. 'Well…we're all learning new things. I'll keep what you say in mind. Maybe I should be doing more. Zulfi, I hope you haven't been offended. People like you and me, we should talk more often, right?'

Zulfi replied with a cursory shake of a limp hand. 'Yes. No offence taken. Anyway, I have to go to the main talk, salaams.'

Ishaq watched Zulfi trudge away. It was obvious that they were going to the same auditorium so he waited, pretending to check messages on his phone. After a short while he followed and took his seat in the packed hall. The temporary seating was arranged as in an amphitheatre, with banked rows descending to a well-lit stage, upon which lay a bare wooden podium. Next to that was a simple trestle table, behind which sat a range of grandees, each ready to take their turn on the soapbox.

The voices from the stage felt edged as they cut and boomed. He struggled to make out words; in his head they were sounded out by the man outside and his megaphone, and then by Abdul-Majid, Zulfi, and finally that *harmless* chat earlier in the day. He looked for the exits but the hall was now full. He was wedged in and couldn't extricate himself without causing needless fuss. He forced himself to settle, cleared his throat, and tried to calm a wagging leg.

The subject for the Panel was the ongoing European Conference on Muslim Affairs. A German minister was out on stage. Germany had taken over the presidency of the council that rotated every six months amongst the constituent nations. The minister spoke with clamant passion: 'The political elites of Europe are becoming emotional and arbitrary. Muslims in Europe are a concrete fact and cannot be wished away. We must find solutions together head on, in an inclusive way. The French model of pretending everyone was equal under the law as citizens has not worked. They do not even count people by ethnicity in their census and many feel it has become a way for to hide bigotry. The English way of accepting and even encouraging difference has led to divided communities. No one way has worked. So we, the countries of Europe, have started to enact pettiness. A poor compensation for the inability to envision a future. The banning of minarets in Switzerland. Then the face veil in France, even though it was worn by the minority of a minority. An attempt to stop male circumcision in my country of Germany. An attempt that was dropped once realised this would affect Jews too. These incidents all destroy the illusion of justice for all. That they were anything but the victimisation of a specific group.'

The speaker said that a blazing spotlight had been turned on. One that seared a community. Europe was letting itself be seen as confused. Inadequate. As if it was not emotionally ready to face up to a new world order. That Europe had to accept that it had changed irrevocably, that maybe it needed to be more like the USA; a melting-pot, not as a dream or aim but as a social reality.

The man was engaging and frank. Ishaq could sense the audience draw within, keen on hearing more. He heard this fissure described as a threat to all. Newly accessioned states such as Poland were aggressive in maintaining the focus on Europe's Christian roots. The minister reported how right-wing conservatives launched diatribes, accusing him of trying to change the very foundation of European civilisation that had brought human rights to the world. He told how many Muslim groups accused him of trying to force assimilation. That they complained that he was seeing them as a helpless and monolithic, rather than containing varying strands of racial, sectarian, social and economic complexity. They saw his proposals as intrusive, trying to regulate thought and action. That he was in fact intensifying light on the issue, stigmatising them, undermining their status.

His words came in a flurry, not yielding to any silences, or the pensiveness of the crowd. Towards the end he paused, took off his glasses and rubbed at his eyes. He looked out, squinting at the lights. Past the stage and lip of light, he must have only been able to see a pitch black. His words slowed, he insisted that many right-wingers did see Muslims as an annoyance. That these politicans were not interested in civic values, they were solely identity-protectionists, fearful and guarded of their privilege. He wanted a different approach. He wanted to emphasise that Muslims were a welcome and integral part of Europe, who could not just be used as cheap generational labour, or to fight in Europe's dirty wars. But that required talk, demanded honest effort on all sides. As the minister left to applause, Ishaq was surprised at how impressed he was. This man seemed to have a vision for a way forward; for the way things could be. He was brave and talked a lot of common sense. Ishaq could only surmise that this would see his career fail.

As the evening ground on, a variety of speakers stood at the lectern. One after the other figures paraded onto the stage. A Conservative MP, then a member of a right-wing think tank. Some self-styled leaders of Muslim communities, followed by others who had been handpicked by some arcane, government-backed process. Like actors in a theatre, reading some shared anodyne lines, all parties, from wheresoever they came, used the same script. They called for working together, for peace and harmony, and they all applauded one another. Ishaq felt it was strange and defeating that they all had the same formulae but actually meant totally different things. 'Working together' really meant accepting the word and ideas of one party over another. For the Right, this meant de-Islamicising Muslims. For some of the others this meant legitimising Muslim practices in the UK. Welcoming 'discussion' and 'debate' really meant mollifying the opposition by allowing them to vent their spleen and, once sated, the more powerful interest groups could go about their way as usual. Both sides of the argument remonstrated through the language of their own experience, that only produced a grainy myopia. Although all putatively native English speakers, it sometimes felt to Ishaq that one side was speaking Latin and the other side Arabic. Unintelligible and isolated.

Maybe Marwane was right: this was a waste of time. Ishaq's leg wiggled involuntarily as he looked around to gauge the reactions of others. They all hung intent on the words produced by this roll call of VIPs. Some, it seemed, were happy and placated simply by the act of a powerful person pretending to hear them out.

The next speaker had been part of an extremist group. As a teen he was already recruiting others to his certitude that the Muslims needed saving, and by his group alone. After periods in jail and burning out at thirty, he started another organization. This time combating the original one. One that he was now positive was dangerous, and led by the very people he had recruited. Ishaq thought of Abdul-Majid: he had the same hip-hop stories, and supposedly rough upbringing in some small town somewhere outside London. Combining the vengeance of a spurned lover and a convert's zeal, this guy attacked his former group and then spread his ire on Muslims displaying religiosity. Once again in ironclad certainty that he was the one to lead British Muslims, this time out of the darkness of belief, he had even convinced the government to fund his new think tank to the hilt.

Yet another speaker followed who disagreed with these previous solutions and put forward those of *his* new think tank. This new man was supposedly an actual Jihadi but was now another poacher turned gamekeeper on the government's payroll. Ishaq's mouth hung open while listening to them. Splinter upon splinter. People arguing over slivered fragments so fine that they were invisible to the normal human eye.

Some people just didn't know when to shut up and take a back seat. Ishaq thought that these guys had never had real jobs. They first sponged off vulnerable people, then the state. They always thought they were right, and loved to tell everyone else what to do. They were truly assimilated, in that they would make wonderful British politicians. They were better off in their natural abode, the Houses of Parliament.

The final speaker came on. A Muslim academic, he struck a very different tone. Bespectacled and wearing a tweed jacket, he was the personification of English academia. His honeyed-words flowed and made the audience feel safe. Straightaway, Ishaq didn't trust him.

'We need to create a British Islam. One that is at home and at ease more so here, in the UK, than some ancestral siren from foreign lands. Something that resonates in the hills of Yorkshire rather than those of the Punjab. We have a veritable Tower of

Babel in our mosques, speaking in Bengali, and Urdu, and Farsi, and Turkish, when we should be reaching out to our people in the language of their own country: English. We need to remove any of our former cultural baggage from Islam and find its pure and true message.

'To our non-Muslim friends and colleagues, I would say that this has been done before. We must remember that Christianity, once a middle-eastern creed, found its way to these shores and became a prime source of spiritual fulfilment. To my Muslim brethren, I say that we should not fear and cling on to an empty ritualistic approach, and to each other. We must remember that we are all God's creation and part of one British community, that we have been given reason, and a mind in which to navigate matters that sometimes cannot be broached with a rigid orthodoxy.'

Pleasant and soothing words. Altogether meaningless words. Yet again something everyone could agree on, yet meaning absolutely nothing.

'It has been done before. We look at the example of Moses Mendelssohn, a Prussian Jew who paved the way for Jews to integrate and gain acceptance. Along with others, via the Haskalah movement, he paved a way for Jews to join as equals in the European enlightenment.'

Ishaq's errant, juddering leg stopped still. He had studied the Haskalah movement at uni and was surprised that the speaker would push this model of integration. Moses Mendelssohn had started his attempt in 18th century Germany. *And didn't that end well*, thought Ishaq.

'We, the leading Muslim thinkers, should join hands with our colleagues in government and push forward a more cultivated and pragmatic education amongst those who maintain a tight grip on the hollow safeties of literal scripture. Show them a better, more egalitarian, way. We should take a more active approach with their offspring. Especially those of the most extreme, who we should take into our bosom with affection and great care. The burden is ours.'

He went on and on. The speaker extolled a hands-on approach with communities and the education of their children, including intervention. Questioning them in their schools, taking them into care if under risk. The threat of children-snatching was a sinister fairytale seeping into reality. Ishaq had grown used to such outlandish proposals when they came from outside, but from someone supposedly within, it stung.

Unconsciously, Ishaq raised his hand. Not waiting for acknowledgement and before he was aware, he shouted out, 'These words are all nice but what does this actually mean on the ground? Are you seriously threatening to take people's children?'

His eyes blinking under the glare of the lights, the academic placed a hand over them and replied, 'Not quite. Just in very extreme cases. It is very complicated. Maybe could you leave the question until the end when we have more time?'

Ishaq's voice gathered force. 'I'd prefer to have an answer now. You've waved around some big statements, but how does this relate to people actually on the ground, people who work everyday? To me, all of these speeches just seem to be one posh class talking to another.'

Murmurs rippled through the audience as necks turned to see where the question originated. The speaker made a calming gesture with his hand, as if he wanted to pat the question down. 'Well, we have differences of opinion, sir. We should struggle to find commonalities. Discussion like this is important.'

Another voice cast out from the crowd towards the speaker. 'All parts of society have differences of opinion, whether it be race, class, geography, whatever. The fact is that Muslims already accept the rule of British law. Muslims are three generations in, and there's no getting round the fact that we are permanent.'

The speaker, neck stretched, tried to locate the second voice. 'Yes, but they should accept Britain's culture and not seek to change it.'

Buoyed by the support, Ishaq shouted, 'So, anyone can seek to change something in Britain as long as they stay within democratic norms, unless they are Muslim? So if I want the council to start collecting the bins weekly instead of fortnightly, I have to think in my head, "Hang on mate, I'm Muslim, I can't ask that. I'll just suffer in the stench like a good citizen."' A smattering of laughter was heard across the auditorium.

'No, that's is a caricature of the argument. I am saying that we should integrate into society, and look more at our reason and the western intellectual tradition...'

'And discard all our traditions, or stop looking at any other. And, if we don't, you'll nick our kids?' Ishaq felt his face heat.

'Ok sir, thank you for your point. Next question...'

Ishaq stood up, pointing and gesticulating at the man. 'Hang on, I haven't finished. You know, what really pisses people off about discussions like this, especially from our own, is the desperation to be accepted. You have no idea how people live!'

'Ok, thank you, I think that's enough. Please sit or I'll have to ask security to intervene.'

Ishaq's voice reverberated. 'As for this bullshit about a Muslim enlightenment; the Haskalah reached its culmination, it's ultimate expression, in an individual like Fritz Haber, did it not? A self-hater, who boasted about the chemical weapons he was producing for Germany, who in turn rewarded him by using his inventions to try and wipe out his people, who he had denied. And in your own way that's what bootlickers like you are trying to do, wipe us out or erase us from the picture...'

Ishaq felt a hand on him and turned as an irritated security guard, who barely fitted into his uniform, shirt buttons bursting, tried to usher him away. With two more coming, he continued yelling, yet as loud as his voice rose it felt lost in the immensity of the hall. 'While accepting a worldview of a society that has committed so many atrocities that they should hang their head in shame, before telling completely powerless people what to do.'

Some people started to jeer, telling him to shut up. Others started to clap. A shout went out, 'He speaks the truth.'

Puffing and bent over from having run to Ishaq's position from the bottom of the auditorium, another guard said, 'Seriously kid, I don't get paid enough for this crap. Let's make this easy. Just calm down and let's go.'

'I ain't going nowhere.' Even in the struggle, Ishaq noticed his intonation and language code switch to a more 'street' type of talk.

Ishaq tried to brush the man's swollen hand off, but the security guard held a tight enough grip that gave time for others to come as reinforcement. Ishaq struggled as they physically ushered him up the stairs and out of the room. As he was transported to the top of the staggered arena, he caught the sullen face of one of the other audience members. It was Professor Harell. Trying to be charitable, the professor averted his gaze in an attempt to maintain some of Ishaq's dignity, but the damage was already done. Ishaq shouted at the top of his lungs, 'This is the reality of the discussion you type of people want.'

Banished, Ishaq tried to control his emotion. He could feel his face burning from anger and embarrassment. Shame mixed with righteous indignation. Escorted outside, he looked back at the doors and saw two guards with crossed arms. Implacable, standing in front of the venue. He could feel the bile rise again, the guards' faces looking like they were challenging him to give it another try.

As he stood there, contemplating another confrontation, a fan walked by. Dressed as one of Dr Who's enemies, the

Cyberman ostentatiously paraded a considered robotic movement. As the steel grey automaton walked past Ishaq it stopped, and pivoted its head left to give what could have been a stern look of judgement. Ishaq eyeballed it, then the security guards, and gave a performative smile in the pretence of being in control. He turned around and put his hoody up, blocking out the world. Ishaq thought at least it wasn't a Dalek shrilly screaming, 'Exterminate!'...or did they say 'Assimilate!'? He couldn't remember which.

He shambled his way to the nearest train station and got on the Docklands Light Railway, an automated unmanned light metro system. Like a self-guided drone, it weaved its way through the metallic towers of the financial district, and then through eerie boarded-up residential streets. Taking no notice of other passengers, Ishaq stayed on until the last stop by St Katherine Docks. His hands started shaking, and he decided to walk it off by following the Thames Path to Waterloo.

Crossing Tower Bridge Ishaq thought how much of an ugly sore it was, especially compared with the jewels of London like the Houses of Parliament; the bridge's Victorian gothic style a pastiche of what someone thought a fairytale London should look like. It was big, and one rule of life was that anything large, or powerful enough, could defy the rules of good taste. It created its own language, its own reality. It rendered any critique futile. He saw tourists, heads back, exposing their camera-strapped necks, looking upwards and gawking. Ishaq saw their awe. He saw how we wonder at monuments and relics of the past, when we should be judging societies on how we treat our weakest, on those small petty kindnesses we do when no one is looking. But history doesn't record those so, like Ozymandias, we make an arrogant fight against the inevitable fading of the permanent.

On the south side of the river Ishaq immediately felt at home, more certain and balanced. A bit closer to the familiar sounds of emergency-service sirens and the curious cries of a busy South London street. Along a stretch of a few miles the northern bank of the Thames held the Tower of London, St Paul's Cathedral, the gleaming offices of The City, and the Houses of Parliament. For the first time in its history the southern side of the river was rapidly gentrifying, to mirror the north, but echoes of what had been still lingered . It held narrow streets that had once hosted boozy inns, whorehouses, docks, and a wretched prison. He wondered whether people from that other time looked across the water in the same way. Unimaginable wealth poured through those offices, in instruments and methods that the general public could hardly imagine. Everything was centred around servicing the needs of those few. Maybe that was the real London.

London was ever-changing but the constant was trade and money, for some small obscure elite that had been trained from birth in schools and societies and organisations that Ishaq would never come into contact with. The lives on the south side, those of the poor, were footnotes. Wealth being sucked-in from around the world, followed by people from around the globe trapped in the city's magnetic hold; an invisible hand herding them to this bygone-Empire's beating heart of darkness.

Ishaq walked past the Pool of London. The river was at high tide and swollen. Always looking on the verge of breaking its banks and wrecking the city, the capital calmly stared this threat down and watched it subside. The wind chilled his face and he wound his hoody tighter, casting his face in shadow. *And so what?* Ishaq thought. Smarting from being told what was the norm, and that people like him had to capitulate.

As if they had got everything right? All that wealth and the English were still miserable bastards. They had lost any religion; they poured scorn on any spirituality. The void couldn't be filled by intellectualism, as they distrusted that too. They had no real shared culture across their classes except for crap television and consuming in excess. They were inhospitable to foreigners, sometimes to the point of being hateful. But then they did not seem to like each other too much either, or even themselves for that matter. Their family units looked cold and uncaring. They needed copious amounts of alcohol before they could even dare to think of connecting with another human being in anything other than a superficial manner. If they didn't constantly treat him and his family like shit, he would actually feel sorry for them. All that wealth…for what?

Yet, for all that, they could create systems. Muslims could learn from that. He, himself, should learn from that. Amazing systems and organisations. Who cares if you were a self-hating arsehole, if a group of self-hating arseholes could create something as amazing and compassionate as the National Health Service, or social services, or a decent justice system. They were generally pliant, did what they were told, were able to work together and just get on with it. Maybe the effects of that were far more compassionate than any religion or ideology that concentrated on building good individuals. Far more moral than Muslims, in constant turmoil, destroying each other and any chance of progress via rivalries in righteousness; people whom, whether religious or secular, held a pliable attitude in using violence to coerce each other.

A thousand thoughts went through his head, vacillating between love and hate of his situation and this country. Always crossed-messages in this city. Giving refuge to the developing-world displaced, yet at the same time providing shelter for rich tyrants, and generals who instigated coup d'etats and would have their opponents executed. London, in all its iniquity and all its glory. The centre for separatists and warlords, agitators and autocrats. The home of Asian intellectuals, Arab newspapers, and Pakistani political groups. Grace-and-favour given to a churning rolodex of despots, dictators, and dissidents, their roles forever rotating, but the money always welcome.

Ishaq could feel his heart pound. Each heartbeat raising to a maximum pressure and then releasing to its lowest. From systolic to diastolic. *Is this the way it will always be? Thinking and feeling like this?*

He reached St Paul's Cathedral. In his path, at the edge of his vision, he saw a young white woman walking towards him, slightly off-kilter. Dressed in a formal gown and wearing a tiara that glinted in the moonlight, like a princess that had just come from the ball. Stopping in front of him she gave him a strange vacant stare. Someone looking like him would probably be seen as a threat to her virtue, in this late, lonely spot. Ishaq thought that, with his hood up, he might be scaring her. He gave the woman a wide berth and raised his pace, to get past as quickly as possible. Before he could do so she gave him another vacant look, took a squatting position by the wall, pulled-down her knickers and started pissing, with a satisfied smile planted on a boozy face. Sprinkled steam emanated, as acrid urine hit cool air. Her midnight had come. Her fairytale over. Crumpling his nose he dipped his head , then looked to the beautifully-lit dome of St Paul's. Ishaq moved on.

7.

On the wall, above Ayub's head, lay a canary-yellow clock. Probably a plastic Made-in-China jobbie from Tooting Market, or the pound shop. The second hand was stuck. Ishaq stared as the hand attempted to move forward, only to be rebuffed each time. Forcing its way onward, only to instantly snap back. There was something captivating about the movement, the hand seemingly destined to repeat the same moment, endlessly thwarted by some invisible force.

He was sitting with his legs crossed in front of him. His body leaning back, petitioning the wall to support him and keep him upright. He had given up trying to be attentive. As Ayub finished, Ishaq looked down, gazing towards his navel for revelation .

As the great companion of the Prophet Muhammad, peace be upon him, Abu Hurarrah, may Allah be pleased with him, narrated: "The believer is the mirror of the believer." As you do before you leave your house, you check in the mirror, for dishevelment in your hair, or dirt on your clothes, and you rectify this. Accordingly when you see your brother, his shortcomings are your own and you should advise them, in a nice way and with wisdom, on what reformation is needed. Of his character and soul.'

Ishaq looked up and saw Marwane sidling nearer, breaking into a simper. He met those conspiratorial eyes and returned them with exaggerated intensity. Marwane must have heard of his humiliation.

'The prophet, peace be upon him, also said: "This religion is sincere advice." So your intentions should be pure with regard to your brother. You should show kindness and humility. Advice should not be given with the intention to make one feel lesser. It should be a reminder to you both. As Allah says in the Quran: "The believers are indeed brothers, so make peace and reconciliation between your two brothers and fear Allah, that you may receive mercy."

'And this mercy spreads out into your community. There are many sayings of the prophet, peace be upon him, that whether in love, pain, and kindness, our people, our community, we are like one body. What is felt in one part spreads and is felt in the others...'

As Ayub finished Shams came towards the boys ,bearing a tray with rattling cups of tea that chimed, and a crumbling pack of digestives. Giving his salaams he sat down, giving each a hug, and dished out the cracked porcelain as the boys scrambled for the best biscuit. 'Assalmu alaikum, ain't seen you both for time.'

Ishaq looked away, fished his mobile out from his tracksuit top pocket and checked the time. 'Wa alaikum salaam, we've been here Shams. What have you been up to?'

'Just a bit of this, bit of that, ducking and diving etc.' Shams gave a nervous laugh that petered out under Ishaq's sudden gaze.

Marwane came in closer and put an arm around Shams, clasping him tight. 'It's good to see you bro, you should come round more often. So, how's the job-hunting going?'

'I can't find any job, can I? I haven't got qualifications like you lot. Plus you know how it is? They screen CVs. If you have a Muslim name, you're loads less likely to get to the next stage.'

With faux solemnity Marwane said, 'True dat.'

Ishaq shrugged his shoulders while playing with his phone. 'Well you just have to keep on trying. Life is tough for a lot of people.'

'Well add brown skin to the name and you're automatically in trouble. Didn't you hear me? I said they sift-out CVs. There was a program on telly where they sent a bunch in with two different names and all the English ones, the Smiths, got interviews. The Abduls got jack.' Shams looked at Ishaq for a sympathetic word.

Marwane reached over and put a hand over Ishaq's screen. 'Well, change your flippin' name then. You could be Sam and Ishaq can become Isaac. Actually, he's totally more like a right Kevin.' Marwane started laughing at Ishaq, looking for a response, but only received a roll of the eyes. 'Honestly, like that Gandhi actor…what's his name?'

'Ben Kingsley?' Ishaq volunteered, while trying to prise Marwane's concealing hand away.

'Yea, Ben Kingsley; his real name is Krishna Bannerjee or something.' Seeing the incredulity of his friends, Marwane continued: 'Seriously. He changed his name and now he's a proper-successful rent-an-ethnic. He gets hired as anything from a Zambian to an Eskimo.'

Ishaq gave up on the phone, wiping the screen with a thumb and stuffing it back in his pocket. 'That's not dumb ya know, I bet he's made loads of money.'

'Nah, I'm not down with that.' Shams' speech sped-up as he talked, emphasising points with waves of his hand. 'That's really sad. I hate it when you meet some guy called Abdullah but who's named himself Joe just to get on. That's some proper Uncle Tom, bounty bar, coconut crap going on. You live like that, you'll hate yourself.'

Shams looked at the boys, making sure he held their attention. 'Anyway, I've got a hook-up with a cousin in Bangladesh who knows a factory that does clothes for a lot of the stores here. He can get a good deal, and I may be looking to do a bit of import-export. I just need a bit of seed money…'

Ishaq interrupted the excitable flow. 'Sorry akhi, you know I'm a skint student.'

Shams looked at Ishaq, folding his grey thobe under him with a violent tug. At sixteen Shams' family moved away to the much larger Bangladeshi community, in East London. He made the effort to come back down and hang out with the boys. They never came up around his yard. When Shams struggled at his GCSEs, just about getting a place in that technical college, it was obvious they had gained good grades. Ishaq and Marwane didn't go into details, their parents' smiles and their unspoken confidence told it all. Shams had plainly asked for their results but they wouldn't tell him. He could tell that they didn't want to make him feel bad. They didn't need to be like that. He was as strong as any of them.

'Astaghfirullah, may Allah forgive me. I wasn't angling for some money. I'm getting it together myself.'

'Thought you said that you weren't working?'

Shams could see question upon question in Ishaq's eyes, in his tone. From warm friends, who would share, Ishaq had started talking down, constantly trying to 'educate' him. Marwane was a bit better, but his interest ran hot and cold and he used Shams only to get in sly digs at Ishaq. Anytime he asked them about uni they would blurt out appeasing sentences. As if he was too dumb or unsophisticated to understand.

'I'm doing some odd jobs…'

'Who for?'

'One of the brothers.'

'Which brother?'

'You know, just one of the estate lot.' Shams bowed his head.

'No, I don't know. Who are you talking about? Spit it out.'

'...Mujahid.'

All three boys went silent. Marwane and Ishaq exchanged concerned stares. Ishaq put his hand on one of Shams' wrists.

'Shams, Mujahid is dealing drugs; what the hell you doing with him?'

Shams jerked his arm away. 'Astagfirullah, Allah forgive us, you can't say that. That's slander and backbiting.'

'I know that he...well, that's the word on the estate. He never comes here any more and I always hear about fights with wannabe thugs,' said Ishaq.

Marwane saw Shams' face fix. Pulling Ishaq's arm back in his direction he said, 'Shams is right. Ishaq, you can't say that, unless you got proof. Still Shams, that bro is a bit off his head. I've seen him around, eyes always bloodshot, looking scary. Be careful.'

'It's legit, he's got a hook-up at the airport to bring some stuff in cheap and then he sells it o...' replied Shams.

Not paying heed to Marwane, Ishaq continued, 'You seen this "stuff", have you?'

'Yea, of course...I ain't stupid, man.'

'Who's this hook-up, then?'

Shams scanned the room, noting-out who was new and who he remembered from before he left the area. Around that time these two started attending circles. He couldn't get them to go on any excursions. The swearing stopped, and it went unspoken that they would not countenance anything with the hint of illegality. They were good at just getting on. Shams felt the distance, a lingering gap that he couldn't even enquire about. That there was some secret to life that they had decided not to pass-on.

'I can't say. Some friend from the estate.'

'Alright Shams, it all sounds well-shady but you're a grown-up now. Just be careful. If you get in trouble, even if you've done nothing wrong, you and me don't get second chances like posh white boys do. Remember that...so, other than clothes, you got anything else going on?'

Dry air, in the flat, pressed his cheeks; Shams pulled his collar to let some of it flow around his skin and felt his finger slide against perspiration at the base of his neck. 'I've got plenty of ideas. All you need to do to make money off of rich white guys is to sell them an experience. They'll spend money on any crap, especially the Yanks. It doesn't even need to be anything decent. I saw this report about one guy who became a millionaire by making USB keys shaped like food. Like sushi or hamburgers. He just buys these cheap ones from China and gets them to add some plastic mould, and then the jobs a good 'un. Can sell them for ten times what you buy them for.'

'Yea, classy, Shams. That's really what the world needs, an endless supply of crap electronics shaped like fast-food.'

Marwane laughed. 'Mr Negativity straight-in there, killing it like a bullet. I'm with Shams. Who cares, as long as it's a halal living.'

Ishaq smiled. 'You mean like making no bacon sausage shaped USB keys?'

'Yea...right...good one...that was nearly funny. Just saying it's not like you're selling haram-drugs or anything. If you made a few grand doing that then you'll be laughing. Then you could do something proper with that cash. You can't be picky from the start with everything. The point is that Shams is just looking for something to set him on the way, right bruv?' Marwane said, as he pumped Shams' shoulder with a fist.

Shams broke into a broad smile. 'Exactly bro! That's what I'm sayin'!'

Ishaq perked up at the chance to wind Marwane up. 'Well tell me, what's halal then? You're using a bunch of plastic that's polluting the earth, and probably using a load of child-labour down the line...'

'Subhanallah, seriously, who made you governor of the earth?' said Marwane. 'If you try and be perfect on absolutely everything then we'd all be naked and homeless.' Marwane and Ishaq eyed each other, waiting for one to budge.

Shams slumped back, away from the other boys, pushing the tray towards them to give him space. 'Anyway, I'm just using it as an example; the best thing is to try and sell it with a story. Take it how you want. They like experiences, no need to know if it's true. Like you can do a restaurant and do a bunch of dishes and say they were from Kashmir, for some Mughal prince who wrote poetry.'

All three broke out in laughter. The flat was a small one-bedder, and the living room was just large enough to hold about a dozen people if they were all sat on the floor, Bedouin-style. The brother who provided the space had thrown out all of the furniture just for this purpose, leaving only a bookcase situated on the wall furthest from the boys, shelves that were filled with ornately-bound books in Arabic. Ayub was kneeling by the case, flicking through a tome while deep in conversation with some new white brother bearing a large bushy beard. Ayub looked around at the three. Marwane caught his eye and nudged the other two, pinching his lips, indicating to them that they should quiet down.

Shams looked round his shoulder at Ayub and then, in a considered hush, said, 'I'm serious. We get such bad press, but you can sell stuff by being exotic. I had another idea, about selling food in tiffin boxes. I was reading about those dabbawallahs in Mumbai. They deliver thousands a day without any mistakes, you could make a great story out of that.'

'But Shams, you're not Indian or Kashmiri,' said Ishaq.

'Yea, but I'm brown. Most people won't know the difference. Our lot won't be coming anyway.'

Marwane chimed in, 'You know, that second one is a really good idea. Properly cynical, but could work.'

The Study Circle

It went quiet for a moment but then Ishaq looked at Marwane. He tried to stifle a laugh while he said, 'Alhamdullillah, some good ideas, but selling yourself on being exotic? It's like just accepting you're a slave to their stereotypes. What do you think M?'

'Wooooahhh, subhanallah, man, you is properly mental bruv. Ishaq, I respect you a lot, bro. You're deep and all that. But seriously…you get dealt cards in life and you deal with them. Shams isn't thinking of walking around in a salwar kameez shouting "a thousand apologies, effendi."' Marwane bobbled his head from side to side and tried to put on what he thought was a generic South Asian accent. Unfortunately, it came across as a sorry mix of Michael Caine meeting Amitabh Bachchan. 'So what does Caliph Tabrizi say to that?'

'Firstly, man, don't try that accent again. It was pathetic. Secondly…secondly…' Ishaq could see that he was getting a rise out Marwane but saw Shams expectant face. He recognised it as the same one that Shams pulled when they used to run for the ice cream van and it looked like they wouldn't make it. 'Yea, sounds like you've got some really good ideas, Shams. Inshallah, make dua, and try your best. That's all any of us can do.'

Ishaq and Marwane continued to exchange volleys, Shams slurped contentedly on his tea. He made a decisive dip of his biscuit into his chai. Everything tasted better with a dunk. He kept it submerged so that it softened as much as possible but overplayed his hand. He looked in horror as his biscuit broke free and crumbled into the milky swell, like a house tumbling off an eroding coastline. He checked if the others had seen and, although tempted, resisted the urge to retrieve the whole soggy mess with his hand.

'Ok boys. If I come up with something decent, maybe you could all give me a hand. That is if Ishaq isn't too busy boycotting Starbucks or something. By the way Marwane, are there any more biccies?'

'There's a pack in the kitchen if you want to grab it.'

Watching Shams get up to fetch supplies, Marwane threw Ishaq a glare. 'You are proper taking the mick, you know that?'

'Look, I know. I backed off, right.'

'Whatever problems me and you might have, we still have more options than Shams.'

'Calm down. We've been friends since we were kids. You want me to still treat him like one?'

Marwane replied, any previous amusement doused, his long torso slanting forward, '*No*, I want you to treat him with a bit more respect and listen to him, and not give-off that 'it's beneath me vibe'. Be a friend. The guy needs encouragement, not verbal waterboarding. Seriously?'

Ishaq, his aspect slightly pained, tested the carpet with a finger. 'Ok, may Allah bless you for the advice. You're right. He just raised some interesting issues, and I was just messing.'

'I know that. No one wants to be a 'sellout', and we want to do what we want to do. But this isn't about having some random intellectual conversation. He hasn't got that luxury. This is about life.'

'And you're not worried about Mujahid?' asked Ishaq. 'That brother is bad news. He's always slating people from the circle, saying we are like the kuffar. We should be fighting for Islam… whatever that means in his head. He's even talking nonsense on the streets about creating a Muslim-only zone. Stupidness. He is going to cause big issues one day.'

'Well…just keep an eye on him, yea.'

They parted as Shams returned with a new hoard of biccies, eagerly handing out some Jammy Dodgers. 'So, Marwane, how's tricks; keeping busy yourself?'

Seeing Ayub peering over again, Marwane puffed his chest and raised his voice, bringing it down an octave. 'All praise is due to Allah, we pray that he guides us all, brother.'

Ishaq's face took on a mischievous grin. 'Shams, you haven't heard, but Marwane doesn't watch telly anymore.'

'Well brother, I try to remember Allah often,' said Marwane with mock solemnity, 'and try to not indulge in frivolous activities, but then again here I am talking to you two?'

'Frivolous activities. Joker. Remember that time you played skateboard warriors and scrapped-up your face on the paving. You went home bleeding; your mum took one look and gave you bare licks,' said Ishaq. 'Didn't let you out for two weeks, after that.'

Shams and Ishaq laughed as Marwane pouted. 'Well I was a proper Braveheart as a kid. Kill a man for being too damn brave, real guts, not like you two midgets. Issy, you were proper sly in games, getting digs in without anyone noticing. I see you.'

They would find an incline somewhere, steeper the better, and two lots of two would sit on skateboards. The boards sped-up, kicks and punches thrashing-out as they rolled down helter-skelter. The speed, or opposing bandits, would always get you.

Games got serious, got out of hand. It was always getting out of hand. That was the fun of it. One winter some chief had the bright idea of hiding rocks in their snowballs. You always retained the shock of that first smack in the head. That fluffy John Lewis scene slamming you in a combo of pain and sharded ice. Your head reverberating as it smarted from the pop. Balls were already being scrunched as hard as possible. And it became an arms race after that. The projectiles getting bigger and bigger, experiments with size versus flight. Testing arcs through the air, and the sharpness of rocks. Kids split into shifting teams, staging pitched battles and ambushes. Until you realised this wasn't fun at all. It hurt. A lot. So you stopped going out until the melt came.

There was also British Bulldog on a epic scale. In between the towers there was kind of a plaza. Kids used to line up against one side, and run from one side to the other. There were brawls but it was hilarious. Always finding bruises in random places days afterwards. Shams and Ishaq were both shorter than the rest, but Shams was a bit on the larger size then. His mum called it 'plus size'. If they were watching him huffing and puffing, 'Don't worry; Shams is just 'plus size'.' 'Your son is getting fat, no?' 'No, he's just 'plus size'.'

If someone sucker-punched Shams, or tripped him from behind, Ishaq would make a note and get the kid back in the next round. The estate was great for playing hide n'seek. Shams would always choose the same place, the large bin-areas where the chutes ended, sometimes even climbing into the skips. He would take it seriously. Some kids thought it funny to leave him there hiding for hours, but Ishaq always made sure to do a round of the bin-stores to fetch him.

If any kid, especialy an older one, dared him, Shams would bite. Wall of Pain: a handful of kids would line up and face a wall a couple of steps away, bridging the gap by resting one arm. One kid would pass under the bridge and be punched and kicked until they managed to get out. Shams was always up for it, pleading that he could do it, but Ishaq never let him play.

'What's that thing you used to say when we were playing tag?' asked Ishaq.

'Oh that, if you were out then…' Shams hunched forward, his voice just above a conspiratorial murmur, 'there's a German in the grass with a bullet up his arse, pull it out, pull it out, pull it out.'

All three started with a soft chuckle.

'Oh yea, and that other one, remember? When you were 'it'.'

Shams' head dipped lower. 'Can't tell you in here, tell you outside.'

'Saddos. Only us losers who couldn't get their hands on a proper phone played that stuff. I would have preferred

Playstation. Billy had one, remember, everyone kissing his backside trying to get an invite. He had Fifa,' said Marwane.

Ishaq detached himself from the huddle, leaning back, eyes softened. 'I remember him. Nice kid. Haven't seen him around for time.'

'I see him around. Tries to call himself Will, now; see him with his workmates sometimes, trying to be big. Always on the verge of saying something but too scared in case we're alone. You know the type I mean.'

'Sounds like an idiot. Anyway, Pro Evo rules,' Shams said. 'So, seriously, you don't watch television?'

'Firstly, like I said, I don't waste my time watching television, my honourable brother. I read Quran or take part in more beneficial activities…' Marwane saw the white brother look over and shake his head, so turned down the volume, '…Seriously. It's all bad news now and it vexes me, and most films vex me too.'

Ishaq, nose raised, sniffing blood. 'Yea, right, you watch enough. Go on, tell Shams why you don't watch Western movies. What you told me last week.'

'Chill, I'm not embarrassed. Well, Shams, take *Pride and Prejudice*. The elephant in the room is that Mr Darcy, or whoever would definitely be a slave-owner.'

'Shams, let me clarify this for you…Marwane won't watch an imaginary period-movie because the imaginary character might have had imaginary slaves,' said Ishaq.

Marwane looked on Ishaq as if he was a naive child. Pursing his lips and with an exaggerated shaking of his head he said, '*Pride and PREJUDICE*. You may laugh, but all the rich white people in these stories probably got their money from slavery, so I don't care who they get married to or how they do it. All their petty issues, talking about love and relationships, when they were oppressive, forcing everyone else to just think about survival. Yea, I said it. Mr Darcy. Racist.'

Ishaq observed Shams, who was moved to give his input. 'Ishaq, thinking about it he's right, you know?'

Ishaq held his head in his hands, one hand sliding down pulling at a cheek. 'This is why I don't like joking with you lot. I just hear madness. You guys are cracked. Ok M, what about *Chariots of Fire*?'

'Well, yea, a story of triumph, at an Olympics with no black people. It doesn't count when you win like that, does it, really? They only win because there are no ethnics. An Olympics with no one of West African descent, no Kenyans, Ethiopians, or Moroccans. Proper joke. Just like slo-mo black and white Fred Perry. No proper opposition. As they say round Shams' area, 'Innit'.'

Ishaq looked at Marwane trying to ascertain if he was being serious. It was hard to tell sometimes.

'Bruv, that is proper off-key. I love that movie. Like the Scottish guy who wouldn't run on a Sunday because it was against his code and religion. See, there were people like us back then. It's about personal struggles. An individual in their world. When there were things more important than making money or just consuming. You know...what you're saying is like non-Muslims asking why no one is talking about suicide bombing in a documentary on Zidane. Or like reading the *Arabian Nights* and complaining it doesn't talk about Hamas.'

All three boys used to stay at each others on the odd occasion when their parents needed a sitter. Ishaq tried to avoid Marwane's as his mum always gave chores. He tried proclaiming that he was a proper guest, like some white person, but would receive a bunch of ironing in the face. Shams' mum was pretty cool, though, as they were allowed to watch old movies together, as long as they just shut the hell up. 'Ok how about *Zulu*?'

'You're taking the P.I.S.S now. I know you're trying to wind me up. Proper transparent. Won't work. Bunch of colonialists, dying while killing natives, and even then they are supposed to be heroes. Bollocks. I don't watch that stuff. All these stories. When they are brave, we are aggressive; when they are smart, we're crafty. Playground stuff. Pure wish-fulfilment.'

Shams said, 'Yea...but *Zulu's* got Michael Caine and he married an Indian. He's cool, right?'

'Even if it's got Michael Caine in it, my distinguished brother,' said Marwane, reverting to a playful solemnity.

'Man, you can't watch anything.' Ishaq kissed his teeth and waved a dismissive hand at Marwane.

'I'll make my own movie then,' said Marwane.

'You won't be able to make jack unless it's some half-arsed story about some random repressed Muslim girl who secretly wants to wear lipstick and a mini skirt, or a guy who becomes a suicide bomber. They're not interested in any other stories.'

'I'd do it. I'm slick. I'd break the mould.' Marwane passed a hand through his fuzzy mop of hair as if he were combing it.

'Mould? You need stereotypes, otherwise how does anyone understand each other?' said Ishaq, enjoying the taste of sarcasm. 'You have to have the call to prayer at the beginning or something. It's like the oldest cliche in the book. It would ring around the desert and show how romantic and alien we are.'

'Nah, I'd be like an Algerian James Bond.'

Ishaq punched Marwane's thigh. 'Hahaha, you're the brown guy who gets killed in the first ten minutes. At best you'd be of ambiguous morality, or a noble savage, and in your case M, we can drop the noble part.'

Wide eyed, as if he had had an enormous epiphany, some grand realisation, Shams spoke up. His interruption startled, hushing the other two. 'How about *The Italian Job?*'

After an extended moment Marwane gave a generous grin. 'Brother, everyone loves *The Italian Job*. 'This is the Self-Preservation Society.' Makes you proud to be British.'

III

8.

Ayub stood watch as the youths walked away, a conjoined trinity in impish delight at each other's company. Their laughter rippled the air and dissipated, leaving a sleepy lull. A bearish white man, with a large mane of greying hair, came out to join him on the balcony. The man's beard was unruly and unkempt. Large strands collided and argued as they tried to forge their own fractious path.

'Subhanallah, what was all that movie nonsense? They talk some real bloody crap, don't they?'

Ayub smiled. 'Laughter is a gift, it softens the heart.'

'But as the prophet, peace be upon him, said, "Laugh not excessively for this deadens the heart."'

Ayub's smile receded. 'Yea…true…nice to see that you have kept your happy-chappy ways, Adam…it's really good to see you too…honestly.' They gave each other a quizzical look and started chuckling. They embraced, hugging each other tight.

Letting go, Adam saw a look of concern in Ayub's face and gave him a warm smile. 'Well just keeping it real, as the kids say.'

'They are good boys, just passing the time. I'm pretty sure we used to be like that.'

'They have it easier now. Islam surrounds them, and practising Muslims and knowledge are everywhere. Circles, Internet, conferences. Not like us growing up. We were freaks.' Wearing leather Birkenstocks, Adam reached down and rubbed the skin of his feet through holes in his socks. Ayub had seen this plenty of times and once bought clothing for Adam, only for the gift to be indignantly rebuffed. Ayub tried hard not to take Adam's pride as a personal slight, but he wished his friend would allow him to help, even if it was to allay his own concern.

'C'mon, if someone runs out of loo roll they blame the 'Mozzies'. When I was a kid we were 'Asians', chucked in with the Indians. We were seen as servile. Loads of jokes about the 'paki' shop, and eating curry. Then one day I woke up and suddenly we were all 'Muslims', bringing chaos, disorder and a threat to their women. These kids don't remember a time being anything other than Muslim,' said Ayub, looking outwards onto stone and a stillness. 'No jokes anymore; they don't get messed around on the street like 'Asians' did. No, instead they get messed around by the government.'

'Different situation now, different issues.'

'Dat is true, bruv,' Ayub said, mimicking the tones of the street. 'But I miss those days. The most exciting thing then was when Mr T used to to walk up and down Tooting Broadway.'

Adam did a double take. 'Is that really true…was Mr T around here?'

'Nah. It was just some random massive guy with a latex wig and mohawk. He wore some real looking gold chains as well, but it was just some bloke on day release from Springfield, the mental hospital...still, as kids we knew no different. Gutted when I found out.'

They both shuffled sideways towards the wall as a young white girl pulled along two even younger children. They wore tracksuits that looked as if they had seen time up a chimney. As one of them passed he looked Adam up and down. Baffled, seeing a largely-framed white man in a pristine white salwar kameez, with a bald, shaven head and a large bushy beard, he asked Adam: 'Hey mate, why have you got your head on upside down?'

Ayub started laughing. Adam began to issue words of protestation. 'You cheeky...' but was stopped cold as the girl gave the kid a horrendous slap. The sound of the strike resounded so hard that it cannoned off the walls and Ayub touched his own cheek in sympathy.

'Shut the fuck up. You don't talk to people that way. Sorry, Luv,' she said, turning to Adam.

The boy rubbed his flushed face. 'Just a fuckin' joke, Mum.' His mother grabbed the boy by the scruff of his jacket and dragged him along with her as she stamped away.

Adam's eyes followed the mother and children along the balcony until they disappeared into the stairwell. '"Head upside down"...cheeky little git; what were you saying about kids again?'

'Haha, that was a good one though. He didn't deserve that slap, I thought his head was going to come off.' Ayub was happy to see Adam actually join in with a laugh, too.

'I've been called worse...some kid actually called me Gandalf the other day.' Adam looked at Ayub with such innocent hurt that Ayub started sniggering like a schoolboy.

'So what have you been up to?' asked Ayub.

'I was working down in Cornwall on a site there for a few months. It's a really beautiful part of the country. But I'm all done there, so now I've decided to head back up north. I thought I'd pass through. It's been too long.' It was still startling to Ayub that Adam's considerable presence produced a humble, mellow timbre.

'It's been way too long. You're always welcome. I remember you in my prayers often. Always on the move, Adam. Are you not interested in laying some roots?'

Since his youth Adam had hitchhiked around the country, looking for work like a winged creature, forever migrating to new horizons; a habit that was hard to break. Behind his barrelled figure and bedouin nature, and in his meekness and fragility, there existed a man at odds with the illusory solidity of the world. Someone who sought out temporality as a reassurance.

'Not yet, maybe soon, inshallah. The kids are growing up so I'd like to spend more time around them, if their mother allows me.'

'I wasn't going to ask about it…but any chance of reconciling?'

'Allah knows best; I can't provide as she expects me to. I send pretty much all my money but it's never enough.'

Ayub nodded. 'Subhanallah, may Allah make it easy.'

Ayub looked Adam over to see if he was truly in good shape. Adam was the deepest brother that Ayub had ever known; he saw the wonder of God's creation and magnificence in everything. He had a poet's soul. From the structure of seashells to the pollination of flowers by bees, from the perfect ecosystem for conditions on life on Earth, Adam saw signs of the Creator in them all. Ayub enjoyed the way he could see wonder outside the constriction of the estate. He loved Adam's wonderment and articulacy, and had a wistful desire to be able to see the world that way. However, even in other, happier, times, Adam's continuous stream of profound thoughts could be exhausting. Adam had such intense feelings for the ineffable and transcendent, that Ayub could not immerse in. They instigated a playful need in Ayub, to vitiate and sabotage Adam's train of thought with more trivial and purposefully doltish suggestions.

'Jazakallhu khair, may Allah have mercy on us all. Have you read this?' Adam took out a crumpled newspaper from a brown leather satchel that he wore around his shoulder and opposite hip, courier style. He had turned the pages back at an article and gave it to Ayub:

A delegate to the EU Conference on Muslims has asked for all European Muslims to sign a declaration that they reject violence and support the text of the Quran being changed to align with European values. When asked what happens if they do not sign, he replied that, 'We are the most welcoming of nations. I cannot see why reasoned and moderate Muslims will not sign it. If they do not they must have something to hide. At least we will know where we stand, and life should be made hard for those people.' As a member of the European Parliament, he had previously proposed a ban on all mosque building in Europe...

Ayub quickly scanned the rest and decided he had read enough. He clenched the newspaper in a fist, handing it back as if he were discarding a piece of trash. 'It's bit like dunking a witch and, if they drown, they're innocent. I really don't know what to say anymore. It's going on every single day. Has he been sacked? Of course not.'

'No, it's all gone quiet. The fact that people can say this, with no one saying aught to them, is scary though. It's pretty much like open season.'

Ayub clenched the balcony handrail, his knuckles turning white like a hot iron. 'What more is there to say about it?...It's the way it is, isn't it. It's pointless reading this stuff. It inflames the soul, puts us off-balance. Belief is difficult, Adam. The prophet, peace be upon him, said there will be a time when holding onto faith is like holding onto hot coals. In the end, life and Islam is simple. You worship God, work hard, spread the word and goodness as much as possible, and then depart, letting someone else take their turn.'

Adam's face turned remonstrative, his hands and arms coming alive. 'Getting work is harder, people are treating me differently too. I used to go to villages or building sites and people saw me as one of them, and they were always welcoming. You know? The eccentric English convert with a big beard. But with the climate now…nowadays…people I've known for years don't look at me the same. The trust is gone. It hurts. I used to live across different worlds and they didn't mix. Now they crash and it's messy…what's a moderate anyway?'

Ayub took up Adam's rhetorical question. 'It's childish politics.'

He paused. Both men went silent for a while, looking out onto the estate. The rest of London was visible through the flashing slits of daylight between the estate's tall buildings. If you scanned the scene, from left to right, the city looked like it existed in stills, as if within a Kinetoscope.

Adam broke their interlude. 'I've been reading some of my old school books. Reading newspapers. Thinking about the past. I think it's time to try settling again, to try and not block everything out…' Adam paused and then recited.

'"*Twas brillig, and the slithy toves. Did gyre and gimble in the wabe;*". Man, I loved that stuff as a kid.'

Ayub looked amused. 'What's that, *Beowulf?*'

'"*And, as in uffish thought he stood, The Jabberwock, with eyes of flame,*"…'

'Ah, you must have gone to some posh country school, I bet. We got stuck with war poetry. "*Dulce et decorum est pro patria mori.*" It is sweet and right to die for your country. Heavy stuff, and about all I can remember. Death, country, sacrifice, futility, all there.'

Both men embraced the silence once again. They listened as gusts of wind hit the building and were forced down the sides by impenetrable walls, creating bursts of air at the bottom.

Gusts that plucked up plastic bags to dance in the wind, happily pirouetting and buoyed to new dizzy heights by the estate's restive breath.

Adams face turned stern. 'Do you ever regret going?'

Ayub looked at two bags that had reached his eye level, whirling around each other as if in a waltz and then thrusting into deep dives in a dogfight. He hated dredging up the past, raking over memories, excoriating them and making new lacerations, never uncovering anything new.

'What…Bosnia? No. Forget everything else, but Muslims should never forget Bosnia; the British mujahedeen who went over should be proud they did their duty. Why do you ask? You regret it?' said Ayub, his speech mournful.

Adam replied, almost in a hush but his inflection carrying an edge that cut the air, 'No, but I've been thinking about it a lot lately. Especially when I read stuff coming from that conference. Bosnia was three hundred years of living together. They married each other. The Muslims drank like them. They looked exactly the same, talked the same, and yet…the man who was your neighbour, broke bread with you, the man who married your daughter. The next day that man would be at your door stabbing you like a stranger. As if everything was nothing. As if they were seeing each other for the first time.'

Ayub inhaled deeply. 'Yea, all that mixing and it still happened. And they were the moderates that these conference types would love us to be. If you can dehumanise someone you can justify anything. Exterminate like vermin. Look Adam, we're hated and it's tough, but it's a good forced-reminder. It compels us to remember our identity and think about the reality of our situation…forgetting is destruction, annihilation at our own hands or others. Always remember. Even if it's painful.'

A chainmail blanket of silence came over them, stifling the screams, muffling the battle cries.

Adam ventured forth, his voice tentative. 'It encouraged the Jihadis though. We should never have been so soft with them, or allowed them to fight. I remember we were once on a hill overlooking a Serb village and one of them took an old woman in his sights. This bent-over, ancient woman. She was just getting water from a well. I pushed his rifle down and explained to him how this was wrong. So wrong! How it was against the Sharia. He listened on that day but I knew there would be trouble.'

Ayub closed his eyes and pinched his nose, and placed his other arm on Adam's shoulder. 'It was a war. You took help from whoever you could. It wasn't our call. And what was the option? Fight Muslim versus Muslim while everything else burned. At least we didn't indulge in that sin. Muslim blood is cheap for the West, and nowadays it's even cheaper between ourselves. But, yes, they thought they did it by themselves, they don't remember the American airstrikes.'

'That wasn't to help us, that was settling a beef with Russia.'

'Whatever it was. Who knows? Adam, there is so much that goes on that we have no clue about, or power over. That's what I try and tell the kids. Don't get confused with all the hundreds of issues and spread your energy thinly. Try and concentrate on something and be good at it. Do things for the sake of Allah, not because you are angry or hurt. We should act out of nobility, not because we want to lash out.'

'And does it work?'

'Well, I struggle to follow my own advice most of the time.' Ayub smiled as Adam attempted a sympathetic laugh. 'Why this serious talk, Adam? Unearthing the past...it's like opening an old wound again and again. For what end?'

Adam reappeared every few years, with the same questions, like a ghost from some Dickensian tale. Their shared history brought up feelings of sorrow. Grief and mourning that emanated from another lifetime.

'Just taking stock you know…I was young when I converted. I had just turned twenty. I moved from youth home to youth home, and I'm still used to moving. Sometimes you have to stop and think.'

Ayub nodded. 'True, I wish I had that option, but I'm here. In a way I'm jealous of you. You're as free as a bird. You go where the road takes you. Like the prophet, peace be upon him, said, "Be in this world as a traveller."'

'Yea, but I have to take my mind everywhere with me. I'm not as free as you think. May Allah bless you, I've always wished I could be as strong as you, staying and looking after these people. Everyone looks up to you,' said Adam, one hand grasping his beard and pulling down, in an effort to calm its erratic strands.

'I don't do it too well. I'm not sure anyone listens. If they only knew how difficult it is sometimes. I struggle too, Adam. Like for the kids on this estate who go the wrong way, violence is easy. It's easy to lose yourself to the violence. I see the simplicity and clarity in it. How attractive it is. That's what I want to tell these kids, stealing from each other or stabbing each other. What I want to tell our idiots, and their idiots, who want to reduce everything to a simple brawl.'

Ayub continued, 'The takfiris and men of violence…they are bombing people away from the religion. We can't allow them to bomb us into taking away the good of Islam. Adam, we have to cling onto our civilised ways. Not let these people denigrate and erode our values. To bring us down. And as for the West. We remember. We remember our histories.'

Adam had been listening as if it was a sound from afar, distant and disconnected. A faint echo. He looked to Ayub and said, 'I knew there were some crazies, but the amount of pain and hate you must feel to do some of that stuff…they've caused everyone suffering, especially themselves. It's totally out of control. And as for the West…who remembers anything.'

The Study Circle

In a drowsy lethargy, almost slurring his words, dragging them across the floor, Ayub said, 'We must remember, though. Remember everything. Just like we remember Srebrenica.'

Still, Ayub thought going had been the right decision, as near to a righteous war as was possible. A responsibility to stop the slaughter of those within a day's drive of London. Ayub was born as a Muslim during that war. He never had the cynicism of the youth. Boys like Ishaq, Marwane and Shams. They did not notice how their being had formed in a climate of distrust and harsh realities. Like their bones, their character calcified deeply until it became their essence. At their age, Ayub still believed in systems, he had a natural belief that things would improve and get better for all people. Srebrenica changed all that. Besieged by the Serbs on all sides, Bosnian Muslims gave up their guns as asked. They trusted Europe, trusted the United Nations, trusted their 'safe haven'. A leap of faith that did not seem that wild, that delusory, at the end of the Cold War when everything was changing, when history had ended. But, when the town fell, eight thousand ended, forgotten in mass graves. Their bodies discarded, industrial bulldozers lumping their carcasses on top of each other.

Bosnia had many lessons. It destroyed the illusion that anything other than might is right, that Europe could be trusted. Ayub remembered. He had a clear vision of talking to one Bosniak in an old ramshackle cafe in Travnik, its roof collapsed like a broken back so that it was now really no more than a lean-to. Its stony faced walls riddled with bullet holes. Slumped and staring, the man had said, 'Never give up your guns. Mercy is the privilege of the strong. Suffering, the reward of the weak.' That wizened, striated, face and those absent raisin-eyes had stayed with Ayub.

'And how do we do it?' Adam asked.

'By being better, that's all there is. Work harder, be more

honest, be kinder, persevere. Worship Allah for his sake alone, not for the trappings of the world. There's no other way. No sensible alternative.'

Both men watched as the sun disappeared, its coral presence shimmering out of existence. Estate and night fusing, so that there was no horizon.

Adam said, 'I'm sorry, Ayub, I've brought a proper downer with me.'

'No, no, it's good. Too much laughter does deaden the soul, like you say. It's good to think about realities. It's good to have some grown-up conversation.'

'I don't know how to say this...but there's another reason I'm here.'

'What's that?'

'I'm being hassled again. They're back.'

Impassive, Ayub used a soft guiding hand to steward Adam back into the flat. 'It's time for prayer.'

9.

'Who was that guy Ayub was chatting to?' Shams asked, as he shuffled along, short legs struggling to keep pace.

Ishaq as ever forged an urgent path. Hands in pockets, his head dipped and his mouth sipping the drawstring of his black hoody, Ishaq offered a smothered reply. 'Don't know. Maybe an old friend; I haven't seen him before. Anyway, what was that 'it' thing you couldn't say?'

'Well…ip dip dog shit fuckin bastard silly git. You are IT,' said Shams, as he tagged Marwane.

Marwane looked around at Shams, shook his head and gave a shrug.

The boys reached the Broadway as radiant tendrils of foaming-pink dragged down a curtain of twilight sky. This was punctuated by neon signs, glowing crimson, that adorned shops. They passed an amusement arcade, filled to its extremities with one-armed bandits, and roulette machines, and pub quiz cabinets.

On video screens greyhounds chased digital manifestations of a hare. Simulacra of Arabian stallions and thoroughbred horses jostled to victory.

Ishaq noted one man sat at the front, torpid and gaping upwards at a display that produced floating colours, like a stained glass window. Without looking, the man took notes, not coins, out of a plastic bag and fed them into the gluttonous machine. Ishaq felt the urge to go in and pinch him hard to see if he would feel, to see if he would flinch.

The arcade swapped regular traffic with a pub next door. A tapas shop had popped-up and was conspicuous as a rare enclave completely populated by white faces. A new organic deli had elbowed its way in, among halal meat butchers and curry houses dripping with ghee. That clean-eating nirvana hosted economic migrants fleeing the tumult of rising London house prices in Chelsea and Clapham. Now, locals sometimes stopped in their tracks and stared at colourful sightings of the lesser-spotted yummy mummy and men who wore plaid.

Marwane kissed his teeth and nudged Ishaq in the direction of the pub. 'See, that's a proper ghetto.'

'You should go in there and make some friends.'

As they passed outside they saw one man, drunk, eyelids almost fastened, waving a crutch at a friend as he hobbled round in a circle, incoherent. His equally paralytic pal returned fire, protesting about money or a round. Marwane looked at them and said, 'No thank you.'

The smaller, unkempt man with the aid wore an Adidas two-stripe tracksuit rip-off, probably bought from Tooting market. Clouded in fury he swung his crutch in an arc that nearly took Ishaq's head off, forcing him backwards onto Shams. The swing took in a wide area before its centrifugal force escaped and the man collapsed in a heap on the floor, face planted downwards. The other, with a grey chapped beard, in his forties or fifties, knelt down to try and pick his mate up. 'Don't be like that Tommy, it's just a fuckin' pint.'

With his help Tommy got up, bleeding profusely from his nose, effin' and blindin'. He staggered away, his friend trailing him warily.

Marwane returned to the middle of the pavement looking after them. 'It's sad you know, to only be able to connect to another through alcohol. What kind of life is that?'

'That's a bit deep for you. Anyway it's their culture, we don't have to respect it. We tolerate it.' Ishaq gave a brief thought to his father.

Shams, Marwane and Ishaq made their way further down the road. Down the high street they passed by the familiar. An Asian man proudly displayed his fruit and veg on the paving outside his shop, making a haphazard display. Another sold mobile phone accessories, with a side venture in hair extensions for black women. Customers who were oblivious that the hair came from some girl in penury. Someone who'd had their head shaved in some Indian temple far away, as an offering to the local deity. People scurried in and out of money exchanges and international-call shops. The boys rushed on, passing all of this by. They wanted fried chicken.

KFC wasn't halal so local entrepreneurs had created their own versions, so you now had chains of 'Dallas' and 'Tennessee' fried chicken battling it out to be the main source of Islamic coronary heart disease.

Marwane pointed at Shams' head. 'What the hell is that?'

'Whaddya mean?' Shams touched his head. He wore a baseball hat that almost resembled a public school cap. Slightly flat, it had a small felt peak with maroon and grey quarters. It made him look like a character straight out of *Just William*. 'This? It's designer from the States. It's cool, don't you think?'

'Like you said, Americans make all sorts of crap. Now it's

designer Harry Potter. Give it here.' Marwane ripped the hat from Shams' head and ran down the street. Shams gave chase and, after a pause, a begrudging Ishaq ran too. They slowed down before the takeaway, bent over, grabbing air in between gasping laughter. Marwane flung the cap at Shams. 'Ah, I didn't want it anyway.'

Passing the Gurdwara they arrived at the fried chicken shop and noticed a cop car. Ishaq whispered, 'Five-O.' A feeling of dread creeping upwards, inverse to the slowing of the patrol.

The boys stalled their pace to the point where you could hear their feet scraping the ground. They turned their backs, hoping to avoid eye contact and giving them an excuse to make them even more uncomfortable walking their own streets. The driver looked at the other officer, in the passenger seat, who nodded. They parked, turned off the engine, exited, and walked towards the group.

'Alright lads, you from round here? What you up to today?'

Shams and Marwane looked away while Ishaq said, 'Nothing Officer, just getting something to eat.'

The Officer paused, surveying the three. 'You looked to be in a right rush there. Where were you coming from?'

'Typical bullshit, why don't you just leave us alone, we weren't up to nothing,' blurted out Shams, until he was stopped by a stare from Ishaq.

In a calm manner, and with empty hands held out wide, Ishaq said, 'We were just having a laugh on the street.'

'And where are you from?'

'The estate.'

'Ok…the reason why we've stopped you is that we're looking for a group of lads who have been involved in a fight, and a mobile's been stolen and you match their description.'

'Ok, what description is that?'

'Two Asian males and one black. In tracksuits. One with a cap. You lads fit that.'

Marwane's eyes lifted; he was used to being mistaken for all sorts by the police, once being told that he was 'ethnically indeterminate.' 'Mate, I'm not black for a start…'

'And we've got nothing to do with what you said anyway,' finished Ishaq.

Both officers looked at Marwane. Unsure, and studying him as if they were trying to ascertain whether he was black, mixed race, or Arab or what. Ishaq shook his head and stifled a laugh at the coppers' inanity.

The silent officer whispered into the other's ear. Police sometimes said that gangs could hand-off to other sets of people as a petty excuse.

The first officer nodded and turned to the boys. 'A member of the public witnessed three people. Two were definitely Asian, therefore we have grounds to search.'

'Well that describes just about everyone round here. What race did you say again? Just like us? This is dumb, I'm outta here.' Shams started to walk away but was blocked by the arm of an officer.

'Look, no one is going anywhere. If this is a mistake, then this will all be cleared up quickly. This has only happened in the last ten minutes and you are the only guys matching the description.'

'Don't touch me. This is bollocks.'

Ishaq held Shams' back to draw him back in case he faced up to the coppers. 'Shams, just let them get on with it.'

'But Issy, we're only here minding our ways. It's not right.'

'I know, just trust me.'

Happy that the situation was in control, the officer proceeded, 'Ok, as I said, I have grounds to search you, based on the information I've told you. The fact is, a theft has occurred and the individuals involved were three males with your description.'

Shams butted in, 'We're here outside the estate just doing our own thing and you think your job is to intimidate us. Why do you guys never come into the estate, you just leave everyone to rot.'

'At this moment we're dealing with this. We can discuss any issues that you gentlemen have with the estate afterwards,' said the policeman, in that exaggerated tone that was supposed to exude training and control.

'You know, you guys just poke, poke, poke. Petty tings everyday, until it builds up and someone lashes out and then you claim the high ground. You guys are just trying to vex us up, waiting for the slap,' said Shams.

On the 'p' of 'slap' both officers' gaze fastened on to Shams. Ishaq's fingers coiled biting into the palm. 'Shams, just leave it, you're not helping.'

The other officer twisted his neck and started talking in the radio perched on his tactical vest. Something about IC4s. The men's walkie-talkies made abrupt noises; electric static and a screeching fizz that crawled into Ishaq's ears.

'As I've explained, we've got grounds, and there's an authority from our Superintendent that we have a power under Section 60 as there has been violence in this area. If you're not involved you'll be on your way.' The man held Shams firmly by his wrist. 'I'm PC 8921 Jenkins from Lavender Hill Station. You have been detained for the purpose of search under Section 60 of the Criminal Justice and Public Order Act.'

Another police car arrived, all blues and twos, parking at an angle. The siren and bleary flashing of lights brought attention from people in the chicken shop. The siren let out one final primal scream but the lights still went on undulating, gathering people at this now nocturnal hour.

One onlooker not impressed with the scene, box of chips in his hand, wiped ketchup from his lip and, in between considered ruminating chews, said, 'Five-O, why you trying to aggravate, treating us like animals.'

The officer ignored the comment and gestured towards Shams. Shams pushed his arm away, and then pushed the policeman in the chest and stepped back. 'I said don't touch me.'

The officer gave his partner, and those newly arrived, a quick look. Their handcuffs came out and they pulled Shams down to the floor with force. One kept him pinned down, a second was at Shams' side, and a third was on top of Shams' struggling body. Shams strained, trying to push them off, with his body arched like a crawling caterpillar, keeping his arms tight underneath his torso and not releasing.

'Relax, give us your arm.'

'What the fuck for? What have I done?'

'Just relax, give me your arm.'

The policeman nearest his head reached round under Shams' neck and used a knuckle to put pressure on his mandibular angle. Shams let out a yelp, his body twitched, collapsing flat. One arm came free, and this was enough to get both out and cuff him with his arms pulled to the rear.

Hoisted up to a kneeling position, Shams was asked, 'Are you going to be quiet?'

Shams looked downwards distressed, flaccid hair covering his eyes, refusing to answer. Taking this as assent, the police positioned the others in a line.

Ishaq took a look at his friend's indignity. The police won't listen. Shams doesn't listen. There's no point pretending in the possibility of control or reason. He looked on as an ambulance sped down the high street, lights blazing, but it didn't stop. It was rushing on to some other Friday night scene in South London.

A blinking infinity of eyes cast out from the shopfront window, bulbous and cyclopean like charms used to ward off the evil eye. Cars slowed; Ishaq locked eyes with the drivers. Some nodded in acknowledgement or beeped their support while taking in the show. An officer started to pat them down. Ishaq felt disembodied hands examine his pockets. One floating on his head, another holding an arm and a third ruffling through his clothing and then touching him from behind.

Ishaq looked up to the stars for a firm point of reference. They always held the potential to navigate a way out, but all he could see impressed upon the firmament was a purpley-black bruise of throbbing industrial light. He tried to give Shams a reassuring look, pleaded with his eyes for him not to blow up again. Ishaq had been through this enough times to know the score. This was a rite of manhood. A form of ritual humiliation. In other societies they had bah mitzvahs and fraternity hazings, but those had some sort of implied consent. They came from within the tribe. This was London's largest gang enforcing a rite against unwilling participants. An admonishment that they are of age, and a contingent threat. A process of enforced tribal scarification by outsiders, putting them in their place.

They did the same with Marwane and a now acquiescent Shams, who was back on his feet but still cuffed. One officer trawled one, and then a second, mobile from Shams' puffer jacket.

'Why have you got two phones?'

Shams shook his head as if trying to regain some of his senses. 'Everyone carries two phones. One for family and one for work.'

Marwane and Ishaq exchanged glances, looking to each other for confirmation that Shams had said he was unemployed.

Handling the battered Nokia candybar, a policeman asked, 'And the family in this picture, who are they?'

'Uhhh…they're relatives of mine…'

The policeman nodded and passed the phone to another, who dipped his head inside a patrol car, chatting away and typing on some machine. Ishaq had caught sight of the photo.

It was a low-res pic of a couple with two kids. Even with the low granularity the wife and child definitely had blonde hair; the whole family was white and Ishaq was pretty sure that the father was wearing an England football top. He spat out a whisper in the direction of Shams, 'You dozy twat.' The main officer asked if Ishaq had something to say, but Ishaq shook his head and responded with, 'Nothing. Nothing at all.'

The guy with the chips had finished munching. Dropping his empty box on the pavement, he wiped his greasy hands on a brick wall and gave a final self-satisfied swipe on his cargo pants. He took out his phone and started to film. 'Look here...proper police harassment, I've got it all on video. YouTubing this, you know. Police brutality, aye.'

One of the silent policemen was young. Not far from their age. Healthy and rosy cheeked, he looked nervous. 'Stop filming. You're not allowed to film us.'

'Boss, I know my rights under the law so mind your own business. I'm peacefully standing here minding my own, just filming you guys harassing these lot. Make sure Five-O don't do wrong, bruv. So what's your names for my records?'

'You don't need to know anything else.'

With his phone the man stepped nearer and filmed the badges on their shoulders. 'Officer 4901. Officer 4679, and 'I'm a man not a number, '8921'', aye, got you. Better mind your p's and q's.' Brandishing the smartphone with a perilous sweep near their faces, both officers turned their back on him.

The officer from the car returned, covered his mouth with a hand and whispered to the guy in charge, who walked back up to Shams.

'We've done our checks on the IMEI code and they've returned that the phone was reported as stolen on November 17th. As this was found in your possession you are now being arrested for handling stolen goods.'

Ishaq turned his neck to Shams. Shams refused to look back. They heard another wail and all swung to see another police car park up. He spied the yellow dot stickers at the back that indicated it as an armed response vehicle. Ishaq looked on, his mind refusing the image, as yet another policeman came towards them. This time with a Glock 17 in a holster on his leg, a yellow taser held on a utility belt, and wearing ballistic Kevlar body armour. He was also carrying a Heckler and Koch assault rifle that was balanced across his arm, with the tip facing down, his trigger finger on the outside.

Ishaq stared at the sleek weapons, their attractive and inviting burnish. If a copper ever went full automatic, and had the ammo, he could shoot eight or nine hundred rounds a minute, shredding the high street. Ishaq imagined what it would be like to have a bullet rip through you. He caught the officer in charge's look of surprise, and his signalling the new man to go away. A member of the now enlarged crowd shouted, 'Budget Robocop coming. OCP. Gunshot. Charles De Menezes.'

'Listen,' Ishaq said to the main officer, 'this is getting stupid. Why the gun?'

'It's just part of their uniform, you've go nothing to worry about.'

Another discarnate voice cried, 'Nothing to worry about? That's what that Brazilian electrician probably thought before he got pinned down and shot seven times in the head. Up the road from here, wasn't that De Menezes?'

Ignoring the comment, Ishaq heard the officer say to his younger colleague, 'Why the hell are they here. Tell them to get lost,' and then talk into his radio, 'Control, cancel any further units. Situation is under control. Sufficient on scene.'

The man who was videoing bobbed up and down in excitement, weaving a flight path around the spectacle. 'More of them, bringing bare mens down. Proper army down here, for what?'

'Move out of the way, do all the filming you want, we're dealing with the situation.'

'No, this is police oppression, you get me?'

'You're not helping, just move back.'

'Ok, just one quick question, just for community chat; where you from? Round here?'

The young officer paused then said, 'I'm originally from Devon.'

The man started laughing and swapped resigned looks with the held boys. 'No wonder. You country folk couldn't tell the difference between a Mongolian and a Masai warrior.'

Whooping emanated from the crowd as the older officer shook his head at the younger. Ishaq scanned the mass of people and passers-by, some of whom rubbernecked. Elongating and twisting their necks in grotesque contortions, many chewing away like giraffes. He hoped that a family friend or acquaintance would not pass-on this whole embarrassing scene. He didn't fear the shame or hit, on reputation, and the ensuing gossip. He feared his family's concern.

Ishaq thought about what the right response should be. He could keep quiet, let the process wash over and take its toll, its pound of flesh. But was being quietly compliant just a form of defeat. Disappearing into an insensate fugue and allowing these people to go on, with impunity, does them no good too. Sometimes, you did need to challenge. Ishaq just wasn't sure when and at what time.

The head policeman had been standing there trying to ignore the circus around him. Calmly, Ishaq said to him, 'Do you really think that this helps anyone?'

'What do you mean?'

'Causing this fuss over nothing. Look around, how many of these people here think you're doing a good job?'

'Your friend has a stolen item.'

'A crappy phone that you can pick up for a couple of quid from anywhere.'

'Just trying to do the best to help the community. Without us it would be bedlam. We speak to schools and to community elders all the time'

All three boys started laughing.

'Community elders?' Marwane interjected, 'Breh, you're having a laugh aren't ya? What do you think we do, sit around in a circle passing each other the peace pipe? Every time someone like you opens their mouth, it shows that you don't know nuthin'. Elders…It's you who've been smoking something.'

Marwane looked away from the officer and spat on the floor by the officer's feet. At that last action the policeman retorted angrily, 'Well, that's the price to pay when saving you from being blown up on the tube.'

Marwane's nostrils flared. 'Maybe we get saved from the bomb only to be shot by one of you lot. Great life that is. Missing explosions from nutters or avoiding dumdums from dumb dumbs in the Great Met Police. Like Forest Gate back in the day, where you mashed up a family's house on made-up shit. What happened there?'

'Don't be silly. No one is getting shot here.' The officer in command looked at Ishaq for a calming influence.

Ishaq pursed his lips and grimaced, 'Yea, when you lot do it it's a "mistake". When we do anything it's a crime.'

Marwane started laughing, the fear of getting shot accidentally. And it was always the dark guy. Seemed to happen everywhere. Always another 'mistake'.

Marwane added, 'Or that fake ricin plot. Fake weapons of mass destruction. Fake crimes. Fake, fake, fake. A long time, fake. Are you guys even policemen?'

One officer said, 'Nothing to do with us, son. We're outside a chicken shop in South London.'

The man videoing replied, 'Yo, leave it out, man speaks truth.'

The officer shook his head, ignoring them as he went through some documentation with his colleagues. Not happy, Ishaq shouted after him, 'As for your justice, some guys got just three years for firebombing a mosque. People got a decade in the Bradford riots for throwing pebbles, after people like you wanted the NF to walk all over them.'

Ishaq surveyed the scene. Every policeman was ignoring them. All of them white. The man filming with the mobile moved around the police like a court jester, dangling his phone in front of them like he was tormenting a baby with candy. Visibly shaken by the camera in his face, the young policeman's rose-cheeked face turned even redder as he looked the would-be auteur up and down.

'Take out your hand from your pocket.'

'I ain't got nothing. Just my wallet.'

'I said. Let. Me. See. Your. Hands.' Without giving the man time to respond, he continued, 'I believe you may be harbouring a weapon. I'm searching you under Section 60. Put your hands out.'

'No, I'm doing jack. Fuck off.'

Before the others could stop him the officer grabbed the man. Begrudgingly, two others helped grapple him down.

'See this?' the man yelled, now prostrate, amongst bones and greased wrappings, his limbs splayed like a collapsed marionette.

The young officer said to the prone individual, 'I am arresting you under a Section 5 public order offence'

The older officer rubbed his eyes with the beaten pinch of one wrinkled hand as a police van arrived. Ishaq watched on as Shams was led to one car, and the newly arrested interloper was led to another as the gathered crowd let out whoops.

'We've found nothing on you two. I'll just give you a copy of this form. It outlines the reasons why you were stopped. I need just a few details. What are your names and addresses?'

Ishaq replied, 'You really nicked my mate for a crappy phone? I'm tellin' you nuthin.

You've already searched me.'

'I just need it for the form, and you'll get a copy…'

'I don't want a copy. You can shove it. I'm not like my mate. I may have been quiet but that's because I know my rights.'

The officer puffed; he looked fed up. 'Look lads just give me your details and you'll be on the way.' Getting nothing from Ishaq, he looked to Marwane. 'How about you?'

Marwane shrugged his shoulders.

'One more chance, give me your details.'

Someone from the crowd called out, 'Take them all in, why don't you take us all in, pigs?' The crowd started chanting, 'Ooh', 'Ooh', 'Ooh', gesticulating at the police, trying to capture a reaction.

Buoyed by the pack, Ishaq persisted, 'No. You know you can't do anything now. This is a joke. You're a joke.'

Taking off his cap and wiping his brow, the policeman's forehead showed deeply raked lines. The situation out of control, he just wanted a quick resolution to keep the peace.

'Alright, Steve Biko, I'll take that as threatening a police officer. Take them both in. Section 5, abusive and insulting language in a public place.' He nodded at the young officer.

The young officer, beading droplets, his face dissolving in acid, looked at the two and, to everyone's bewilderment, said, 'Have you got anything in your shoes? Take them off.'

Ishaq laughed. From an early age local support groups had given out leaflets on procedures concerning being stopped by the police, or if your house was raided.

'If you want me to take my shoes off you need to do it back at the station, or in a private place. That's the law. I'm not doing that in front of all these people here. Are you just trying to be humiliating?'

'Under Section 44, I can ask you to take your shoes off here.'

'Mate, that's to do with terrorism. You've stopped us under Section 60, then Section 5. This isn't pick and mix. The street isn't your sweet shop. Seriously. Read a book.'

One officer tapped the youngster on the shoulder and took him away to have a word, while another dealt with Ishaq and Marwane.

Marwane shouted after him, 'You're a proper muppet. Let you out of the work experience scheme early, hey? Didn't swot up on your City and Guilds course.'

One at a time, to cheers and whoops, Marwane and Ishaq were led into the waiting van. The policemen's faces had melded into one, it was difficult to discriminate between them, but one said,

'Look straight ahead. No looking at each other.'

10.

He hated their looks, like shit on a shoe. Something repulsive to be wiped away quickly, processed out of sight. The policemen disgusted Shams. He fazed out as he was escorted into custody. While the Arresting Officer talked to the Duty Sergeant, he took a look at the waiting others. Mostly silent and sullen men, even younger than him, looking downwards, shuffling their trainers. Plasticised masks as faces, they looked like they had either stabbed someone or been told by their parents that they couldn't watch TV.

One brooding juvie, in a black and gold Adidas tracksuit, looked up with raw baby blues. He caught Shams square with a defiance that dared for a challenge, right there in the station. Shams disregarded the dummied test and looked to the custody staff as they reeled off their rote questions. Their inflection worn, through weary repetition. Shams answered routinely and nearly pre-empting their queries. Are you injured? Have you ever harmed yourself? Are you seeing a doctor? Can you read and write English?

Shams broke out of his stupor at this last question. 'Obviously a lot better than you, that's why you're doing this job.'

The duty officer looked at him and smirked, shaking his head as he went on to explain the circumstances of his arrest.

'Do you understand why you have been arrested?'

'Yes, for walking down the street like a normal person…'

Another admonishing shake. Another patronly smile. Shams' phones were seized and placed in plastic evidence bags that were then sealed. His rights and entitlements were explained. When asked if he wanted to call someone, Shams felt a slight shiver and declined, but heard himself hoarsely accept when he was offered the advice of a solicitor.

The police searched him again and made him take his shoes off. Shams made an affected show of struggling as they held his hand on a glass screen to take his fingerprints. He watched as one-by-one they came up on the computer screen. Ridged contours and swirls forming in a way that was unique to him as an individual. He wondered how far down those impressions went before everyone was the same again. Not satisfied with what they had taken from the outer, they took a buccal swab to Shams' cheek and snatched a piece of him forever. DNA for the national database.

Shams was taken to a cell and heard the door shut with a sharp click. He sat on a padded bench with his back to the wall and pulled up his knees, curling into himself. A man shouted from one of the other cells, carrying brutality down the corridors, 'Fuckin' pigs. Why don't you just kill me? I swear I'm going to shit myself and shove it all over these stinkin' walls.' Shams heard an officer shouting back. Then the sound of flailing limbs. Then nothing.

He waited. For a long time he thought. Then a knock on his door and a guard said to him, 'They want you. Get up.'

'Has my solicitor arrived?' The guard stayed silent, cuffed him and led him away, physically manipulating him when he needed to turn a corner in what was a labyrinth of corridors.

Shams was escorted into a bare and narrow room where he was uncuffed. It held nothing more than a table and two chairs. The guard motioned to him to take a seat. Shams sat; he had expected something like a one-way mirror but this enclosure was spartan. The only indication that the room was different was a CCTV camera in the corner. It did not move and bore no active light, but Shams thought someone must be watching him and he guessed that they could listen as well.

There was no clock and no window. He was not sure if twenty minutes passed or two hours. As he sat, he sometimes exchanged looks with the taciturn guard. Shams started to make a rhythmic rap of his knuckles, on the table, that faltered under a stymied stare. Shams asked, 'What's taking so long? Why bring me in if no one is coming?'

The guard, expressionless, said, 'Don't worry, someone will come for you.'

Shams tapped his toe on the floor, ignoring the guard. Were they looking for something to jail him on? Was his lawyer here? Was this a good sign or a bad sign? Was the guard a bit dim? He rested his forehead on the table but, as soon as he did this, he sprung up as a new man entered. Not in a police uniform but in a navy blue suit that was smartly cut, in an expensive cloth, with a crisp, white shirt and a striking blood-red tie.

He took the chair opposite, settling himself and a few folders on the table, as Shams studied him. 'Shamsuddin Haque? Mr Haque. My name is Theodore and I'm with the Security Service, also known as MI5. Do you know what we do?'

Shams sat upright as if a rod had been inserted into his spine, 'Uh…what's this about?'

Striking, athletically built and straight-backed, Theodore looked like what Shams envisioned a spy should be. Shams noted his silver cufflinks, a sure sign of sophistication. Theodore continued; his tone was light, airy, yet economical and straight to the point.

'You're someone we've been keeping an eye on. You have been keeping, shall we say, 'interesting' company recently and we would just like to have a chat. Don't worry, it's nothing serious.'

Shams immediately thought of Mujahid and couldn't help a concern wash over him. Could this guy tell? 'I don't know nothing about anybody's business.'

'Well…we think you do, or at least you have some basic information that could help us,' said Theodore, fingers meeting and arched as if in pious contemplation.

'Like what?'

Theodore kept up a fixed stare. 'That's a nice beard you have there. Tell me, Mr Haque, would you call yourself a devout Muslim?'

'Yes…no…yea…depends what you mean? What's that got to do with anything?'

'Just getting to know you. Do you pray five times a day, for example? Do you regularly attend a mosque?'

'Yes… of course I do…I go to just the local ones…I don't understand why you're asking this. It's got nothing to do with nothing.'

'Don't worry, I just want to get to know you. Nothing sinister,' Theodore said, as he affected an oversized smile.

'If you're MI5 then you would know me already, right?'

Theodore laughed, to reveal two tracks of browned and rotting teeth which veered off in unpredictable ways. Whenever he smiled, or laughed, his teeth made him look carnivorous, as if he had been gnawing on bloodied meat.

'Well Mr Haque, we're not the Gestapo. We do have our limitations. Are you part of any political organisations?'

'No…nothing.'

'Ok, ok. Out of interest what are your views on the British Army abroad?'

'I have no views.' Shams failed to control his lower lip from flapping like a bird's broken wing.

'Come now, I find that hard to believe. You must have views on our best lads going abroad, defending our country, no?'

Shams bit down on his lip and tasted some of his own blood as it oozed, the pain giving him focus. 'Like I said, I have no views.'

Theodore nodded, opened a brown foolscap folder, took out a wad of papers, flicking through a set. 'You don't work – or at least don't do any work that contributes to the tax system. Signing on too, I see.' Theodore looked up.

'No. I'm not signing on, that's a mistake.'

Theodore looked again. 'I stand corrected. Not signing on. That's a surprise. Anyway, the other two lads who were brought in with you are doing well. Studying. Have good prospects. You're a bit of the odd one out, aren't you? Must be difficult to be left behind.'

Shams gave a contemptuous sniff, anger darting over his face; he was sure it had betrayed him before he reined it in. 'I've known these guys since we were kids. No one ain't leaving anyone behind. They're my best friends.'

'Ok, fair enough. But we have been told that you, yourself, do hang out with extremist groups. You have been seen at gatherings with the Caliphate mob. Do these childhood friends of yours know that?'

Shams pursed his lips. A man like this could know things, or was it another fishing expedition? Either way, he should get to the point as he was getting amped. 'Who told you that?'

'Well you were at a rally supporting the veil? Funny, since your sister doesn't even cover her head. Another one, by the way, who is doing a lot better than you.'

Theodore took out some photographs and handed them to Shams. They were shots of him at rallies. Captured so close that you could make out where he shaved his cheeks to keep his beard trim and well groomed.

As if he were reading Shams' thoughts Theodore said, 'It says in your Koran, about Allah and the believers, *"We are closer to him than his jugular vein."* Now, Mr Haque, although we aren't God we're the nearest thing available in this country.' Theodore smiled, smug and self-satisfied at his flourish.

Shams looked at Theodore, needled at this brandishing of God's word in frivolity, as something to bait him with. He hated the sneering as the man made an elaborate intonation of the name Allah. And in his hate, Shams lost some fear.

Theodore seemed to see something shift in Shams, some discomfort. 'Oops, that was sacrilegious wasn't it? Never mind, it really would be in your best interest to be helpful and truthful. Theres not much we can't dig out, eventually.'

'Actually, I don't support the veil. I don't care one way or the other.'

'So why were you there?'

'Well, just because people like you are against it.'

Theodore looked to be taken aback by the answer, eyes narrowing, and took to flicking through his foolscap for more.

'And the other demos?'

'Well…I just have friends who go.'

'Ah, another set of friends. You're a very friendly person, Shams. Very friendly. I can call you Shams, can't I? That's why we're interested in you. These other friends, they are the types of people who picket dead soldiers. Why do you go? Just to cause unrest?'

Shams had never gone to one of those death pickets. If Ishaq and Marwane were to find out they would be furious. He couldn't deny a light thrill when he heard of British soldiers dying, but he dared not speak of it. He felt both delight and shame to the point that it confused him. Delight in an act of revenge, however small. Something that was absolutely nothing compared to what these soldiers and their governments had done. Ashamed because it was a human life, after all, he felt diminished by this instinctual reaction. It was his dirty secret. One time he had skirted around mentioning the subject to Ishaq, but received such a lecture. Ishaq said he could understand the anger, but how wholly unacceptable it was to feel that way. Everything was this way with Ishaq nowadays.

'I don't get involved with that stuff. Listen, I want a lawyer.'

'Relax, this is just a friendly chat,' said Theodore, with a Chehire Cat grin. 'We can get lawyers involved but it will become a lot worse for you. Now, do you know how reprehensible, how offensive, these types of demos are to normal British people? These brave men fight for all of us, including you.'

Shams' ears caught the word 'offensive' and rolled it around in his head, groping and poking at it. This man didn't know that meaning of what real offence was. The world was just a game of Cowboys and Indians for them. These people who liked to remember their dead but not those they killed.

'Not against the law are they though, and like I said, I don't go.'

'But you hang around people who do go. You boys honour terrorists and killers.'

'I've done no such thing. I would never call for the death of civilians...'

'But soldiers?' interrupted Theodore.

Shams was puffing, his nerves threatening to overwhelm him. However advanced society was, he knew the world was like the street. You could still batter, bully, and kill your way to legitimacy. Games and films all lauded the violent man taking charge of his destiny and rising above. Like all mythology, they were stories of the unreal that allowed escape from the petty vicissitudes of the mundane. Open shows-of-strength were seen as honest, concealed-thought seen as cowardly. Right and wrong was just an application of power. The power to say: this was a justified murder, and this was not. People would always gravitate to those of influence; in their fear and desire they would compromise their senses and morals when it came to the most lauded and successful. Might was always right. These people said they wanted capitalism, and a free market for all, yet they treasured a monopoly on violence.

'I'll always support people protecting their home from invasion. You call some poor villager who's never heard of the Houses of Parliament, or the Eiffel Tower or whatever, and who's defending his country...you call him a killer? Soldiers here have armies...and history, and structures...and lines of command...all of that hides them from their real actions... you make it like they're not *killing*, they're 'serving', like they're not '*responsible*'when they're always the ones bossing-in other people's countries. I do nothing against the law. I've n-never h-hurt n-obody.' He finished his outburst, his insides spasmed and convulsed, lips and tongue trying to draw strength from the air.

Theodore concentrated elsewhere, a finger giving an idle flick to some pieces of lint . One silver piece of fuzz on his suit, and then another, while he waited for Shams to finish. 'True, not against the law, but not exactly conducive to society. We are this thing called a democracy. You can write to your MP or vote.'

'I'm peaceful, I've done nothing...nothing against the law.' Shams looked upward at the camera, both hands gripping the table.

'Not yet you haven't, but you hang around people who do. Do you think those people care that you're here, alone, and by yourself? We can get them on something else and throw the book against them. Just like we could do with this stolen phone. Alternatively, a lot of the policemen here or in the prison service are ex-squaddies; I could just let them know of your views and leave a door open some day. What do you think to that?'

Shams looked straight at the door, expecting it burst open at any moment. He must have heard of a dozen or more deaths in custody. Whispers dancing around the estate about someone's cousin from an estate in North London or somewhere else. Always a brown or black man. Always someone poor, or without big-time family and friends. Someone who wouldn't be missed or made a fuss about. Someone like him. And he couldn't think of even one copper going to jail over it.

He looked around the confined room and saw it warp and buckle as it constricted his chest, and he struggled to take in breath. He looked at Theodore through a strobing effect, his stuttered view making him nauseous.

Slowly in a whisper, he forced out, 'Please...I just want to go home.'

'Look Shams, we have enough on you. If you don't help us then you will be considered a terror suspect under Schedule 7. We can initially hold you for up to nine hours, and then if we're not happy...well, after that, anything is possible.'

Spasms of fear rushed over him. Coming in he had felt weak and scared but, as that subsided, he now felt angry and forceful, wanting to strike the man in front of him. Shifting between the two left him confused.

Theodore pulled out more photographs. This time they showed brothers from the circle exiting the flat: Ishaq and Marwane coupled in laughter; lots of shots of Ayub, and even of that white guy he saw him chatting to; close-ups taken with a tele-photo lens, but at an angle from a concealed vantage point. They had probably been through his bin bags, too. Like unhinged paparazzi, snipping away slices of your life, except where the celebrities got cash, and fame, he was being threatened.

Theodore continued, his voice calm and mellifluous like an avuncular Sunday school teacher, 'But if you help, home you will go. I just need to know a bit more about the other two with you? What groups are they involved with? Anything you know of, other than this gathering?'

'The other two are just friends…'

Theodore paused offering nothing back.

Shams looked at him and felt the silence. The room's darkness flooded his eyes. One hand palpated the other arm. He remembered an old bible story from his C of E middle school. Samson and the Philistines. He always daydreamed about wiping the smile off someone like Theodore, bullies and wrongdoers, by bringing the whole stinking edifice down around them all. A righteous reckoning. But for now he needed to fill the void in another way. 'They all attend this circle. This talk that's done weekly at that flat, but nothing dodgy goes on. Just talk, nothing more. Believe me.'

Theodore nodded slightly. 'Good, good, we're getting somewhere. See, it's just little things like that that we are looking for. Harmless isn't it?' Theodore pointed at Ayub and Adam. 'So what do you know of those two? What do they talk about?'

'I don't know the white one. Ayub normally gives the talks. He's a good man. A peaceful and religious man.'

'And are the other two active in the community?'

'Not especially. I know my rights, you're not allowed to ask me about anyone else? Shouldn't you just be asking about me?'

Theodore pushed back his chair and swung one of his legs onto the other, tapping the toe of his top brogue against the steel leg of the table.

'You have quite the sense of humour. What rights? You're quick to talk about rights and at the same time try to undermine those rights. You're lucky that this is a country that has rule of law.'

'I know my rights…' insisted Shams.

Theodore stopped tapping. 'Go on then. What are your rights?'

Shams was silent. Talking about terror, it was terror that possessed his body. His mouth dried and held a bitter taste. He looked at the door hoping that it would open with help, but it stood there entrenched.

Theodore broke into another delicate laugh. 'Listen, I've been doing you a favour. Going softly-softly like a friend, but if you can't help us that may need to change. Now don't panic, this is friendly advice. We are not charging you with anything but you do need to give us a bite. No one will know. Give us something and you're free to go right now.'

'I can go?'

'If you actually have some info for us. Plus you should probably think about why you're in here with me, while those two have already been let out.'

'What do you mean?'

'Well, let's just say that individuals with your profile can be a worry, and concerned friends can sometimes be a source for mentioning such individuals.'

'What are you sayin'…they reported me?'

'Like I said, we can't discuss sources but you do need to have a think about where people's loyalties lie. I want to help you. I can see that you're not a bad lad. Not in too deep. Just confused. We get loads of people through here but we don't offer them such an easy way out. If others have given us harmless bits of info and got on with their life, why can't you?'

Shams was positive that Ishaq and Marwane wouldn't have reported him. But when he told them about Mujahid, they did ask a lot of questions. They were always concerned about who he hung out with. He looked at Theodore anticipating an answer, and thought that all he needed to do was give him something. Anything. Even if it wasn't true. Just to keep him off his back.

'There's a march by that anti-Islam lot outside East London Mosque. They were discussing whether to go to the demo against it.'

'To start a fight?'

'No. No. Just to show support for the mosque.'

'But, if things got out of hand, would they be the type to get involved?'

'Yes…no…probably, I don't know. They just get on with their own thing.'

'Are you sure? Like I say…be truthful and you can leave.'

'Yes. The only people I know like that are your lot. Those who like getting pissed on Friday nights and then beating the shit out of each other,' said Shams, in a sudden rush of acrimony.

Theodore looked like a disappointed parent. 'Now, now, Shams. No need to be rude. A bit more and you can go. You are doing very well.'

Shams thought Marwane and Ishaq probably wouldn't go, and if they did it would be harmless. They would stay well away from trouble.

'Well, they know how to look after themselves. Let's say that. They are estate lads. And they do talk about protecting the community a lot.'

'Ok, good. Well at least we have their photos,' said Theodore, as he tapped their pictures with a stern finger. 'See, we highlight individuals from both sides to the police beforehand. It's better for them and for everyone. Keeps everyone safe. See, that was easy wasn't it?'

'Yes.'

'Ok, that's enough for now. Here is my number. It would be in your best interests to use it if you hear anything.'

Theodore shuffled and organised his papers and then knocked on the door for the police attendant.

'By the way. I'll be keeping an eye on you. I may call, or bump into you, from time to time. Be a good boy, yes?' said Theodore, lofting over a casual wink as Shams left.

Shams was quickly processed out. They didn't ask about the phone. He walked outside; the cool night air brushed against his face, providing relief, but sent shivers down the rest of his body. He noticed that his shirt was impregnated with sweat and his face felt dirty. He saw the figures of Marwane and Ishaq playfully wrestling at the bottom of the steps.

Marwane came up smiling. 'Well, that was a waste of time. Flippin' pigs. Got nothing better to do than give us hassle.'

Ishaq gave Shams an odd, disquisitive examination. 'You look like crap. You get scared? What took you so long, anyway, what did they ask you?'

Shams looked at Ishaq and Marwane. He noticed how unaffected Ishaq looked. How unkempt Marwane's hair was, how carefree. They were starting to look older. Could these friends really have reported on him? Shams wiped his face with his hands and looked around at the now lightless sky. 'How did you know I was coming out?'

'Well we were delayed because custody was busy and there was a wait in the booking queue. That intern wannabe screwed everything for them so they let us go, and they told us you wouldn't be that long after. What happened with you?' insisted Ishaq.

Shams stared at these two strangers, these two unfamiliar beings. 'Nothing brother. They let me off. Exactly the same as you.'

II.

Shams left Mujahid's flat. Hot coals of rolled fifties, in an envelope, created an obtrusive bulge in his puffer jacket. If he got mugged, would Mujahid believe him? Embarking on his journey, going underground, he looked around with his hand placed over the burden. A woman opposite him shifted in her seat, looking at him with concern as his pincer fingers struggled awkwardly at something within his bulking coat.

Shams arrived at the industrial compound just outside of City Airport in East London. He wandered through a maze of rotting pallets, piled steeple-high and teetering Jenga-like. The sky was overwhelmed by amorphous clouds; Shams strained his eye to see if he could make out any shapes but the patterns always changed as if out of spite. Planes roared continually over the area, flying so low that you could identify the carrier and even their tail numbers. They loomed so large that he lost himself in plumed shadow, feeling that he could reach up and touch one. Mouth slightly agape, he wondered at how they kept aloft in the air. Shams had heard that one had once clipped the top of a local hotel. He couldn't imagine having responsibility for so many people.

Raising his pace in case a pallet-tower collapsed, he neared an opening. Just before the exit Shams saw a stringy cat cornered by a far larger dog, a mangy German Shepherd that shed fists of blackened hair. Quivering, with no hope of escape, the wan feline arched its back to a distressed breaking point, trying to roll into a furry ball and make itself as unthreatening as possible. The canine, eyes fixated on its prey, approached — stately, imperious, savouring the exalted power it held. Nearly eye to eye it lowered its head and tensed its neck muscles, baring jagged teeth, globs of saliva dripping down the sides of its expectant mouth. Shams was about to move away when the cat, gecko-eyes blood-red in terror, let out a piercing scream and flung a set of claws that ripped at the dog's head. The shrill pitch of the cat's howl hurt Shams' ears. Bloodied, the dog returned a timid welp and ran away in shock. The cat crooked its neck and stared at Shams, who raised his hands in anticipation of it pouncing. But, after one brief look, the cat jumped and vanished into a nest of pallets.

Shams found the work unit as the text on his phone indicated. An abandoned portakabin stood outside, looking quite empty. The metal loading doors of the unit were down. Shams reached and took a tentative tug at the handle but it would not budge. He walked around the side of the building and saw a door. He heard sharp voices from behind it, and the disturbed frequency of a radio blaring out the day's news.

'I don't know what this country is coming to. Some guy shoots some Taliban terrorist and he gets life. Some other guy is a dirty paedo and he'll probably be out in a few years.'

'Yea, it's sick, but to be fair that guy was in custody. In cuffs, they said. On his knees.'

'I don't give a fuckin' shit, you don't think that raghead wouldn't have done the same to our lad. We'll probably get all his relatives coming to Britain claiming benefits and houses, we're so pathetic. What's happened to our country?'

As he earwigged, Shams tensed and steeled himself. He knocked twice like it was the beginning of a bad joke. A wiry white guy opened the door. Shams caught sight of a tattoo of St George's flag within a shield spread over the man's skinny upper arm. Shams thought the face somehow familiar. The man looked Shams up and down, not impressed, his red-veined countenance showing disgust.

'What the fuck do you want?'

'I'm looking for Charlie.'

'What the fuck for?' The man was spitting out his questions, just as he inhaled through his nose and also spat out a green globule of phlegm, that flew and splattered close by Shams' right boot.

Shams took a slight step back away from the gooey detritus before him. 'Just some business. He knows.'

The man took another good look at Sham through his spider's web of a face and slammed the door. Although muffled, Shams could hear him give out a shout. 'Charlie! Some little fat paki at the door. Say's he's got some business with you.'

Whenever the 'P' word was used, Shams felt fear, anger and helplessness, a potent cocktail that made him want to lash out. Such a rancid mix of casual racism and violence. The perpetrator hurling it onto innocents, absolving themselves of all responsibility. The onus was suddenly on the receiving person to be a victim and ignore. Or agitate, possibly to the point of violent conflagration, by making sure his honour, and any others the opponent might meet, is upheld. Maybe they wanted an overreaction and ignoring it was indeed the best action. Anyway, every time it happened, a decision had to be made. Be a victim or aggressor, there was no middle way.

The door reopened and a belly came into view that moved as one solid mass, like a ripened jelly. The lump's adjoining host, presumably the man known as Charlie, came out, looked around and ushered Shams into the portakabin.

Within the cabin, Shams saw signs strewn everywhere. 'WE WILL NEVER SURRENDER OUR LAND, OUR ENGLAND' and 'STOP FOREIGN OCCUPATION. NO MORE MOSQUES' and 'NO TO FASCISTS AND PAEDO RAPISTS IN ENGLAND. SAY NO TO MUSLIMS'.

Shams couldn't believe that Mujahid had done a deal with this guy. Barely standing near to this obese, sweaty-faced man made Shams' skin crawl. This was the type that would insult him and his parents when going out, like it was routine. Some filthily cast comment about their skin colour, or going home to their own country. Shams had promised himself that he would never take such humiliation.

He recalled his witty mother feigning incomprehension, pretending not to understand English. He remembered his father acting as if he had not seen or heard a verbal assault, or tirades of insulting invective. They dared not raise their head. Deaf, dumb, blind; rather than their humanity, they embraced disability.

Shams didn't want to please these guys with his emotion. 'Nice guys you work with.'

Charlie replied, 'Who, little Billy? He's harmless. Fuckin' idiot. I'm pretty sure that the nurse used forceps on his head when he was born and pulled too bloody hard. So, have you got the fuckin' cash or wot?'

'I know you. Why did I need to come all the way out here?'

'That estate is heaving, if you know what I mean. Nobody gives a shit what happens out here. Why didn't that black guy come? Too busy banging his head on carpet?'

Shams' eyes narrowed 'You've got a thing about Muslims, then? What's with all these signs?' Shams indicated the placards with a jut of his chin. Shams had seen these placards just the other day on the news. An Islamic group had rented out an amusement park in Windsor near Slough, for a Muslim kids fun day. Britain First had taken umbrage and decided that their Battle of Tours, their titanic Battle of Lepanto, the coming of the apocalypse, was to take place at Legoland.

Ishaq and Marwane had considered making their own signs for a counter-picket. *Legoland for Legolanders only. We will never surrender our Lego. Take the Mecca out of Meccano.* In the end, the day had to be cancelled due to Neo-Nazi threats. Shams could not understand how the other two could take it so lightly. He had decided if he had seen one kid crying, because of some rancid picket, he would go nuts.

The man's face took on a sheepish air but then he caught himself and replaced it with defiance. 'Just freedom of speech. Just expressing a viewpoint. They're for the march against the mosque expansion. Anyway, I'm not here to chew over this politics shit...so, you just gonna stand there gawpin'? You got something for me or you fuckin' wastin' my time?'

Shams felt this man's eyes laughing at him, as if he was a nobody, an annoyance, a fly to be swatted, or gum on his shoe. Yet, who was he to think this way? An out of shape, ageing nobody, with a crap job and no prospects, surrounded by toadies who would probably turn on him given the right incentive. How dare he think he was superior? He should say or do something? Defend his own...but, if he screwed this up, Mujahid would be furious. Shams put his fingers down into his chest and lifted the envelope from his internal pocket. Eyeing the leery man, he passed it over warily.

'You should count it.'

'Don't worry mate, I will.' He gave his sausage-shaped fingers a lick and flicked the notes, bludgeoning his way through. 'Ok, that's fine.'

'We done, then?'

'Of course we're done, you muppet. What the fuck do you want, a chat and cup of tea? You fuck off now and tell your mate it's all sorted.'

Shams looked at the thick pieces of plywood attached to the signs. The man saw Shams' face turn. After a pause, the man smiled and said, 'Just messin' with ya kid, no point getting your knickers in a twist. Tell your boy it's done. I'll call you when it's all ready. We cool?'

His teeth clamped shut, Shams affected a reply. 'Ok, fine. See you next time.'

Shams walked back to the station. His body lighter but mind heavier. This was England. There was no distance, no space in this tarmacked landscape. They had no choice but to interact. But it was like two sticks being rubbed together, waiting, just anticipating some strands of scrapped kindling to catch a cruel blaze. Shams was unsure how this had all gone but the payment was made. He had done his bit and could forget.

12.

Ishaq tripped head first into the flat, mounting an unforeseen jumble of shoes in the hallway. Kicking his trainers off he managed to jump three steps before he heard his mother calling from the living room. 'Ishaq, come here, son,' she said, in polite Urdu, 'we have guests, give salaam.'

Ishaq looked upwards at the landing. The summit was within reach, but he thought of his mother losing face in front of guests. Pivoting one hundred and eighty degrees on a big toe, he took thudding steps down and rambled through the beaded curtain into the living room.

Scanning the scene from left and then right, he saw his mother in one chair, wearing a pristine salwar kameez with a golden-lined dupatta, worn with an ostentatious piety. His father, in another, was holding a saucer precariously between the thumb and finger of one hand, and stabilising a cup on top with the other. On the table there was a pile of crisp and flaky samosas and a few juicy seekh kebabs. A teapot sat there smouldering, giving off smoke signals. Mother's best china. He'd never been allowed to even touch it. On the three-seater he saw a smartly dressed Pakistani couple, about the same age as his father. Sandwiched between them was a young girl of roughly Ishaq's age. He knew what this was: an ambush.

His father introduced the family. 'Son, these are very old friends of ours, the Shaikhs. Uncle Amir and Auntie Ruby. You know, when we first came here in the sixties, they stayed with us in our small, poky flat. Two couples, and lots of friends coming and going. It was difficult in those days.'

Ishaq returned his father's genteel smile and tried to break the air of formality. 'Well the poky flat hasn't changed, has it, Dad?'

Ishaq's smile was battered down by his father's admonitory look. Ishaq took the visual chastisement and gave salaam to the guests. He shook the elder man's hand and slightly bowed his head, so that both the man and woman could touch it. He gave a cursory nod to the girl.

The man asked Ishaq to take a seat. All the settee spaces were taken. Ishaq saw that the only dining chair in the house had been brought to the living room. It was a rickety wooden affair with no padding and a painfully rigid back panel. More of a medieval instrument of torture or a savage cure for scoliosis than a functioning piece of furniture. It was only ever used by Ishaq's mum to retrieve spices from high cupboards.

Ishaq took the seat, ready for inquisition. He was placed facing the three seats but he made sure that he was near the table. At least he could satisfy himself on those always-delicious appetisers, rather than on the prospect of other-worldly desires.

His father pointed to the other man with an open palm and said, 'Amir bhai was on the buses like me, but then they moved to Dubai. Alhamdulillah, they have become very successful with import-export.'

Everyone was smiling at this point and Ishaq heard himself say, 'Mashallah, that's nice to hear.' He had heard of a lot of Asians with import-export businesses and was never sure what that actually entailed. He managed to control his urge to ask what they actually imported and exported. He knew that it wasn't his role to start any conversation of interest.

This Uncle Amir was a very smiley chap, with a happy girth. He wore his brown flannel suit well, along with a white shirt, paisley tie, and a golden tiepin. His chipmunk cheeks inflated and deflated as he gnawed at some samosas, until a paper napkin was forcibly shoved under his eyes. Catching his beloved's hand, then her stare, he put his plate down, giving a quick lick to his oily fingertips before a grin broke out. Taking the serviette to wipe his hands, he said, 'Ishaq, you've grown up quickly. Last time we were here you were at my knees. Do you remember us?'

'No, Uncle, I'm sorry, I don't.' Ishaq replied politely, while noticing Auntie Ruby wipe a finger across a plate and then inspect it, presumably for dust.

'Your father tells me that you are a very good student, mashallah. What do you study?'

'Mostly history, with a bit of political science.'

Before the husband had time to respond, Auntie Ruby leaned forward and said, 'Oh no. Not proper science or computing...What do you actually study? And what kind of job will you get?'

Ishaq had been through this with elders many times. He found it tiresome and it narked him. Somehow he was a slacker for studying something he was actually interested in, rather than getting a degree that licensed him to print money. His parents had no qualms about his studies. They were just relieved that he had made it. However, whenever they heard a comment like this he could see their concern and doubt.

'Well, everything after this point is the future. Everything before this point in time is the past. The past is history. That is what we study. Pretty simple.'

The room went silent. He forced a staccato laugh, as appeasement. 'As for work, well I might study on. Plus, most major companies, including accountants, have training programmes for people from any degree.'

Auntie Ruby looked pleased, tapping her husband on a knee. 'Oh, so you might become an accountant.'

Ishaq detected a statement rather than a question. 'No, I think I'd find that too boring. I might do something in the social sector. I'm not sure yet.'

Ishaq's father abandoned his tea, the glass table top giving sharp reverberations from the strike of bone china. 'He will probably study on. He is not sure yet. He is young but very responsible. He will do what is best.'

Ishaq wasn't sure whether this was fatherly support or parental pressure.

Auntie Ruby talked with certainty, like she had it all under control. 'In Dubai you will have much more than you have now. A house and car. A good area and nice neighbours. Your mother says you are religious. That's good. You have big Islamic banks in Dubai, you can get a good mortgage and make a good life.'

Ishaq watched as she swapped looks with his mother. Auntie Ruby had a dyed boy-cut, and was wearing a black pantsuit with a ruffled shirt that was white with black polka dots all over. She guided a hand through her hair and then pulled her suit tighter over her breast. He thought these people would really prefer someone like Zulfi.

'That's nice.'

Auntie Ruby did not look assured, eyes briefly raised upward, making calculations at quantum speed. 'Our daughter Firdaus is studying Pharmacology in Dubai. There are many good jobs in this sector. She gets top grades and it will be easy to get a job afterwards – until she has children, of course.'

Firdaus gave an awkward grin as everyone chimed in with their requisite 'mashallahs'. Ishaq noticed her cheeks turn red; he wanted to say something friendly but her mother kept on.

'It's important to make enough money to support a family, and you have to make sacrifices in life. Ishaq, we told your mum and dad to come with us to the UAE, but your dad insisted on staying here for you to get an English education. I think they suffered enough, in this area and place, to do this.' Auntie Ruby looked around at the unassuming room, taking in the anaemic furniture.

Ishaq looked at his parents. Quiet. No reaction. Looking smaller in their own home.

'Firdaus has many families and successful matches interested in her and us, but your parents were very close and helped us a lot. Her father...' Auntie Ruby looked at Amir Bhai, who was now licking his fingers again despite not eating anything, '... decided we should come and see you first.'

What an immense favour they were doing. Such an endowment out of their colossal hearts. Firdaus was really pretty. Maybe she was smart and they could get on. Poets would have described her as almond-eyed, and she had pleasant curves at the hip and breast that showed through her kameez. Ishaq averted his gaze as he realised he was sizing her up her like a camel for sale. He repressed the urge to make a joke about checking her teeth. Hang on, maybe she was looking at him in the same way. Aware of his slouching he sat up straighter, and made a quick dig at his straggled hair.

He could settle down with this girl. Have lots of babies to keep everyone happy, while they both worked away earning money for new mouths, and as a pension-policy for ageing parents. He did quite like the idea of an arranged union. It was a spin of the coin, either way. At least here they could discuss their values and aspirations in a sober way.

Maybe he could move like this woman said. Live in a country where a clement eastern sun would annul his visibility. They could live in some suburb, where he could wash his saloon car on weekends. He could invite his polo-shirted, beige chino-wearing friends round for a barbecue, and they could discuss their amazing prospects for promotion. He could forget that the estate ever existed. It would all cloud into a hard-times origins mythology for his suburban children, who would smoke pot or dye their hair in their oh-so rebellious phase.

He looked at Firdaus, as if a thought bubble would appear above her head and reveal what she was thinking. Did she have doubts? What hopes had she outside of ending up with some random ragamuffin from South London? Ishaq looked at the mother. He could not criticise anyone. The culture of British Muslims had changed: you were told to look primarily for character and piety in a partner. This exchange of security and obligation was an old-style transactional relationship. A trade of blood, based on an old bond or promise. Firdaus could be the most amazing person in the world but he couldn't allow himself to be corralled into something suffocating. The values of security and social advancement seemed illusory. He didn't believe in any such thing. Far too often he had seen life overtake such petty dreams. Economic success was an accident of birth as much as the result of any hard work. As for social mobility, it didn't matter to him, all he could see was doing good and doing bad. There was nothing else.

But maybe this family had it right. Maybe they just lacked subtlety. Maybe this was the outside world in totality. Everything was about swapping value. The drop of a name, the casual mention of a wage packet, showing-off your car, or posting to social media a ton of pictures that highlighted your amazing life. You did not get ahead by being a better man, instead you flourished by telling everyone how great you were and hoping they didn't find out anything to the contrary.

Five pairs of eyes settled on Ishaq, waiting for a word. He reached over to the table and poured himself a cup of tea with tender ceremony. He lifted it to his nose and savoured the aroma of the infusion. Putting his cup down, he pursed his lips and looked at the eager crowd.

'In one of our history lessons we had a parable, a story that was given by a man who became Muslim amongst other things. He split oppressed people into House Negroes and Field Negroes. A slave owner owned both. House Negroes had the better food, a roof over their heads and served their master well. They got sad when their master was sad and happy when their master was happy. They didn't want anything to happen to their master as they were scared of what would replace him, and then what would happen to them.

'Field Negroes, on the other hand, had little food, and rags for clothes. They lived and toiled under the elements, suffering beatings from their master. They hoped he would die, as anything was better than how they were living now. But they knew the truth of their situation, and of their evil master, and once they had that truth they could not live without it. They couldn't swallow it and pretend it did not exist.

'Now I don't know what's better, and what I'll end up as, but at the moment I'm more like the Field Negro, and I have no intention of becoming someone's House Negro. I respect your family's achievements, but my parents worked and provided for us and that's enough for me. I don't really care about being rich, or living in a suburb and sending my kids to an expensive university so they can repeat the same cycle of constantly repaying debt all over again. I may be a young idiot who doesn't know anything but I'd rather take my chances out in the sun and rain and keep feeling them beating down on me. Your daughter looks wonderful and I hope that you find a suitable match.'

Ishaq stood up and walked out.

The toilet seat down, he sat, not doing the act but definitely feeling it. Gone way too far. He felt his face tingle as he imagined his parent's awkwardness as they explained their ungrateful son. Their shame at dishonouring a guest.

He adjusted his cheeks as they deadened on the hard surface, and then listened to the vibrations of pipes as a tap was turned on next door. No real escape, even here. The bathroom didn't have any outside facing windows. Early on they couldn't afford a shower, so Ishaq would take a bucket bath, ignoring the bangs and shouts from his sister. On those rare occasions when another member of the household was not screaming for the bath, he would lay there pontificating, allowing the warm suds to envelope him. Each flat was a mirror image of the next, so the bath and toilet rooms that were on the left side of their flat were adjoined by the bath and toilet rooms on the one next door. In a daze from the humidity he would sometimes hear the conversations of the couple next door. Their voices palpitating through rusting tubes.

He had lived next to them for his whole twenty years, but did not know their names. The husband was in his seventies. A full head of white hair, that crowned and flowed backwards like a lion's mane. Outside of the flat he wore hobnailed boots, woollen trousers that had seen numerous attempts at patching, a gingham shirt and scraggly tie, topped off with a black, gentleman's blazer. To Ishaq it looked like his clothing had come out of a time capsule, just like the man himself, who shared a slightly musty impression with his attire. Led by thick, black-rimmed glasses, he used to march everywhere with a battered leather bag and a fierce frown. It took time to dress like, care that seemed at odds with their frayed state.

The Study Circle

All the kids used to be terrified of him. Energetic whispers in each other's ear about him killing people in the war. Not a clue which war, just THE war. Some said he was an old gangster who mixed it with the Krays, back before YouTube and when telly was in black and white; that he used to dish out 'Chelsea smiles' using tools in his bag. The kids used to be in rapture disseminating the method. The key to such a grin was the making of small incisions on the corners of the victim's mouth. You would then beat the wretch pitilessly in the stomach, until they couldn;t stop their face muscles contracting and make obscene ripping tears through their cheeks up to their ears. Ishaq remembered a posse of seven and eight year olds mimicking the action with a plastic knife, taking turns to be perpetrator and then victim. One girl brought her mum's rouge lipstick down and, as they got a victim to laugh and convulse, they would draw long red lines showing the lengthening cut.

His wife was delightfully mad. Ishaq would spy her out of a kitchen window, peeping through gaps. She would sometimes pose and pirouette to imaginary tunes on the balcony and, bashful, curtsey to an invisible admirer. Her grey arrow-straight hair reached her knees and she wore flowing garments, dark dresses and wintry cardigans. The other kids thought she was a witch. Once, Ishaq asked his mother whether it was true and received a rare show of real anger. Mum shouted at Ishaq, saying that they were an old couple trying to get on and that he should know better than to indulge in gossip. As she did with other neighbours, Mum was always dropping-off food or sweets to them whenever she made too big a batch, which was often. Ten-year-old Ishaq would keep his head dipped outside the door, lingering until he saw his mum come out safe, ready to flip his head back in like a Pez dispenser if the man came out, instead.

One time, while bathing, Ishaq could hear clear words. He could hear him encouraging his wife to take a wash. She would moan, kicking up soft protestations while he tried coaxing her into washing her hair. Gently admonitions, then encouragement, then pleading. The hollow tap of bucket or tub to wash his wife. He heard them gently chat as he brushed. The sorrow in his speech as he struggled to get her to eat enough, gently chiding her, his voice near breaking. Ishaq felt shame that day. It was the first time he thought of white English people as truly human like himself and his family. All he had ever encountered was racist, violent people who wanted to stamp his kind out. Who acted brutally to people like himself and to each other. It was novel that they were also capable of being gentle and loving, like his own.

Every argument on the estate seemed like the proverbial bald guys fighting over a comb, but with consequences so serious that it felt like a cosmic joke. Stabbings over disputes concerning pennies, massive family eruptions where the mother tries to nick the daughter's man, fistfights over the wrong look and a bump of shoulders. It was a competition to reach a new depth. Ishaq thought this new world must be as incomprehensible to the old man as it was to him. The old certainties were long gone and this new England was so terrifying that you can only stare it down with ferocity.

One morning, Ishaq awoke to find ambulances and police below. The medics went to the man's flat. The old woman had departed in her sleep. Disconsolate, his defiance cracked and finally crumbling away, the old man was led away by one of the medics. He was never seen again. A month later, a Ghanaian family moved in.

Ishaq heard the front door shut downstairs. He listened out for movement. After a few minutes cloistered away, with the only accompaniment being the low-pitched buzz of his throbbing ears, he opened the bathroom door and gingerly occupied the landing. Peering over the bannister all of the shoes were gone, including those of his parents, and their coats. They must have escorted the guests back to their car and were hopefully walking off any anger.

Ishaq navigated his way down the stairs on the tips of his toes, taking two steps in his stride to avoid the squeak. He opened the front door and a slash of razored light came carving into the hallway. No one was on the balcony, so he walked out and leant on the metal balustrade. Filled with expanses of clotted rust and flaking paint, he poked at it with his normal expectation of seeing it give way. It didn't. Looking around, and down towards the car park, he was satisfied that he was in the clear. He sealed his eyes. He felt the air cool them, and took in a heady breath.

Bang. Ishaq heard a boom, his shoulders jumped and the balls of his feet nearly left the floor. His ears steered him to the sound of the gunshot. Two small school-age figures were jockeying on old mopeds, one backfiring sooty pestilence into the air, their steeds' whinnying enlarged by the tinny sound of their exhausts. He could tell that the boys had drilled holes in them to mimic the bigger sound of proper, grown-up bikes.

'Hahaha. Gunshot.'

Ishaq looked to his left and saw laughter emanate from a delighted Mujahid.

'Assalmu alaikum. How long have you been there?'

'Long enough. You thought you were in some gang warfare, right? Dadadada, hahaha.' Mujahid shook both hands to simulate a machine gun, before returning to a rapid laugh. 'You'd be useless in Jihad. That's man's work.'

Ishaq bounced forward and grimaced as Mujahid slapped his back. 'Well, I suppose I won't be declaring Holy War on Clapham Common anytime soon.'

'Haha, I like that about you, always funny. Maybe too funny though, heh?' Mujahid paused. Ishaq was still looking at the bikes so Mujahid pushed his shoulder so that he pivoted towards him. 'Hey, I saw that shawty come in with her whole clan. Proper dressed-up. Is that some arranged marriage ting?'

Ishaq saw Mujahid smiling in his overly familiar and sardonic way. He thought that Mujahid liked to feel that he was all-knowing and in control but that his slightly taunting manner was just a shield. Ishaq was never quite sure what his game was, and he didn't want to know. It was that unwritten rule. You mind your own business. Ishaq heard that he somehow had other flats too. Mujahid would disappear for days, and then turn up smoking fetid weed on the balcony, leaving a pathway of raised voices from behind his door. He seemed to take an inordinate joy in the glowering looks of Ishaq's parents, and those of the neighbours as they passed by, and showed proud defiance to people who weren't all that interested in defying him, or anyone. Ishaq made sure that he never gave him that satisfaction. They had only had a couple of minor altercations about the smoking, before and after he went to jail and conversion. And here he was again, with an oversized spliff, smoking the evening away.

'Something like that.'

Mujahid managed to break out an even bigger grin. 'She looked fine. That family looked like they have a few quid too.'

'I don't know, Mujahid. I didn't force them to a cashpoint to check their bank balance.' Ishaq looked away, hoping that his withdrawn demeanour would end this. However, it only spurred further interest.

'Man, you look upset by it. You against this arranged marriage stuff? It's the Islamic way, too.'

When Ishaq was younger he knew Mujahid to be a small-time dealer. Mujahid converted to Islam at a time when many well-meaning brothers instantly suggested the name Bilal, for Afro-Carribean converts. Ishaq couldn't decide whether it was funny or distasteful when brothers, mainly Arab, always mentioned the name Bilal to those converts. Bilal's story, like many of the other companions of the Prophet, was inspiring, but Ishaq always thought that shouldn't mean you had to foist the name on any random guy who converted to Islam. Bilal ibn Rabah was an early convert and a famous follower of the Prophet Muhammad. A slave of Abyssinian descent, he had been emancipated due to the prophet's decrees regarding the excellence of manumission. Bilal had a strong and steady voice and became the first Muezzin or caller to prayer. Of Jamaican parentage and a decade older than Ishaq, this man had taken the name Mujahid instead, someone who struggles for Allah and Islam. A strong name, a soldier's name. Ishaq wasn't so enthused about this soldier's name but, as Mujahid said, 'I chose my name myself. Didn't let anyone choose it for me.' Ishaq agreed; everyone has a right to their own naming.

'Hey, Issy. You had posh company today. All those colours.' A third voice forced its way between them. Mujahid and Ishaq looked over the balcony to the ground and saw a white woman with tissued skin and permed, fox-red hair. Her hands trembled as she held a couple of coffees in a cardboard holder.

Mujahid shouted, 'Pauline, Ishaq is having an arranged marriage.'

'Oh, she was pretty, but oh Issy, you're not like that, are ya, luv? You could find a nice girl round here, not some random bint.' Pauline shielded her eyes from the sun as she looked up at the two dim figures.

Ishaq looked at this woman, who nowadays could barely shuffle along, just active enough for her daily Venti Decaf Vanilla Latte run, an ersatz facsimile of the ferocious woman his childhood knew. A failed madam, she turned tricks until she fell in love with one of her clients, Dr Habib. Ishaq went to school with her daughter and she told him that the doctor freely gave her mum prescriptions for all sorts. He was always visting for a 'check-up'. Even as a kid Ishaq connected the dots, but there was a genuine fondness. Even now after he passed away, Pauline mentioned his name often, and wistfully. Ishaq remembered how he and the other kids used to wait for Dr Habib's visits and then stand outside, tongues playing lasciviously, making lustful noises and using their hands all over their bodies, moaning, 'Oh Dr Habiiibbbb.' How she would rush out swinging a broom, heedless of what contact was made.

'It's not like what he's saying. Anyway how are you?' shouted Ishaq.

'Good, hanging in there. The medication makes me slow. Lucy is up in Enfield, she just had her second. She asks about you every time I go up. You should give us a knock when she's down.' Pauline paused for Ishaq to answer, '…anyway, give my regards to your mum.' They watched as Pauline limped off, scraping the stone paving in her fluffy bunny slippers.

'You think it's right, shouting people's business?' Ishaq turned so that they were nearly toe to toe. Mujahid looked like he had gone rat-catching but had caught something far juicier instead. 'And talking about business, what are you doing with Shams?'

'He told you? No matter. He's doing work for me. I take care of him. He's more my younger, more my type of people, than you are. You know that the Prophet, peace be upon him, said that only a minority will be on the right path. Shams is like me, struggling to find the right path. You don't see that. You look at him but don't see him.'

Ishaq listened-out for any others around.. Once something was outside, it was earwig central. Any drama providing easy entertainment. Loves, fights, domestics, deals, hustling, all human life could be assayed on the balcony. Naked souls, people who were stripped and truly revealed, without the common places to hide.

He could see why Shams had bonded with this guy. People love glorying in the ascension of struggle and significance of victimhood. Especially if that's all they've got. You still need to take a step back and look at what is right and what is wrong. Sometimes there is no meaning, no abstruse message. Life is just graft and shovelling shit, and you cope as best you can. Ishaq saw Mujahid bring his spliff to his lips. It looked like a burning tumour eating away at his face.

'Shams is a good kid. He's easily influenced. Don't let him get into trouble, yea?'

Mujahid put out his fat joint and stuffed it into an inside pocket of his army surplus jacket. He craned over at an angle into Ishaq's face. Threads of saffron spread through to the stalks of his eyes. 'Awww, Issy is just upset at having a fine one just drop into his lap like that, is he?'

'Yea, she was a good looking girl, but it's not that.' Returning Mujahid's look, Ishaq laughed. He was actually making him feel better. 'Ok, so you want a proper explanation? I'll give it to you as long as you promise not to get offended, whatever I say. Ok?'

'Ok…' Mujahid had seen this kid running about for the best part of fifteen years, and other than a short period of salaams, the most they'd exchanged was 'hello', 'alright', 'night', 'laters' and, as the kid had grown, 'I wish you'd stop smoking weed around the kids on the estate' and 'Fuck off man, don't you dares tell me what to do'.

Ishaq outlined the Field Negro and House Negro conversation. He explained it, being careful around the N-word, gauging Mujahid's response, hoping that the much bigger man didn't punch him in the face. After Ishaq finished, Mujahid retrieved his joint, lit it using a match that he struck on the sandpaper surface of the railing. He took in a massive draw.

'So you pakis are nicking our words now?' Mujahid stressed the word 'paki' as if he were trying on a new coat, feeling how it draped over his shoulders and fell in a clean line around his body. 'Only joking, we brothers ain't we?'

Ishaq normally felt the violence of the p-word but coming from Mujahid he wasn't bothered a bit. 'Well, the guy who came up with that allegory was a mainstream Muslim in the end.'

'I know who it was, you fool. I'm not a fucking moron, whatever everybody in this block thinks. I read...like you... "Allegory"...' Mujahid lips curled, as if tasting something sour. 'Tell me, what you up to nowadays?'

Ishaq could see him mulling it all over. Like an autodidact, Mujahid could come up with some sense, use wise words. Arguments that were completely factual, but then he would go on to make random connections with no thorough reason or arrangement. Overeaching. People like him lived life on wits not structure, an inherent instability that shredded at their nerves, making them fragile and volatile. Ishaq took his parent's example that, though lots of people could say perceptive things, the ultimate calculus of their soul was how they lived, and their works; their ability to endure and take responsibility, their capacity to build a dignified life however small, and their self-control.

'Uni.'

'A proper one or one of those ones full of immigrants.'

' It's one of the decent ones, not a visa factory.'

He could see Mujhaid checking him out then viewing the estate. He noticed a slight sheen of sweat on his forehead that glinted in the light. He wondered what he saw. His domain? A place where he was immune from the judgement of outsiders, or was it another prison. When Mujahid starting speaking again, it was different, it sounded humble.

'You think you know it all but you haven't a clue. A boy with boy thoughts. You know, I see you going round doing your business as if you're floating above the estate. You, and your mates, like that Arab one. Something about you guys...it's like you've checked into a hotel and anytime soon you'll be checking out.'

Ishaq kissed his teeth. 'Mujahid, that's bollocks. I know what I'm about.'

Mujahid lightly wiped his forehead, his tongue briefly coming out to wet his lips. 'I don't mean that in a a bad way. I know you guys think I'm some kind of waster but let me tell you, I've lived a life, man. You've lived one small one. And I'm telling you that whatever I did, or wherever I went, I never really left this place. Seen too much, did too much. Too much of a rebel soul, don't no man or woman telling me what to do or when to do it. Whether it's sense or not, I was never no monkey and anyway there's no drumbeat big enough to make me dance like one.

'You guys ain't leaving either. Maybe, if you were like those Sri Lankans on the corner who only let their kids go out to school and come home, you could, but you lot have been running around since you were kids. Poking your eyes and noses in places where you shouldn't have. Difference is, you are smart and got some options. You got given good family. Just like that girl. Some rich family come and offer you their hot daughter, and you'll be all set up. Out of here. And you turned it down. You must be crook'd in the head, bruv.'

Ishaq examined Mujahid's scarlet eyes and realised that it wasn't the ganja but that Mujahid had been crying. He felt a twitch of pity but put it away, he knew how Mujahid would take it. As condescension, being patronised. Mujahid was still the type of person who saw empathy as a weakness or a subterfuge.

The walls of towers bore witness around them, mute and firm. In the washed-up light it was only when you got up close you realised how stained and pitted they were. Mujahid's large frame relaxed. Ishaq saw the man. Mujahid surveyed out over the balcony, looking like he would test the estate with a shout. To see if it would echo his words around the rock and gravel. But words poured out as fine grain.

'But I know what you feelin'. You don't want to be pushed. Whenever I got pushed, I pushed back and harder. With my parents, then school, then any job. I wasn't takin' shit from nobody. I'm my own man. I couldn't see the good if there was any. Now I've got three baby mamas in three different places. I do a bunch of shitty jobs whenever I can get them, and hustle on the side so that I can give them some cash and hope they hate me a bit less. I do the best for my kids and hope they grow up better than me. And, trust me, bruv, I will be there for them. So what I'm saying is, be thankful for what you can and could do. And whatever brave shit every man come up with…actually if I could go back and tell my young self anything, it's that over a life, face up, sometimes it's better to be a House Nigger than a Field Nigger, any day.'

Ishaq stood there static, feet nailed, knees locked. Three doors down, he heard a shout coming from Mujahid's flat. Ishaq realised that for all the years Mujahid had been around here, he had no idea what was behind that blue door.

A female voice screamed 'Michael! Get back in here right now and sort your dumb kid out before you go again.'

13.

A male voice screamed in the night, caroming round the portakabin. A solitary din, that even the odd flight arcing above could not penetrate. The windows fogged up with perspiration, blocking vision, reminding Shams of his isolation.

Charlie looked him up and down once. Then again. 'I ain't fuckin' stupid, I heard you got picked-up the other night. You've got some heat on ya, haven't ya?'

Hands up, palms presented forward, Shams said, 'Where did you hear that?'

'I've still got friends round your ways. You got stopped in the middle of the High Street, no? Your faces lit up like you were on the X-Factor. Just a day before you came to me. Funny that.'

'No, that was nothing. Just the Five-O messing about as usual.'

'So why were you held overnight?' Charlie placed a clubbed hand towards Shams on the table before them.

'I wasn't held overnight, just a few hours. They made a mistake.'

Charlie grunted, rubbing his bald pate. 'Well, me and you are done. Ain't nothing happening between us now.'

'What does that mean?'

'It means, bonehead, that the deal is off. You can sling your hook, son.'

Shams' forehead rumpled, looking like it was collapsing in on itself. 'Look mate…I can't go back and tell him it's off. You know him, he'll go off on one.'

'Don't "mate" me. I can handle some piece of estate trash.' Charlie turned around, picking up a green bomber jacket with an angry tug. The nylon jacket was embellished with a patch exhibiting insignia from the RAF during the Second World War, and an army one from the Great War.

Shams pitted both hands deep into pockets and looked around for help, before he lay eyes on the placards for the protest. 'Wait. The police. I'll tell them that you guys are planning on creating trouble at the march. I can bring a lot of eyes down here. The pigs, they'll be all over.'

Charlie grabbed him by the collar and pushed him against the wall, his body slamming with a hollow thump, the feeble partition feeling like it would give way. Shams could feel the bigger man's sweaty weight slump against him. His puttied face, all folded jowls, rubbed cheek to cheek. Charlie's spewing breath stank of cheap alcohol. 'What did you say, you dumb paki? Did you just threaten me?' Charlie reached for a crowbar on shelving nearby. Shams felt crisp metal as Charlie traced a slow line on a cheek. 'Is that what you were in for? Snitching to the police about us. Tell me. Tell me.'

Shams's tried to turn his nose away from stale breath but felt steel pinch his skin as Charlie applied more pressure. He winced as one of Charlie's knuckles caught the corner of his mouth, the man's chalky-white skin highlighting every scrap of dirt collected during the day. 'No…no…I said nothing. They didn't ask anything about you or Mujahid. Keep my ear to the ground they said. But I don't have to say nuthin' if you just let this one deal through. You won't see me again after this, I promise.'

Charlie let go. As if placated by Shams' quivering. He pinched the bridge of his nose while snorting through it, and closed his eyes in thought.

Although released, Shams kept his back pressed to the wall, heaving air. He tried looking for the door but this blimp was in the way. 'Look, we're all in this together, right? Coppers don't care nothing for people like us. As you said, you're protesting peacefully. Nothing to hide, nothing to fear, right?'

'Ok, ok, but the price has gone up. Tell that nigger friend of yours that I want another five-hundred quid for you trying to blackmail me, or everything's off.'

'I…I…can't do that. He'll ask why. He doesn't know about the police.'

Charlie shook his head. 'You're a right fuckin' case aren't you? Bet your parents wished they'd aborted you when they had a chance…well that's your fuckin' problem, ain't it? That's the deal, take it or shove it.'

Shams looked at the hand with the crowbar and saw it still tightly clenched. He then looked past Charlie's form to the door. 'Ok…ok. I'll tell him.'

Shams crept to Mujahid's, clinging to the sides, not wanting to be caught in the light. Feet on their balls, toes sometimes tapping. He paced up and down, turning and looking at the red door.

The door opened. Shams almost jumped. Mujahid sauntered out, miswak in his mouth. 'Assalmu alaikum, you gonna wear your shoes out bruv. What you doing here this late?'

'Nothing, just came to tell you about the deal.'

'Cool, cool.' Mujahid looked at Shams' empty hands and his hangdog face. 'Why haven't you got the package on you?'

'That's what I need to talk about.'

Mujahid stopped brushing, took the stick out, and shot a stern look that made Shams take a step back. 'You'd better come on in then, hadn't ya.'

Shams saw the pitch black that lay beyond the open door. Darkness poured into that one place. He shivered, but took a step in, guided by his patron's gaze. Once inside, Mujahid said, 'Ok, spit it out, what happened?'

'That Charlie guy wants another five-hundred quid,' said Shams, his words tumbling over each other.

Raising his voice Mujahid said, 'What's he want another five-hundred quid for?'

'Why didn't you tell me he was racist? A proper skinhead type.'

'Don't change the subject. Does it matter?'

'Well yea, he hates us lot. Obviously he was going to pull something like this.'

Shams forced his best poker face, but he wasn't gambler and was sure it was cracking under attention. Mujahid, though, didn't show any disbelief, he just nodded, rubbing under his eyes. The man looked a bit tired, a hint of dark rings appearing.

'I know him from way back. He used to live round here a while ago. He used to breed Rottweilers for a living.'

Mujahid remembered Charlie's ground floor flat with its neglected garden. All discarded rakes, spades and beer cans, amongst high, tattered grass. He bred guard dogs. A great side business that was always in demand and, as illegal as it was, somehow Charlie was never hassled by the police. The wooden fencing at the back was loose enough that you could get a good view of his ramshackle cages. Mujahid would see this massive butterball, this beer bellied brute with his union jack tattoo, constantly poking at his dogs. He would swear at them and, starting off gently, use a wooden strip. Intensifying the pressure until he elicited an angered response from behind that cheesegrater mesh. The dogs would claw at the stick, try and reach Charlie with their jaws. Then the stabbing would abruptly stop, a uncertain moment of respite, before the cycle started again.

Once cultivated Charlie would encourage them to fight. He'd force them on top of one another. Hold one's head, pressing it forward, pushing another into a corner. The only way out was by scratching and biting. Charlie was smart. He wouldn't beat them down outright. That would make them too defeated, too docile. Instead, the constant aggro produced really fierce animals that could be guaranteed to explode in aggression when needed. They sold well.

Mujahid sat on the bottom of the stairs and left Shams standing to attention, ready for inspection.

'I know him well enough…but…it doesn't sound like you is telling me the whole truth?' Mujahid sat impassive and calm, one hand stroking his slight, evenly-carpeted beard while he took in Shams' countenance.

'Like what?'

'You know, Shams…we're brothers and, like family, we survive on trust. Don't be scared with me. Trust me, it's better you're plain with me, than me finding out you are hiding things.'

Jaded light from the walkway cast Shams' shadow onto the hallway floor. He saw it, familiar, like an old friend. But now laying in a puddle beneath him, evaporating into a line that extended towards a Mujahid who was once again chewing on his stick. Shams could see hydraulics as jaws bit, and then relaxed, as Mujahid moved the stick to brush another area.

'Ok…He said…what he said was, there was too much heat from the police.' Shams scraped one shoe on another and looked down.

'Why would he say that?'

'Well…I got stopped yesterday.'

Mujahid reached out and gave Shams a gentle slap, right on a kneecap. 'Good, good. Yea, I heard about it. On the High Street, right? See how easy that was? Don't hold back on me. You know, so what about the police? You should have told him to mind his own business. That happens all the time. I've been stopped like twenty times in the last year. No stress.'

'I told him. Nuthin' doing.'

'See Shams. You come across as too weak, and all this holding yourself back and hiding makes it even worse. People in our world, they feed on each other, like predators. The wolf eating the lamb, Shams. You need to toughen-up. Front-up. Aggression respects only aggression. I remember when people treat me badly. I store it within me like fuel, I do. People can sense it. They back off. It takes practice, I wasn't always this way. You put a front up, pretend you're tough, pretend it doesn't hurt, pretend you're not fussed, then all of a sudden it's all good.' Mujahid presented both palms outwards as if they were pages of a book.

'Thought you said, you don't wear masks?'

'That ain't a mask, bruv. That's armour.'

Shams thought about Charlie, drawing an X in his blank puddle with a toe. 'How long do you keep on pretending, though? At one point there must come a time that we're not pretending anymore. Just an animal. Like that guy. I'm not cut out for dealing with people like that. I think he more than hates us, he doesn't want us to be.'

'Well, out here it's like I learned inside. It's like it's out there in nature, it's survival of the fittest. He's not the fittest so he won't survive. He's just a useful loser needing a few quid. Anyway, don't worry…tomorrow I'll come with. We're brothers right?' said Mujahid, offering a hand.

Shams nodded and shook the hand. Mujahid's felt warm and firm. Shams stepped to the door, stopped, and looked back. 'You said tell you everything. That we're safe right?'

'Yea, of course.'

'The Five-O…they kept us back only for a few hours but honestly I have to tell you, bruv, I didn't tell Charlie…but I got questioned by a guy saying he was MI5. Security service.'

Mujahid pounced on Shams, grabbed him by his jacket and pulled him into the living room. He pushed him onto the sofa. Looming over him, his face only a couple of inches away. 'Spooks. What the hell have you been up to? What did you say?'

'I said nothing. Seriously. It wasn't me.'

'You grassing on me, Shams? I said hold nothing back.'

'That's why I'm telling you. It wasn't me. They didn't even ask about you…'

Mujahid held Shams, pushing down on the sofa. Shams put his hands around his head as if he was about to be hit.

'So why did they stop you? I want an answer or you're not getting out of here.'

Shams looked at the walls. Patches of damp, browned plaster had fallen off in places. Some spots had haphazard but annealed fillings, leaving the room looking scabrous. His mind flailed, grasping at air until he felt something solid, but not sure of its true shape. With an uncomfortable stammer, he threw it out like an offering.

'It wasn't me. It was Ishaq. Ishaq reported me.'

As soon as he had said it. As soon as those words made it sacrificial, he knew he had transgressed. There had always been an invisible boundary that he had skirted well. Until now. He felt an estranging fill him, a gap eaten in by his eyes and mouth. As soon as he had verbalised it, animated it, he also knew that it could not be true. Ishaq wouldn't do that. But it was too late. Shams' lip started to quiver.

Mujahid checked over Shams, and took in his shivering disposition as fear of him. 'You sure? Why would he do that?'

'That's what the MI5 man kinda said. To save his own back… maybe. Maybe it wasn't him but the man kinda said it was…'

'You were all stopped though?'

'But I was the only one questioned by them. The other bros went through normal police stuff.'

'That little chicken-shit. He was talkin' all nice with me just today. You asked them about this?'

'No, I kept it to myself. By Allah, I didn't tell them what happened to me.'

'Good, so what did they want?' Mujahid let go of Shams and started pacing around, taking in a surmising orbit like a bird of prey.

'Just random questions about…a lot about Ayub's circle. They just wanted me to keep an ear to the ground. Maybe it's about drugs and teefing? I don't know.' Shams uncoiled his body and watched Mujahid move. 'It felt bad though, you know? Like I had done wrong even though I hadn't.'

'That's what they want. They want you to feel wrong even if you are doing nothing, walk around with your head low and beating on yourself,' said Mujahid not breaking his movement, not looking back at Shams. It was as if he were talking to himself. 'They want you to take responsibility for everything going on among the Muslims, while they take none for nothing.'

'I was scared.'

'They're scared of you. You should enjoy their fear. People who see clear. They're such hypocrites. You know Shams…about drugs…this country once forced Indians to grow opium and then sold it to the Chinese at the end of a gun. Opium Wars. Look it up, yourself.'

Sham forced a wan smile. Not sure what he was going on about, but Mujahid seemed to be more bothered by the government than

Ishaq. A good thing. 'Like I said...I'm not sure what they wanted. They just want to stop criminals. It's all nothing.'

'Yea, but who are they to judge what a criminal is? Shams, do you think someone stealing an apple because they are hungry is evil? Do you? Yea, these pigs are far worse. They make systems. Massive companies to do their sin-eating.' Mujahid had finally started looking, more like peering, at his lone audience. Shams could not keep up with Mujahid's outpouring as he rumbled around the room, kicking-out at indistinct objects.

'Slaves, they made them into cattle and shipped millions. Taking their names, so they don't know who their parents were, or their religion, or what country they came from. They made people become rootless. A product. The Jews, they wiped them out in Europe. Like they were killing chickens it was so organised. Native Americans and Aborigines, they created laws stealing their land and destroying them. Then they turn around and say "my bad" and expect it to all fade away. Want us to forget, say it's over because they say it's over. They start shifting things, saying it is humanity's sin, not unique to them. Then, after a while, they start focusing on our faults, until we, the boy stealing that apple, is the worst thing that ever happened in history, and they say the sin is ours alone, not spread around like theirs. But here's the thing with that trick; we don't forget history...it's not over. '

Shams waited to see if Mujahid would continue again. The words reverberated around the room and he found it difficult to focus, but the emotion just felt true. It felt right. 'What do you want me to do?'

Mujahid stopped pacing. 'This changes everything. I can't come with you now. I'm gonna protect mine, my family. So you go back and sort it yea? I believe in you.'

'Akhi, I'm not sure he'll listen.'

'Shams, this is your mess now. You're lucky you told me

everything before I found out myself, otherwise you'd be in big trouble. Know what I'm sayin'?' Mujahid leaned over Shams, the iron scaffolding of his face taut, and prodded his chest with each word. 'So. You. Sort. This. Shit. Out.'

Shams started to reply but Mujahid waved him away and pointed to the door. As Shams trudged, his stooped body barely holding him up, Mujahid called after him, 'Next time I see you I want my money or the products, or there'll be big trouble. Trust.'

14.

Ishaq and his father sat in sullen silence as they watched telly. News footage showed an old London riot in full rage. Some pop star's son was in court for swinging like a crazed baboon on a Union Jack attached to the Cenotaph. Ishaq remembered a similar white boy had invaded the Houses of Parliament in protest for his right to hunt down and murder foxes. Ishaq thought that if it had been him, at best he would have undergone 'enhanced interrogation techniques'. Not really cricket that.

Next up was a feminist group called Femen. Women, naked, not a fig-leaf between them. Outside a Paris mosque, they were trying to force their way in to protest at oppressive patriarchy. Ishaq was surprised to see that their troop were still going despite it being revealed that it had all been started by some old white bloke, who only hired nubile models to demo. Youthful women jiggled away, hoping that, by jumping up and down, their undulating breasts would start tremors. Tremors that would reverberate through the Muslim world and make veiled oriental women discard their vestments. Kinda like their version of the Butterfly Effect.

Looking at all the grinning, blithely-eyed youngsters, hands in pockets, coming out of the mosque to take a look, these ladies had miscalculated their effect on the western-born. They definitely had made a gender rise, just the wrong one and not really the kind of rise they were looking for.

With pendulous breasts still dominating their 50 inch plasma, Ishaq, through the corner of his eye, peeked at Dad, saw his mouth ajar, gawping, and tried to imagine that they were watching *Countdown*.

Ishaq buckled under the weighty stirring of silence and bosom. 'Dad, did you know in pre-Islamic Arabia some women used to walk around bare breasted?'

His father looked, not impressed, 'Hmmph' and turned the television off.

'You know when you were a baby we were worried you would be a right dumb-dumb. You started crawling late and backwards. Bloody hell I said. A dumb-dumb, we'll be looking after him forever. Mum went running about for advice. Stayed up night after night praying…You turned out alright though. Smart. Too smart. Your mother has been crying.'

'I'm sorry,' said Ishaq, as his eyes involuntarily welled.

His father's eyes studied him from above Mother's cat-eye glasses, that were perched on his nose. 'What do you want, one of those head to toe covered niqabis, who have a massive list of what you can and cannot do in the Sharia? Create a mini Islamic state in your house?'

'No, but I don't want the Muslim equivalent of all those boring posh girls at uni, who are proud that they read a lot but know nothing.'

His dad shook his head and took in a long breath. 'It was wrong, Ishaq. They were guests in our house. I've told you before, even if your greatest enemy knocks on your door then you need to be hospitable. These are the old ways. Our traditions. The guest is king, and you broke that. Amir Bhai is a good man. We have so few friends from the old days in Pakistan. We must keep our ties.'

'I know. I just want to have a life that means something.'

'I want you to build a happy life. Build that first. In the end I don't care if you marry Brown, Green, Yellow. I don't care. Be Muslim, be happy. Just promise me one thing. Don't forget Pakistan, don't forget your mother's and father's roots.'

Pakistan. The old country. Like a lot of the Islamic world, they were crap at being Islamic and crap at being Western. Honesty, hard work, self-reliance, loving your brother, all of the traditional Muslim values lost. Ishaq felt that giving to Pakistan was like giving, in painful love, to a doped-up sibling.

Yet he heard his father's hunger. Pakistan was once an idea, a whisper in the wind for the Muslims of the subcontinent that were to live as a fragile minority in an independent India. A notion made by men into a destiny. A country made manifest, cleaved in violence from the carcass of a rancid Empire. Hard to believe but, for a while, it was a hope for his parents' generation. A shining light. A fresh start, an opportunity to begin anew, a tabula rasa onto which they poured their hopes and dreams. A dream that quickly soured.

Ishaq had only been once. Pakistan once again had become a concept, more of a faint sentiment. Something far off that occasionally broke the hermetic seal of their lives. It was the early hours, a phone call, piercing the dark, that had his mother crying at the death of a loved one they had not seen for years. It was not knowing how to react as he felt his parents' guilt at not being present among family. It was an inherited identity that that generation clung on to so generously, as if it had always been, even though it was scarcely as old as they. A secular state built in the name of religion. An internal contradiction that would always eat at itself. Pakistan was an idea that hardly worked, and only brought guilt and sorrow, so why couldn't their British progeny themselves set out to create a new identity. One that brought advancement, and built something new with the Turks and Bangladeshis and Arabs that were also born here. But still, Ishaq recognised his parents' need.

'I will always remember, Father. I will do as you say.'

His father made an irritated shift forward in his chair. 'Don't throw everything away. You will regret. You have a language, another culture, for free. No work. How many of these white people would love that. They are stuck in one mind, one head. All these maulvis and maulanas, I'm sure they can tell you from a book how to live, but it's never the same as having to do it. You have a big advantage over many children in this estate. Two parents, stable family. Sometimes, you have to compromise in life. Make life easy.'

He appraised his son's tracksuit bottom and football shirt.

'When I was a child I was walking along the road in Lahore, and a white couple, expensively dressed, was walking the other way. The man shoved me out of the way. He didn't even look at me as he was too busy with making his lady-friend laugh at something. Pushed without a single thought. They're probably dead now and they never knew I even existed. Pushed out of the way, on my own road, in my own country. They didn't make exceptions for us or our ways. The English. The West. And you kids…'

He looked at his son's face. A face that would have nearly fit in among his childhood friends, in their ragged salwars, playing around an abrupt pond during monsoon season. Those large, innocent, lamblike eyes, with glowing, honeyed skin. His beautiful boy.

'…you're just like them.'

Ishaq was open-mouthed, as he search for a response. 'All we do is compromise,' said Ishaq, his words dying.

'I didn't mean that. I mean you kids have turned out very British. You have all of their expectations. Of what life should be…but life never works like that. You think you automatically deserve things. But you have to work at life. And you should give people a chance…she was a good girl.'

His father went to the Mosque on Fridays but didn't mix with the community. Always complaining about layabout 'Tablighis', proselytisers who left the family for forty days to travel between various mosques, visiting local Muslims and calling them to the religion. And he hated the one-upmanship of the local Punjabi community. He knew that his father cared for none of this, only wanting to live a contented life, bringing up happy children.

'But Dad, if you compromise too far, it's a gateway to hypocrisy.'

'Ishaq, son, when you have family and responsibility, when you have others whose well-being is based on you, that's love not hypocrisy.' His father waited to see that thought settle in his son's juvenile head before he continued. 'One good thing about the English is that, even if they want to stab you in the back, they will shake your hand in front, especially if money is involved. Our people refuse even that and cause even more hatred because that is integrity. Stupid. We call it 'hypocrisy', the English call it 'pragmatism'. Maybe we should be more 'pragmatic'.' Gesturing to the television as a helmeted and bulletproof-vested correspondent broadcast from a war zone in the Middle East, his father said, 'All these religious men and politicians, and soldiers with their laws and codes. They're meant for living a good life. They forget that, and they think that the code, what they call their honour, is more important than the suffering of people. In a way they end up worshipping the code. They want control over all things. To control all minds so that people can't sin or make mistakes. Isn't that a form of 'shirk'? You tell me.'

Ishaq looked his father over, slumped in his tatty armchair, his favourite beige cardigan worn over a salwar kameez. His father's only real social life came from occasional and illicit whisky-drinking sessions with his colleagues at the bus garage – Jamaicans, Indians, and Nigerians, away from their haranguing spouses, spending time playing cards in laughter. They bemoaned their destinies and their feckless children, kids they found baffling.

Yet, he didn't dare try to upbraid or chide his father. He was the son. Ishaq thought maybe it was a sign that he had no conviction. Maybe a bleeding heart that was not fortified enough to hold both a moral code and the strength to act on it, without resorting to an extreme of behaviour like some of his peers. All he saw was frailty. He had seen so much of it on the estate. People stuck in a vicious spiral of hardship leading them downward. One bad mistake to another. Cars crashing, revolving and twisting in slow motion, inexorable and unremitting. His parents, like others in the community, had lived lives of struggle, constant loss, and facing up to incomprehensible change. War, partition, migration. Settling among a hostile population. Wanting to do right by their children whilst always pining for home and what was familiar. He felt chastened.

'I know. I know. I understand. I'm sorry. You're right, I shouldn't have been so rude.'

'But then what do I know, Ishaq. I'm simple. I'm not complex…complicated like you are.'

His father relaxed back into his seat and smiled, turning the news back on. 'I liked the story, by the way. I didn't understand it all. You were very kiddish but I enjoyed it. That woman, the wife, she is a pain in the bum. She would have nagged you to death. I was ashamed at the situation, but proud of you too, in a way. Although don't tell your mum.' He reached over and put a palm on Ishaq's head. 'Ishaq, life is simple. You should get an education, a job, marry, raise a family and try and be happy. The world can rage around but, if you get that right, everything else will be good.'

His father pointed at the screen as cameras moved from crying Arabs to grieving Jews from somewhere in the occupied territories. 'Barren lands, like empty homes, all they can produce is madness. Nothing but people telling you what to do. Arabs and Jews are so stupid. Why do you think they had to be sent so many prophets? What do you think Chinamen think of all that? Just get on with it, building their country. Bloody smart are those lot, I tell you.'

His dad saw the absurd grotesqueness of the world. We all secretly knew. Ishaq knew he shouldn't laugh whenever his father skirted being sacrilegious or racist, but he laughed anyway and it broke him out of his mood. His father was far too innocent to be a bigot. 'Dad, I think the better term is Chinese, and I don't think you can just dismiss the wisdom of the old, you just need to sift through.'

'I'm old too. Wisdom? Maybe the old Arabs had it. They want to be accepted as equals, but rather than work at it stamp their feet. The new ones don't know how to live a life, all they know is how to blow themselves up and to teach others how to do that, too.'

The line was too crude but something about it rang true. The hopelessness of that act was as chilling as the finality. It took bravery to spend a life struggling with your family and community, at best seeing some incremental change. As well as the warping of the faith, it just said we should give up. In a supposed moment of clarity, some split-second of glory, just give up. An easy solution. It was a full stop imposed where there should be a question mark.

'Another good thing about the English is that they've given up trying to control the big things, so they save-up the pettiness

and hate for the small things. Spend a day on my bus and you'll
see that.' His father looked at his son's face and then turned back
to the screen. 'Ishaq, you think too much and worry too much.
You're like an old man sometimes. It is not the time for that. I
know you. Do the Phd, see what happens…maybe nothing, but
a few more years wasting, being free, won't harm anything.'

'Thank you,' said Ishaq, bowing his head and averting his
gaze. 'So…if I was going to be a bit backwards, why was Mum
all worried and you were all chilling, relaxed?'

His dad lent over and pressed a thumb against a forehead.
'Because Allah had given me gifts, and if I was to look after them
for the rest of my time then so be it.' Settling back, his eyes glinted,
crow's feet extended and the corners of his mouth curled upwards.
'Plus you know your sister has always been the favourite. Now go
upstairs. If your mother isn't sleeping, say sorry.'

Ishaq scrunched his face, leaving his father looking satisfied.
He liked that about him, his father lived within himself, but that
laughter, that life, was always there bubbling. There was some
inner space that was always his own. Life had never defeated him.

Ishaq went upstairs, tiptoeing to the door, pushing it slightly
ajar. He heard his mother's heavy exhales that verged on snoring,
and gently shut it again.

'Hey Brother Malcolm, Mr El-Shabazz, come here.' He
heard his sister's laughing whisper emanate from her room.
There was a stifling lack of privacy in this place. His sister was
always nosing, and had nicked the bigger room. She could just
about fit a study desk and a chest of drawers into her room. As
for Ishaq, he resided in what could hardly be called a bedroom.
More like a lock up for solitary confinement. He had the 'box
room'. A third of the room was literally taken up by a large box
structure that extended from the walls. He was often told that it
served some structural function, possibly to support the stairs.
He couldn't see how that was possible and was tempted to take a

sledgehammer to it to see if the stairs would actually fall down. The rest of the room held a single bed, leaving a small sliver of real estate for everything else. Ishaq was clean and methodical, but you wouldn't know it. He had no option but to use the floor as a system of storage, layered like an archaeological dig. He knew where to summon clothing and books. Football kit from the Mesolithic layer, textbooks from the Palaeolithic. He drew into a muffled rage when anyone tried to 'clean'. For studying purposes, there was always a battle to use his sister's desk that he invariably lost. So he studied by sitting on the floor of the living room, with his books on the floor and the dining cum coffee cum chickpea de-shelling table as a desk. The advantage of this was a showering of steaming cups of chai and various coronary inducing fried treats and sweetmeats from his mother, joyous at her studious boy.

As he entered her room she slammed her laptop shut. Ishaq walked up and forced it open, overcoming his sister's closing pressure.

'That's shady. What you hiding?' he said, as he input the password.

'Hey, how do you know my password?'

'Uhh, I set it up for you remember? And I know you're too lazy to change it.'

'It's private,' protested Maryam, as her hand covered the screen.

'My dear sister, you know privacy has been abolished. Now shove over.'

Password in, the screen resolved to a YouTube clip of some guys driving cars. Ishaq watched as the shaggy uptight with arrested development, the man-child, and the ironically racist one, lumbered around, carrying out hi-jinks in some foreign land, making bids for the freedom of middle-aged white men everywhere.

'You like *Top Gear*?'

Maryam blushed. 'Yea, so what. I'm not ashamed. It's better than watching the news.'

'It's annoying. I like it, too.' Ishaq sat on the double bed to watch the rest of the clip. 'I heard Mum was crying?'

Maryam eyebrows slightly raised, yet looked pleased. 'She was upset but it wasn't that bad. It was embarrassing for them. They lost face. Dad just knows that, for a mummy's boy like you, their greatest fear is mama's tears. By the way, thanks for telling her to talk to me about that FGM stuff. That was an enjoyable conversation. Not.'

'Hmm, it's like that, is it? I'm being played. It's not like I don't worry about the future. I think about how I'm going to support them when I'm older. They shouldn't worry so much, I'll do it. Plus you're not doing too bad...'

Maryam made a show of clearing her throat, as she clicked on a new clip. 'Excuse me. I'll help out too, but don't you be getting ideas. Anyway, back to the goss; I heard she was a catch. Well out of your league.'

'Uhh no, her eyes were all over me,' said Ishaq, finally breaking out in a simper that immediately made Maryan smile.

'I doubt it. She sounded accomplished. Look at you, you can't even look after yourself. You haven't even got a driving licence. If she was late and needed a lift to work, what would you do? Take the training wheels off and give her your bicycle?'

'Uhh no, I'm a gentleman. I'd lend her my bus pass.'

Maryam laughed and punched Ishaq on the shoulder with a knuckle. She did that all the time, since he could remember, and always a bit too rough for his liking. When he was too small to resist, she and her friends delighted in running experiments. Once they tied him up with sellotape to see if he could get out. Her face when Mum told her off in front of her mates was priceless.

'No way she would have said "Yes".'

'Mmm, nooo. She definitely would've. Anyway, you're not doing much better.'

Maryam had been approached through a marriage site, online, by a white convert. A while back he visited and met the parents. More inclined towards the sufi ascetic than the brand of Islam that was popular round the estate, the biggest turnoff was his staring eyes and his strict adherence to his own religious law. Way too intense. Five minutes of him was enough.

'I couldn't believe it. A man who doesn't drink tea and coffee. Honestly, it's difficult enough sometimes, without completely making stuff up,' said Ishaq.

'He creeped me out anyway.'

'He looked like Rasputin didn't he? Seriously, I think some of the really posh white converts are a bit nuts.'

'Astagfirullah, you can't say that. That's terrible,' said Maryam

'It is a bit predictable though isn't it; if you're from the estates or working class and brown or black then you become orthodox. If you feel hard done by, you go to one of the extreme groups. Now, if you're white and middle class, looking to fill something empty, you become a yippee-dipee head in the clouds spiritual-type.'

'Hmm maybe, but it's loose talk like this that'll get you into trouble one day.'

Shaking his head, Ishaq said, 'I'm just talking to you.'

Maryam gave Ishaq a strange look. A bit like when she had been caught stringing him up. She shut the door, went over to her chest of drawers, brought out a white envelope and handed it to Ishaq. This was weird. He checked for any markings but none were visible; opening it he saw a bunch of fifty-pound notes.

Handing it back, he said, 'What's that for?'

'I wanted to tell you...I got approached in the street by two people who said...they said they were from MI5.'

Ishaq stared, mouth open slightly. She had said that as if she was talking about going to the post office. Maryam, with force, flattened some crinkles in her skirt. 'I was coming out of the tube and I heard my name called, "Maryam Tabrizi". They said they were from the security service and asked for a bit of my time.'

'Ok…What did they look like?'

'I can't remember – it all happened so quickly and it was so surreal. The lady was youngish in her late twenties, but the man was older. He had a strange name and bad teeth but said I could call him Al. They took me to a cafe, sat down, and they asked for my help.'

'What kind of help?'

'It was vague, like they wanted me to go places and get info where they couldn't. For example, go to a place where Muslims gather and give them information on the room, size of the room, who goes in and out. That kind of thing.'

'What did you say?'

'I said I want to be left alone. They went on for a while but once they realised I wasn't interested they thanked me for my time and gave me this.' She held the envelope in a pincer with the edge of her fingertips, as if it were diseased.

Ishaq looked at it, churning through the ramifications of what this meant. Even its existence in the household violated. 'This is dirty money, you need to give it away.'

'I know, I'll give it to charity or something. What do you think it was all about? They actually wanted to recruit me or something else?' Maryam paused, making a tentative move to hold her baby brother's hand. 'Ishaq, you know you can tell me anything. If you have problems…or anything. Have you been up to anything dodgy? You just…you don't seem very surprised.'

'I can't believe you're asking me that. By Allah, I've done nothing. I just…anyway, I can guarantee I wouldn't be of any interest. I should be more offended that they didn't want to hire me. As for what it is really about? I don't know. No point wasting energy on things so out of our hands.'

Maryam looked at her younger brother, studying him. For what, she wasn't sure. 'I never know what you're thinking. Dad says the same thing. We worry you know.'

Ishaq looked down, his hands entwined, wringing them with force. He could tell them about uni, about the police, about boys on the estate, but what was the point. A plague of anxiety when there was nothing they could do but fret.

'I'm fine…you just don't hear something like this every day. Feels so weird, you know? You do everything right. Pay taxes, look after your family, be community-minded, adhere to the law, and it all can get wiped out in an instant.' Ishaq snapped the fingers of his right hand, the harsh click catching Maryam by surprise and making her jump. 'A malicious tip off. Your neighbour maybe. An ambitious officer or politician…all… outside of your control, all unknown, at anytime, any place… that's how I feel sometimes. I'm just keeping my head down.'

Ishaq moved a hand to stop a video clip, which was still playing in the background. His sister noticed his hand shake. He tried to stop it and quell the nausea. Maryam placed a hand on her brother's head and ruffled his hair.

'And do you think this is what it will be like from now on? Looking over our shoulders.'

Ishaq gripped his sister's hand firmly. 'Don't worry, I'll take you to work if it all kicks-off sometime.'

His father used to get Ishaq to escort Maryam to work whenever there was a terrorist incident. Hoodlums courted trouble by targeting woman they thought looked 'foreign', especially those who covered their hair.

And what do you do if you have to confront one. Treat violence with violence? The Quran taught patience in trying times. Excuse those who treat you badly. The prophet, peace be upon him, said the strong is not the one who overcomes people by his strength but the strong is one who controls himself in anger.

The problem was this cultured behaviour. Like being called a Paki or getting into a fight, the accumulation of daily petty harassments went unseen and unchecked by the police or society. The street had its own laws, ones that didn't reward reason, or civility, or negotiation. When you avoid retaliation they rarely see it as someone acting out of strength, someone trying to be better. Like hyenas, they smell weakness. If a man feels it's ok to be racist, call you a terrorist, or take aim at someone's clothing, they feel braver next time. Allow a slur go unanswered in front of a crowd, especially one that has permitted it with their silence, and you encourage it to happen again. Stupid people, bigoted people, don't understand subtlety and morality. They need to know you are avoiding violence out of strength, not out of weakness, and the only way to do that is to crack a few skulls first.

But Ishaq could see the lunacy, and he wanted no part. He wanted to step outside it all. He was disturbed from his thoughts, as Maryam's head flexed back in laughter.

'Haha, that's a laugh. Look after me? Like a few years ago, when you were a small, skinny thing. It was more like me looking after you. That's part of the problem with this world, lots of skinny boys, even if they don't look like it on the outside, pretending they are grown men who have to do manly things. Anyway, you don't know any self-defence?'

Ishaq gave a look of mock-indignation. 'I do.'

'Yea, right. Like what, boxing, or MMA?'

Ishaq paused for thought, scratched his nose and then said, '100 metre sprint.'

Maryam patted her eyes as she laughed, as if she was trying to put tears back in. She put her hand on Ishaq's again. 'Good, that's the best one. Ninety-nine percent of the time, there's no point fighting. I hope you never ever see the one per cent. Promise me you'll run if something happens. There's no shame in it.'

Ishaq looked at his sister. The only time someone had dared touch her in the street, it was another Muslim. A woman had grabbed her — brown, with an accent — she held Maryam in two desperate hands. Shaking her, clawing at her hijab and shouting, 'If it wasn't for you, we would all be ok, they would leave us all alone. You've made it hell for all of us.' The shouts on the street were nothing, that was the only incident that hurt, that got past her defences. Ishaq was in awe of his sister; he had no idea how strong you had to be to wear clothing in such open devotion. Despite people wearing special clothing, or holding sacred rites, through all recorded history, in this confined modernity it was seen as pathology. An object for fear, an expression that was the subject of government bans.

'I promise to do the right thing. Don't worry.'

Maryam nodded, as she put the envelope away. Layering it under multiple pieces of clothing in a bottom drawer. Her voice softer, she said, 'She would have definitely said "No", by the way.'

'Uh, definitely would have said "Yes".'

'Na, she sounds too cool, she would have said "No".'

'Naaa, I'm a catch. I'm convinced.'

'Ishaq, COME HERE.' Ishaq heard his father give a pleading shout from the living room. Ishaq swapped a confused look with Maryam and then shot down the stairs. He can't have heard the conversation?

'What is it?' he asked, his insides feeling shaky.

'See what this stupid man has said.' He pointed at the telly, glee mixed with apprehension, like a kid pointing at the Gorilla cages in the zoo.

On the screen were two men coming out of some uniform building in Europe – Strasbourg maybe, Brussels, or Luxembourg; drab men against dreary backgrounds surrounded by a jaded mob of press. One was that German politician Ishaq had heard speak at the conference; he seemed to be in an argument. His colleague was proposing a charter for minorities that specifically targeted Muslims. The German said that we might as well start sticking yellow stars on. He defended an integrated Europe, welcoming all to work within a common framework, excluding extremists on all sides.

Ishaq closed one eye and rubbed it with a knuckle, his stomach settling. 'I thought something big had happened. I've seen this plenty of times.'

'No. Wait.' His father grabbed Ishaq by the wrist stopping him from leaving. 'Watch the rest.'

The German's opponent was a man from a Dutch far-right party, in an expensive suit, swept-back hair. All ruddy and chubby cheeks with an upturned nose that gave him a porcine air. He had no real political base or influence but was far more at ease in English than the German, and had a populist forthrightness that commanded more attention than was his due.

'What my esteemed colleague doesn't understand is that this is a fight for civilisation. We are civilised and tolerant, and our European values will triumph.'

The man checked to see he had the full attention of the stalking cameras. Flashes of light lit up the dusk and bathed his face in a lambent glow. He was smiling, hands outstretched in openness. Annointed, he held court in full flow, while the German stood silent beside him, looking small and pressured.

'When I was a child I used to play with a magnifying glass and ants. You put it up and, from the outside what can seem the clearest surfaces, reveal imperfections. Even if I held it up to a beautiful young lady I could reveal some flaws,' he said, squinting with one eye and making an O with the thumb and forefinger of a hand as he held it up to the face of a young reporter: a once antagonistic questioner who now instantly went flush. 'That's what we can do with the Muslims, bring light onto them and reveal. And of those imperfections, of those who abuse our trust and our history of justice, we can expose them. And with all the light that Europe can muster, we can concentrate it so that they burn like ants.'

The crowd gasped and murmured. The flashes intensified, calls and texts were made as the swarming pack smelled the wounded scent of headlines. The young woman recoiled from the politician, her flattered face turning to disgust. The Dutchman patted down the crowd with his hands and they heeded.

'Now, we, the enlightened West, we invented the magnifying glass, we hold it, we use it, and I shouldn't be blamed for ants being ants.'

Ishaq clutched the arm of his father's chair as his nausea returned. He felt hairs on his arm rise. Ishaq was used to politicians talking like this, talking about them without them, but it still sent a quake through to his marrow. Like members of a rarefied banqueting club, these men flung statements into the ether that served their own gluttonous agenda. But this was no vacuum, no blue-skies where they could conduct thought experiments, their self-determination at the expense of others.

What hurt was not the casual references to taking away citizenship, the taking of children, travel bans, torture and deportation. Not the prisons of Guantanamo and Abu Ghraib, or talk of collective punishment until they get their house in order. What vexed was that, in actuality, these men could not care less about these issues, because they did not have to. They did not need to. Obese in their entitlement. They were in thrall to their own voice, their own ambition. They would ditch any conviction for lurid exigencies. They had room to equivocate. They could make throw away comments and wake-up the next day and turn to opining on the decline of the grey squirrel, or the wretched state of their football team. They lived lives with no consequence, existences with no repercussion.

Ishaq looked at his father, who now looked concerned. 'The man is a nobody and obviously psycho mad. He's going to cause loads of headlines, and chat ,and then nothing as usual.'

'But wait, there is more. They are repeating this on all the channels now,' insisted his father, as he hurriedly thumped buttons on the remote until another channel was found.

The German man, his glasses shaking as he adjusted them by pressing a finger against the bridge, came forward.

In his German accent, and halting English, he said, 'This is a disgrace. We have come ... hundreds of years of fighting... each other. Have not learned a thing. We cannot blame. We need to help them more. We do need to find a final solution for Muslims in Europe.'

The crowd started roaring, and glaring flashes blinded both men as they were peppered with further questions. Attendants and security pulled the politicians away, even as the German was protesting, having realised his mistake, his face masked with revulsion.

Ishaq grabbed the control and turned off the television. *Well, that was a major fuck-up, wasn't it,* he thought to himself.

'Don't worry, Dad. Nothing will come out of it,' he said, as if to himself.

'Well, I want you and your sister to be careful for the next few days and no mixing with any hot-head friends.'

'Okay,' said Ishaq, as he went and grabbed some trainers by the door.

'Where do you think you are going? Haven't you bloody seen what happened?' His father had both hands out towards the television as if he was presenting a cart full of steaming horse manure.

'I'm going out. Local.'

'Where?'

'Just footy with Marwane. I need some air. Don't worry. It may kick-off in Europe but it'll be different here. We're not like them.' Ishaq walked to the corridor and started lacing his trainers.

'And no going to the march?' shouted his father. 'Trouble makers are everywhere. MFI will sort it out.'

'MFI was a furniture store; I think you mean MI5.'

'Anyway, they will sort it out.'

'Don't think they can sort anything out. No one is in control, especially those who think they are,' said Ishaq, in a mumble.

'What did you say?'

'Nothing. Don't wait up, I'll be fine,' and Ishaq exited the flat before his father could shout anything further.

15.

Ishaq loved the freedom. It was perverse; that they played in a cage but felt ever-so free. Ishaq would run, ball at his feet, air on his face as it rushed past, penned in by meshed-fencing that would ripple and sing as a body or ball punched into it. The jangling of caging, providing percussion to an orchestrated movement of passes. The thrill of passing an opponent through speed or guile, the heady buzz of scoring a goal and taking in the acclaim of your mates.

Ishaq even enjoyed the needle between opponents. Ishaq, Marwane and his friends enjoyed a skilful passing style. The aim was to create beauty. To display skill and panache by humiliating your opponent in exposing them through a nutmeg or an intricate buildup. Scoring a goal was incidental to this sophistry and even frowned upon if it did not contain some scintilla of flair.

As well as infuriating opponents it also caused frustration among friends. They berated Ishaq and Marwane. Shouting at them that winning was everything, as they hoofed the ball upfield whenever they could, huffing, and puffing, and shooting at every opportunity. Playing like Vikings. It was all good though, especially on those sticky summer nights when Ishaq held a secret hope that this would last forever. He, being ever-responsible, guided the defence and came out with the ball in control. Marwane, indisciplined, capable of great skill but infuriating in his inconsistency.

Ishaq and Marwane left the cages on this still evening, the air calming their perspiration. The two lads took seats on a railing while Ishaq vigorously rubbed his football sock into his shin, and then peeled it down to look at the result of someone's errant kick. He did not look impressed, shoved the sock down, and then raised his face to the sky to let air cool his eyes.

'No stars.'

'What you say?' Marwane looked sideways to Ishaq.

Ishaq looked at Marwane and jabbed upwards. 'No stars. Would be good to see some, sometimes.'

Marwane was in the middle of a gulp from a can of coke, carbonated bubbles expanding and moving upwards, nearly overwhelming his nose. He was uncertain of what to say to such a random remark. 'Just make sure you only talk to me like this; I think only I can handle your weirdness.'

Ishaq jumped off the rail and, with Marwane following his lead, started to walk.

'Whatever. Anyway, guess who I bumped into? Father Horan, from the community centre days.'

'Oh, Father Ted. How's he doing? He must be a fossil now.'

'Nah, he looked fine. He was just taking care a few odds and ends at the building. Was asking about ze Muslimz. Talking about the IRA, and the bad ol' days for the Irish.'

'Was he now?' Marwane said, in a mixture of amusement and derision. 'Man, hate it when Irish people go on as if it's the same. They should leave it out. Seriously, don't try and 'relate'.'

Ishaq looked at Marwane walking beside him in his elongated but lolling style. With his height and explosion of hair, he looked liked a monochrome Ronald McDonald. Ishaq stifled a laugh, his shoulders purposefully hunched. Father Horan had said there was a chance to resurrect the centre, but no point telling Marwane, he would just hide behind a joke and belittle the idea.

Mistaking the reason for the laugh, Marwane retaliated with his own triumphant cackle. 'We haven't talked about you going-off on one, at that inter-faith thing.'

'Yea, yea, you told me so…Well done. If I had a hat, I'd take it off to you ,' Ishaq made a bowing gesture.

'Ah, you a bit sore about it,' said Marwane, his grin widening. 'Look, that's what happens when you mix with the super-annoying, intellectual renewers of the Ummah. The only ones who can bridge Islam and the West, blah blah blah. You should let them get on with it.'

'I just feel that we need to make more of an effort with them. We can be insular and scary to those lot. We actually have common ground. Did you hear that guy on telly today? He doesn't make distinctions.'

Marwane started laughing again, this time showing gently crooked teeth. 'I heard it, but you trying really worked out for you, didn't it? Look, these guys will always be more comfortable with middle class non-muslims . They're just as insular. They can't connect with us. They don't want to anyway. They just want to kiss arse and get along. All their talks are about stuff like Muslim representation on TV. Stuff we don't give a crap about. And anyway, the ways I heard it was that the speaker was calm and super-slick with you, you came out of it sounding like a foaming-at-the-mouth fundie. Honestly bruv, I would have paid to see it.'

'Go on, laugh as much as you want,' said Ishaq, kissing his teeth and shaking his head. His footsteps slowed until he was lagging a bit behind, making Marwane twist and walk backwards to interact. To a bystander it would have looked like Ishaq was being dragged forward by the other man with an invisible rope. 'It just bugs that they look down on a lot of the kids. They think of them as simpletons who need rules and regs to navigate their lives.'

Marwane's grin dropped and he looked back, over Ishaq. 'Well that's right isn't it? A lot of brothers do need a lot of hard rules. I need it too. What's wrong with that? Man is in loss, nothing shameful about that, and it doesn't make it less true. Look, these guys want to cure poor people of being poor, without actually having to meet any. Man, you're making me angry now!'

'Ok, let's drop it. I acted like a tool. I don't want to talk to you about it,' said Ishaq. Marwane had called him Mr Negativity but all he offered instead was apathy and cynicism, and sometimes it just grated. He could now see that it was just hiding. It was funny now, but it was getting harder and harder to talk about anything.

' Speed-up Ishaq. I want to get home. You got me going now. You know they've got that poster campaign, as well. The one that has pictures of model Muslims. You know, like a doctor who wears hijab, or a policeman, and they've chosen fair-skinned people or white converts.' Marwane made a loud inhale of breath. 'It's just so desperate…the need to be included…'

'Look, I actually understand what they are doing with the posters though. It's not saying, "Please let me in, I'm just like you", it's saying to people like that politician today, "Please don't smack me in the face, I'm normal."'

'Well, then it's a humiliating plea.'

'Bruv, no point pretending we're strong. What are we? Like four percent of the population and all different, all divided. Anytime, the outside can squash us like a bug. Nah man, we're just the bogeyman.'

They reached a tunnel. The underpass marked the end of a sparsely built-up part of the estate, where the cages resided.

Their footsteps made cavernous echoes that fled away from them in a pitter-patter, descending down the singularity of the sloping path. As they exited they saw a cityscape lying passive under a waxing moon. A silver sheen spilled over the concrete. Laid out like an ice rink, this silent world was when the estate was at its most deceptive. An easy seduction into thinking all was right.

Marwane opened his arms up wide, in protest at the emptiness around them. 'And really? How would we have ended up, if we didn't say no? Islam says don't drink, so we don't. It says don't take drugs, so we don't. It says, don't sleep around, so we've managed not to get a girl preggers at fifteen. You know, people get a bit of ease in their lives, or get education, and they think it was all up to them. Not luck, or destiny, or a privileged background or anything. They think they're so complicated, and we are all so simple, in our wants.'

Ishaq tried to intervene but Marwane's hands rebuffed him, whirling away while he ranted, his eye's trenchant and fastened somewhere else.

'Money talks, Issy. In those posh areas, they can afford to make mistakes. They can afford to look down on people like us, with our rules. Imagine you or me banged up before a judge with some coke. We're screwed. We have to be stricter. It's the only way and that's part of the wisdom...Maybe we are needy, but then there's some truth in people's needs, not deception.'

Ishaq was happy to let the words echo and settle, but Marwane kept fixing him with his triumphant 'whadya think' mug. 'Well, M, that's a bit deep for you. Where'd you get that from?'

'Nowhere. Just made it up. See it's not only you arty farty students that think a bit. It's not good to be alone in that head of yours 24/7. You and your weird ideas. You have to live in the real world. See, what I'm gonna do, inshallah, is graduate. Get a job that pays, marry a good muslimah and raise a family. Simple.'

'That's fine, but this other stuff has a habit of breaking down your door at five in the morning, terrifying your wife and kids, and then carting you off to prison.'

Ishaq changed tack, charging forward, Marwane sidestepped in a hop, facing him to continue the conversation. 'That's scary. But I ain't involved in anything like that, so if any great injustice like that happened, then I'll just accept it and rely on Allah.'

'Really Marwane? That's so easily said, but if that did happen, and you were innocent, then wouldn't you want people to be around to help you out? People who cared about something other than just their own backside.'

'Look bro, Allah says save yourself and your family first. So I'll do that, then, if I have the strength and resources, I'll help outside of that. It's not being selfish, it's about foundations. You can't do anything unless the foundations are strong, and that's your family, then your local community, and so on. Any racing ahead and trying to save the world, when that stuff isn't right, is vanity, just causes more aggro. Don't be like those uni guys who are only interested in cool causes that suit their ego.'

The same rote lines. Ishaq could hear the uncertainty, more of blind hope than real conviction. As if repeating them, again and again, was a comfort in itself. Nothing had ever pricked Marwane's protective bubble, and it wasn't his place to pierce it, either.

They matched strides as they forged homewards, making headway, the hush only broken by three barks of a dog that had been chained up someplace. They stepped through a small field that had been left boggy by rivulets of rain. Marwane cursed himself as one foot landed in a deep patch and he felt water spill over his shoe, down to his sock.

'Speaking of marriage. That sister who gave you the leaflet, she was nice,' he said.

Ishaq smiled. 'She was super-political and thought you were a twat.'

'She thought WE were twats. Anyway, next time I see her I might slip her my phone number. Give it a chance. All through the parents, legit and all. Or Shams stylee.'

Towards the end of their time together Shams had discovered girls. Ishaq remembered how stricken Shams was when he took a fancy to someone. He'd go mute and self-aware, fixed to the spot, pretend he was looking away. Once, he even spent hours outside a girl's place, hoping for just a glimpse of a face. Ishaq had to bale him out sometimes, explain that his mate wasn't strange, just having a moment. It was sincere though. For a time. The odd thing was that, once a week had passed, Shams' ministrations found another target. A new arrow, piercing his heart. Layla after Layla, to his one Majnun.

'I do miss that guy.'

'You sure show it,' said Marwane.

After a moment's deep thought Ishaq said, 'Ibn Hazm, from Cordoba, Spain, thought that courtly love, one that was chaste and from a distance, could be edifying. It could ennoble your character.'

Seeing Marwane give him a look of pity, Ishaq said, 'What?'

'Don't know whether to slap you for talking about "courtly love" or for using the word "edifying". Honestly, Ishaq, I think the stork that brought you to the ghetto must've been on crack that day.'

Ishaq laughed. 'Just reading, expanding my horizons, you bonehead. Back in the day, Islamic scholars wrote and talked about everything. And edifying means something that raises you morally...'

'I know what it means, you arty farty ponce. Anyway, sounds like Ibn Hazm would have a coronary if he came round these parts. You're pure if you hold out beyond the first time you get wasted together.'

'Well, good luck then. Her dad might be like Obama. You know what he said he would send, if someone tried to date his daughters?'

'No, what?'

'Predator drones.'

Marwane's mouth flattened and his demeanour chilled. Ishaq followed suit, realising his mistake. Marwane said, 'Everything is a joke to those people, they've lost their souls.'

They reached the old community centre. More of a hut, it was a shoebox-of-a-building. The walls were pock-marked from errant shrapnel thrown by passers-by. The windows were mostly smashed, and covered by rusted grating. Once a beneficiary of council funding, it had a good set of play equipment outside. In between the scattered trash there lay a carousel, multiple climbing frames, and swings. Yet no movement, petrified as in an exhibit. A sole lamppost bathed the area in a lambent pool, separating it from the field, and, once within, the rest of the estate looked indistinct. Two paths led to parts of the now adumbral estate which, while screened, was only a hop, skip, and a jump away.

In the light they saw a boy wearing a green puffer vest over a marl hoody. He took his over-sized headphones off, and brought down his hood.

'What's up? Long time, man. Ishaq, bruv, you've gone awol. Don't see you much since school days.'

Marwane whistled, and gave the new boy a hug. 'What's happening, Levi? Ishaq's having an identity crisis.'

'Ah shut up Marwane,' said Ishaq, as he clasped Levi's hand and slightly bumped his chest.

'I. Den. Tee. Tee.'

'Proper dry. You're really not half as funny as you think you are, you know that?'

Levi nodded. 'I see. I see. So what's that about?'

'Well, it seems to involve lots of posh words, and mixing with posh rich-kids discussing poshness. Ya know, how much pain is in the world,' said Marwane.

Levi said, 'Nah man, Ishaq's a homeboy. He knows what he's about, don't ya?'

'Yea, he does really, but he also spends too much time on the Internet, and reading newspapers about how much people hate him. He gets-off on it.'

Levi folded with a snicker, bringing a fist up to his mouth in an abortive attempt to quell it.

Ishaq made a theatrical shake of the head, emphasising slow and long sweeps to show his pity and patience. 'Course I do. Course I do. I would love to be you, M.' Ishaq's hands were out like a showman at a circus. 'I'd love to be dumb enough of our situation so I could be happy in my ignorance. You see Levi, Marwane just likes to stick his head in the ground like an ostrich. He never developed past five years old, and still thinks if he covers his eyes and can't see people, then, they definitely can't see him.'

'Whatever, Ishaq. Go and spend all day on twitter. Hashtag killallmuslims.'

'Marwane. Xo xo my backside.'

Levi continued his snorting, as Ishaq gave Marwane a playful punch in the chest and Marwane bent over, pretending to wince in pain. 'Man, you boys don't change.'

'Anyway, enough of our stuff. How are things with you? What's new?' asked Ishaq.

Levi's mouth fell into a grim line. 'Where the fuck have you been? You haven't heard? My cousin Leon got stabbed last week. Bled-out on the corner of the estate under one of the bridges. You haven't been past there? Seen all the flowers and the incident sign?'

Ishaq nodded. 'I did see that, bruv. I'm sorry I didn't realise who it was. What went on? How's his family?'

'His mum's in bits. I don't know what happened. He was sixteen. Some random beef. It's fucking mental. Maybe he did something stupid, I don't know, but I'm pretty messed-up about it, too. Someone said there was a group of them, just bounced on him like a pack of dogs. Fucking sick. Man, I'm sick of this place. Police don't do nuthin'.'

A fox darted out from the darkness. Levi recoiled with fright. With its neck rigid, the fox strolled its way round the edge of the play area. It kept a disconcerting stare on the boys as it sniffed out any discarded food.

Marwane, trying to do the civil thing and not laugh at Levi's jump, 'You alright?'

'Nah man, I is cool,' Levi replied, his face telling a different story as his body still shuddered. 'Those foxes are becoming bare brave, ya know. Vermin like rats. They carry disease. We should be shooting them all.'

Ishaq said, 'They breed like rabbits; you kill one, they just get replaced. You just have to put up with it.'

Marwane ran up to the fox, his arms wide as if he were attempting a capture. It gave him a stare and then scampered off. 'See Ishaq, all mouth no action, like you. In fact worse than that, they can't even bare their teeth to try and look scary. They don't have the face muscle for it.'

'Nice one. Who told you that? You can't have been reading a book.'

'Haha. Shams – he knows his stuff, man.'

A voice spat out at them, gatecrashing their shelter. 'What the fuck are the three of you hanging around here for?'

Ishaq looked in the direction of the sound but couldn't see anything outside the bubble of light. All the boys could hear was was their own pallid breathing – Levi's with a choking rasp – as Ishaq started to see three formless sketches approach. He placed a hand above his eyes and squinted, while his torso dipped as his body prepared to run. The watery shapes were just outside the lit area and, though bathed in the moonlight, it was hard to make out any features.

The first broke through the barrier of illumination. 'I said, what the fuck are you doing here! This is our area.' The voice belonged to Mujahid.

'Flippin' hell, bruv. Mujahid, you scared us,' said Marwane. Levi relaxed, taking his lead from the relieved expressions of the other two.

'Ah, brothers Marwane and Ishaq. I didn't see it was you.' The voice sounded robotic, somehow devoid. 'Did you boys not hear what that man said, on the television? It's all going to kick-off now. I want to make sure that Muslims are safe on the estate. I'm making sure round here is a safe zone.'

'Like a Muslim-only one? That's cool, it could be like our version of Chinatown, except instead of hanging lanterns, you lot can start hanging televisions, Taliban stylee,' said Marwane, who started laughing with Ishaq and bumping fists.

'You two are both very funny. Laugh-a-minute kids.' Mujahid pointed at his own severe face, that he extended out from the darkness. 'Do you see me laughing?'

The other spectres resolved into men. One came behind Mujahid and pushed at a swing. He prodded it with a single, extended, finger. Enough to make a line of swinging shadows that swayed along the ground, as the chain made a desperate squeak.

'Who is this, here?' Mujahid asked, indicating Levi only with his eyes.

'Just a friend from school we bumped into.' Ishaq felt a tingling down his spine that peaked and crashed. His skin felt clammy, he thought probably from all that running about. The silence intensified, and he smelled the pack of men mix with the whiff of decomposition.

'Ok. We'll leave you to it. Good seeing you bruv.' Ishaq moved away, but Mujahid stepped forward and placed a contending hand on his chest. The other members positioned around the three, to make obstacles of their exit.

'Not so fast. I asked who is he? Ishaq, don't disrespect me. I'm a Brother, just like you and Marwane.'

Levi looked at the new men, was made unsure by their frosty interaction and tried to warm them up.

'Fam, I know Ishaq from school. We are friends from way back.'

'Don't 'fam' me. You and me are nothing. So are you Muslim?' Levi hesitated and looked at Ishaq for guidance. 'Don't look at him; what are you doing out here so late?' Mujahid put his face into Levi's, foreheads touching. Levi cast his eyes downwards, his body hung.

Ishaq pulled Levi away. 'He's not Muslim. He's a friend, he was just telling me how he lost his cousin last week. He's in mourning. Just on his way home, like us. You're right. We should all be getting back.'

The one who toyed with the swing joined his friends. They all waited for Mujahid's response, silent while children's amusements created playful shadows, their motion at odds with the static figures of men. Ishaq knew this was not the tranquil quiet of long summer nights.

One of the men came just behind the shoulder of Mujahid. Ishaq recognised Saeed, he was the son of one of his father's colleagues from the bus depot. When younger, Ishaq used to visit their house and Saeed would let him play on his games console, knowing that Ishaq's family couldn't afford one. That soft teenager was a world away from this shaven-headed guy. Someone had once made an inappropriate comment to his sister and he and a group of friends steamed into the guy's phone shop and beat him senseless. So he done time. Stupid time.

As a group they didn't look like much. Maybe they found some some affirmation and brotherhood. Some comfort in each other's assigned guilt. When he looked at Mujahid, he thought that he was internalising it all, and taking others with him. Allowing it to become woven in to the fabric of his being, losing hope of anything better. Just playing-up to an imposed identity, realising a destiny of malevolence endowed by others. That was what scared him about these people. They were so unknown.

Saeed looked timid, an echo of that former life, as he whispered into Mujahid's ear, 'Why you hypin'? We know these guys, let them go.'

'Shut the fuck up. Who asked you?' Saeed shrank back.

Looking at Ishaq, Mujahid said, 'Friends? With him?' Returning to Levi, 'So, your boy was the guy who croaked…I heard he was runnin' for some other lot round here, causing trouble. You should know we don't allow that here. So, what you doing?'

'Nothing fam, I was just on my way home. I don't want any trouble.'

'I said don't fam me,' shouted Mujahid, bawling at Levi, whose eyes widened and face opened. 'Let's see what you got on you. Jump up and down for me…I said jump.' Levi looked again at Ishaq, and then a made a couple of half-hearted hops as Mujahid listened for signs of anything loose and metal.

There was no method to this, it was just humiliation. Something you do just because you can. Ishaq stepped in and stopped Levi. 'Mujahid, itaqullah. Fear Allah. What do you think you are doing? This is too disrespectful.'

'What did you say? You fucking little shit!' Mujahid grabbed Ishaq by the neck and pushed him against the metal A-shaped frame of the swings. With his free hand, he brought out a knife. 'Don't you fucking dare talk to me like that! Always the same with you lot, looking down on people like me, when you're the snake.'

Marwane moved to grab Mujahid but was held by the two other men. Pinned, Ishaq was helpless as Mujahid brought a glimmering blade to his throat. He summoned up all his resolve to stop his lower lip from quivering, offering a silent prayer that, if his life was taken, he would at least die with some dignity.

The Study Circle

Breathless, Ishaq said, 'I don't look down on anyone. You are my brother, and I'm telling you this isn't the way. Why are you acting like this? I haven't done anything. He hasn't done anything.'

'You haven't done anything? You haven't done anything? You've threatened me and my family. If I go back in, there's no one to feed them. And you say that you've done nothing? As for these kuffar, they give us no dignity so why should we give them any. I'll take what I want from these people and this system, no man can tell me anything else.'

'Threaten you, what are you talking about?' Ishaq stared at Mujahid's eyes. He looked frenzied, but those eyes were clear and held a harsh focus. 'At least let this guy go while we clear this up? He's got nothing to do with anything?'

Mujahid release his grip ever so slightly and, after some calculation, nodded at Levi, who in turn looked at Ishaq.

'Go on, I'll be fine. Don't call anyone, leave us to it,' said Ishaq.

Ishaq's voice was betrayed by his shaking hands but Levi nodded in thanks and ran.

Ishaq addressed Mujahid straight on. 'You can't violate other people's property. Brother, you're fooling yourself if you think this is halal. Look where it's ended, a knife against another Muslim's throat.'

'You guys, in your mosques and circles, and your scholars.' Mujahid broke eye contact and spat onto the rubber matting. 'You heard them. They've called for our end...and they've spread their little moles and grasses, like you, amongst us. You haven't a clue. It's a war, out here. We do what we need to do to survive.'

It came out in a spitted gush. His demeanour and words confused Ishaq. 'Survive? By selling drugs? By eating your own people!'

'Drugs? Foolish child, what you talking about? What's the difference? You want to be like Mummy and Daddy...pay taxes...work 'til you're dead?'

Marwane had been struck dumb, but manged to coerce some words from himself. He sounded foreign as, for the first time, Ishaq heard tremors in his voice. 'Mujahid, this has gone too far. You're scaring us. Allah knows what we've done, but we apologise if we've dissed you. We're just on the way home. Subhanallah, you used to come to the halaqah. Why you acting like this?'

'The circle again; all you people know is being a slave to the system. What kind of Muslims are you? If you are Muslims at all? What's the difference anyway, we are all stuck here. You and me, both. Rules are different here.'

Ishaq struggled against Mujahid's clamped hold, finding some new energy. 'The difference is the halal and the haram. Allah sees what we do!'

'And you say that after what you have done?'

'What have I done? You're not making any sense.'

'Leave it, bruv, you've made your point. Let them be. You can't be hurting one of them, one of us, like that,' Saeed implored Mujahid; but he was implacable, not even acknowledging him.

'You stood with me just a day ago, chatting like a friend. You're a liar! A traitor! You threaten me being able to provide. A guy who just wants to go about his business. You like talking about truths, don't you? So I'm teaching you one now. Tell me Ishaq, for all your big words. Your big-man words from your small-boy mouth. What can you do if I decided to put out some justice on you, right now?' Mujahid strengthened his grip on Ishaq, who could feel a crushing just below the neck.

Ishaq's eyes bulged and glided downwards, then over the group, as he gave out one limp, paling, word. 'Nothing.'

'Exactly.' Mujahid finally smiled and released his grip. 'Ok, you lot can clear, I better not hear anything about this.'

Ishaq collected himself and adjusted his clothing. He could hear formerly-heavy breathing around him retreating to a normal pattern. He gave Marwane an uncertain look, but his friend looked away. He moved his gaze onto the others. Hesitant, he looked outside the light and went to step out.

'Just one more thing,' said Mujahid. 'I want to give you a reminder to behave in future.' Mujahid grabbed Ishaq and pinned him, again, and slashed him on the arm. Ishaq let out a powered cry. As the sound carried across the dark space into the estate and into homes, lights, that were illuminated, extinguished. The obligating burden to see, to be accountable, was too heavy a responsibility.

Time slowed as Ishaq fought the fog of consciousness. He felt a slashing of skin. Cutting that continued for an eternity. Mujahid threw him to the floor. Ishaq saw a clump of rust invade the white of his football shirt and looked on as crimson drops collapsed on the floor. His own blood. His own blood oozing out. Blood dripping out from his fat and muscle, cut by another Muslim.

He tried to cover the bleeding with his other hand. Marwane struggled to get to Ishaq, but was still held by two men. Breathing rapidly, Ishaq said, 'Mujahid, this is madness.'

Mujahid pinioned Ishaq with the toe of his boot. 'This is mercy, considering what you done. One more thing. Tell me about Shams. Would he double deal me? Are you two in it together? Tell me the truth and I'll let you go? Just a little word.'

Ishaq could not believe the sheer amount of warm ooze that the cold ground leeched. He wondered if he was going to die, in his own squalid puddle. He half-heard his own words, as part of him prepared for this final destination.

'...Shams is a good lad. He wouldn't double deal.'

Mujahid moved his foot to Ishaq's upper arm and Ishaq screamed, this time with a chesty gurgling as he struggled for breath.

'Say it again, tell me the truth. If you tell me the truth, that he's been lying, I'll let you go.'

'I'm telling you the truth. He's done nothing.'

Mujahid moved his leg away. 'Tell Shams, I want that money, and I better not get any more messin' from any of you guys or it'll be a different story next time. You're lucky I used my knife instead of something else…you know what I'm saying?'

Mujahid and his cohort walked-off, disappearing into shadow. Saeed had tried to kneel to take a look at Ishaq but was grabbed at the collar and told to move. Marwane helped Ishaq up so that he could lean back against the posts. Marwane's hands shook as he took off his football top and tied it above the cut.

Ishaq could hear a scratchy pounding and looked, his mind wandering for its origins until he realised it was his heart. Drowsy, he started to feel a chill as his clothing saturated with sweat. He stayed there, slumped across the post, for a while. At one point Marwane stood, as if he were getting help, but Ishaq used his good arm to cling weakly to a sleeve of Marwane's t-shirt.

'I think it's ok, just get me to the hospital.'

'Don't be crazy.'

'Just get me up and help me in to St Georges. It's not too far.'

'It's way too far to walk, the way you are.'

'You can borrow your cousin's car, right?'

Marwane closed his eyes and rubbed his forehead in thought, while Ishaq lay there stealing spasmed breath. Ishaq tried to concentrate on inhaling, but the tugs of splintered air hurt his insides, as if he were choking on pins. Ishaq looked at Marwane, tall like a tower but with no fortification. Ishaq had seen the fear paralyse him. Now it struck him hard, how that tall tower was now collapsing in on itself.

'Marwane, it's going to be ok. Just help please. Let's get going.'

'But what are you going to say?'

'I'm not going to say anything.'

'The man's crazy. An animal; he overstepped the mark.'

'And, if I tell the brothers, it'll start a war. I'm just going to keep quiet for now.' Ishaq struggled with his answers, as he used his left hand to wipe moisture from his eyes, his breathing now laboured like a man ascending a hill but afraid of reaching its peak and journey's end.

'And your parents?'

'Please, Marwane, no more questions…no more bloody questions. Just help me. Please.'

16.

Europe seethed in a jealous foam; rolling, gathering astringent mass and momentum, a map of ever-shifting acrimony; each altercation different, yet always with the same result. An overzealous stop-and-search of a Moroccan woman in Rotterdam, a triumphant shout at a group of Turkish men in a Berlin cafe, the surrounding of a mosque by police in Paris for their 'protection'. In Marseille they started burning French flags and barricading streets. French youth brought out their passports to add to the pyre, their blood-red covers melting into crimson flame.

In London the streets were thronging and, just below the hubbub of discordant voices, you could feel a racked tension, a fraying string held so taut that it could be rent apart with the blow of a kiss. People took second-takes at others, concentrating on strangers' hands and what they were pulling out of pockets, stealing looks over their shoulder as they went about the business of the ordinary.

The Study Circle

In South London Ayub looked at a menu. When they were doing their A Levels, Ayub and his friends always used to stop by this café and satiate their hunger on pieces of buttered toast, at six pence a slice. This sometimes descended into ludicrous food competitions, involving tottering mountains of cheap sliced-bread and inordinate amounts of dripping butter. The owner put up with this with great resentment, even on occasion kicking them out, berating them for being time-wasting students and wasting his space. And this also became part of the game, seeing how long they could go on before the owner went ballistic.

When even younger, they used to come round with a half-made effigy of Guy Fawkes, bugging the Cypriot owner for a 'Penny for the Guy'. The old man would chuck them some shrapnel in the form of coppers. Happy, they would move on until they had enough and end-up burning Mr Fawkes' towelled and ragged body in some lonely car park. The smell of carbon wafers and burnt flecks floating away, crawling with a spreading glow. Poor old martyred Guy Fawkes, what happened to that night? Ayub could not remember it stopping but he had not seen any Guys on the streets for years. Old customs died quickly now and without notice. It had all seemed so innocent then. Those times were long-gone.

Hit by a wave of paranoia he put the menu down. He eyed his backpack lying on the floor, picked it up, gently, and with great care placed it on the seat beside him, securing its important load. He took a look around at the punters, especially those passing near his bag. They were going about their day like any other, oblivious to the world outside and unaware of what was about to take place in this cafe. How the netherworld was about to visit upon them, and how utterly blameless they all were. The determined time was nearly at hand. He closed his eyes in concentrated readiness. He placed his hand until it was hidden inside his jacket, and then reached and pinched, until he felt it release.

Ayub opened his eyes with some relief. He worked to release some other stiffened muscles around the rib, and then wound his way up and around his neck, rolling it left, then right. Once the aches and pains of approaching middle age were alleviated, he placed the bag between his legs. He did not want some local guttersnipe making a grab for it and running off with the day's takings from his father's grocery. Cash was king, especially when people like the one he would encounter any second now could close their bank accounts on a whim, destroy their lives in a whisper. He was ready to meet Simon, the friendly ghost, his neighbourly spook.

The thudding tones of Lupe Fiasco played in the background and Ayub could not help but nod his skull-capped head and, under the table, tap a sandalled foot, to the rhythm.

The music stopped and Ayub looked up. He saw Simon whispering into the ear of the remonstrating waitress, having changed the station of his own accord.

Simon always struck Ayub as a slovenly type. He frequently wore that dirty blue suit, with a red tie mottled from decrepitude. He had thin arms and legs, but a bowling-ball belly that protruded in a white shirt over his belt. His dirty blond hair and his spindly limbs gave him the air of a floppy scarecrow, which was, apt given that that was essentially his role in life. Apart from constant pithy remarks he showed little understanding. Ayub wished Simon would go on a quest, looking for a brain.

'That's enough of that. Just mindless noise. I can't see what people see in that stuff.' Simon grabbed Ayub's hand and shook it with vigour. 'Ayub, it's been a while.'

'Not long enough.'

Simon smiled at the mouth, not matched by the flat look in his eyes. 'Don't be like that, we're old friends aren't we? I love to give old friends a surprise.'

'I was told that you were back sniffing-around. Tired of grooming fifteen-year olds online to get them to make a bomb?'

'Ah, yes, our itinerant fakir. How proud his parents must be?' said Simon, as he slid onto the benched-seating opposite.

Ayub felt a pang of anger. Simon knew Adam's background as well as Ayub did. 'So why am I here? You could have just sent me a message.'

'Not really. It may surprise you that we still do things face-to-face. Plus I'm not on Facebook.'

Ayub laughed. 'But your boss was, once. In his undies, wasn't it?'

'No, it was speedos. And I agree, that was pretty disgusting but he's MI6. Bloody amateurs, compared to us, and I don't think he'll be inflicting his pasty body on the general public anytime soon. Anyway, I thought it would be good to have a chat.'

'About what?'

'About what? The end of the world. It's all kicking-off now, isn't it, haha...Just a polite catch up. Your mate Adam, doing well, is he?'

'He's fine. I have to say this is really tiresome. You have all our names, you know we're peace-abiding, so I don't see the need for a chat.'

Simon picked up a laminated menu and spoke, face covered, nose down, his eyes flittered upwards from the top to look at Ayub. 'Your next generation doing what you did. Afghanistan, Syria. A road once less-travelled but now well-trodden, indeed. Trodden by you. People like you are a sure conduit, for the young. Just indulge me, it's getting hairy out there. Also, it is now against the law.'

'Of course it's against the law. As soon as a Muslim does something, you make it against the law. George Orwell went and fought in the Spanish Civil War. One of the Eton boys though wasn't he, Eric Blair? Had he called himself Abdul Abulbul, or whatever, it would have been a different story.'

'Ayub, come now, you're better than that, be reasonable. This time it is different. People returning from war zones are a threat to us all. Their acts are barbaric.'

Ayub had been in front of this flippant mouth many times. Since Bosnia the security agencies had managed to get a few of the names of those who went. A tap on the street, or a visit like this, was a regular occurrence.

The waitress stopped at their table and took orders, not batting an eyelid at the sight of a suited white guy and a thobe-wearing Asian man chatting away, but she gave Simon a retributive look in retaliation for the radio. He ordered a full English and Ayub, after some prodding, made do with a couple of pieces of toast and a cuppa.

Simon nodded in the vague direction of the world past the window. 'In those talks of yours, do you still condemn extremism?'

'As much as all the other isms you've given us; socialism, communism…maybe even Islamism.'

'As well as spreading democracy, human rights. Everything that stops people like the extremists putting us back into the Stone Age,' rebutted Simon.

Ayub leant over the table and lowered his voice. 'As you know, I've never threatened anyone, nor has anyone else I know. We don't do that or condone it but, again, it's a bit rich. You've declared the whole word as a battle zone and you can go in and kill people with drones, or special forces, anywhere…Somalia, Yemen, Pakistan, Iraq. Hundreds of thousands of lives wrecked, and yet when just one idiot does something stupid you want all of our heads.'

'Ah, and here was I wanting a pleasant cup of tea and chit-chat, not a litany of Western sins and how we're to blame for everything from Eve eating that damn apple onwards.'

Ayub saw Simon's smug satisfaction at his reference and thought how strange it was to live among people with no concept of sin, with no notion of the sacred; no idea of its demanding burden, carrying none of its brought humility and salutary guidance; that, just because you do not believe in it, it does not mean you do not bear any.

'You don't want our condemnation, you just want us prostrate, controlling how we respond and react to everything. No matter how many statements we make, and bleat, and cry, it's never enough.'

Simon looked at Ayub as if expecting more. Ayub returned the stare, eyeballing Simon. After a long pause Ayub said, 'We can sit here and be silent as long as you want. I don't find it uncomfortable. It's really just a crap journalistic trick to try and get more out of someone. If you have questions ask them, or stop wasting my time.'

Simon said, 'I don't want your head bowed but it would be good to see anger at them, not only at us. Large unsolicited demos would make us less suspicious. And all your talks… What's the point of your circle? At some point you have to assimilate to Western norms? Not always get out of control, like the protests about the Danish cartoons. Look at what happened next…'

Ayub picked up a fork and jabbed it in Simon's direction. 'I hate what happened in France but the cartoons were different. That wasn't an exercise in free speech, it was a statement of power. Some jumped-up guy saying to us, a minority that is already being hammered, "Hey, you will abide by our rules whether you like it or not." No conversation. "We will dictate to you." And a bunch of us, saying, "This isn't 100 years ago when the conversation was one-sided." See their PM now, kissing the backside of Arabs they hate but whose investment they need.'

Ayub was in no doubt that press-attacks on his community were acts of violence. As much as a slap in the face, they were attacks on people without funding, status, or elected power. And that was what he felt the cartoon demos were, a response to that violence. Telling Europe that, now, you have limits on behaviour, not just us. Europeans wanted the freedom to shout 'fire' in a crowded building that wasn't theirs. They were atheists who wanted to create a world in their own image.

Ayub studied Simon for a response, but saw a man who was just grinding through the gears, going through the motions. Simon looked tired. When they first encountered each other, a decade and a half before, he used to have the air of a proper boy scout, like out of the Enid Blyton books Ayub used to read. Someone who went on toothsome adventures, with their exotic jars of potted meat, hard-boiled eggs, and lashings and lashings of lemonade. Now he resembled someone who had slept uncomfortably in the office, had it tough at home, and didn't even have the recompense of being the big-man at work.

Ayub leant over the table again. 'Simon, why all this intrusion with people like me? I've made my choices. I'm not a burden. I don't kick up a fuss. But that's not enough. You want an act of complete self-abnegation. All you have destroyed is a bunch of people coming together to discuss issues. Now they'll be scared to talk, so everything will fester, and problems be repressed until they become bigger, or some fall into bad groups, or look at the Internet. You should listen to me and think. I'm giving you the best type of intelligence-gathering. I'm giving you understanding.'

Simon put down his menu card and placed both cuff-linked arms on the table, one folded over the other. 'We think about things very carefully. We have doubt.'

Ayub noted Simon's sleeves, that some of the cufflink's silver acrylic paint was peeling off to reveal a base plastic. Ayub found it hard to take that a jumped up civil servant had such power over him. A self-appointed pharisee. 'Ha. Doubt. That old thing. You think it makes you human. It's up there with "Let's have a debate." A way of nullifying opposition. How does it go? "I have doubts, and so should you. I listen to you. That should give you pause for thought and keep you happy." But, in the end, what's the difference between a politician who doubts and one who doesn't? Nothing. Same result. They still bomb. Give me two presidents: both send drones and kill faceless, unknown people far away from their leather chair in a cushy office. The President who is assured gets vilified. The President who says he thought a lot about it and has doubts, maybe he gets a Nobel prize, instead. Doubts...'

'Now, now, Ayub, all this talk about killing. Especially when it's likely that only one of us has, and it's not me,' said Simon, with a sly look of contentment.

Ayub's lips opened in response but were thwarted by the returning waitress, so he pulled back his fork and placed his hands on his lap. She smiled at Ayub, put down his plate, and then almost dropped Simon's onto the table with circling vibrations. Once his plate stopped trembling Simon made a massive inhalation and a show of breathing in the aroma of his bacon rashers. He wafted a hand, wheeling it and trying to take in more, while dispersing the hoggish odour. 'Mmmm, marvellous, some proper English scran.'

Ayub couldn't stop his face turning at the smell. 'You're a proper wind-up merchant, you know that? For your information, this cafe is halal and that's turkey bacon. Low quality meat-ends that will probably give you cancer but, yes, I still find the smell distasteful. Happy?'

'Well, really, in this job I have to amuse myself, somehow. People look at me like some Torquemada but, trust me, behind the scenes it's more like working for the Inland Revenue. You do have to work for your kicks in this job.' Simon started cutting into his rashers and sausage, taking them down with large gulps, hardly bothering to chew, and punctuated his speech by pointing his knife at Ayub. 'You know it must be frustrating, a man of your capability just working away in his father's grocer's. You've got a good education and...what is it...three languages you are fluent in? If you weren't so obsessed with this Islam thing, maybe you could have been somebody. Interest. Free mixing. All these prohibitions...you just make yourself poor.'

'A big somebody like you? You think if I'd changed, I could be sitting where you are. My languages, my knowledge is useless here?'

'It may surprise you, Ayub, but we are sitting in the same place.'

'It sure looks that way from the outside, doesn't it?'

Ayub had to look down every time Simon opened his mouth. *We are a civilised country*, he thought, *we did have a publicly funded healthcare, so surely he could get those bloody disgusting teeth fixed.* They looked worse every time they met. In a way, they had grown up and were now growing old together. In a kind of stasis, not quite knowing each other, a grudging respect mixed with a sliver of disgust. 'My mother became ill. My father struggled to work, so I had to chip-in, early on. That's life, and I *am* somebody. Somebody to someone. Being a working man isn't a punishment.'

'I checked your internet connection, too. You don't even look at porn, which is a bit odd. You would be amazed how many pious Muslims, Christians, or saffron-robed Buddhist monks like a bit of five-knuckle shuffle before browsing the latest deals on Amazon.' Simon demonstrated by curling his right hand and jerking it up and down. He then allowed his words to settle as he mopped up some yellow drip from his eggs and added, 'You could move more towards the Gandhi side of things but I actually think you're a good role model to the kids at your circle.'

That wasn't a wind-up attempt. That was him. People like him always called on others to produce Mandelas and Gandhis, while lauding Churchills and Andrew Jacksons. Ayub laughed. 'And what would you know about what's needed in their lives? I always wonder what you actually see through your eyes. I'm not sure you understand anything. Honestly, you probably think that they're walking down the street, see a wonderbra advert and next thing decide to blow themselves up.'

Simon sighed, looking Ayub over. 'I really don't care what they're thinking, only how to stop their violence. Some of the ones who have made it abroad are truly moronic. They text each other about getting loo paper and Nutella and video games while planning murder. I don't understand.'

'You can't have it both ways, be scathing of them and also say they're an existential threat to the country. The kids I see – the ones I try to talk to – they have it hard. In my day we could learn and speak in private. And really it was without the responsibility of having to actually change anything. Nowadays, everything is monitored and up for criticism. You're a target and object of vilification, and at the same time expected to take the brunt of responsibility for building bridges between communities.' Ayub rubbed his bottom lip to indicate to Simon that he had some milky residue hanging from his mouth, and chucked over a bunch of napkins from his tray.

'They can be dumb, but still dangerous.'

The cafe lit up briefly as something greasy blazed on the cafe's main griddle. Ayub saw the flames shoot up as the cook rushed to manage the frying load. He wished to tell the man in front of him that they were the children of partition, colonialism, immigration, racism, and terrorism. That every part of them was formed in an act of violence whether physical or verbal, over generations. That they lived in constant convulsions of which glib Little Englanders like Simon, with their parochial view of humanity, had absolutely no comprehension. But it was pointless. It was like trying to use a shallow breath to blow down a brick wall.

This society only sympathised, it only listened, if it had made a great sin against your people, neutralised you as an apparent threat. Until then it pressured and wore you down until you collapsed. Just like with the invasion of countries, they hit you and justified intervention with the issue of the day: insurgency, then the plight of women, then drugs. Each time succeeding in making that problem even worse. Focusing on one errant thread that, when pulled away in isolation, unravelled everything else.

When your people ceased to be a threat, or simply ceased to be, they could enjoy pitying you. They could show sorrow in retrospect. The Left would highlight your strained forgotten-voices to no avail, serving only to sap away at your passions. The Right would clap, using it as a sign of their culture's largesse, carry-on doing whatever they wanted and then cuff you. The Left liked you as a pet victim, the Right as a rabid threat. The Left defanged you for the Right to dominate. Society was a giant game of good cop, bad cop. Ayub was not interested in either. He was not interested in their game or their caged limitations. *Please, just let me be.*

In the background, interspersed with the sound of raw meat sizzling, cracked eggs frying, and steam hissing from the coffee machine, the radio provided a soundtrack to their conversation. A debate was being held about young girls in the North who had been sexually abused by Pakistani men. People rang in to excoriate the community, saying they were in denial over sexism and misogyny, and sheltered the abusers. Others on the defensive said that the flurry of BBC presenters and MPs caught abusing women and children were never talked of as a 'white' issue.

Ayub cupped his ear. 'Listen to that debate. Yet another with us as the football. You and me have major differences but we can all agree that those men are animals, yet the police said they went softly because of race. We didn't ask for that. You don't hesitate to stop us, target us, when it comes to terrorism, but when it comes to homeless white girls, or black kids stabbing each other, you don't care. Easier to put the blame on people like me, though?'

'Again, Ayub, that's PC Plod, nothing to do with me. But go ahead, use me as a punchbag. You're lively today.'

'No, you guys are the fake yellowcake from Nigeria, the dodgy dossier on WMD in Iraq. Guantanamo, Iraq, Afghanistan, Abu Ghraib, you are the thousands of renditions. You're all no better. At the height of your civilisation, you failed. You can't compare it to some guy on a council estate...'

Simon banged a clenched fist on the table. 'These are trying issues and circumstance. Our intentions are good. We're only human...'

'So are we.'

Simon and Ayub fell silent, auditing each other.

Simon's plate was empty and Ayub used an errant piece of charred toast to swab some remnants of butter off his own. The waitress came and collected their plates and Simon proceeded to order two teas, this time not bothering to ask Ayub.

'You've got a lot on your mind today. All this European stuff will blow over. Always does.'

'I have a lot on my mind everyday.'

For a moment Simon looked almost human. His face slackened and the soft wrinkles around his eyes flexed. 'I'm a government employee. I won't apologise for defending my country. I make choices everyday that are difficult. Sometimes, you should see that too. You should see what I see. I'm not your enemy.'

'You push the kids outside, treat them like scum, and soon enough people are hopeless enough, and give up, and play-up to it. You don't understand the world we live in, but we do. You should encourage our voices even if you discard the bodies, otherwise you'll just stare at your bloody screens thinking none of it makes sense.'

'Again I don't understand, but then you're mistaking me for Oprah. It's not my job to care or feel. My job is security. As far as who started all of this, and the sorrows of the world, I haven't

233

a clue. Again, chicken or egg – not my concern. And what my current concern is, is to keep an eye on you and your associates and to make sure that you're quiet while the latest events run their course. I'm doing you a favour.'

The tea arrived, and a glass ramekin of sugar cubes came with it. Simon picked the sugar and held it up, squinting in study. 'Ooh, not sachets. This part of the world is up-and-coming, hey?'

Ayub watched-on as Simon played with the brown cubes, using his fingers to push them one way then another. As if he was undertaking a thorough examination of a strange substance.

'Maybe they were better off in packets, without you placing your manky hands all over them.'

Simon look abashed, stopped playing, and plonked a couple of white cubes into his tea. They made a plop as they hit the hot liquid and caused concentric circles that radiated outwards.

Simon took a sip, gave out a satisfied sigh and leaned back. 'Ayub, don't you get sick of all this bloody moralising. It's oh so tiring. There are more subtle ways to get your point across.'

'Tiring? I'm disturbing your sense of decorum, am I? Emotion and earnestness too vulgar for you? We live in a time when someone thinks it's ok to travel from here and cut a head off on YouTube. On the other side, people disappear into a legal black hole, imprisoned. Both are people that look and sound like me. There's nothing subtle or sophisticated about what's happening to us…maybe it's time for a bit of moralising.'

Ayub's voice had raised and people were looking at them. Simon shook his head, indicating for Ayub to calm it down.

'I just have a problem with organised religion. The carrot-and-stick approach to it all.'

Hushed, Ayub said, 'Well, doesn't look like it's even good at that. Anyway, what's your alternative? Interest rates and CCTV?'

The Study Circle

'Ok, ok, enough, Ayub. Enough. We need to tone it down on the preaching. Times have changed and we won't allow it.'

'Allow it? Be careful, don't you represent my elected government?'

'Now it's your turn to stop winding me up, Ayub. Things are different. You need to be more like...' Simon waved a hand around the cafe '...everyone else. Here, I have something that might be helpful.'

Simon took a book out of his satchel, placed in on the table and slid it towards Ayub. 'It's worth a read, it helped me out too.'

Ayub was worried that Simon had turned Jehovah Witness and was giving him a copy of Watchtower, but then he scanned the front: *The English* by Jeremy Paxman, and thought, *You cheeky bloody bastard.*

Their conversations always came close to having to justify their existence. Ayub didn't need Simon's approval for that. He didn't need to explain his right to be. He would not do that. *I'm not the strange one*, thought Ayub, *you are.*

Ayub smiled. 'Why thank you Simon. You know, I think people in power truly believe it's a choice, between Islam, and going to the Opera, quoting Shakespeare and taking high tea. No, it's a choice between Islam and what you've done to the rest of the working class. They have nothing. You've taken it all. You use benefits as bribery so they don't riot, to keep them out of your view and then batter them for it. Reduced to fighting for scraps while their MPs pig-out on expenses.'

'That's ridiculous, Ayub. You're better than that. Come on.'

Ayub picked up a cube of white sugar between a thumb and forefinger and flicked it away. 'You think that we landed in Mary Poppins-country, where people sing about a spoonful of sugar, and dance. What we landed in was more like Lord of the Flies. You have to struggle and hustle, and develop an aggression, to survive. An aggression that you guys have made systemic.'

Simon's pallor turned a rustic cherry. 'I've had enough. You're being very unreasonable, today. I admit I'm a very shallow person, Ayub, and I get as pissed-off as the next man, but we have law, tolerance, democracy, free press. A standard of living that the world dreams of. All that, we created. Institutions that are worth defending.'

'All of which are there more for some, than for others.'

'Will you stop?'

'No.'

'We get new laws and powers everyday. Someday, to my regret, you might get banged-up for it. I'm trying to help. We're a bomb away from internment. What do you teach, that's worth that?'

'Piety, compassion, and duty.'

Simon let out an immense shredded roar of laughter, tea dripping from his mouth as his body convulsed. He wiped his smeared mouth with a sleeve. This time the rest of the cafe turned their heads to stare at him. 'That's the real problem. You're a bunch of romantics. The mortal world will always disappoint you.'

Ayub sat impassive, letting Simon's laughter wash over him.

'Who knows what the results are of what we do with our lives. Whatever happens in your life, don't you want to come to work and feel like you have made a difference? Ultimately, I don't think you do make a difference. You just stick plasters on wounds – it's teachers that heal the wounds. That's why I won't stop.'

Simon started tapping the fingers of his right hand, one by one, getting faster, as Ayub talked, until it was a roll. He suddenly stopped and said, 'That's all very interesting and all remarkably besides the point. Maybe you should start a political party, Ayub, or better still get yourself up to Speakers' Corner and rant at the tourists in Hyde Park. I'm only interested in my job, which is to protect the security of this country. That means disrupting networks of groups of potentially violent people.'

'And, like I said, neither me nor anyone I know is, or wants to be, violent. Ultimately, we like being Muslim. And somehow that's incomprehensible to you. If you think banging-me up is going to change anything then you're kidding yourself. Whether you go home to your wife and kids, or some bedsit, on a civil service wage, you're lying to yourself.'

Ayub looked at Simon's now humourless face. Simon had previously mentioned a family. Ayub thought it had been made up, his references to them had faded as time went on, but with Simon's increasingly forlorn attitude, he knew he had hit a raw spot.

'Keep your nose clean, or you'll be in big trouble. Anything dodgy, like going near that march coming up…'

'Or what? What are you actually going to do, Simon?'

Simon picked a brown cube of sugar, pinching and crushing it between two digits until it lost shape, crumbling into granular pieces. He then rubbed those two digits together so there was no residue on his hands. Simon lent over and, in a hushed tone, whispered licks of wet spittle into one of Ayub's ears. 'What is the biblical equivalent of your name? Job, isn't it? The most tested one. You know. You're a good man. A good 'good man'. An honourable man. And I enjoy our conversations. But know this. When it's four am and your front door is smashed in, when your mother is crying and your father is wheezing for his heart-medication as he has a panic attack, and any other family is cowering in a corner, when your head is pinned to the floor – when that happens, do not say I did not warn you.'

Ayub swallowed and bit at his lower lip. 'You have rules.'

'Of course, I'm not the man from Spectre.' Simon rearranged his cufflinks and straightened his neck. 'But Ayub, you're right about systems. Once a decree, their will, comes from on-high, it spreads throughout and can't be stopped. There are no rules.'

Ayub knew that's why Simon had let him go on, and vent. Because what Ayub said didn't matter and Simon knew that. He could talk and talk, and express and be impassioned. He could pour out his soul in a neverending stream, and it wouldn't change a thing. Simon had the privilege of silence, and the assured inviolability of his own thoughts. Simon was a representative of his, Ayub's, government, yet was not answerable to him. Because of people like Simon you needed a permit to remain kind in this country, to think good thoughts of your neighbour. But, to acquire one, you needed to fill forms in triplicate, navigate through indecipherable legalese, and surmount the use of invisible ink.

Ayub clenched a remaining fork on the Formica table, looking at the three, sharp, elongated tines. Lives with no consequence, existences without repercussion. And there begins the temptation to reach out and make them feel, change them so that they understand, impress on them your reality. But Ayub freed his hand and pushed the fork away, as he knew that that was a warping and twisting rabbit's hole, from which you could never return. That was the beginning of madness.

'Maybe that's so, but I have rules. Thank you for the book.'

17.

Sitting on the steel table, Ishaq placed three fingers on his upper arm to test its throbbing. He placed more relieving compression on the pressure dressing and padded wrap. Once Marwane had helped him into A&E the triaging nurse had rushed him through, more concerned by the fact that he wasn't responding well to simple questions rather than the sight of blood.

Once satisfied they sat him in a curtained area, waiting for an hour. Between the gaps of furrowed curtains he saw other patients being wheeled past. An old man was trolleyed-in and placed in the section beside. Ishaq caught a glimpse of blighted, swollen, eyes that started red at the base but ended in fungal mounds of black. Ishaq watched as the man's white hairs, on an even paler chest, poked up then retracted. An attendant closed his curtain, but the man's breathing accompanied Ishaq's thoughts, a syrupy hoarseness that peaked and troughed.

They moved Ishaq to his current room where they stuck two drips into him, one in each elbow. One took blood, and Ishaq looked on as red essence looped upwards, sucked out as through a straw. The other elbow held a cannula that put fluids back in. He was told that they needed some time to take tests and his blood count.

Minute by minute he started to feel better, his head and vision was clearing. His breathing was stronger. He caught sight of himself in a full-length mirror. Sallow skin, his eyes drooped and sunken. A pathetic sight. He looked away.

'I'm Doctor Faisal, and I'll be dealing with you.' The doctor had a strong accent and friendly eyes. He bore a large wiry beard and a zabiba or 'raisin', a darkened patch of hardened skin on his forehead that showed where he prostrated during prayer. 'You've had a bit of a scare tonight.'

Ishaq was unsure whether this was a statement or an inquiry so just nodded, thinking a silent rebuttal would deflect any further inquest.

'So what exactly happened here?' insisted the doctor.

'I was messing about with a friend and I tripped over and cut myself on a chucked beer bottle. It was a bit freakish.' Ishaq hoped that a slightly trenchant tone would convey that he knew how pathetic an answer this was but also that he did not want to engage further.

The doctor smiled. 'Must have been a very long, straight, and sharp broken bottle, and you must have landed right on top...' He stared at Ishaq for a reaction. 'You know I should report this?'

'It's all under control, it was just an accident. I'm near my finals at Uni, so I can't afford any hassle.'

The doctor appraised Ishaq, looking over his tracksuit and face. 'Hmm Hmm, well, you're lucky. The police have their hands full at the moment. As we have, too, with everything that's happening. Lots of stupid people hurting each other. Where are you from?'

'The Estate.'

'No, I mean where are you originally from?'

'London.'

Still not satisfied, the doctor consulted his notes.

'The Estate? That's rough, I heard there were raids there last month. Boys. Your lot.'

'There's always something going on. And it's not my lot.'

'The police said that they have evidence of them buying-up chemicals.'

Seriously give me a break. Ishaq's shoulders dipped and his body buckled slightly. 'They are not my lot. I don't know anything about it.'

Ishaq heard a sharp scream from outside the door. The tannoy sounded soon after: *DOCTOR TO RESUS.* The doctor grabbed his stethoscope and rushed out of the door. Ishaq was left alone once again. He still had a pulse oximeter on a finger and leads on his chest. For amusement he studied the monitor beside him. The numbers, high and low, were incomprehensible but the lines and waves of his heart rate were fascinating: red, green, and blue pulses, that pinged up and down like in a video game. Ishaq first held his breath and then, after a moment, panted rapidly, testing to see if he could make the display change, but had to stop after once again feeling faint.

He thought about Mujahid, still confused by his behaviour. He remembered one of the last circles that Mujahid had attended. Mujahid would always go on and on about Islam's golden history and how everything was perfect in those halcyon days, snatching random names from history as evidence.

Mujahid had said, 'We should be be proud, and respect our heritage. Gain some dignity from the achievements of people with our beliefs who came before us. Our societies. I was reading how we invented the zero, we should be proud.'

He remembered joking and throwing the arguments back. It seemed so light-hearted but, looking back, it wasn't. There was something fundamental at stake. Deep-seated ways of looking at the world that were at odds.

'I read too, Mujahid. Indians and Hindus can claim to have invented that too, and people like al-Kindi brought it over. I'm not saying that what happened back then wasn't amazing, like ibn Hatham creating the scientific method…'

'See, Ayub. The boy is disrespectful,' Mujahid had said, kissing his teeth.

Marwane had laughed as usual. 'Mic drop.Don't mess with Ishaq, boy.'

Ayub had tried to make a soft, smiling intervention, 'Yes, the West would like to believe they invented everything and, yes, we should talk about it and learn this history ourselves, and make sure it's not forgotten or discarded, but I'm not sure we should link it to anything deeper.'

Ishaq said, 'See, Mujahid, the Greeks made amazing breakthroughs and they worshipped multiple idols. Isaac Newton was an extremist Christian nut, yet that didn't stop him being a genius, scientifically.' Ishaq remembered the feeling of showing-off, that he was pushing it too far. 'Arabs use it for nationalism, which is a joke, too, when half of the famous guys like Al-Khwarizmi, the algebra guy, and ibn Hayyan, the chemistry one, were Persian. Just like they go on about Saladin and forget he was Kurdish.'

Ishaq had shown him up, but still, he didn't deserve being here in this disinfected room. He saw that old scene as through a mist, time blurred and replayed. Speech sounded low-pitched and elongated. He remembered Marwane's chuckles and Mujahid's abashed look around, before a silent withdrawal. There was still some comfort in harking back to that past.

The doctor returned.

'I thought you had forgotten about me.'

'Sorry about that. We are really understaffed. I'm a locum myself. They like getting foreigners like me in. We are disposable. You can easily blame us if anything goes wrong. Ha, ha.'

'Was it the old man? What happened?'

'Why do you want to know what happened? What does it matter to you?' The doctor took off the pressure pad and examined the clotted wound. He took a swab and some iodine and started to cleanse the area. He then relented to Ishaq's obvious curiosity 'He died.'

Ishaq wondered about what kind of life the man had lived and whether he had family. He thought of how little we knew of our end and, in our finality, how death was the absolute equaliser.

As if reading his thoughts, the doctor said, 'You shouldn't be so morbid. It ends for all of us, sometime. But not yet for a young man like you, not tonight.'

The doctor consulted his notes and checked the monitor. Assured, he took the leads off Ishaq. Talking his way through the procedure, he took a syringe with some local anaesthetic and injected some either side of the wound.

'Ok, we have to wait a few minutes for the anaesthetic to kick in. Ishaq? That's a strong name. A prophet's name. Ishaq, Yaqoob, Ibrahim. Do you know where I am from?'

'Egypt.'

The doctor smiled, tickled and pleased by the correct answer. 'How do you know?'

Ishaq looked at the much older man. The dome of his head shining, but cosseted by greying and white bolsters of hair. 'Your accent, a guess from the way you look and, I heard in the corridor, you sometimes pronounce 'j' as 'g'.'

'Ah, so you are familiar with Arabs? And your parents are from…?'

Ishaq was now feeling relaxed, brain-fog lifting, so submitted to the inevitable. He was used to the interest from English people who lived outside London, and co-religionists who were overly-familiar. 'Pakistan. They're from Pakistan.'

'Good. Good.' The doctor's tone lowered and he peeked around, even though the room was empty. 'By the way, you're right not to trust the police, they make things up all the time.'

The Doctor was warming to this conversation. First the distrust, then a sudden rush into confidence and now he was his co-conspirator in idle discussion. Ishaq nodded timidly, forcing a smile. The Doctor carried on stitching and talking, talking and stitching. Ishaq wanted to ask him to stop the chat and concentrate on the task at hand but thought better of it as he looked at latex-gloved hands sewing the wound, metal forceps in one, to hold his mutilated skin together, and a curved needle with nylon thread in the other.

'Ok…so will I get a scar?'

'Oh, yes, but it's a pretty clean cut. You might get away with a faint line,' the doctor said, as he smiled like someone hoping something away in the face of incontrovertible proof.

The doctor examined the sutures once again, looking at them intently, rubbing his forehead.

'Whoever did this likes jokes, too, I think. Or maybe the cinema.'

'Why do you say that?'

'Well, look at the cut. It's marked like a Z. Have you been fighting with Zorro?'

Ishaq took a look at the railroad of stitches, that turned one way then another. It did look strikingly like a Z. But did he really mean to cut him like that? Ishaq remembered his jokes about the spelling of 'Muslim Boyz', but he never told Mujahid. 'Well, maybe more like a wannabe Robin Hood.'

The doctor fetched a fresh dressing from a cupboard. 'Out of interest, those boys on the estate? Do you really believe that they were making and buying stuff to hurt people?'

'I don't know what to believe anymore.'

'I think it's all made up,' repeated the doctor.

Ishaq was exhausted. His brain felt muddled. The constant fluctuation between the compulsions of fight and flight, assessing friend or foe, was depleting. Conversations like this exacted a toll. Each time, the intrusion took a chunk, a slight bite, of you. And it didn't matter what the issue was, it was always somebody else's fault. The whole world thought themselves innocent, everyone thought they were doing their best while impotent in the face of the bigger picture, yet people still did bad things. Shit was still happening yet no one was to blame. How does any of it happen, if no one is ever to blame? No one was ever in error. Everyone was human. Everyone had flaws. Were we supposed to just give shrugs of the shoulder, be decent and accept that we were powerless, and get on with scratching along, fumbling in the dark, sitting, chatting and bemoaning, stewing in uncertainty, and be intimidated by complexity. And who did that leave? The only people who could rise above and break outside were kooks and extremists. People with surety and visions so clarifying, so dazzling, that they bleached out those things of the most importance: other people. It was not acceptable.

Ishaq took another look at himself in the mirror. He saw someone weak and subdued. A boy in a stupor. He decided to take charge of his features: rearrange them so that he had control.

Ishaq said, 'The thing is, we do have dodgy people among us. The thing with these conspiracies is that you can't prove them, one way or another.'

The doctor stopped and responded as if Ishaq had just made an accusation. 'I'm not into conspiracies. I'm a realist. I don't trust anything. You can't keep on denying all conspiracy theories, as so many are true. Just look on the Internet.'

Great. That wonderful invention, the Internet. Where every issue seemed so serious that in the end nothing was. Where spreading falsehood and abuse felt as substantial as throwing air.

'Yes, but…'

'If you send an email, or say certain words on the phone, do they track you?'

'Yes.'

'In Birmingham, did someone write a fake letter about Muslim schools, and did they once put traffic cameras around the whole community to check who was coming in and out?'

'Yea..'

'So what do we do when all the conspiracies are true?'

Ishaq shook his head. The doctor sounded like a more educated form of Mujahid. Even among men like this conspiracies spread. And he was right, what *do* you say when so many conspiracies are true? When paranoia is a sensible awareness?

Ishaq looked at the doctor and the room around him. Doctors and teachers were once the last position of trust in society. Now, it wasn't uncommon to hear about a doctor trying to bomb an airport. Now, it wasn't uncommon for academics in their ivory towers to debate torture. One Harvard law professor pontificated on how one could cause excruciating pain without lasting damage; he surmised that it was ok for sterile needles to be pushed under nails with agonizing force. Needles like the one the doctor had used, on people like Ishaq and everyone he loved. Now it was ok for your own university to spy on you.

'It's all a mess…but still…you have to try and live a life, right?'

'Maybe.' The doctor nodded, and seemed to take in and accept it. Ishaq was relieved. The doctor checked the cut a final time and, happy, he placed a bandage on it and then some padding, and covered it with a white dressing. Smiling, he handed Ishaq a leaflet. 'This will tell you how to look after the stitches and wound. Make sure they are clean and you don't get them wet. No scratching, as the irritation will make it worse. You can go to your GP and get the stitches taken out in a few days. Please keep out of trouble.'

He took off his latex gloves and shook Ishaq's hand. Ishaq walked to the seat where his shirt lay, now stiffened by flakes of blood. He put it back on, hoping Marwane had gone and fetched some new clothing. He gave one last look to the doctor, who was still speaking '....but these boys making that stuff and then storing it in that garage, I still think the police could have used a computer to change the image of their faces.'

Ishaq stared blankly at him in disbelief...and then it popped into his head, diverting his train of thought: the Z: the only people he could remember joking about it were Marwane...and Shams.

18.

As Shams climbed the stairs he passed an Arab couple. Immigrants. The man always had the saddest smile. Their English was halting, and sometimes they gave an obligating look as if wanting something more. They shared a faith but how could he explain his life to newcomers who were just grateful to be here. Even before they arrived his father's status had already been as a British Overseas citizen, one of the Empire's favoured.

On the balcony Shams looked down, checking which flats had doormats as he walked. When his mother was alive she used to say that you could tell the civilised peoples from this. Having somewhere to wipe away the dirt of the world. He made it home, dragging chained feet, his pinched back aching. He opened the door and entered the front room. As usual his father was sitting in his beaten leather Chesterfield, with the television on full blast. The neighbours never complained. They were too fearful of confrontation.

The Study Circle

He differed from Father, he liked turning the volume right down. He enjoyed seeing them mute, the roll-call of reporters, experts, and politicians. To see them miming like comics, as they tried to explain concepts, peoples, and struggles. To see them profess and feign influence. With the sound absent the pretence disappeared and it was the images that showed the stark truth of the matter, not the court scribes and actors. People who shouted too loud in outrage, when they were hated not for their freedom but that their freedom came at the expense of others, and they dare not acknowledge it.

'Where have you been?' His father stared straight into the blaring pictures.

Shams sat on the two-seater beside him. 'Just to see friends.'

'Friends.' Shams' father articulated the word with contempt. 'The same friends who got you into trouble the other day.'

Shams looked at his dad, still looking ahead, acknowledging great problems but never him. 'There was a mix up with the police and I was taken in.'

'And you didn't tell me? I had to hear this at the mosque from others. How embarrassing for me, your father.'

'I'm sorry, but it was nothing.'

'Nothing.' Shams' father reached over for the remote and changed the channel. On one a debate on segregation, on another the war in Syria, and on another the results of a drone strike on a wedding party in Pakistan. His father dropped the control, his limp hand releasing it and letting it fall.

Shams rubbed his forehead, trying to bring some life back and ease an oncoming headache. 'I don't want to discuss this again and again. Nothing happened.'

'You're nothing but trouble. Of course your sister, Shazia, was the good one, and she left.'

'Yea, so good that she never calls. I don't see her looking after you. What would you do if I wasn't here?' Shams raised his voice and was rewarded with a look from his father.

'That is up to God.'

'I'm tired. I'm going to sleep.'

Shams's father attempted a stern face, but that papyrus face looked weaker each day, dragged down, with sagging cabled wrinkles that had given up any pretence of support. 'You and those bloody boys. You call yourself Muslims. All you do is bring calamity.'

'Baba, they didn't do anything. It was all a mix up.'

'I don't believe it. We came to this country, worked hard, and your generation has wasted it, flushed it all down the toilet.'

'And don't I work hard? Don't I try to work hard? What do you want me to do? You want me to look after all of the family but then create my own life…I can't do both.'

Shams' father bent over in his chair to pick up the remote control. His arid skin agitating as he reached out slowly. Shams got up, picked up the control and handed it over. All the years had caught up with him. Where once he had been the giant of his childhood, Shams now saw a withered, scared old man.

At night his father would wake, dazed, in fear of the dark, and he would call. He would call out the names of his wife, his parents, and then his ancestors until, unheeded, he made a final mournful plea for Shams. He complained of dark spirits clawing at him, snatching at his feet, trying to drag him away. He heard windy howls of lament for lost civilisations. He saw hundreds and thousands of twisted limbs, shattered faces, flaking skin, chipped bone. He made choking gasps, talked of suffocating dreams of blood, bile, and phlegm. He feared his slumber as it no longer provided rest. Shams had sometimes taken to sleeping just outside in case he needed a glass of water, occasionally woken by a frozen cheek on a numbing door.

'We sacrificed everything for you. We hoped that you would have better lives than us, and your children even better. It breaks my heart…my head…Muslim countries a mess, here a mess. I'd like to turn on the television and ,when I see a bombing or shooting, I would like my first thought to be about the poor people and the suffering. But no it isn't. Instead…instead I'm thinking, "Please don't be a Muslim."'

His father pointed to the television, that showed fighting and explosions against some sweeping desert scene. 'Look here…every side fighting each other. All have beards and call on Allah. Just like you and your friends. This is the mess.'

Shams watched on as his father sat in that hateful chair day after day, shrivelling away. His father was a pious man who nearly lived in the mosque after retirement but had started attending prayers less and less. He saw as his father stayed lashed to the television, transfixed by the news. Syria, the West Bank, Kashmir, back home, here, everywhere, there was a tumescent chaos. Libya, Egypt, Iraq. Violence so overwhelming that it consumed even the passive onlooker. Each bombing, each bit of inter-fighting, every upheaval, chipped-away at his father's belief in his religion, his belief in people, and his belief in living. A porcelain soul fractured into pieces. Each time it took Shams all of his effort to gather his father. Each time he would display more cracks. The bloodshed and sheer brutality robbed him of all illusion, because it was people, that looked like him, harming others, who looked like him. He recognised their hearts and tongue. No imperial force, no oppressing power. And there was no safe place; the baying of the outside world had collapsed the walls between public and private. Everything living outside, lived within. He was forced to live all those distant battles within his own being. A never-ending punch in the gut.

'Muslim, muslim, muslim , I'm fed up of the word,' Shams' father muttered, as if to himself, tasting the syllables. Shams also rolled the word round in his mind to the point of semantic saturation. Picking at and kneading it until it lost any form, and lost any meaning, just a combination of ejected sounds.

Shams' father reproached him further, 'You people had everything. Peace…education…So much more than we had, and you've done nothing with it. We came here so you could have a better life, not wrap your head around with politics. This country has opportunity. Don't blame the country for a lack of opportunity.'

'It *had* opportunity. Now it's just decaying and drying up. All that humiliation, all that you and your friends put up with, and for what?'

Shams, tired and wrought, could not bite his tongue any more. 'Dad, the fact is that you came here for money. For cash. You left your parents, and brothers and sisters, and yet you ask of me what you never did. To look after you. And I do it. Out of duty. I can't do any more…'

'Don't you dare talk back to me in that way. I'm your father.' His father held a walking stick aloft; vibrations in the air followed the tremor in its guiding hand. They both knew it was an empty gesture and his father halted, lowering it. 'It was all for you children.'

'For us? So that we have bigger problems, that you did nothing to prepare us for.'

'So you blame me?'

'No, I don't blame anyone. It's no ones fault. Not you, not me. It's just the way it is. Coming here, you just saw the money and power, and were made small by it. You didn't grow here, you don't know the ins and outs of it like we do.' Shams' hands were apart, with the palms up, as if he were pleading. 'But it would be nice if you tried to understand…whatever I do, I can never please you. I've never been involved in crime. I've never taken drugs…been on benefits…I got as much education as I could and I'm stuck here. And it's still that's not enough.'

'You could have worked harder, got better grades like your friends. Like your sister.'

'That's all a lie, too. Even if you get the grades they look at the colour of your skin, or your funny name, or that you don't talk like them at their dinner party. Working your way up is a big fat lie. Overcoming adversity is a fairytale that you all believed. Like a story on that dumb TV you watch all day. It doesn't exist. The reality is that struggle is a constant. There's this background pressure day after day…It ain't gonna change, and that's what we need to deal with. You don't understand…'

Posh people loved stories of people facing adversity. Of overcoming it all. Of beating the most difficult obstacles that they never themselves faced. They loved how there could be a message in suffering, that it was a vessel for building character, that it could be beautiful. It made them feel good. It said the world was fairer than it really was, and they found that reassuring. But really it was a sinister judgement upon life, because its natural logical conclusion was that if you do not overcome outrageous odds then it's your fault. You just aren't trying hard enough. Ishaq and his dad were like those posh people.

Shams looked at the rolling news again. His father could not comprehend. Even if we say it's not us, the outside world did not believe. Shams refused to have them affect him like they affected the old man. They didn't feel that way, so why should he. Recently there had been a spate of lone wolf attacks on soldiers. Shams saw whole societies panic. How their leaders would eulogise and make gloried pronouncements invoking their highest ideals, all the while displaying shock at how this could happen. He watched their rituals, full pomp and ceremony, bathed in military regalia and drowning in flags. They would seek safety in simplicity and, in fright, hide from complexity. But their claim of innocence, that mantle of virtue, was poached from others. Their claims were offensive, their shock obnoxious. America, Australia, Canada, New Zealand. The myth of virgin lands, stolen, like jewels in the crown. They only showed bravery in surrendering the rights of others.

'No, I don't. I don't understand. I don't understand this,' his father jutted his chin towards the television, 'I don't understand your friends. I don't understand you.'

And I don't understand what's happened to you, Shams thought. He closed his eyes and rubbed them, half in the hope of seeing something different when they reopened. Father and son sat in communed silence transfixed by the screen, watching on as a thousand years of trust and civilisation was destroyed in savage convulsions. Slaughter, beheadings, executions and mass murder. All their good was being lost in a mountain of violence, it could no longer be seen through the fog of capricious men. They were bombing people out of the religion, refuting people into not caring, desensitising them so that they ended-up turning within and looking after only themselves. You didn't know what to think, what to feel. It was hard to keep up with who was killing who and for what. Children of a cultural revolution, they were destroying what we were and glorying in it, readying themselves for a phantom future.

'Shams, a lot of the time, strength is saying no to violence. Saying no, and getting on with your life.'

'But people think you are saying no because you are weak. You have to show your power first, so that saying no is seen as strength. It's the rule of the street. Of everywhere.'

'That's the rules of animals…the rules of the jungle.'

'There are no rules for people like me, Baba. We are learning from scratch. Security and getting on…all an illusion…it's all a lie, and you just believed it. How about if I want it to be different– to make my own way?'

Shams' father's hand massaged the crook of his walking stick. 'We had such high-hopes, Shams, such high hopes…'

'So did I Father…so did I.'

His father repeated himself, muttering. 'I wanted the best for you. For the family. I came here for a better life for you…better than we had…'

'It didn't happen.'

The old man took the stick, tried to lift himself and put his weight on it. Shams stood and helped his father up, guiding him. Once his father gathered momentum he pushed Shams' hand away. Shams watched as his father shuffled up the stairs. His father disappeared, ascending out of view, but Shams could hear the creaks as he climbed, and listened-on as the pulsing beats of steps came to a still with the shutting of a door.

19.

Shams spent day and night in a floating daze, his body held aloft on currents, his mind anaesthetised. He picked up his father's effects from the hospital, obtained his body's release, then a trip to Wandsworth Town Hall to get the death certificate, and at the same time called Muslim cemeteries to procure a burial place.

Traditional Muslim funerals take place as soon as possible and are a simple affair. A wash of the body, the saying of prayers by the community, a journey to the graveyard, and then a quick burial without complicated ceremony. The priority was for the arrangement to be a mercy to the soul of the departed, to ease and quicken their journey forward. Rather that than the burden of a busy speech-filled event, that was meant more for the catharsis of those that had been left behind.

The mosque's morgue had been been created from a small adjunct to the main building. It kept a few basic cold chambers for temporary storage and a sizeable basin, but the room was dominated by the steel washing table. Shams breathed in the dulling smell of unknown chemicals, closing his mouth to avoid taking in too much. He felt the walls pinch his ribs, and the low ceiling close in on his head. As he moved round the room he put a supporting hand on the table, drawing its clinical coolness to keep him alert.

The body arrived from the hospital. Shams and the mosque official gently lifted the body onto the table. Shams felt some shame as he struggled to lift his father's torso. His father's corpse was extremely heavy, a result of those last few years of ignoring all his loved ones' health warnings. His father had had a passion for gulab jamuns, the sweet and oily sweetmeat. Shams remembered him always slipping him some after work, and winking. A trusting code between them that he was not to tell Mum. When working he also used to surreptitiously discard his pack lunch, of lentils and a simple unbuttered chapatti, to indulge far too often in the fried chicken from next to his place of work, one of those that were called something implausibly southern American. He saw it as one of his few pleasures. Shams' mother would always find the branded red and white sachets of wet-wipes in his pockets, but no amount of encouragement or admonishment swayed him.

Shams expected to see a lifeless grey cadaver lying on the table but his father merely looked asleep. Not quite at peace but at rest. Helped, he removed his father's outer garments. They ensured that his private parts were not revealed by placing a large white cloth over the lower part of the body. Carefully, they washed the body with warm water, softly pressing the stomach to ensure that anything foul was expelled. Shams' hands flinched as they touched bare dead skin. He could not not shed tears. His swollen head ached, and at times he had to stop, but he contained himself, wishing to finish the washing with some dignity. At these times the Imam's assistant took over, or guided his hand, offering soft words of solace and comfort, reminding him that this is the final destination of all of mankind. As friends would say at times of calamity, *'Inna illahi wa inna ilayhi raji'oon'* – *'Surely we belong to God and to Him shall we return.'*

They proceeded to wash the body in the manner of ablutions before prayer, taking special care with the nose and mouth. They then washed his father's hair, still strong and full, grey with black flecks. They spread lightly scented oil over stiffened skin. After drying, they shrouded using three white cotton sheets. It was done.

They waited for duhur to finish before starting the janazah. The word had gone out, and the mosque was busy with extended family and the local community. Some had traditional words, some hugged him, some avoided his gaze, not knowing what to say or how to respond. Shams was grateful to all for their attendance. Some inappropriate comments were par for the course, and expected. One uncle told Shams how the family in Bangladesh would be angry that the remains had not been repatriated. All he could reply was that this was the example of our prophet. We are buried where we die.

The Imam led the prayer, standing by the middle of the body. The funeral prayer differed from normal daily prayers in that there was no bowing and prostration. Another defence against idolatry. Once finished the men set off for the burial plot. This graveyard had special dispensation for burial without a casket, so the shrouded corpse was taken out and placed in a dug out indent within the sidewall of the grave. The people who had followed the procession then proceeded to throw three handfuls of dirt into this final resting place. When they finished the gravediggers were left to complete the internment. He was gone.

Shams had always been told to remember death as a guide, a marker for life. The prophet, peace be upon him, said, *'At evening, do not expect to live till morning, at morning do not expect to live till evening. Take from your health for your illness and from your life for your death.'* He was not sure what to make of his father's life, now buried in cold, rain-sodden ground in a small island off northern Europe. He had been born in a hot country, surrounded by people who, though changeable, were warm and sociable, people who cared for him – gossipy people who were always in your face and overly-worried about your business. Sharing people who touched, and joked, and sang about the minutiae of their lives. He had migrated to a tough and lonely nation for a life of struggle, in the hope that his progeny would have a chance for something better, to be more successful. Shams did not understand what that better and more successful part meant, and he wondered whether his father had ever known. Life in Bangladesh was indeed a struggle under the arbitrary whims of the powerful, and this had been swapped for living with people who had little understanding of him, who never really reached out to each other, but who had order. The swap of constant existential worries for some semblance of material wellbeing. Maybe this was better, however hard it had been. All Shams knew is that, ultimately, his father had been a good parent, one he had been blessed to have. Shams only hoped and prayed he would also have a child that would wash his body and bury him when he died.

Shams shook the hands of, and hugged, the mourners who gathered around him. He struggled while watching the weeping of people who he did not recognise, who he did not know. He yearned for his opportunity to escape and mourn.

20.

Rain drilled into bloated ground, rupturing the earth and splashing mud on his trainers. He scanned the headstones blighted by creeping fungus and tried to imagine what it was like to be buried. They were corpses, but he couldn't help but imagine that they still felt the wet chill.

Ishaq shivered, waiting for the crowds to dissipate, not knowing what he would say. He felt a tremor down his spine as he saw, through steel bars, Shams exiting the cemetery. He saw how he clocked him. He saw how he quickly put his head down, in the pretence of not having seen him. Ishaq should have left this for another time but the action angered him more than if Shams had come up to him and chatted away as if nothing had happened.

He strode after Shams, brushing the mildewed railing with a hand, the metal spikes resonating to the impact of his fingers and dislodging raindrops that clung to his hand like glue. He put a hand on Shams, who tried to pull away, but Ishaq held his sopped jacket, forcing him to turn around.

'Look, Shams, I'm sorry for your loss. To Allah we belong and to him we return,' said Ishaq, knowing that he had to keep some calm and respect.

Shams finally acknowledged him but remained mute, and continued to walk away. Ishaq stepped after him and stopped him once again.

'Is that it? You aren't going to talk?'

'Do you think this is the right time, bruv? Look what happened.' Shams looked tired and fraught, the rain washing away any tears but not relieving the strain. His eyelids trembled and he could barely look Ishaq in the face.

'One thing I'm learning, Shams, is that there is never a good time. I'm truly sorry for what's happened, but you owe me.'

'No salaams, you just go straight in?'

His hurt was obvious but Ishaq was hurting too. 'According to your new friends people like me aren't Muslim, so my salaams aren't worth it. Anyway, not much peace about these days.'

'Look, I'm sorry. I didn't know he would do that,' said Shams, his voice giving way to something approaching sympathy.

'So you did hear?'

'Seriously, by Allah, I did not mean it to happen.'

'So it was just 'one of those things'?' Ishaq's throat gripped in a hunter's trap. 'You never mean anything to happen but you're still responsible. Don't you understand that you told lies. You made stuff up, just to save yourself. Always looking after number one, even if it's at other people's expense.'

'I didn't know what to do. Please let me be. We can talk tomorrow.' Shams moved but Ishaq had not loosened his grip. He made a feeble attempt to pull away but gave up all too easily, his papier-mâché arm flopping loosely, like it was unhinged.

Marwane walked up behind Ishaq, coming from the burial. He prised the two apart and gave Shams a hug and a kiss on the cheek, before holding his face in his palms.

'I had to ask around. You told people that Ishaq was spying and reporting on them. Why didn't you ask him to his face? Or ask me. You know I would have helped you.'

'I should have. I'm sorry.'

Ishaq couldn't understand what he was doing here. Marwane had elicited an apology but he could see there was no real understanding. What was he expecting to happen? His friend's father had died, yet Shams' shifting behaviour, his hiding, had caused this. Shams' capitulation, the lack of even some pathetic denial, upset him to the point that he nearly forgot why Shams was here at this graveyard. Nobody was ever culpable. Shams did not understand that Ishaq had a chance to do something more, even in a little way that could take them all forward and not just stagnate in this little pond. He just brought him down. Ishaq could not go forward with Shams holding onto his coat-tails .

'I'll tell you why you didn't do that,' Ishaq said. 'Because you're a coward. You crapped yourself and just chucked whoever was nearest under the bus, to save your pathetic backside.' The rain increased in volume, washing down their faces, battering them down into mulched mud. 'Man, what happened to you?'

Marwane said, 'Leave it out, Ishaq, he's got your point. Just listen to him for once.'

Ishaq raised his voice to overcome the pounding of the rain. 'No, I'm not leaving it. Shams, I'm tired of all of this crap. You have no clue how much discipline it takes to get as far as *you* like to keep talking-on about. You always need looking-after. Always need, and never give back. Maybe we've all been too soft on you; always being there for you has made you soft. How do we know that it isn't you who's been talking to the spooks and pigs about us?'

Shams thought about Mujahid. He didn't want to make things worse. 'I wouldn't do that.'

'I just don't know, Shams, you're flakey as hell. Don't know what to make of you.' Ishaq threw a dismissive hand and started to turn, but this time Shams stopped him.

'You don't understand. There's so much against me. I'm never given a chance. Can't you see that? You? Of all people?'

'It's the way it is. Just the way it is. And going on about it doesn't change a damn thing.' Shouting, Ishaq felt the dull pain on his upper arm reminding him. 'Shams, this is what we've been born into. No escaping, no point complaining, no point moaning. How about just getting on with it? You've always got an excuse ready for your latest screw-up, always something that makes us forgive you, but there are no excuses this time.' Ishaq only just managed to stop himself from saying, '*Not even your dad dying.*'

'Please...I need help...I'm in trouble.'

Ishaq flung a hand through the air in Shams' direction. 'Don't talk to me about trou...'

'C'mon, let him speak,' said Marwane.

Water formed creeks and crows-feet tributaries on Shams' cheeks. He poured out the story of the deal with Mujahid and the dog trainer, and how it had all gone wrong. He pleaded with them, asking them if they could they get Ayub to talk to Mujahid, or lend him some cash to pay-off the white guy.

Ishaq said, 'Is that everything? Are you telling me everything?'

Shams' eyes shot upward in thought but, after a pause, he said, 'Yes, that's all there is...please...help me.'

Ishaq looked back and forth between Marwane and Shams and shook his head in a slow arc, as if his head was tied by invisible restraints. He did not have the strength to break free.

'No, not this time...You know, Shams, I've got a chance to do something more with my life. Something small that can take our people forward, but we're always held back, held back by people like you. Hotheads. Shams, you bring me down, you bring us all down. One by one everyone gets involved, because you can't control your tongue or hand, and then you expect everyone else to bale you out.' Shams looked like an admonished child, his face sullen and red, droplets of rain and tears indistinguishable.

'I'm your brother and you won't help? You live in your head.'

Ishaq couldn't but laugh at Shams' audacity. 'Brother this, brother that – it's only 'brother' when it's convenient. You don't believe me, but I've always had your back. So I've got a bit of ice in my veins. Maybe it's the best way to be…selfish. Maybe what you call selfish is actually looking after yourself, and not being a burden on others.'

'And that's why no one likes you, Ishaq. You're just like them, all of them. That's why you have no friends. You're becoming a loner. Even Marwane thinks so, ain't that right?' Shams looked to Marwane who refused to corroborate his claim.

Ishaq looked at the boy before him, surrounded by the whipping of rain and crackle of leaves. 'That's right, I finally agree with you. Because everyone prefers a fuck-up. He's interesting. He makes them feel better about their own crap lives. He doesn't challenge people to raise their standards, or think. You're like a loveable pet that poops all over the place, except this time you've taken one dump too many.'

Bare trees bowed in the wind. Leaves slapped against their trousers. Some, green and lush, were nailed into the ground by rain, forced into a sludgy compost. A watchful bird on a gravestone took flight and sailed through the boys, the irregular flapping of its wings interrupting them.

'You know what I was thinking, just before I was lying there thinking I was dying?' said Ishaq. 'You know what was going through my mind? What *is* bravery? If I fought, and killed, and died, is that brave? If I just accept it, and hope he lets us off, is that wiser? What is wisdom, or bravery, or cowardice? Maybe surviving is the ultimate bravery? But then, I thought, you know it isn't the answer that's difficult, it's the whole bloody question. The question is always out of order, it's loaded, and there's never a right answer. It's the question that should never be posed.'

Shams looked at Ishaq, dumbed.

'Just go. I've got nothing more to say. We're done. Ask him for help for once,' Ishaq said, nodding towards Marwane.

Ishaq walked away, his silhouette disappearing into the storm. Shams looked to Marwane who said, 'Leave it a couple of days, Shams, let him calm down. I'll have a word with him.'

'I don't have a couple of days.'

'You're my brother. Always. But you do know you've done wrong? This is heavy stuff – you could have wrecked his life.'

'How about you? Just a little bit of cash.'

Marwane shook his head. 'I've gotta go. See what he's about. Keep your head down.'

Shams stared as the two left, not sure whether he was feeling too much or too little. His sister was at the Mosque, amongst the competing moans and wails of grieving women doing their part, playing the act. He walked there, refusing a lift, feet dragging a trail. Dirt stuck to his foot, in the grooves of his sole; unable to shake it off, he tried wiping it, yet only succeeding in muddying his already marked hand.

He met his sister and they went home together. She had been their father's favourite, even if she had refused to acknowledge it. Their own Ishaq. Once, she had gone out with their father to buy groceries. As he examined some purple aubergines, for the first time she saw rows of unyielding wrinkles collapsing on his once flawless neck. She came back in tears and was never the same again, and then she left. For years. Maybe she had known something that Shams didn't, that it was best to give up on sapping lost causes. No point having another's inevitability take you with them.

She had some posh office job somewhere and didn't come back often. Her partner and friends were all white. He sat on the stairs while they talked in the kitchen. Shams could see that he was fearful of what might happen, her white knight. But the guy had never talked to him, so what was his fear? Shams did not know; the guy did not know.

He listened as his sister talked and talked. As if this was a daytrip to real life. At the end, he asked, 'So when you're at some posh dinner table and they think you're some brave Muslim woman who escaped from oppressive men…do you ever defend us? Do you look at things through our eyes or do you just let them feel good, damning us through ignorance? Do you let them know how it really was?'

Uncertain, she paused, and then said, 'I wanted a different life. I wanted at a chance at something different.' Shams thought, *So did I*. He didn't bother pressing further or asking for help, and watched his sister leave.

Now Shams was alone.

21.

Ishaq rocked back and forth. Shouts penetrated the room, of a woman hanging washing and debating with a neighbour. Something of ordinary life when all was anything but. The unrest had spread across the city and intensified in outbursts of wanton damage. Politicians stood with any community leader they could ferret out and assured everyone of the strength of British values. But people, especially the young, were ignoring them and went roaming, looking for trouble, whatever kind that may be; the world had opened like one giant fracture, the streets muttering a febrile chant, and they were responding.

He assured his father he wouldn't go out, and here he was stranded at the circle while it was all happening out there. Ishaq traced the line of the cut up to his shoulder, back and forth, the sermon thrumming in the background .

'Brothers, we must look to the story of the Children of Israel. Allah, may he be glorified and exalted, sent them the great prophet

Musa and released them from bondage. However, was this enough to be free? They were free from the evils of the Firaun, that tyrant, the Pharaoh. However, once Allah rids us of dictators then the work has just begun. Their bodies were free, but their hearts and minds were still those of slaves, still in servitude to fear. They were accustomed to simple thoughts of immediate need. Those of shelter and sustenance. When this was at risk, even after their victory, they panicked and turned to familiar Egyptian ways of idolatry and rebelled against Musa and Allah. In a crisis, they did not have the courage to abandon familiar ways.'

The door creaked open, the hinges making a protracted squeal. Air scratched at attendees' faces as shuffled steps sounded. Then he entered. Marwane and Ishaq exchanged looks. Marwane lent over to whisper something to Ayub but was stopped by a signal from Ishaq. Standing above everyone, all eyes upon him, all mouths now in locked silence, Mujahid tried to find a gap. There was no space available but he sat down anyway, pushing in with his shoulders, nudging those to his left and right. The circle broke. His neighbours recoiled, moving away to give the intruder his own space. Ayub did not break his flow as the rippled disturbance spread, only targeting his eyes as if he were solely addressing the interloper.

'Slaves. They were truly slaves. For years, they continued to wander the desert, searching for the Promised Land. A generation died-out during that nomadic time. A time of constant change and uncertainty. They were replaced by people who had been born free and had the ability to create, people with the potential for renewal. This process, of the new replacing the old, was necessary. The servile can only react and destroy, they cannot build. They didn't have the fortitude to look at higher ideals, the wisdom needed to create a just society. One of mercy and forgiveness. Living for the moment, they lacked patience, sabr, to see what could be, what should be, and what needed to be.

'Maybe we are like those souls wandering the desert. Our minds still recovering from the colonial West. Although free, we get angry beyond just boundaries when threatened, or we cower and are unsure when left to our own devices. Allah knows best, but I say to you that we must always hold fast to the rope of Allah. Stay away from the doubtful and create just individuals. Be soft on each other, soft on the non-muslims. Work on purifying our hearts, firstly working on ourselves and then helping to create better communities. And remember the golden age of the Prophet sallahu alyhi wa salam, and his companions, and the early generations. They were the exemplars. And as Allah says in the Quran, "Those who give in times of both ease and hardship, those who control their rage and pardon other people. Allah loves the good-doers."'

As Ayub spoke, Mujahid examined each individual in turn. His face a smooth shield, yet displaying damning judgement, he started to clap, a slow dissonant slapping of flesh, his hands slipping and sliding across each other in lazy observance.

'You're doing the job of the West for them, sitting here, gossiping like women. They steal everything under our feet because people like you talk and don't do jack. You see that danger too late. Syria, Iraq, Afghanistan, all destroyed because of your 'forgiving' and 'mercy' and 'patience'. I don't see any real men here, let alone free men. You should be outside, defending our people, not huddled inside like cowards.'

Mujahid's eyes met Ishaq and his mouth curled . 'When we were strong people, strong on our way, everything flourished. We were the leaders in all the sciences, literature, mathematics, medicine, and education. But look at us now. Weak. Nothing.'

Again this romantic nostalgia. Ishaq recognized it for something that you had never known but believed could be. It was warm, you could slip it on and feel comfort, yet he did not trust it. Seductive half-truths wrapped in mythology and auspicious perception. A distraction from the here and now. Everyone had a version, from his assailant in front of him, to the doctor, to the white guy ranting at the conference, and Ishaq had had enough.

He clamped his eyes and slowly freed them. In a whisper, his voice skipping beats, he said, 'We've been through this before. That Golden Age stuff is crap. People like Ibn Rushd and Ibn Sina, nowadays some random would have found fault with them and tried to chop their head off. Someone like you.'

A couple of the brothers started laughing, not aware of what was taking place in front of them. One said, 'Bruv, that's so true.'

Mujahid quelled the laughter by turning to the new voice with his own smirk. A smile that warned and suffocated.

'I don't know who that is, but maybe they deserved it. Sometimes you have to send messages. Like when an oppressed people riot. Because a judicious use of violence can get attention. Messages. You should know all about that, Ishaq.'

Ishaq could feel Mujahid's eyes burrowing into him. He raised his head and returned the focus, forcing himself to maintain a gnawing embrace.

'The trouble with violence is that it is normally unhinged. It snakes around like electric wire. Its head cut off. It jumps, pounces, and threatens all. It's not even in control of itself. Violence again, Mujahid. That's all you seem to know.' Ishaq's voice was shrill, contorted, his eyes swallowed his courage and cast themselves downwards.

'Nice words. You're good at words…going to that university where they brainwash you. All you learn there is misguidance. You get above yourself. We have nothing to learn there. And funny you use the word snake, though. You don't know anything about me because you've never taken the time. What do you know? You're a spoilt brat.'

'I may not know the A-Z of who you are but I know the Z, Mujahid. That's the only character I need to know. You would be funny if you weren't so dangerous.'

'Both of you, fear Allah,' Ayub said, intervening in this strange mesmeric dance. 'Do you think this is the way...'

Ishaq cut him short in a scream. 'And Ayub...you, Ayub... in a way, Mujahid is right. All you always do is produce words – the same words – while out there it is all happening and you don't have a clue. No. Bloody. Clue. We sit here week after week and nothing is solved, or really said. We're left to read between the lines and make our own way. Look what's happening on the streets right now.'

Ayub went still, looking older, tired, obsolete.

Mujahid shuffled forward to take the centre, nose slightly held high as if he had sniffed out Ayub's weakness. 'Brothers. Look at how little respect is here and how few answers. And the same goes for this system, in this country. This would not happen if we had our own state. This is a system for slaves. You have mortgages round everyone's necks, which forces them to work, forces them to be productive for the system. They can't get out otherwise they'll be homeless. They give enough free speech so people are relieved of complaints but a small group still dictates everything.' Mujahid banged his fist twice on the floor, his voice rising and filling the room with an augured grotesqueness. 'It's a beast, and a beast that demands more and more of a sacrifice. Soon the houses prices go sky high and the women are forced to go out and work. But the beast still needs feeding. It starts sucking the money skywards. It starts devouring any protections, anything good. Soon we will be back to children in poorhouses. They throw you enough rope to hang yourself in unpayable debt. This whole thing will eat itself as interest traps itself. Work harder and harder, get poorer and poorer. That's why we need Sharia. Not idle words.'

The words fell onto the gathering. Embers falling. They had a momentum that impressed or confused. In a few minds some marked, and caused pause, in others they crumbled with frailty.

But it was enough to cause a new uncertainty. A gap, a silence appeared, that poured over and no one was brave enough to pierce it.

'And what's your alternative?' Ayub's gentle whisper, returning a rhythm, waves of calm that pacified the room. He stayed Ishaq with a hand held forward. 'These takfiris – these people who decide who is acceptable or not – would you want them ruling over you? Such a little level of toleration that they live in fear of each other. They start killing each other. Sharia? It's not about chopping hands, and executing people willy-nilly, and picking on the weak. There is the welfare state, rules for economics, and governing in justice and mercy. People like you say they want Sharia but they mean they want control. Their own Sharia. They make the word meaningless. You can't be so rigid that you break backs. Is that what you mean by going outside, and being brave and protecting us? By causing further harm?'

Mujahid looked around, uncertain. Ayub's expectant face seemed to disturb him and all he could do was shake his head, as if at himself.

'But why are you here, Mujahid, after so long? Why have you come?'

Mujahid wiped his face with both hands. Drained eyes that softened as he looked at the faces around him. 'I've come to warn you. Warn you all that we have vipers in our nest…that before we *purify* ourselves, as you put it, we should cleanse our homes of vile traitors. This boy, this child here, is one. And maybe his friend Shams, who is stealing from me.'

Ishaq's voice was weak in comparison but he forged on. 'What are you on about? You're with the fairies. Ayub, this man cut me with a knife only a couple of days ago, he's unhinged and dangerous.'

The rest of the gathering passed whispers, still unsure what to make of the exchange. Marwane moved up next to Ishaq, to try and reassure him.

'I hardly touched him. Just a reminder. He has been consorting with the security services and passing on information,' said Mujahid, jabbing a finger at Ishaq. Mujahid stood, grasping in the direction of Ishaq, his eyes burning, any hesitation purged. 'He has fallen into error and needs to be punished. Maybe I got angry, but the sin is on the boy. I've got family.'

'I'm not passing info to anyone.' said Ishaq, his voice floating with a strange sterility. He looked around for support, but faces blanched away.

'Shut up. You've said enough.' said Mujahid.

'I don't know what he is talking about.' Ishaq took a large swallow, a distension of his neck that did not appease. He felt Marwane steady his shaking body.

'Sent by security services to entrap us. He's a viper. MI5 have been all over this estate, and why? I have been told that it was him, and it all makes sense. Why else would they be here?' Mujahid took another step forward, nearly over Ishaq. Everyone but Marwane had moved, afraid of what could happen.

'It wasn't me. Someone's telling you nonsense. I swear by God that I haven't done that.'

'Shut up or I'll hurt you again,' said Mujahid, his face scaffolded in iron.

'One more step and by Allah I will get up and stop you myself,' shouted Ayub, sadness mixed with wrath. Mujahid turned and saw an Ayub that had no gentility, no forgiveness.

'This is all to do with me. They are here because of me. Ishaq, leave us now. We will sort this between us,' Ayub said to Ishaq, who remained rooted. 'I said leave. I'll talk to you later at the mosque. Marwane, take him outside. Calm him down. Please Mujahid, sit.'

Marwane pulled Ishaq up and ushered him outside. He yanked him forward, Ishaq seemingly lost, his eyes elsewhere. Down the stairs and out of the block Marwane placed both hands on Ishaq, to take a look at him, but they were pushed away.

Marwane grabbed Ishaq again and pushed him against a wall.

'Ishaq what were you doing up there? The guy's dangerous. You should let the bros sort it out.'

'The bros sort it out. The bros sort it out?' Ishaq, his mouth curling. 'They can't sort themselves out. I'm not being lectured to by a guy…by a guy who cut me.'

'And attacking Ayub? You're going to spoil your rep amongst the community.'

'What community? I don't care anymore.'

Marwane shook his head. 'You're burning so many bridges, you're going to end up alone. Adrift.'

'Like with you. Like you've been useful, just standing there happy to do nothing.'

'See what I mean? I've got enough shame about what happened.'

Ishaq adjusted his jacket, wiping some dust off the back where he could reach and straightened it out. 'You cutting me off?'

'Of course not. Never. But I am advising you. For a while all you have been doing is having a go at others, just moaning and criticising. Have you got all the answers then?'

Ishaq mulled it all over. A lamppost stood tall at the edge of the block to their right, its light filtering through a bundle of satellite dishes. Antennae pointed to every section of the sky, searching for the orbit that would bring news from Asia or Africa or the Middle East. Shadows spread their ambit, boxing the boys in.

'No, but I have questions. So many.'

'Ishaq, you're not happy with the liberals, or the traditionalists, not with us, not with the kuffar. So who is right, just you?'

'No, Marwane, no. I'm the biggest idiot of all, because all of these people – here, there, everywhere – are so convinced they are up on the truth that they power through life. Secure in mini-kingdoms, acting, having their mistakes forgiven. No, I'm the biggest fool. Too educated for what I really am. Exposed to too much, for a life in which I'm never really going to leave this place…I know that…I don't need to be told.' Ishaq made a kick at a flattened tin and saw it skim down the road. He thought about how stupid he was, how arrogant it was to want something more; about the absurdity of dreams.

'And the MI5 stuff? You sure you don't know nothing?' asked Marwane.

Marwane's face betrayed some fear, which riled Ishaq even further. 'Do you honestly think I have a flippin' clue? Seriously?'

Ishaq looked at Marwane and for a brief moment thought about telling him about the Security Services at university. He followed Marwane in bowing his head. Marwane had his hands in his pockets while Ishaq scuffed the floor with a trainer.

'Alright, chill. I'm on your side,' said Marwane. 'Let's go.'

'Where?'

'To the masjid. We can wait for Ayub and get this all sorted.'

'Listen M, I'll sort it. I'll go. I don't need you there.'

Marwane's body tensed for a plea, but Ishaq gave him a hug and left him in the shadows, as he made his way out of the estate.

22.

*Truly in the body there is a morsel of flesh, which, if it be whole,
all the body is whole, and which, if it is diseased, all of it is diseased.
Truly, it is the heart.'*

Saying of the Prophet, pbuh - Sahih Bukhari

Police cars ramped up and down in posses with ambulances following. Blinking, he felt a fever, a rising heat as revolving red light cut his face. So many sirens wailing that they melded into one high-pitched tinnitus.

The Mosque used to be situated in an abandoned warehouse with a leaky corrugated roof. It had always been busy, but in this last decade it heaved under the weight of visitors. Sweltering in the summer and freezing in the winter, it was especially uncomfortable when worshipping through long Ramadan nights, when the community's souls gathered in unison for Tarawih. Ishaq, now sitting inside, recalled the fragrant smell of lentil soup that local Arabs made during that blessed month of revelation, how it satisfied, sating an empty body.

During distant Fridays the mosque overflowed with believers. Local streets inundated with cars parked at strange obtuse angles, and some discarded even more haphazardly. Far more perturbing for local residents was the sight of worshippers stopping, laying out their mats and prostrating. Local garage and postal workers, with short lunch breaks, taking a strategic approach to their prayers, added further bottlenecks. They refused to go in too far past the main entrance in case they ended up stuck trying to escape after prayer had concluded. The Imam would implore the congregation to leave their cars at home and be good neighbours. It was futile but, as usual, there were some who profited from the chaos. Traffic Wardens couldn't help their smiles as they congregated on the honeypot. On bonus schemes, they dealt out thick ticket wads every Friday, thinking of that XL hi-def telly.

After years of council inquiries and fundraising, planning permission was given for a multi-storey mosque on the site of the original warehouse. It didn't completely solve the parking problem. The mosque remained brimming, as the next generation started to come of age in abundance. However it did allay the fears of those behind shaking net curtains, translucent screens that were so sheer they gave the illusion of openness but in actuality blocked all visibility. The concern at illegal Islamic annexations on South London roads was placated.

A harmonious equilibrium had been reached, but that maturation, and then progression, led to a third transformative stage: the mosque disappeared. When a pig's carcass was dumped at the entrance, an ignorant attempt to defile, CCTV was installed. When a Muslim, however distant, carried out an atrocity, mosque telephones pinged with death threats. Non-muslims were then barred from visiting except in official groups. When a string of mosques were subject to arson attacks, the railings of this House of God grew higher. They shot upwards like vines in crenellated bunches, topped with arrowed tips, and grew so dense as to obscure. The mosque had gone from clanging visibility to being draped in a steel cloak of silence. And now the net curtains started agitating again, quivering in whispers about what happened inside.

This was a serene home for Ishaq. The one place where his mind felt clear and his heart did not feel heavy. A normal worshipper. Not under siege from endless talk about the future. Safe from overwrought Chicken Littles. He knelt on the floor, leaning forward, his back bent over like the bough of a tree, tremulous under duress from an imposing wind. Eyes closed, his mind discordant, he felt a sharp tapping pain as he tried to impose order on stalking thoughts.

Ishaq peered out through cut eyes. He saw the mosque inhabited by old men who spent all day here, growing beards, increasing their religiosity as penance for wasted youth, and who were waiting out the final act of their lives. Ishaq's father used to tell him about what some of these now feeble elders used to get up to in their youth. It was hard to reconcile the image, before him, with those that lay behind them in blurred senescence. Ishaq felt the real test was to be moral and god-fearing in your youth, when vigour and ambition coursed through your veins in convulsion and tumult. When desire clouded your judgement and beguiled your senses.

Not one could provide advice. He was as foreign to them as the country itself. Still, he held a deep love for those resting in their well-earned dotage, however vast the distance. At the time of the prophet, the mosque was a centre of social change. A vibrant place of consultation, a venue to settle disputes, a centre of radicalism where people were exhorted to look at their faults, within, and struggle to be their better selves. Now it was a place of chanting sermons, by robed Imams in languages the youth did not understand. In bygone times, these were once leaders, rising in resplendence as the best amongst them. Now they were imported from abroad. Modern clerics reduced to mendicants, asking for funds at the behest of nameless committees, to make ever larger domes and minarets that the people cared little for. Ritual and theatre entwined, worship reduced to esoteric liturgy.

Change did come, initially moving like a glacier, indomitable and incommunicable. The youth brought their new religion as a thawing recrudescence. This is why circles were set up in people's homes, where they could discuss freely, outside the strictures of mosque and prying stares, and those greedy ears.

Ishaq's eyes looked caved. He rubbed at them, trying to reintroduce some life and test their fragility. He thought about Mujahid, his refusal to listen. He thought about Shams. He couldn't understand why Shams had been so weak. He thought about their pain, and how easy it is to just succumb. You could do a lot with pain, you could wallow in it and drown, you can use it as fuel to drive you to greater heights, and you could also weaponise it. Make it something to beat others with. Indulge in a competition to prove who was at more risk, whose life was under the most duress.

Your own pain and hurts were special. Hardly contained, it was difficult to endure and still be open with others. In fact the grief of others was a threat, as it felt like their suffering diminished yours. It was easier to deny theirs. That was only human. Ishaq remembered seeing a TV debate between two famous Jewish writers discussing the latest invasion of Gaza, one for and one against. Both of them prefaced their arguments by stating how their parents died in concentration camps, so as to add credibility to their argument. In other conflicts, antagonists clinically swapped ghoulish numbers of how many children the other side had murdered. Pain used as a currency in decreasing trades of poverty.

He had to be honest with himself. He had to make an admission that, however much he had tried to block it out, he too felt pain. At university, on the street, via the internet and television, he was barricaded in, just like the mosque.

Constricted and attacked on all sides, betrayed by friends, and unsafe. He also had to admit that he desired, that he wanted much more than what the estate offered. Maybe to admit that wanting that much was a sin, or that aspiration was something for other people. Allah says in the Quran *Kun fayakun*, 'Be and it is'. He wills it so, and it happens. New creations, new realities. That is God's attribute alone, but aren't we made from clay? Can't we mould ourselves into something different, something that can rise above any given situation? Ishaq closed his eyes and leant over again to aid his thinking. He felt a hand on his back that made him shiver.

'Assalmu alaikum, I'm sorry. I didn't mean to make you jump.'

Looking around he saw Ayub, kneeling beside him with a look of concern. Ishaq watched as Ayub reached into a small pocket in his pristine white thobe. He pulled out a rollerball vial containing fluid that clung to the sides of the bottle. Ayub took off the cap and offered it to Ishaq. As was custom, Ishaq did not refuse and rolled it over his hands, proceeding to wipe the liquid over his clothing. A distinguished white musk, the oil's fresh clean tones spread over Ishaq, covering what was redolent of the day.

'A lot has happened lately,' said Ishaq.

'Yes, it has.'

'Why didn't you tell me about the spooks bothering you? We've sat there week after week listening to you.'

'I thought it was ancient history and I didn't want to make things worse.'

'I trusted you,' Ishaq said, observing Ayub through rheumy eyes.

'And you don't, now?'

Ishaq looked behind Ayub. The mosque thrummed with resonating murmurs, calls to the unseen that normally made Ishaq want to sit in a contemplative languor. He peeled back from Ayub onto his haunches and then set back cross-legged. 'What did you say to Mujahid?'

'I told him a few things and I told him to back-off. He can be controlled.'

'He's not in control of himself, so how can you control him? What happens now? It went too far.'

Ayub tended to his beard, grabbing at his chin, sliding down, and then starting from the top again. 'I don't know, Ishaq. I don't know what to do. We try to control everything, sort it out between ourselves, and it just makes things worse.'

'You can call the police?'

'And bringing in outsiders will make things even worse. I know a man...men... that can bring absolute disaster with them.' Ayub wrung his hands. 'One wrong step and so many lives could be wrecked.'

Ishaq looked at the elder man's face, on the tipping point of aging, about to follow the other men in this mosque. 'You know, over the years, your talks were exactly what I needed. I still appreciate them, but you never checked the attitudes of the brothers.'

'What attitudes?' Ayub said. Ishaq was unsure of whether to continue but Ayub prompted him further. 'The privilege of silence has passed. You might as well just say everything you need to.'

Ishaq nodded. 'Ok, ok, it's just that we sat there, as a group, week after week and some attitudes just didn't change whatever happened. There just seems a lack of any...any real thought. You give amazing advice but left it at that...Well, it all got a bit lazy; as a group we're insular and there's no questioning of...'

'Of Islam, of our way?' Even sitting, Ayub was taller than Ishaq by a head as he leaned in.

'Hey calm down. That's a bit heavy. No, not that at all – just the bigger issues...here, now. It's always...anyway...'

'Look, that's fair enough. But, as I always said, I'm not a scholar, nor is anyone else. We do what we can and we were doing our best to remind each other of the basics.'

'I understand that but there has to be recognition of our circumstance, our drivers in striving for the truth…a truth. It's just sometimes that…it's all very predictable. Why we do what we do…I'm really not making sense. I'm tired.'

His words drifted like his thoughts, formless and without shape. Sometimes they piled up in heaps, indistinguishable, and other times they carried him along, wandering, buoyed by whatever light breeze or tempest was blowing that day.

Ayub softly wrapped a knuckle on Ishaq's thigh. 'No, I think I know what you mean, but that's complicated stuff, akhi. You're talking about intention, and the contents of one's soul. Only Allah knows that, and in a far better way than ourselves.'

And sometimes those thoughts hinted at form, you could almost reach out and discern a pattern. It felt like, in that reach, you opened yourself. Exposed yourself to something that you may not come back from. Yet, it excited. It animated.

Ishaq said, 'But if we are striving for a moderate middle way, a path, then shouldn't we try to be aware of these things. Otherwise we could be just kidding ourselves.'

'I agree with that, but we must be soft towards each other, in thought and deed. You know Ishaq, you're in a very blessed position and have the luxury of being in a dream world. Studying, no bills to pay or people to support. Mashallah, you come from a stable family who are there for you.' Ayub placed a hand on Ishaq's shoulder to reassure him that he was not attacking him. 'You can think about these things. You have time and little responsibility. Of course you should use that time, but remember that your thoughts also have their biases. A lot of the brothers have heavy family responsibilities. Jobs to hold, wives and kids to feed, extended families to help. They do this without your education, and far more limitations. They struggle really hard to rectify themselves and not to fall into old harmful patterns of behaviour. Some of these bros have done time, or made other mistakes in the past. And you and me are not better than them, we are all trying to get along.'

'Even Mujahid?'

'Even Mujahid.'

'So I'm spoilt and had it easy. Did I deserve this? Because of my *luxuries* and *position*?' Ishaq looked around and then partially brought up his arm and shoulder through the neck of his shirt.

Ayub's face cleared and fell vacant at the sight of the cut. 'No, of course you didn't.'

'And this is where our softness and understanding has led us...I want solutions, not questions that lead to more questions.'

'I can't offer that. All I know is we can offer up the struggle... the constant struggle to live in dignity...that's all that we can promise ourselves. Companions of the prophet, peace be upon him, used to weep in the struggle to purify the heart from disease.' Ayub paused, a sole finger resting on his temple. 'And as for Mujahid, please leave it – at least until we find out where Shams is.'

'Why? Shams went too far. Why should I care? Would he do the same for me? Why bother with him? Maybe, I'm better off alone. Maybe I can make my own way.'

'I don't think you mean that? You do need community. Its annoyances, its bonds. You have to be careful that you don't straddle so many worlds that you get lost in between and are nothing.'

Ayub spoke inwardly as if he was warding himself, and then Ishaq saw it. Ayub was as confused as he was, fumbling in the dark, looking for something to hold onto. He must feel like he did, every day with the irritation of nagging concerns, that you can't shake off, that remained voiceless and elusive yet irritated the pit of your stomach. That uncomfortable feeling of constant harm, that at any moment all of the walls around you would collapse and take with it every person you loved. A life of constant apprehension in which every minor step was deliberated on, where you stuck a toe out to test the ground, even though you could see it was concrete.

The boy and the man stopped talking for a while, gazes cast elsewhere, guarding their own counsel. After a while, Ayub said, 'Whatever has happened Shams is your brother. The prophet, peace be upon him, said you should make seventy excuses for your brother.'

Ishaq clenched a fist and pressed into the lush carpet. 'But, Ayub, some mistakes are worth a thousand others. This isn't about a missed invite to a footie game, or being tight and never paying for chicken and chips. He brought me into harm.'

'Yes, he did. But what now…cutting ties with him? You know…'

'With respect, Ayub, don't quote me another hadith. Sometimes that's a cop-out. I know. I know.'

Ayub moved to touch Ishaq on the shoulder again but thought better of it and moved back. 'But then you…we have ignored him. He feels left out. Vulnerable.'

'Ayub, I feel left out. I feel vulnerable. Why is the sympathy one way?'

'Because you're stronger. All Shams wants is some love and care. What is it that you want?'

'To live honest and true. I want the truth, Ayub. Unvarnished, even if it hurts. Because, even if it's painful, at least it makes you aware of reality. I don't want to be a hypocrite. I want my faith to be real, and I want to do something with my life. Not just survive and tick along.'

'And you can't do something with your life here?'

'I don't know. That's what I'm figuring out,' Ishaq said, his voice surging.

An old man, back bent, shuffled past them and put a battered copy of the Quran back on a shelf, admonishing both with judging eyes.

'Ishaq...maybe it's just an illusion, but all these debates you've been having lately. Your head wandering in the clouds somewhere far away from here. All alone. It's not healthy and it's not our way. You have to reach out to other souls.'

Ishaq didn't know if he was a thinker or a coward, someone of reason looking at the longer game or just small and fearful. A man could organise his life, live well, be successful, look after number one. He could look after a family and be a good citizen, wasn't that enough? Who was more moral a person, one who could be a role model for others, maybe starting a business leading to thousands of jobs, or the one who smiled and gave reassuring platitudes, who was kind but aimless, who achieved nothing?

Ayub said, 'It's fine to chase after the truth, or a truth, or truths, but leaving and hurting people in the process isn't. Go for painful examination, be harsh on yourself if you want, but be soft on others. Don't let your search become the product of narcissism and greed.'

Ayub's tone had changed, more pointed, and Ishaq could hear irritation. Ishaq was taken aback by the slight aggression . He had not seen him talk in such a manner before.

'Ishaq, you're despairing. As believers we hold fast to the rope of Allah. We hope for his mercy, we fear his wrath, and we love him for all that he has done. Hope. Fear. Love. It's the same for society, too. Always hope for something better. Don't despair. Fear consequence. And love, love each other with an open heart. We lurch and see-saw but we must have a balance between the three. We lean too heavily to one and then we fall. That's part of life's struggle.'

Ishaq listened carefully. The voice sounded exactly the same as when he gave the circle, yet it now lacked something. The timbre was controlled and dignified but it had lost its complete hold.

Ishaq shook his head. 'It's all so confusing.'

'Yes, it is. There's so many times I want to run from my responsibilities. To give up the fight. Like you I think, where else could I have gone? What could I have been? But, in the end, you have to decide what man, and you are a man now, Ishaq, what kind are you? What will make your heart rest easy?'

Ishaq used his right hand to lean on, making an ineffectual grab of the carpet's fibrous strands. The matting was made up of panels that mimicked the portals of the Alhambra in Andalusian Spain. Ishaq followed it up to its edges and then up the whitewashed walls, until his eyes met the geometric designs on the ceiling. None of the star-shaped motifs that he liked, but rigorously ordered shapes in a never-ending pattern, simple in isolation yet amazingly complex as they extended and interlocked.

Ayub and Shams, they were both right in a way; we did have obligations to each other. Hunkering down in your head, with the rising bile coming their way, was sufferance. Real strength came in extending your arm outwards. Helping, assuring. In that extension you may indeed reveal too much, show weakness, a fragility that can be exploited, but there was no other choice. Enjoin the good and forbid the evil. Listen to each other, be kind. A mixture of his parents' homespun cod philosophy was maybe not a systematic approach, but a necessary one. Ayub was right; there was no restful peace when everyone who came from the same place as you stayed in poverty and disrepair. Class, or tribe, or race, you needed their uplifting, too. Any success without that tasted like a bitter fruit. Wholesome and inviting but, as you ate into it, its acrid, biting, kick shocked the system, causing an instinctual violent refusal.

Ayub put a hand in his pocket once again and pulled out a folded piece of paper that he handed to Ishaq. 'This is the address of where Mujahid sent Shams.'

'Why can't you go?'

The crow lines under Ayub's eyes grew more marked as they curved and extenuated. 'By Allah I would, but I have to be careful at the moment.'

'To do with Bosnia?' Ishaq had always known that Ayub was frightened by bumps in the night – apparitions from the past that he could not shake off. He saw the angst in Ayub's face, and surprise. 'We've always known. It looks like a city but it's really a village. You didn't talk about it so we respected you, protected you.'

Ayub nodded, he leant over and kissed Ishaq's forehead, and then pressed his head against his. 'I love you all for the sake of Allah.' As Ayub scrunched up the piece of paper Ishaq stayed his hand, unfastened his fingers and took it.

'Peace be upon you. I'll see what I can do.'

Ishaq looked on as Ayub walked away. Once he was gone he stood in prayer, and then prostrated. It was the steady interruptions of the five prayers that gave rhythm to life. It was the primary ritual that united. A constant renewal of faith, a purifying ritual that reorientated. It reminded him of a greater vision of life, as compared to day-to-day banality. An act of submission.

Ishaq, kneeling, finished his salah. He noticed his shivering had stopped and his fever had subsided. Ishaq felt a new conception within him, a fresh soul had broken through, one not without doubt but one that harnessed his fears. All life, love, joy may be subsumed by the world he had found himself in, but he could retain an inner place, sustain a sanctum away from the terror. He could refuse to spend an existence in entreaty on those that despised him. Ishaq decided then and there that he would try to do the PhD. He would go to the university the very next day, to speak to Professor Harell and talk about the incident at the conference. He would explain how he would handle disagreement in a different way, and that he hoped the place was still on offer. Ishaq also decided he would contact Father Horan and try to help resurrect the youth centre project. It would be something that he could get Shams involved in, too.

It was not the life he had envisaged, but he could make it a good one. No lax fatalism. He may have to live his whole life within a rift, against shuddering clashes and in a state of constant schism. He may need to bear permanent exile from himself, but he could be of use, be an honourable man, a good man. And that's all he really wanted, a modest opportunity, the affording of that slim chance, to be dutiful and upright. In doing this, as he had seen Ayub before him, Ishaq decided that he would never be leaving the estate.

23.

'When will God's Help come?' 'Oh, verily, God's Help is always near!'

Qur'an 2:214

A shop window shattered. Fragments lay over the pavement holding viscous colour as within an oil spill. The shop owner brushed pieces up with a broom, pulling at them with a tug, until he tired and paused, rubbing his kufi cap over his skull as he surveyed the damage. A seller of vegetables and other conveniences, his store had been ransacked by a group of English men during the night. The police were busy around the city dealing with flashpoints and were too stretched to respond. One scared neighbour said a woman with a walking stick had accompanied them and had actually returned not once but an additional two times to fill her shopping bags. In the morning the police told the shopkeeper that a local pub had been firebombed and he was unfortunately the first Muslim shop in a retributive path.

In light of developments, in Europe, the march had been cancelled and coaches from round the country were being turned back. But still they came. Streets were cordoned off, but people managed to find gaps, like mice gnawing at barriers, squeezing their pressed bodies through tiny holes

Police, irate residents, a broken shopkeeper, Shams didn't notice any of them. He walked on, away from the troubles, back to the industrial estate. Shams was tired of being scared, tired of being looked down upon, tired of being a victim. He would take the package. He would show Mujahid that he was worthy. Show that racist twat that he shouldn't be messed with. Show Marwane and Ishaq that he was a man to be reckoned with.

He waited around a corner, and spied the man with his comrades. He looked on as they loaded a van with placards, and also saw them chuck-in some iron bars in the back. With the skinny one in the drivers seat they drove off, leaving Charlie to himself. Shams peeled himself around the bend and walked to the hut, slightly crouched, tempering his breath as he tried to regulate a pummelled heartbeat. He placed a hand on his waistband to reassure himself of his guaranteed safety. Entering, he saw the man bending down, playing with some signs. The floor creaked and Charlie turned around and looked on Shams like he was seeing the postman.

'You couldn't have picked a worse fuckin' day to sort this out. You're lucky the others didn't see you, they're out for blood.'

Charlie returned to his sifting at the back of the cabin.

'I thought you wanted this sorted quickly? I'm here now,' insisted Shams.

Charlie drew an impatient sigh and his gaze turned again but made a lingering stop on Shams' face. Shams' face felt taut yet his palsied muscles wanted to twitch independently of his control and betray him.

'Yea, well, come on then. Spit it out, where's the cash?'

Shams stepped forward, stiffened in statue form then screwed his rusting neck and looked around.

Charlie stood. 'Come on. Chop chop. Are you fuckin' retarded or somethin'? Don't stand there like a dumb paki. I've got places to be.'

Shams broke free of his stupor and stared Charlie straight in the eyes 'Don't speak like that to me, or this will all kick-off, right? There'll be problems between your lot and my lot. We can do business but don't be a cunt about it.'

'Your lot? Your fuckin' lot?' The man's hot-plated head reddened. 'Your lot is why this country is in such a mess. Just like this; you fuck around and make a mess. Nothing runs smooth.'

'Your lot just enjoy hating things, makes you feel big and powerful.'

The man started laughing, holding on to his stomach with both hands to stop gelatinous wobbles, afraid they would change his centre of gravity and topple him. Charlie's mirth came to an abrupt end as he saw Shams lift up his coat and reach for an object in the waistband of his trackie bottoms. He watched Shams raise the paring knife he had bought for his mum. Charlie's voice dropped an octave, and levelled off. 'What the fuck are you going to do what that bloody toothpick? Don't be silly, be a good boy now and go home. You've fucked this up.'

'Give me the package.' Shams' voice came out in a quiet tremor that issued from deep within but barely had the momentum to exit his throat. His right hand extended forward, with the knife pointed in Charlie's general direction. The arm was shaking and Shams felt his legs wanting to give way.

'I'm not giving shit.' Charlie put both hands out in a grappling position. Shams' shaking, and his mask of thoughtless despair, had unnerved Charlie. He had the instinctual notion that you could not control a man not in mastery of his self. Charlie's hands waved up and down, pre-empting any charge on Shams' part. Shams stepped forward, taking arid swallows, trying to introduce moisture to his mouth.

Charlie's voice took an uncertain pitch, shorn of its previous confidence. 'Look, I don't want any trouble. My mates have seen you – do something stupid and they'll be after you. I can see that this ain't you.'

Shams coughed and cleared a parched throat. His legs felt steadier and his own voice held. 'They ain't here now though, are they? They're too busy causing shit elsewhere. Give me the package.'

'Look around, can't you see we're still shifting signs for the protest? They'll be back. Just put it down and we'll forget it ever happened.' His hands still feeling the air looking for holds and gauging no response from Shams. 'You're scared shitless, and I'm not liking this, too. That's why, just now, my mate has managed to park up outside, and you ain't heard jack. It's over.'

No other smell, no sight, no other sounds, he could only hear Charlie's voice, see that pudgy face, and smell his wrenching sweat. Only the two of them existed, only the package had meaning, and the sole reality was the knife. He perceived a dark void behind him. He felt the sense of falling, plunging in an endless drop. He jerked his head to look back, to stem the panic, to take in the wider picture, to see if there was a larger truth.

The van was not there. Shams' coiled head sprung back but, too late, he felt a pain in his right arm that made him lose grip on the knife. Charlie had made a grab at a placard and swung it into Shams' arm at the elbow. The knife bounced on the hut floor, and the fat man and Shams went head down in a scrum. Tackling each other, trying to knock each other's hands out of the way, but only succeeding in pushing the knife around. It was bobbing around like a baitfish hooked to some arcane line and lure. Charlie could hardly shift his blubbery anatomy but his sheer weight impeded Shams from pushing any further forward. Shams pulled back, stood, and attempted a penalty kick at Charlie's orbed head, but the man grabbed his foot and pulled, taking the other leg from beneath him. Sham hit his head, then fell flat on his back with a reverberating thump that made the floorboards judder around them, and dust mushroom-up into the air.

Tongue out and panting, Charlie got off the floor, propped-up by his hands, and booted Shams in the midriff, winding him and eliciting a hollow lament. Tottering, his legs shaking, Charlie knelt on both knees and crawled towards the knife, putting one hand over another until his right hand felt the chill of the blade under a palm. He pushed to get himself up but, instead, felt pain and pressure on his hand that led to a reflexive roll of the palm, which forced the sharp side of the blade into his hand, at an acute angle. Charlie screamed. Looking up, on his hand he saw a boot with its edged heel cutting into it. Crunching his eyes in pain, he followed the boot up and saw a taller, athletic-looking Asian youth staring at him.

'Try anything stupid and I'll finish you.' The man looked at the boy and thought this face was different. This one was all unforgiving lines and cold, still and more certain. He felt more pressure on his hand and cried in pain. Ishaq leant down and prised the knife out from under Charlie's splayed hand.

'You're still hurting my hand.'

Charlie's vision blurred. He heard the new boy's voice say, 'Ok, I'm going to let go of you, and you're going to stay on the floor. Are we clear?' Charlie nodded in blind acquiescence.

In a slow movement Ishaq drew his foot up, and the man pulled a bloodied hand back and sat on his inflated backside. He brought the hand to his chest for nursing, cradling it and yet ashamed of it, like one of his pups.

'Ok, stay on the floor and shuffle back.' Charlie did as asked, and saw a third guy. Much taller with loud, fuzzy hair.

Ishaq looked at Charlie and recognised him as being, once, from the estate. From its dark ages. From within the dwindling white population that had become more uncomfortable with each passing day. They fled. To places further out of the city. Ishaq had been to one, once, to see an old friend and had seen many faces like Charlie's. In some ways those areas were even scarier than the estate. Running from London, a seething human wave with a white crest of resentment, collapsed into suburban housing estates that were low density but drowning in government dependency. The only acceptable integration was one where they had their foot on his neck. Hidden away, from the spotlight of the big city, they did not even have the media fetishisation of 'ghetto' and 'urban' life to make them feel special. Ishaq saw the same impulsive hate in this man's eyes. But still he wanted to say, 'You don't know us? You don't know me? I don't want this either.'

Ishaq saw the protest signs. A right grubby mess, this was. He half-expected there to be something about 'Muslamic law' or 'Never submit to Aslan'.

'Where's this package?'

Charlie thought Ishaq's voice was stern and, though juvenile, rigid. Charlie jutted his head in the direction of a large office pedestal at the back of the hut.

Ishaq looked at Marwane. Marwane walked over and opened the pedestal, taking out a large cardboard box. Within the box he found rectangular cuboids wrapped in brown paper. Marwane picked a package and started unravelling it.

Ishaq eyed Shams. 'Let's see how much trouble you're...we're in, shall we?'

Marwane threw a package over to Ishaq, who started ripping at the paper. After a few layers he uncovered a printed box, packaging for the latest hi-tech smartphone. He opened the box and chucked out the manual and cables. He took out the phone and polystyrene, discarding them on the floor. When it was empty he levelled the box with his eye to make sure he had not missed anything. Confused, Ishaq asked Marwane to throw him another, this time from the bottom of the box. More packaging and paraphernalia became trash on the hut floor.

Both phones in his hand he looked for an opening, tracing edges with a finger. They didn't have an obvious battery compartment. Ishaq took one and looked at it in silhouette, noted how thin it was, and then twisted it round and round, looking for an opening. Marvels of modernity that had no room for flaws, no obvious entry points, or vulnerability. He looked at Charlie, who remained disinterested, too busy wheezing and catching his breath. Ishaq took one phone and slammed it into the edge of a table. Once. Twice. Then in a countless flurry. At first the casing just warped more and more, until the screen and tiny screws started coming apart and the casing spilled industrial secrets from its innards. Nothing. There was nothing in the phone except for a battery, chips and sensors, and memory. Severed silicon arteries and a spaghetti mass of metal.

Marwane opened a couple of other boxes and it was the same thing. Ishaq looked at Charlie and demanded, 'Where are the drugs?'

Charlie sat on the floor, coughing and heaving. 'Drugs? Why the fuck would there be drugs?'

'Did you know what was in the box?'

'Of course I know, I'm the one that processed it. I work as a loader and know people in customs.'

'So what's the deal with Mujahid?'

'He just tells me that he's getting shipments in at the airport and I look the other way, or get it sorted out. He avoids taxes, like that. Sells them on. I'm a family man just like him, I wouldn't get involved in anything shady. He cleaned himself up way-back, too.'

'So, no drugs?' said Ishaq, his manner insisting and trying to force an affirmative, ignoring Charlie's dubious definition of shady.

'Bloody hell, no. What are you talkin' about? Who said that? I'd lose my job that way. This is just a bit of money on the side. I live at home with my mum and dad, I'm so skint. This keeps the kids in presents and stuff. Look, there's a picture of them on my phone in my coat over there. My darlings.'

Ishaq put a hand up declining the offer. He looked at both Shams and Charlie and realised that the only person who had mentioned drugs was him. He was filled with a flooding shame, but still the situation had to be solved. 'So you two were about to kill each other over a bunch of mobile phones?'

'Don't look at me, look at him,' said Charlie, rubbing his face and then directing flabby arms towards Shams. 'He had the knife. The dumb shit.'

'Why did you double the money?' said Shams, in retaliation.

'You looked as green as anything, thought I'd chance my arm.' Charlie moved to get up but Ishaq shook his head. 'I would've backed down if he had pushed it. It was just a business deal, pure and simple.'

Ishaq tapped a couple of signs with his boot. 'You're like the EDL, are you? Off to that dumb march today? What did you expect to happen?'

Charlie's face wobbled, he put his head down between his arms. 'C'mon, nothing against you lads. Just protesting against extremists. People who don't adapt to our ways. You know… when in Rome do as the Romans do, and all that.'

Shams, invigorated by his backup, took a step towards Charlie. 'He started it all, he kept on calling me a paki. He was being well abusive.'

Ishaq looked to Charlie for a response. 'I didn't mean anything by it…just short for Pakistani, ain't it?'

Marwane started laughing. 'Why don't you and me go down to Brixton or Harlesden and start calling random black people what your short version of Nigerian is, then?'

Charlie went silent. Ishaq looked at him dumped on the floor there, bald, teary-eyed, with a misshapen body that had fat spilling out at all sorts of angles. He had no real form at all. He looked like an ugly baby that had been ejected out into the world, confused and dejected. Ishaq walked over and stood over him, watching the man take fright and cringe.

'Do you really think we asked to be here? No, but we are and we're not going anywhere. We're here, now, because you lot went out there, then. We're not the barbarians at the gate, we are the Romans.' Ishaq put out a hand and saw the man scrutinise it, to see whether it was a trick, an open palm that would quickly curl into a fist. The decision was made to take it and Ishaq helped the man up. 'We'll pass the phones on.'

'How about my money?' Charlie took on a look of puppy-innocence, as of the aggrieved party. 'A deal is a deal. I promise nothing more will come of this. Mate, be reasonable, it was all an obvious misunderstanding.'

Ishaq took an envelope from his coat and threw it at the man's feet, making another shake of his head to ward-off any questions arising from Marwane's startled look at the cash. The man leant over to pick it up and perched his backside on the table, careful to avoid the entrails and guts of the smashed phone. He opened the envelope, licked a finger, and flicked through the notes.

'That's not enough. The deal was...' Charlie's protest was stopped by an unequivocal stare.

Ishaq looked at Shams, who was standing a bit prouder. The boy who would be king. 'You give these to Mujahid and it's all sorted yea? Seriously Shams, what did you think was going to happen? You stab him, no one notices?'

'It was just a threat. I didn't expect it to go down like that.' Rubbing the back of his head in acrimony, Shams spat out the final bit of his reply with pestilence. 'Where did you get all those notes from? I didn't need your help anyway.'

Ishaq shouted, the hut echoing with his voice. 'You didn't need my help? You didn't need my help? You were about to stab a man over nothing, just some crap little deal. Of course you needed my help. You, this guy, Mujahid. Brawling over scraps while the rest of society sneers at how pathetic you all are. That guy's right, you're a fucking idiot.'

'Don't talk to me that way.' Shams threw a punch at Ishaq. His fist impacted in the groove where Ishaq's nose met his cheek, knocking him down.

Ishaq stayed on the floor, feeling a swelling in his face. Shams must have caught his upper lip as well, as he could taste his own blood dribbling into his mouth. The tinge of pain was a confirmation of everything. 'Brave now, Shams, and you haven't got the shakes like you normally get. Full-on fighter. Scared in front of the non-muslims, but to your own you're full-on ready to use violence. Brave man. Go on, hit me again.'

Marwane tried to help Ishaq up, but he pushed Marwane's hand away and stood up, dropping the knife. Light from the hut's windows reflected in Shams' eyes. Ishaq could see the world there and it was on fire.

'You just don't understand…it's difficult, so difficult. Ishaq, you're such a fool, you think it's possible for us to live decent lives and that it will all sort itself out. That people see the difference between you and me, and Mujahid and Ayub. But that's not what's happening. Damned if we do, damned if we don't. Just damned.'

Shams took gulps of air, struggling to breathe. He tapped on the side of his head, two straightened fingers like poles, banging into his temple. Like a deranged woodpecker trying to get at his brain. Tap. Tap. Tap.

Shams screamed, primarily at Ishaq but releasing his ire at it all. His friend, the golden-boy. Proper mummy's-and-daddy's boy. Oh, Ishaq is good at sports. Ishaq is good at studies. Ishaq is pious, wise, even-tempered. The brothers respect him. The kuffar talk to him nicely. The one who glides along, while all the shit sticks somewhere else.

'And why do you always think you can talk to me like this? Where have you been all this time? What the fuck do you know? You're always right. You've always been the golden-child. You stopped giving a fuck about me and anyone else a long time ago. You're just selfish, man. Self-centred, self-involved and selfish. Don't talk to me like you're helping me out. There's always a bottom line for you, for Mujahid, for him, everyone.'

Ishaq felt like his face had been slapped. He didn't recognize this kid. The one who thought he could prove he wasn't an animal by acting like one. The screw-up everyone loved. The one who had the freedom to be thoughtless.

Ishaq hit back in a stuttered shout, 'That's not true.'

Shams said, 'And where has it got you, Ishaq? You're going be stuck on the estate just like the rest of us. Study, being *good*, for what? The only difference between you and me will be some cheap certificate your mum can put up on a wall.'

Even while being present here the two boys couldn't bear the memory of each other. Distorted mirrors of who they are, what they might be. They spent time in examination and just increased their unease. The ensuing silence was broken by Charlie. Looking jolly, with his cash stuffed in his pocket, the white man said, 'Look, I don't know what the fuck is going on, now. I don't understand and it's not my business anymore, so I think it's best I just go home and leave you to it.'

Marwane and Ishaq exchanged bewildered looks. Marwane said, 'You cheeky bastard. You're as much a part of this mess as everyone else. You're not going anywhere. Now just sit there and shut the fuck up.'

As a shy Charlie slinked back, Ishaq felt a beat, the pounding. They were all babes like Charlie, like Shams. From the safety of the womb you came into this world. You came with screams and spent your life clawing for lost comfort. 'I feel it too, Shams... being surrounded by people for who life is just a game. I want to lash out, but where does it end …where does it end? Look where it has got you? Please. Look where we are now, you with a knife, scaring people, bleeding.'

Shams nodded at Charlie. 'People like him. If he got really scared that would be good, we can force them to feel what we feel.'

Ishaq could see in Shams the terror of life, the uncertainty. The shock, when exposed to the world, in learning that they were seen as violent, and sexist. Rotten to the core, atavistic and recidivistic. All the compassion that Ishaq knew added up to nothing, for the outsider. Yet the greatest assault was that somehow they were irredeemable, it was part of their being, somehow impure. This shook Ishaq so much more as he realised that was exactly what he used to think of them.

Stories, no…slurs, came at a pace like a beat to a drum, the frequency more rapid year after year. He knew that their objective was to get a reaction out of him, get him to prove their point and make him jig, but he was not their monkey and he would not do their dance. There was a difference between the two boys; Ishaq couldn't think of himself without hope.

'You think our lives are small. They're not, you just don't see it. All our history, Shams. You, me, Marwane, together, has to count for something. Just trust me. I won't let you down again.'

'You always say that success isn't on your self, that it's our group, our people as a whole, but what's the point of doing anything when the goalposts shift? It's like we're building lives on a pile of sinking, shitty, mud. It's like being shouted at constantly. No room to think…no room to breathe.'

The narrow light carried Shams' anger. He was there, standing, his face twisted, using a fist to bang at his head from above. Drip. Drip. Drip. Like Chinese water torture, each issue falling on him, collectively driving him insane.

'And do you plan going through life with a mass of resentments? I have my own, and you need to just let go. You can't just be a collection of likes and dislikes, of sorrows and wounds. You are what you intend and do, however difficult. You can't package everything up and solve it all. That's impossible, these questions are so much bigger. You can't take responsibility for all that,' said Ishaq, his plea showing in his voice.

' You?…it's all words, you're just leaving everyone behind, just charging ahead. You're a cold fish, cold and into yourself…'

'That's not true…'

'Let me finish.' Eyes closed, Shams brought a flat palm downwards in a scything motion through the air, his face red, straining with some internal pressure that threatened to break. 'You don't want us to own our own pain. You even want to deny me that. You want us to go through life like robots, not feeling what other people feel. All logical and shit. What kind of life is that? To have nothing of our real self. Look in the mirror one day and see a stranger. Not sure if he exists. I'm not sure if I exist.'

Ishaq's footing became unsure and he collapsed onto a metal crate to rest. Shams was right. He restricted himself, cut bits off that could catch. It was the only way he could cope. He didn't want to feel everything. He couldn't feel everything. Easier to feel nothing.

'I can control what I do, what I say. As soon as I try to do more than that it becomes confusing…I get confused, Shams, and I don't know what to do…' Ishaq's voice had lost its vigour. He was shorn of all strength.

'See, why don't you speak to me like that? Instead you try to manage me like a problem. Speak to me like a person.'

'…I'm so sorry…please…honestly, I had no idea…I always thought of us all as the same…' Ishaq understood what those closest were saying. He had taken the world's problems on his shoulders. Not in vanity but as an honest desire to work out a way to help his friends. But what was important was the now, with his boys. '…I'll do better, I'll be a better friend. All I know is that this isn't the way.'

Tears streamed down Shams' face. Words twisted and strained, forcing their way through. 'And what way is it with these people. Our countries were invaded and the locals made second class, but we need to forget?! Our parents came over and were treated like crap, and we're supposed to let it slide. We're stopped and hassled . These lot have gone over the whole planet and fucked so many countries up. Every single problem on the planet they started, and we're supposed to pretend that's not the case, pretend, instead, that it all started with us. Forgiveness? Patience? They ask us to do what they've never done or would never do. They only stopped when they're weak. I'm sick of them. Fuck 'em! All they do is screw us over.'

Ishaq let Shams discharge, he let the air electrify and then go still and saw the dust settle. Softly, as if any sudden noise would break them into pieces. Ishaq put out a hand. As if surveying the fragile crucible of the cabin, he presented the panorama of broken technology, shattered ties, tribal rivalries and the airing of sweat and blood. Slow and steady, almost in a whisper, he said,

'But look around, Shams. That's only half of a truth. We do it to ourselves. We do it to each other.'

Shams was in the midst of sobs, bent over, chest expanding in raspy breath. Ishaq walked over and lifted him up. Holding Shams' face, between his hands, he wiped away some of Shams' tears with a thumb. 'It's all shit. You're right. All we…I can do, is try.' Ishaq looked over at Marwane. 'Not be consumed. It destroys us, Shams. Yes, I've failed. I won't let that happen again. I'm learning. I hope that you'll forgive me…please, Shams.'

Life was asking them questions so grand that any answer was an impossibility. To burden lone souls with so much was an oppression. They had the right to make mistakes, the agency to start anew, and the right to anger. There was remembrance held in that fury. They would not stand as ciphers for whichever ill society wished.

Ishaq looked into Shams' eyes and saw them clear, a calm return to an even-keel, after thunder. He took his head and buried it into his shoulder as Shams continued to sob. Marwane came over, picking up Shams' schoolboy cap and carefully placing it on his head, and gave Shams an embrace as Ishaq pulled away.

A loud cackle broke through the ensuing stillness. Charlie said, 'You boys are flogging a dead horse. I've got mates just like him. Once a fuck-up, always a fuck-up. You can't change your nature. One day you two boys will wish his dad had worn a johnny when he was banging his decrepit old mum. Stupid fuck.'

Sham let out a roaring scream, and jumped for the blade on the floor. Getting up, he swiped at Charlie, who had a forearm out to protect himself and caught a slash from the knife. Marwane pulled Shams back, but he pushed backwards, smashing Marwane into a set of metal shelving. Shams took turns to look at the other three men, turn by turn.

'I'll fucking show him and his mates.'

Shams ran out, the door making a loud bang as it slammed open. Charlie's arm ran crimson as Marwane lifted it up and scrambled on the table for any cloth to stem the bleeding.

Ishaq said to Marwane, 'How bad is it?'

'It's not good, he needs a hospital. What do we tell them?' Marwane looked on as Ishaq stretched his neck out of a window. 'Let him go, Ishaq, it's done.'

Ishaq looked back at Marwane. 'Take him, tell them whatever you need to to get him sorted. Tell it all if you need to.' Ishaq addressed Charlie. 'Your mates, they headed to that march?'

Charlie nodded with a grimace. Ishaq ran out of the cabin.

24.

He ran as fast as he could, legs shaking, heart beating with an excavating thud. Down the escalator, three steps at a time. He saw a train about to leave and jumped for the carriage. The doors were shutting and he jammed them, with his torso partially through, and then pried them open with his free hands. He squeezed through, with the help of another passenger pulling him in. As the train left the station the passenger asked him if he was ok but he could only hear a drowned warble of speech. His running had produced a clogging sweat that reached up to the middle of his ears. Ishaq's drained lips mumbled something appeasing and he felt the travellers' presence retreat as they took fright.

The driver's voice announced that Whitechapel had closed, so Ishaq came off a stop early. At the station gates his Oyster card refused to work. He swiped it multiple times, scraping the card reader, getting frustrated at the 'Seek Assistance' message that displayed on each swat. His pleading face turned to a guard, who dismissed him without even a cursory look, instead waving a silencing hand as he talked to another customer. Ishaq looked at the closed gates and then listened, as the underground employee explained some Odyssean route. Ishaq vaulted the gates, both hands apart. As he rocked through the air he ignored the timid plea and delayed grasp of the guard. People hesitated and looked at him but if there was a shout behind him Ishaq refused to hear.

He started running again and, as he ran, he tried Shams' mobile. His call was blocked; the cell towers here must have overloaded. He shoved his own phone back into a pocket and slowed, as he saw the golden dome of the great mosque. The protest had picked one of the most civic-minded Muslim institutions in the country. A great achievement of the local Bangladeshi community, it had taken great strides in developing links with greater society, even sheltering a tiny synagogue. Seven thousand people could attend prayers in the cluster of buildings that had started out, a hundred years ago, as a rented room. Over a century it had been supplemented by the donations of cloth-factory workers. Layer upon layer of immigration was the sediment that had firmed into foundations and had produced the latest inhabitants of the area.

Coming near to Whitechapel Road, Ishaq heard a mighty crescendo, and as he turned a corner he saw crowds, thousands of people, blocking the wide thoroughfare. Finding Shams would be impossible and he almost turned back, defeated, but then gathered his determination and went towards the throngs. Eyeing a lamppost he scrambled up on a bin beside it, and shimmied up the pole. Nearing the top he saw such heaving crowds they almost looked like celebration. Riots of colour, accompanied by shouts that erupted into the air. A tapestry of people extended to the horizon. Ishaq could see pigmented layers that blended into the skyline. First there was a motley mix of all sorts of browns, then an empty expanse of grey concrete road, and then a further band of pinky-mass, before all the colours hit the now-violet sky, as evening descended on all.

Enforcing the grey no-go zone were bands of black-armour-clad police, holding riot-shields and wearing visored helmets. They were sandwiched between the two battle lines. Two serried ranks of foot-soldiers agitating for their just cause, pawns, in someone else's game, who gladly gave their lives to the swell. Even over the clamouring, from his side, Ishaq heard savage, discordant cries coming from the white side, modulating between insults and taunts. Vicious calumnies and screeds were catapulted across the divide at a stinging pace. The two sides were feeding off each other, goading and amplifying each other's hate and righteousness. Each side stood behind their line trying to incite the other to do something to break their own, to do something outside of their normal boundaries.

Ishaq could make no sense of it. He closed his eyes and all he could hear was one mass-harmonised scream. Shrieks by people of scripture, ritual, or tribe, frozen out by streamlined industrial society. Those who felt so cast-aside that all they could do was throw their bodies on the tracks and try to break the whole damn thing. People who, on normal days of monotony, would shop, work, and go to school. Different, yet distinct. One thousand points of contact held the rift together. Friction holding them united, yet retaining a power so monstrous that, when unleashed, it was out of anyone's control. An earthquake that could shatter societies.

Ishaq slipped. He clung on, desperate to avoid a crash to the ground, overcoming the sudden shock of pain in his right arm. He fell only half-a-foot yet his eyes caught Shams' cap weaving a path. It was taking a crooked but driven direction to the front of the Muslims, to the first black row of police. Ishaq, taking a mental marker of Shams' flight path, slid down and started pushing his own way forward.

As he navigated his way the crowd became denser. Thickets of bodies had to be nudged aside as he gently advanced. He reached where the road met the start of the mosque complex, spreading eastwards. An old man, wearing a fluorescent helper-bib, had made an impromptu platform from plastic boxes. He was urging the men from his own side to go home, but his frail voice failed him and was usurped by more virile shouts. His white beard dripped worry, his face ashen. A voice from the crowd told him it was too late, that now was the time to make a stand or never. That once you allowed these animals to march past they would do so forever-more, without compunction. The aged man made entreaties, asking them what example they were setting for the youth. He implored them to step back and think, but was besieged. Defiant voices that said it was better to die a shaheed, a martyr, today, than live a whole life as a coward. The old man was pulled down and bundled away, and a more triumphant, rallying howl took his place.

Ishaq came to a stop, unable to push further past. He could not see any gaps to his side and those behind had closed tight. Through the bow of someones arm he could see the nationalist lines. Revelling in their bigotry like pigs in mud, enjoying their big fuck-you to the world, that looked to them as strength. He could make out red puffed cheeks as they made their taunts, arms outstretched, grasping for a fight. Bodies swaddled him, and the sounds became muted. A message passed through the crowd, trouble was starting around the city and they were being kettled until police could get a handle on the situation. People with radios tuned into the news as looters used the day's events as an opportunity to go shopping. The police were responding to incidents all over the city and were stretched.

Ishaq waited. He tried his phone but still there was no signal. He asked others but they had the same problem. He could feel a panic set in as a wave of claustrophobia washed over him, a spread of nausea that was made worse as he tried to take in more air. Ishaq asked for more space and pushed at the huddle around him but they were all in the same position. There was no one to hear Ishaq's plea.

Time dragged on and day turned into the fullness of night. Over the course of hours his personal space receded until his arms were pinned by his side, his head nearly resting on someone's shoulder. Ishaq felt pressure on his chest but this time he managed to suppress his anxiety and keep some calm. Others, however, started to push and complain. He heard a grand roar from the other side as they tried to push through the police line. An older man fainted and water was passed from beyond to the man's aid. A whop-whopping sound was heard as helicopters passed over-head, reminding the crowd that their penned-in plight was known, yet nothing was being done. Ishaq thought about Shams and was satisfied that, once freed, he could go home. Shams would have had time to calm down. The biggest problem for Ishaq would be what story to make up, for his parents.

The night was at the height of its blackness, everything still and unchanging. The local shops had been boarded-up, so no light escaped their frontages. Street lamps cast their jaundiced light over the quieted crowds, stilling the scene, fossilizing them in amber. Yellowed skin and eyes of ivory-white accompanied a silence that gave the occasion the quality of the unreal. The calm occasionally broke when the police made sorties at the edges and snatched a body. They took their guidance from security service spotters, up on the high, overlooking roofs, who watched through binoculars for people of interest.

For a moment Ishaq viewed the scene out-of-body, as if seeing an ossified diorama. People started to use their mobiles as flashlights and were joined by the flashing of police cameras taking shots. The constant adjustment of eyes to differing sources of light made his head ache. Whispers went through the crowd, colliding and contradicting, about how long they would be here, and what the police were saying. Someone said that the police were not sure themselves what the next step would be.

Ishaq heard another roar from the other side. They were hurling abuse at the police and pushing forward. What looked like a brick flew through the air and hit a policeman on Ishaq's side. Despite the man's visor it caused a bloody-cut and he was led away by a colleague. Ishaq started to feel more space around him. First, the rubbing of shoulders subsided and then he could actually move his feet without stepping on another's. A rippled message came through that a gap had been forced in the other crowd, and they didn't have enough heads to keep both sides contained. As if they detected a coming moment, people started wrapping scarves around their heads, leaving a slit only for their eyes.

From opposing lines, rocks, then stones, then hewn slabs of paving, hailed their way onto the police's heads. Someone shouted push and everyone pushed against them. Ishaq saw a boy, just into his teens, break some paving and throw a concrete fragment. The police broke their cordon, creating a Roman shield wall, lines merging behind to get the culprit. The testudo, moving at tortoise pace, gave-up and came back as it took battering hits from all angles.

The slow boil of the kettle came to a sudden steam. Against the darkening sky molotov projectiles flew through the air, searing their fiery trails into the night, most bursting in no-man's land, but they pierced the gloom, and provided a background to the shouts that broke the previous hours of peace. Ishaq felt the space enlarge around him so that he could take more steps, but still no-one was sure what was happening. Flares were lit that gave out a vermillion aura. They pierced the gloom and their burning smoke reached Ishaq's nostrils, bringing the rotting smell of sulphur. Fires were started elsewhere and smoke billowed through the crowds. A gap opened that let a couple of EDL badged supporters cross the forbidden concrete. They ran the distance between the two lines and slammed with a thud into the next line of riot shields and visors, who turned their backs to pin them to the floor. That enabled a few, then many, Muslims to get through. The police struggled to stop both sides pushing-through to start fighting. The lines broke, and two phalanxes met in the no-man's land. The Children of Adam collided. Cruelty burst through, violence won the day, it was the language of the street writ large. A syntax of brutality, a cycle of reaction.

Policemen dropped their batons and tried to flee, caught in a vice, two jaws of society's inflamed animal-spirits chomping down on them. Ishaq saw the frame of a woman through her police armour, and watched her drop to the ground as an EDL member punched her in the gap under her visor. Her body folded and lay prostrate, like discarded cardboard. The authorities' abandoned weapons were picked-up, their own truncheons used to batter them. Ishaq tried to make a path away from the trouble but was buffeted, pushed back, by the rush of people choosing to run towards the danger. Ishaq could not tell by whom, but canisters of tear gas were released. He took breaths of fire that incinerated his innards. He inhaled a stinging pain as black smoke spread. His eyes streamed as the fog reflected light, producing a strobing effect.

Out of the gloaming a pale-grey horse charged, snorting blackened smoke and making a squeal, its visored rider wielding a baton like a sword, dipping his head to take a swipe. Ishaq dived out the way to avoid being trampled by panicked hooves. He looked back as the horseman was grappled by a masked assailant. The steed reared and shook-off its doubled load. Unburdened, the beast galloped away, the smog reclaiming it.

Ishaq heaved for breath and wiped his eyes, he drove himself upright and staggered away from the main crowd, hoping to find sanctuary. He moved between pockets of clear air and woollen smoke, holding his nose and mouth, coughing on sooty particulates, trying to stem the phlegm. He smelt the putrid decay of sewers and the burning of rubber. With the lines completely broken a surge of white men came through. Pissed-up, and angry, they initially exulted in the fight, as if this was their wildest dream come true. Shouting 'English 'til I die', 'Britain first', they had the chance to have their grievances answered with fists. Their cries gave way to panic as it was clear they were out numbered. Small packs and individuals were isolated as Muslim youth rained-in on them with whirling arms, punches, and armaments. The men started running, first back, and then in all directions, chased by the revengeful.

Ishaq saw a large gap and tried to run through, but stumbled. He looked around. He had tripped over a fallen policeman, eyes vacant. As he tried to rise his hair was grabbed, his head thrust into the tarmac. Shocked, he managed to spin round. A white man grabbed him by the neck and punched him, but only made a glancing contact. Lips bleeding from the brush of the man's signet, Ishaq struggled as the man tried to strangle him. Legs pinned down he reached for the man's neck, and gave faint hits to tattoo-sleeved arms. The man was wide-eyed and joyous. Ishaq closed his eyes as he drifted in pain. He opened them and saw an image of Frankie, red hair aflame, sweaty hands wilfully embracing his neck while smiling in gleeful friendship. Manic fingers crawled his throat and pressed inwards. Maybe a due retribution, a vengeance formed from failure that now had its time. He let his eyes close as he lost consciousness but then heard a sickening crack. The pressure on his neck alleviated and Ishaq gasped for breath, his lungs wanting to explode out of his chest. As his eyes cleared he saw a defiant-looking Asian man in a pristine butchers apron, holding a discarded nightstick. His absurd smile targeted Ishaq and was joined by a thumbs up. Enraptured, the man ran on and threw himself back into the delirious fray. The white man was at

Ishaq's feet, face downwards giving testament to the earth, hair black like soot, skull cracked, a trickle of blood moving down the side, unmoving, probably a corpse.

A couple of shots rang out unseen, an incentive to move further away. Touching the walls, and walking in a crouch, he got to the edge of the crowds and then navigated a mazy warren. He could see scuffles at every junction and street, with no police to be seen. Somehow he ended up on Commercial Road. Ishaq knew the river wasn't that far, south, and that he was nearly in the clear. Men ran around him; Ishaq braced himself on a couple of occasions for a strike, and then started a shuffled jog down a long, straight road. Outside of the confusion he started to feel pain, on his arm, and around his neck and mouth, and somehow on a knee. He was constantly overtaken by other people fleeing as he hobbled along, his tongue tasting salty blood.

One chunky white man overtook him, his cheeks puffing in and out like a bellows, eyes panicked. Ishaq took a look at the man's stumpy legs and, out of some still-intact ego, tried to raise his pace to match but failed. The man was followed, chased, by a stocky Asian wearing a hat like Shams'. Ishaq jogged a couple of steps and then his head shot up, 'SHAMS', but the second man paid no heed.

Ishaq heard a thunderous roar, a clash of steel, and vibrations of air. He looked up and saw a train on an overpass, fulminating sparks floating downwards. He had reached Cable Street. Under the bridge he saw Shams tackle the fat man to the ground and launch a fist into his head. The man, now dazed and on the floor, lay still as Shams stood and landed a hefty kick to the ribs. The man welped and covered the back of his head with his hands, while curling into a ball. Ishaq started running, pushing through his pain, struggling with his breathing. He saw Shams launch a punch into the man's head and force the man to look at him. Shams paused and then brought out his knife. The man looked terrified.

Shams raised the knife in two hands with his back to Ishaq, who jumped, launching into his friend, rugby tackling him down. Both now on the floor, Ishaq saw the white man cautiously getting up and in a firm imperative shouted, 'GO.'

Shams had lost the blade but saw it on the ground and crawled to pick it up. Ishaq grabbed one of Shams' feet, who pulled his leg back and then launched it into Ishaq's face. His nose stinging, and having bitten his tongue, Ishaq still held on.

Shams said, 'Let me be, Ishaq. They deserve it.'

Shams swiped Ishaq with the back of his fist, but it was too tame to knock him off. Shams managed to get one hand on the knife, but Ishaq managed to get a hand on Shams. They struggled, bodies twisting and merging and then apart, grappling on the floor facing each other. Ishaq gripped Shams' strained hands and tried to prise the fingers away from the handle, one by one. Ishaq rolled on top of Shams to try and pin him down. The knife turned inwards, pointing towards Ishaq's stomach. Shams felt the weight of Ishaq's body on top of him, felt the knife push through and heard Ishaq let out a shout. In fright Shams' grip loosened on the knife, and Ishaq pulled away. Shams pushed himself away as he saw Ishaq reel backwards on the floor, his eyes widening as he saw the knife, pierced into Ishaq.

'I'm sorry...I didn't mean...'

Breathing laboured, Ishaq slowly pulled himself off the floor.

'It's alright...it's alright...everything's going to be fine...'

He took a moment to wheeze, as he kneeled on one leg as if genuflecting in prayer. The knife held steady in his right hand as he pulled it out. Ishaq pushed-off from his knee to stand. He used two fingers, wiggling them like bunny ears, to explore the newly created hole in his clothing. 'Haha. It went through the side of my jacket...'

Ishaq smiled and laughed, at odds with the frown of fresh blood on his face. He stood slightly over Shams, collecting gulps of breath. He held the knife aloft, high and out of Shams' reach, displaying it to reassure that no harm had been done. Ishaq extended his other hand, reaching out to help Shams up.

'...haha, look. Nothing...no blood...let's get...'

Ishaq was lying on the floor, looking up at the throbbing bridge above. He had been knocked back as he heard a crack like lightning, his ears now thundering. Ishaq looked at Shams, whose skin looked milky and was staring somewhere past him. He felt a numb pain that became a burning sensation in his chest where he had felt the knock. Looking down in detached fascination he saw an inky-blot sprout from his jacket, and then flower, in youthful bloom. Ishaq didn't understand and looked at Shams again. Shams' eyes were tearing. Ishaq felt fear. He felt scared. A fear so acute that it was as if the sky would be rent asunder and judgement had come. His vision turning into a dark mist, he looked towards the direction of sound, and Shams' gaze, but first caught sight of the knife on the floor in front of them, still manifesting danger.

Ishaq started to stand but felt a crackling pain in his ribs and had the sense of nearly passing out, seeing an insoluble blackness. He collapsed to a kneeling position and reached out for the blade. As his eyes rose, a young man came into hazy perception. He seemed to be wearing a police uniform and, wide-eyed, with legs bowed, was shaking and pointing at him with an implement of metal. Ishaq shook his head, trying to clear his eclipsed vision and disperse the fog of his mind. And then. He saw stars. Falling stars against a cloak of midnight. Wonderful speckles of light that scored his sight and drew prodigious fading arcs that made Ishaq smile. With all his summoned might, he raised his head. With all his strength, he urged his eyes to see. Ishaq met the rosy-cheeked boy's gaze and heard one final thunderous clap.

Epilogue

He placed down two styrofoam cups of tea, sat down on the plastic seat and pulled the little table towards him. He looked up at a sliver of window, where the wall met the ceiling. Although reinforced with criss-crossing steel wire it was still slightly cracked. The rest of the prison's meeting room was barren, a dreary off-green. He looked around and could see inmates and their visitors sat at tables, a few shedding tears, some holding hands, and others swapping deserted silence, missing each other with remote stares. Every time the door swung open he looked up, expectantly, until finally Shams came through. Shams looked healthy, well-fed and with a relaxed face. Shams extended his hand to Marwane.

'Assalmu alaikum, bro, really good to see you.'

Marwane took his hand then stood, pulling Shams into an embrace. 'Akhi, you look good. How's it going, in here?'

'Alhamdulillah, it's all good. I'm getting by. What you up to?'

Marwane and Shams sat, looking at each other across the wobbling table. 'I'm working now. I've got a job in the city. Pretty rough hours but it's a start. So, seriously, how is everything?'

Shams took his styrofoam cup of tea and rolled it between the palms of his hands, taking in its dulled warmth . 'It was difficult at first, but the Muslim bros in here look after me. They own this place.'

Marwane didn't bother hiding his worry. 'What type of guys are we talking about?'

'Listen bro, I'm in with a good crowd, who don't want no trouble. I know better now. I'll admit they are a mixed lot, but you do need to be part of a group in here to survive.' Seeing his concern, Shams tried to placate Marwane. 'I know what I'm doing, I won't get into anything dodgy.'

'No, Shams. You listen here, you keep your head down and don't mix with anyone. Keep your nose clean.'

Shams looked down at the table while Marwane spoke. He started to tap his teeth with nervous energy. 'I don't discuss politics or anything. I'm really getting on. If people talk foolishness I just nod my head.'

'Ok, Shams, I hope so. You are looking settled. I'll give you that.'

'Alhamdulillah, it's all so clear in here, Marwane. My mind is at rest.' Shams took in a deep breath while making a vague indication to the world outside. 'Here it's straightforward. I like that. I read, do my prayers, do the bits of work they give us, read, have my meals, exercise, and that's it. Just count the days down. How is everyone? How's Ishaq's family?'

'Not good Shams. Not good.' Marwane looked downwards; he tried to lift his gaze but found it too heavy and returned to looking down. His eyes started tearing. He felt his throat constrict. He still found it hard to hear that name. He tried to still his upper lip and pushed and rubbed at his eyes, trying to force the tears back in. As he wiped he felt some of the bitter taste. 'They are going through a rough time, bruv. His dad is toughing it out, going to work. His mum doesn't go out anymore...but Ayub is helping out a lot. I don't know if you heard but he married Ishaq's sister.'

Marwane looked for some sense, some recognition but Shams looked blank and calm. No emotion, no tears. 'Yea, I heard. It seems an obvious match now, may Allah make it easy on them,' said Shams.

'Yea, may Allah make it easy on us all, Shams. They got close helping out with the justice campaign. A lot of organisations are really active on all this now. I've actually joined in and I'm doing bits, as well.'

Shams managed a smile. 'Yea, I heard that too. It's pretty funny, you becoming active like that...'

'Well, you know...like he said, we were born into it. Can't stick our head in the sand.'

Shams nodded. 'I still haven't talked to Ishaq's family. I can't do it...'

Marwane placed his hand on Shams' arm, wanting to comfort him but at the same time wanting to squeeze him hard until it hurt. '...Don't worry about it, man, look after yourself. One day you'll be ready, inshallah...and maybe one day they'll be ready.'

'It wasn't my fault. It was all an accident.'

Marwane watched Shams' Adam's apple bob up and down as he swallowed. He thought, *How do you tell those born blind what it is to see?* Marwane swallowed his tears while Shams swallowed sin.

'Do you think they'll get the guy who did it?' said Shams.

'The copper's mates arrived after, and they all got together and agreed on what happened. That's the way it goes. Anyway, he said he shouted.'

'I swear he didn't. I would've heard...but the inquiry?'

'Headed by a bunch of people who went to school with each other. A lot happened that day but it's like it never happened.'

They sat there in silence for a while. Marwane made a circle in the dust on the table, watching his finger go round and round without end, creating a clean space on the dirty surface. Marwane struggled with what to say. 'Does your sister come?'

'Yea, but I've told her to stop. She starts crying, making a scene. I can't handle it. My lawyer goes to visit, to guide her through all the appeal's stuff, but I'm not bothered about that. Not sure she is either, really. Like I say, my head is clear in here. I'd like it to stay that way for a while.'

'Allahu Akbar.' (God is Great)

'Ash hadu an-la ilaha ill allah.' (There is no god but Allah)

Coming from behind Shams Marwane was surprised he could hear the adhan being called. A couple of visitors looked in the direction of the sound and muttered something, shaking their heads.

'Haya ala-salah.' (Hasten to Prayer)

Marwane noted the voice, resolute and resonating. The free voice consoled him like a soothing balm. He wondered whom the caller was and what he had done to be caged here. He knew that, like him, the call transported him elsewhere, outside of this earthly confine.

'Haya ala-salah.' (Hasten to Prayer)

Shams noted Marwane's surprise. 'Yea, the block where the prayer room is is next door. It really annoys the rest of the prisoners and a lot of the screws but, like I said, we're the biggest group in here. Got to be nearing half Muslim. They'll do anything to avoid bad publicity and a riot or something…'

'Haya ala-falah.' (Hasten to Success)

'Anyway, I better go.' Shams got up from his chair, leaned over and gave Marwane a hug. He took a step towards the exit.

Halting, he turned to face Marwane. With a wan smile he said,'You'll come back to visit me, right?'

Marwane got up. 'Of course, bro, I ain't going nowhere. I'll be here. Take care, yea. Be good.'

'Haya ala-falah.' (Hasten to Success)

Shams nodded and gave his friend salaams. Marwane watched Shams turn around and be escorted back through the door. The call went on. As a hundred generations had heard it, before, so Marwane listened, attending to it as if it were new and as if he alone were being summoned. This plangent link to their past. A clarion call to the eternal. He felt a weight at the pit of his soul, a sore that would never heal, yet still his heart was made lighter by the sonorous sound of the promise, the call of awareness, the call to good.

Acknowledgements

To my parents Zainab and Ayub, for all their struggles, and passing me their narrations of Burma and Pakistan. I'll keep them well. Sophia and Soraya for childhood indulgences. My niece Sharifa, I hope you grow to value the word.

Thanks to Saeid for the lowdown, Ursula for being my earliest reader and not crushing, Leon for not judging dead nights, Nicos for finding impossible insanities.

Nathan and Dead Ink Books for making those ridiculous leaps.

Publishing the Underground

Publishing the Underground is Dead Ink's way of publishing daring and exciting new fiction from emerging authors. We ask our readers to act as literary patrons and buy our books in advance in order for us to bring them to print. Without this support our books would not be possible.

Dead Ink and the author, Naomi Booth, would like to thank all of the following people for generously backing this book – without them this book would not be in your hands.

If you would like to help Dead Ink continue this work please check the website.

Sharmin Badiei
Suman Bangera
Yusuf Bashir
Emma Baxter
Charlotte Bence
Jenny Bernstein
Alex Blott
SJ Bradley
Dan Brotzel
Kit Caless
Daniel Carpenter
Khalid Chaudhary
Rizwan Choudri
Oscar Colino
Oscar Colino garcia
Nathan Connolly
Tracey Connolly
Martin Cornwell

Danielle Davis
Daniel de Nieuwe
Leon Driscoll
Julia Edgington
Laura Emsley
Sam Fisher
Harry Gallon
Atar Hadari
Graeme Hall
Paul Hancock
Shahbaz Haque
Robin Hargreaves
Felix Haubold
David Hebblethwaite
Sophie Hopesmith
Rebekah Hughes
Katy Jackson
Sophia Khan
Steph Kirkup
Jkk Kklk
Rebecca Lea
Sally Lines
Dara Lobo
Khaled Majdoub
Wendy Mann
Susan McIvor
Andrew McMillan
Arshad Mea
Monika Melon
Marc Nash
Corey Nelson
Phil Olsen
Stefani Palmerini

Arifa Parkar
Dipesh Patel
Ileana Popa
James Powell
Nicos R
Julie Raby
Meaghan Ralph
Saeid Rasool
Gareth Rees
Asif Rehman
AmberRollinson
Amanda Roskilly
Tamim Sadikali
Stephen Scott
Anthony Self
Kashif Shabir
Matthew Shenton
Yvonne Singh
Kieron Smith
Denise Sparrowhawk
Roshan Thomas
Louise Thompson
Dan Thomson
Simon Tokumine
Adrian Ward
Nick Wilson
Beata Zawislan

Also from Dead Ink...

Every Fox is a Rabid Fox
Harry Gallon

'Every Fox is a Rabid Fox is a harrowing and brutal read. But I fell for its incredibly tender heart. I loved this book.'

    - Claire Fuller, author of Swimming Lessons and Our Endless Numbered Days

'Beautifully executed tale of innocence, tragedy, and the family traumas we all carry with us and many times fail to leave behind.'

    - Fernando Sdrigotti, author of Dysfunctional Males

Robert didn't mean to kill his brother. Now he's stuck between grief and guilt with only ex-girlfriend Willow and the ghost of his dead twin sister for company. Terrified of doing more harm, Robert's hysteria and anxiety grow while Willow and his sister's ghost fight over him: one trying to save him, the other digging his grave.

Every Fox Is A Rabid Fox is a brutal yet tender tale of family tragedy, mental illness and a young man searching for escape from his unravelling mind.

Another Justified Sinner
Sophie Hopesmith

It's the eve of the recession, but who cares? For commodity trader Marcus, life is good: he's at the top of the food chain. So what if he's a fantasist? So what if he wills his college sweetheart to death? So what if it's all falling apart? This isn't a crisis. Until it is.

As misfortune strikes again and again, he goes to help others and 'find himself' abroad – but it turns out that's not as easy as celebrities make it look on TV. Another Justified Sinner is a feverish black comedy about the fall and rise and fall of Marcus, an English psycopath. How difficult is it to be good?

Sophie Hopesmith is a 2012 Atty Awards finalist and her background is in feature writing. Born and bred in London, she works for a reading charity. She likes comedy, poetry, writing music, and Oxford commas. All of her favourite films were made in the 70s.

About Dead Ink...

Dead Ink is a small, ambitious and
experimental literary publisher based in
Liverpool.

Supported by Arts Council England, we're focused on developing the careers of new and emerging authors.

We believe that there are brilliant authors out there who may not yet be known or commercially viable. We see it as Dead Ink's job to bring the most challenging and experimental new writing out from the underground and present it to our audience in the most beautiful way possible.

Our readers form an integral part of our team. You don't simply buy a Dead Ink book, you invest in the authors and the books you love.